"Don & Chris were a dynamic duo when I worked with them in Atlanta, and they've proven they still are with **DEADLY NEWS**, *set mostly in the city they know and love. Their wealth of experience from decades in the news business provides a rich and well-informed backdrop for an explosive, exciting thriller."*

—**KATIE COURIC**, former Today show star, CBS Evening News anchor, host of her own nationally syndicated program, *Katie*

"I've known Don Farmer for years and I'm here to tell you he is the one person uniquely positioned to pen this thriller. He knows the news business, Atlanta and his beloved Southwest Florida. Add to that his irreverent sense of humor and knack for spinning a yarn and you have some great reading ahead of you."

—**NEAL BOORTZ**, Nationally syndicated radio talk show host and author

*"***DEADLY NEWS** *cleverly weaves together the fast-paced worlds of media and crime."*
—**GRETA VAN SUSTEREN**, TV host, anchor

"From the Deep South to the edge of the Everglades, **DEADLY NEWS** *is a riveting must-read that propels you full-speed on a roller coaster ride through intrigue, murder and the underside of the "news business!"*
—**NANCY GRACE**, Host of "Nancy Grace" on HLN network and former felony prosecutor

"Don Farmer and Chris Curle traveled the world covering news as reporters and anchors. They know the people behind the stories and the details that never make the news. **DEADLY NEWS** *captures the behind the scenes drama of intrigue, violence and character flaws that make a story so compelling. You won't be able to put it down."*

—**CLARK HOWARD**, Nationally syndicated radio talk show host and host of *Evening Express* on CNN's HLN Channel

Deadly News

Don Farmer
with Chris Curle

Publisher Page
an imprint of Headline Books, Inc.
Terra Alta, WV

Deadly News

By Don Farmer with Chris Curle

copyright ©2014Don Farmer

Publisher Page
P.O. Box 52, Terra Alta, WV 26764
www.PublisherPage.com

Tel/Fax: 800-570-5951
Email: mybook@headlinebooks.com
www.HeadlineBooks.com

Publisher Page is an imprint of Headline Books, Inc.

ISBN 978-0-938467-71-7 paperback
ISBN 978-0-938467-76-2 hardcover

Library of Congress Control Number: 2013941585

Farmer, Don
   Deadly News / Don Farmer, Chris Curle
   p. cm.
   ISBN 978-0-938467-71-7

Dedication

Dedicated to all the hard-working journalists who struggle to report the news in a changing and challenging media environment. We appreciate their work and hope they will share a few laughs with us along the way.

Cast of Key Characters

Brenda (Bren) Forrest – Founder, CEO, Global News Service

James (Jimmy) Hagan – Tough homicide detective in love with Cassandra Page

Cassandra (Cassie) Page – Talented crime reporter at NewsBlitz3, who loves Detective Hagan

Cav Campbell – Fading movie actor, fiancé of Bren Forrest

Lia Lee – Beautiful Olympics hostess, dying to be a TV news star

Tia Lee – Lives in the shadow of sister Lia.

Ian Phelps – Ruthless British media mogul who wants to take over Global News Service in the worst way

R.E. Lutz – Atlanta Chief of Police; vain, weak, worried

Max Ippolito – Level-headed senior producer at GNS

Ned Bastige – Arrogant GNS producer and part-time weasel with a secret agenda

Sheila Belle – GNS entertainment reporter, pop culture ditz

Yvonne Tender – Phelps's favorite fetish friend

The Milkman – Eccentric owner of TV stations, including NewsBlitz3

Rita Runner – NewsBlitz3 producer whose newsroom habits reek

Liz – A waitress on Marco Island whose "good eye" serves her well

Jerry and Jan Vaughn – Close friends of Bren Forrest, philanthropists, VIPs in Olympics. Their forty-sixth floor lux condo becomes a crime scene.

Prologue

ATLANTA, GEORGIA—The Near Future

"Ladies and gentlemen, we are about to become heroes to millions, role models to more and give the world a life changing morale boost—or this city soon will become the laughing stock of the planet."

Bren Forrest paused to let that sink in among the eighteen people gathered in the tenth story boardroom at the headquarters of the all news TV channel, Global News Service, in downtown Atlanta. This was a glittering assemblage of power players from around Georgia who had major roles in planning the Olympic Games set to begin in a few days.

These Olympic Games were nervously dubbed "Atlanta 2.0" by its supporters, "Atlanta 2.Oh No" by the critics.

Jerry Vaughn, seated at Bren's right in an identical studded leather chair, turned to face the others, a tight smile on his face.

"The lady is an expert in understatement, but she is committed to truth-telling and plain talk, so let's get to it. Are we ready? Are we really ready to bring the Olympic Games to Atlanta for a second time?"

Vaughn, the city's premier builder of skyscrapers and other features of Atlanta's impressive skyline, was the chairman of the Atlanta Olympics Committee.

"As owner of GNS, I know a little bit about public opinion," Bren said. "And I think the games here next week will have to be the best run—no pun there—the cleanest and the most exciting Olympics in anyone's memory.

"We have to show, in spite of the economic crises around the world, we can still put on a show, even after dozens of other cities pleaded poverty and slinked away from the challenge.

"So, let's hear from each of you now about how your part of the plan is going. We'll start with you, Chief Lutz."

Atlanta's police chief stood, smiled and set the tone for the others with a glowing message.

"We're ready, Ms. Forrest," he said with a gesture resembling a fist bump, except there was no one else standing to be on the receiving end of it.

"My officers know their specific assignments and we're getting great cooperation from other law enforcement agencies around the state…"

He droned on for eight or nine minutes before sitting down to a round of applause that seemed mostly to laud the fact he finally finished.

Atlanta's mayor was next, with some reassuring words about what some thought would be a daunting effort to keep traffic snarls to a minimum. He finished his remarks with the reminder the city was about to start a buddy system for homeless people.

"We'll urge our homeless friends who wander around downtown talking to themselves to walk in pairs. Visitors who come here during the Olympics will think they're talking to each other."

Everybody in the room wanted to laugh out loud, but no one did.

"Thank you, Mayor," Bren Forrest said quickly. "Now, I want to call on my dear friend and the wife of our chairman, the person in charge of our innovative Olympics Hostess Program, Jan Vaughn."

She volunteered to handle the hostess project and by all accounts selected some of the best-looking young women ever seen in one place since the previous summer's Victoria's Secret catalogue.

"We have seventy-five lovely and talented young women who will attend most of the major social events," she said. "They'll be charming, multilingual representatives of Atlanta's hospitality, and I know they'll make us proud."

As each of the VIPs spoke, their messages became shorter and more alike, exuding confidence and congratulations to one another.

Bren went last.

"As you know, our Global News Service has exclusive world rights to broadcast the Olympics and we are ready. This is shaping up to be the biggest challenge for GNS since the day we went on the air fifteen years ago.

"It has been my personal privilege and thrill to create GNS and reach this milestone.

"So, whenever something happens at the Olympics, you'll see it first and, in some cases, only on GNS."

Applause filled the room as Bren did an exaggerated southern-belle curtsy. The Olympics committee members apparently also were clapping for themselves for studying Olympics history and discovering other "great cities" snared the Olympics more than once. If London, Paris, Athens and Los Angeles could do it, why not Atlanta?

Some called it self confidence. Others called it hubris.

Bren ended the meeting with a big smile.

"Some comedian once said, 'If you want to make God laugh, tell him about your plans.' With that in mind, what could go wrong?"

1

BUCKHEAD—ATLANTA, GEORGIA

The guy who answered the door looked like a miraculous merging of The Hulk and George Clooney. But when he saw the woman standing there, he mentally withered for a moment.

His smile, as dazzling as the inlaid crystal on the mahogany double doors to the penthouse, was fixed. The only thing about him that moved was his racing pulse.

When the stunning, black-haired beauty made a tentative step into the foyer, the doorman resumed breathing and stepped aside.

"Welcome, miss, uh…" he said, hoping she would say her name.

Lia just nodded, smiled and brushed past without a word.

The chattering and piano tinkling subsided as she moved through the foyer into the large living room. The other guests, glittering in small knots of conversation, stopped talking and stared, as though they were thinking collectively almost out loud, *Who is that stunning woman?*

Lia usually experienced that sort of reaction from strangers. She walked past a white baby grand and toward the bar in the corner without acknowledging the stares. Her raven hair fell almost to her waist, brushing her body as she moved. Her Amerasian eyes and ivory skin were magnets to men and women alike.

The piano player took a long pull on his vodka rocks, then resumed his show tune noodling, pretending he was not distracted.

The eight or ten women near Lia looked her up and down quickly, then pivoted back to their chat partners. The men turned away more slowly, willing to risk the disapproval of their spouses and dates for a lingering look at Lia's remarkable face and gold-medal body.

Standing amidst a claque of his financial backers, the mayor of Atlanta saw the quizzical look on his wife's face and shook his head slightly, as if to say, "I have no idea who she is, dear."

A woman of abundant girth, standing to the mayor's left, leaned over and whispered in his ear, "I think she's some sort of official hostess for the Olympics."

"Sure beats the Welcome Wagon," the mayor whispered back. "She's an athlete, I think."

"I knew I should've been a P.E. major," responded the mayor, a pudgy man who relentlessly insisted double-breasted business suits made him look slimmer.

His focus this night was single-minded, hoping these second Olympics would make him a celebrity known well beyond North Georgia.

Lia walked past an original Warhol, an eight by ten foot self-portrait, in which the artist gave himself orange hair and bright green eyes, the kind of painting eyes that do not follow the viewer around the room.

The Warhol was probably the least expensive piece in the apartment, a museum-of-a-condo on the forty-sixth and top floor of Atlanta's most exclusive high-rise apartment building.

It was the Atlanta home of Jan and Jerry Vaughn, who also had homes in Naples, Florida, in the Georgetown area of Washington D.C. and in Jackson Hole, Wyoming.

This pre-Olympics party at their place undoubtedly would be one of the hottest tickets in town, so to speak.

The bartender looked up and smiled when Lia said softly, "Perrier, no ice please."

Lia preferred other self-medication to alcohol and knew she would get to enjoy that elsewhere very soon. She tipped the bartender enough so he'd recall her later, if necessary. She turned away and "accidentally" bumped into a tall, broad-shouldered man in a dark suit, a hearing device in his right ear. A few drops of her drink splashed onto his lapel.

"Oh, I'm so sorry, can I brush it off?" she asked, noticing the man was looking from side to side, not at her.

"Uh, no, it's okay," he mumbled, then looked down at her.

"Geez," he whispered, staring at the most attractive woman he'd seen in a long time.

Ron was trained to see, observe, watch and remember, but he couldn't recall anybody quite that startling.

"I'm Ron," he said, extending his right hand, approximately the size of a catcher's mitt.

"I'm Lia. Are you working or playing tonight, Ron?" she asked, knowing the earpiece meant Ron was security for some VIP.

"I, uh, I'm with the mayor," he said, still staring blank-faced, wishing he were clever, witty and not on duty. He glanced over his shoulder to where the mayor was impatiently shaking the ice cubes in his empty glass.

"I was getting my boss another club soda," Ron told Lia.

A bead of sweat formed on Ron's right eyebrow. He was a pro, a veteran of at least two shoot-outs in his days as a street cop, but he never was quite so neutralized by a woman as he was at that moment.

Lia smiled, her black eyes sparkling at Ron's discomfort.

"I bet this place is full of guys with guns," she grinned, "all these important people around."

"Nah, just my partner at the door and the uniform in the lobby. And me," Ron said, catching his breath now, able to put fifteen words together.

"I'm one of the hostesses for the games," Lia said.

"I'm Ron."

"Yes, I remember, Ron. And, Ron," she said, feigning concern and looking past the nervous agent, "I think your boss is thirsty."

Ron turned toward the mayor and saw him chewing his ice cubes.

"Hope to see you again, Ron," she teased, then stepped aside and walked past the agent, noticing the room's twelve-foot sliders were open to the balcony of this rooftop castle.

Lia needed to check in with Jan Vaughn, her boss for the Olympics. Jan wanted to do something for the Olympics other than just be Mrs. Jerry Vaughn, so she volunteered to be in charge of the seventy-five beautiful, multi-lingual young women chosen as hostesses for Olympics-related events.

"Good evening, Mrs. Vaughn," Lia said, with a slight nod as she approached. Jan was with the guest of honor, Brenda Forrest, the owner of Global News Service. At Bren's side was her fiancé, the biggest Hollywood celebrity at the party.

"Hello dear, I'm glad you're here." Jan was 5' 3" tops, with a friendly face and sandy blond hair with just enough gray highlights to look distinguished. At fifty-eight, she was very Vanity Fair-meets-Town & Country.

Jan turned to the woman on her left.

"Bren, may I introduce Lia Lee, one of our hostesses for the games. She's also an intern at Global News."

"Good to meet you, Lia," Bren Forrest said, shaking Lia's hand. "How is your work experience at GNS?"

"It's great, Ms. Forrest," Lia answered, noticing the cleft-chinned man standing next to Bren Forrest staring with undisguised approval.

"Oh, and, Lia this is Cav Campbell," Jan said with a smile that said, obviously you know who this is and don't gush or anything.

"How do you do, Ms. Lee, or may I call you Lia?" said Campbell, his eyes dancing in a practiced way known to millions of moviegoers.

"Yes, please call me Lia, thank you," Lia said, almost in a whisper. She forced herself to a near blush, knowing Campbell would expect some sort of flushed unease from any woman lucky enough to meet him in person.

As Campbell started to say something, Lia turned back to Bren Forrest.

"Ms. Forrest, congratulations on the fifteenth anniversary of GNS. It must be very exciting."

Campbell interrupted. "Yes, we're thrilled," drawing Lia's attention back to where he wanted it.

Forrest and Campbell were "engaged" as they chose to call it. They had been sharing her penthouse apartment in the GNS building downtown for almost a year.

In that time, Campbell had not made a movie. He did turn fifty-two and acquired a younger chin, a tucked tummy and an eye job.

Bren met Cav Campbell at the premiere of a movie produced by the small but trendy film studio her company, Global News Service, Inc., bought a few years before.

Bren thought Campbell was good for her, rich enough not to be a gold-digger and just close enough to career over-the-hill-ville to be looking for a meaningful relationship, such as being the husband of a media tycoon.

Campbell was a heart throb once, a shy guy with a throw of hair on his forehead who shuffled his feet now and then and tried to remember to say "ma'am" and "sir" a lot.

At twenty-eight, he was an established star, enjoying the myth he cared more about his work than about his "celebritude," a word some columnist made up.

By the time he was thirty-eight, Campbell faded from the supermarket magazine covers. He did not want to play Ward Cleaver and was way too old to be the Beav.

He didn't deal with it well. Until he became engaged to Bren, the women he dated expanded in number and decreased in age.

After the Party House IV film, his first lead role in a couple of years, had record low revenues making it pretty much a box office dud, Campbell smiled his way onto a few TV talk shows, telling people mostly he wanted to direct.

Then came that film at Bren Forrest's studio. It was better than anything he had done in a while, but not good enough to give him a bounce to other offers. So here he was, a good companion with an easily aroused itch.

Bren watched with a fixed smile as Campbell ogled Lia.

She hadn't noticed his legendary roving eye in play lately, so Bren thought, hoped, he was tamed.

Sure, he thinks this kid is gorgeous. She is. *So what*, Bren thought, as she turned to Jan and Lia.

"To have our network's anniversary coincide with these second Olympic Games in Atlanta is a wonderful happenstance," Bren said to Lia, regaining Campbell's attention with the slightly sharp tone of her voice.

Jan smiled, noticing others socializing in clumps around the room were looking at her little group. And why not? Watching Lia from behind and Cav Campbell from the front offered something for everyone.

Campbell had a tan he could die from. Cynics wondered how many sheep placentas and jojoba plants were sacrificed to keep Campbell's face so smooth.

Physically, Cav Campbell was a hunk for his age, well, hunkish enough, but his career would never catch up with his charisma.

Bren Forrest's angular face was softened by her shoulder-length auburn hair and wide eyes matching her hair color. She looked like the winner of the British royalty gene pool, the slightest bit horsey, but pure, Triple Crown stock. She made middle age seem like first prize.

"Are other Welcome girls coming?" Jan asked Lia.

"Yes, Megan and Brittany take their turns soon."

Eight of the hostesses were invited to this party, a key social event leading up to the opening of the games.

Their job was to be there one at a time, for maybe half an hour, working the room, using their language skills or charm or both to make everyone feel welcome.

The girls were parceled out to different pre-Olympics activities. Lia swapped assignments with another hostess to get on the list for this party at this time, nightfall.

———

"Georgia, Georgia, the whole night through...." Country star Jake Owen was singing now at the front edge of the baby grand. He wore jeans, a black cowboy hat and cobra skin dress boots, quite a contrast with the penguinesque sameness of the other males in the room.

As Lia turned to watch the singer, several men who were staring at her snapped their eyes back toward the entertainment, but too late not to be noticed.

The conversation quieted as Owen finished the mandatory, "...keeps Georgia on my mind..."

Bren and Jan walked slowly toward the piano and stood by it, listening, smiling, happy in anticipation of the formal festivities that would take place there. They would bask in warm words and accolades.

Lia hung back, looking at Cav Campbell, who was looking at her.

"You know, I could use some fresh air," Lia whispered, nodding her head slightly toward the balcony.

"Me, too, maybe a quick hit?" he said, looking for a sign of response from Lia.

"Hmmm, interesting," she said, almost batting her eyelashes.

"Then how about..." he began, but she put a finger to his mouth.

"Shhhhh, give me a few minutes to, uh, cover for us. I'll meet you out there, on the balcony, over in the corner."

Campbell shuddered slightly with anticipation as he watched Lia turn and walk toward the people clustered near the piano.

"Ron, I have to leave now. It was great meeting you," she said to the security agent.

"Same here. And, can I call you sometime?"

"That would be great, just phone the Olympics office. They all know me there," she said.

The mayor watched the exchange. *Handsome bastard, that Ron, he'll probably want to show her his gun. He's lucky I'm not a player or he'd be making a date for me.*

Lia then moved to where Jerry Vaughn was having a whispered conversation with Atlanta's police chief, R.E. Lutz.

"Excuse me, sir," she said to Vaughn. "We're changing the guard, so to speak, so I must go now, but I wanted to thank you for having me to your wonderful home."

"You are welcome, Ms..."

"Lee, sir, Lia Lee, one of your hostesses. I hope to see you again soon during the games."

The police chief, an inch shorter than Lia, bristling with brass and braid on his dress blue uniform, assumed his tallest possible posture and stuck out his hand.

"I'm Chief Lutz," he said with a salacious smile.

"Yes, a pleasure," Lia said. "Do you have the time, Chief, um, Lutz?"

As he turned his wrist so Lia could see the Rolex, she glanced at it, frowned and bowed slightly.

"Oh, I really must go. Nice to meet you."

She moved toward Jan and Bren. Lia thanked them, shook Bren's hand and excused herself.

She walked to the front door, nodding, smiling to everyone, knowing she looked good from all angles, as memorable in her departure as she was in her arrival. Her black dress was a good choice, with its silver threading on the spaghetti straps, around the neckline and at the above-the-knee hem.

The security agent near the front door opened it for her.

She smiled and nodded, walked the twelve feet across the hallway to the elevator and pushed the button.

Cav Campbell lingered on the balcony, the pungent smell of his marijuana cigarette carried away by the warm breeze of the Atlanta night.

Slam dunk, I think. She'll be back and then, well, wonder where she lives.

Campbell knew the Olympics would draw good-looking women to Atlanta, not to mention the "Bambies," his word, who already lived there.

I may learn to love this town, one girl at a time. Bren will never know.

Campbell checked his watch, but couldn't see the dial in the dark corner of the balcony.

He turned and looked out on the city, the lights of Peachtree Road winding south toward the lighted skyscrapers downtown.

Lia opened a door from the kitchen and slipped onto the balcony without Campbell knowing she returned. She glided up to him as he stood looking out, put her arms around his waist and kissed his right ear. "Some view," she said.

"The city looks great, too," Campbell said with a grin, turning to face her, leaning against the concrete railing of the balcony, his back to the city lights.

"And you, my dear, are sensational."

Lia smiled and let the tips of her fingernails brush against his stomach, just above the belt buckle.

Campbell sighed and reached for her. The marijuana joint in his hand touched her dress where it closed at her lower back. It hissed, leaving a small burned spot on the cloth.

"Oh Geez, I'm sorry," he said, fumbling to wipe off the burn.

"It's nothing, no problem," she whispered.

He dropped the joint and stepped on it, then reached for her face with both hands.

Lia looked up, smiled, and purred, "Lean back."

She touched his belt, then the buckle, then the tab on his zipper. She pulled it about half an inch. He closed his eyes.

"Lean back, honey, come on now," she whispered.

As Campbell arched his back against the railing, thrusting his pelvis forward, Lia leaned down and grabbed him under each knee.

With a burst of upper body strength that would have surprised anybody who saw it, Lia jerked Campbell's legs up and shoved them backwards.

He teetered for a moment, grabbing at the air.

She pushed harder on both legs and Campbell tumbled over the railing.

2

BUCKHEAD—ATLANTA

Homicide Detective James Hagan punched in Cassie's cell phone number with one hand as he sped up Peachtree Road in his unmarked sedan.

"Cassandra Page, News Blitz3." She was in the passenger seat of the Channel 3 news van, her video photographer, Daryl Evans, was at the wheel. They were heading south on Peachtree Road.

She was annoyed having to cover the Park Towers party. As Channel 3's most prominent on-air reporter she mostly covered crime, violence and corruption, not chichi social events. But so far this day she couldn't even scare up a convenience store robbery to report on, so when the news director asked to help out at the gala, "just this once," she relented.

"Cassie, Jimmy here. Where are you?" She could hear the tension in his voice. Or maybe it was excitement.

"Hey, Copperhead, what's up, darlin'?"

"Not much, other than some guy just fell from the penthouse at the building where there's a big pre-Olympics bash going on and I'm on my way there now. Other than that..."

"Jimmie, for God's sake, are you serious, come on, what? I'm just a block or two from Park Towers myself. Long story, are you there now? Is this a joke?"

"No joke. That's why I called you. I'm almost there, too. Race ya. Kiss, kiss," Jimmy said, ending the call.

3

GNS HEADQUARTERS—DOWNTOWN ATLANTA

"Get that off the air, you prime asshole!"

Senior producer Max Ippolito, was yelling as loud as he could as he stormed across the newsroom of the Global News Service.

He was furious at what he just saw on the air and his shout made the two news anchors on the set wince. Their viewers could hear it, too, even through the glass partition separating the anchor desk from the production and work areas in the background.

The foreign minister of Jordan had just been shot to death in Amman by a man on a motorbike who then turned the gun on himself.

The producer of the hourly newscast in process ordered a "graphic," the photo or drawing viewers see on the screen, over the news anchor's shoulder.

"Call it 'Jordan Shooting'," he yelled over the intercom to the graphics department.

The anchorwoman, a streaky blond with brown eyes and a cameo type blouse that added a touch of school marm to her look, started to read the story of the Jordanian's assassination. As she did, the graphic appeared on screen.

Large red letters at the bottom read, "Jordan Shooting." The photo above the headline was a picture of basketball legend Michael Jordan.

"Get it off now!" the producer bellowed as he stormed toward the "pit." That's what GNS people called the control room where the director sat facing a battery of monitors and switches, running the video and audio of the newscast. It was not a pit at all, but a step-down area, part of the original studios built at the birth of GNS. The name "pit" was born and survived a couple of control room spruce ups and expansions.

"Jesus, how did that get on, Billy?" Max asked, the two worry lines in his forehead seemingly growing as he frowned. He rushed over to stand behind the director, Billy Olson, whose job was to control what goes on the air, including audio, video, sound, graphics and everything else. He was already punching the graphic into oblivion and ordering the director operating remote camera three to fill the screen with a tight shot of the anchorwoman.

Billy leaned back in his swivel chair and looked up at Max.

"You won't believe it, boss," he said shaking his head.

"As soon as the graphic hit the air, I yelled at Bastige it was wrong. I told him 'Jordan Shooting' was not about the NBA for chrissake. You know what he said? Honest to God, he said 'Don't tell me how to do my job, I've been a full producer for almost a month now.' Can you believe it? Three weeks and he's Einstein."

Max shook his head as the director turned back to the wall of TV screens and said into his headset, "Teases next, then throw to commercial break."

Max leaned in to Billy. "Isn't Bastige the one who once said he shouldn't be expected to know about the Third Reich because he wasn't even alive then?"

Billy grunted, "Yeah and he wasn't joking. He has the sense of humor of a doorknob. But just wait, Max—that incompetent smartass will be a vice president here someday."

Max nodded, knowing Billy probably was right. Ned Bastige was a holdover from the early years, always an associate or an assistant, never a full producer until last month. In Max's opinion, Bastige more or less stagnated in place all that time. He was not promoted for good reason.

"He's just uninformed, in his own twisted little world," Max told his boss a year or so earlier when asked about Bastige's news judgment and overall journalistic savvy.

"Some months ago, he asked our Chicago bureau chief to get us an interview with the mayor there about some political corruption controversy. The mayor refused, and the Chicago guy called Ned and said, 'Sorry, pal, the mayor blew me off. I messed up. I didn't get dick.'

"You know what Bastige did? He snorted at the bureau chief and said, sarcastically, 'Well, forget about it pal, I can get Dick. Just give me Dick's phone number for God's sake and I'll get Dick!'"

Max also told GNS brass Bastige was a whiner who always blamed others for his frequent screw-ups. But the bosses promoted Bastige to show producer anyway and assigned him to the ten o'clock news hour. They also reminded Max that Bastige started at the network when it was founded and deserved a shot."

Max disagreed, but lost the argument. Now, hoping to forget Bastige for a moment, Max turned away from the control room and walked a few steps to the rear, deep in thought.

He had a live truck committed to covering his big boss, Bren Forrest, at the GNS anniversary party at Vaughn's home. The video from there would then fold into the network's TV special at ten o'clock. Already, it was costing him overtime because the camera crews and other techs in the field started before dinner and would be on the clock at least until midnight.

Worse, the on-scene anchor for the live coverage would be Max's least favorite on-air personality, the GNS entertainment reporter, Sheila Belle.

As Max once said to a GNS co-worker, "Deep down, she's shallow."

Sheila could be counted on to do at least one interview in every program with the guest's back to the camera, so Sheila would be seen asking the question, then smiling, nodding and pouting her lips in a way she believed was sexy.

Sheila thought so because some guy once sent her a poem from prison, the last lines were:

Your full red lips are beautiful; I love to see them pout.

Your teeth, your tongue do turn me on, just wait till I get out.

Sheila's boyfriend at the time advised her to tell GNS security about the letter. Instead, she posted it with little stickpins on the corkboard above her desk.

"It helps keep me centered," she explained when anyone asked.

Max also was up to his ear-buds in plans for a huge, star-studded, live gala the next night to tout the GNS exclusive TV coverage of the Olympics and to celebrate the network's fifteenth anniversary.

It would be held in the fourteen-story atrium of GNS headquarters downtown.

A success with the special show would be a big plus for Max. His next career move could be a vice presidency at GNS or even a higher-paying job at ABC, NBC or CBS.

PARK TOWERS, BUCKHEAD—ATLANTA

"What the hell was that?" Jody Portier said out loud. He was sitting on the roof of his live truck, sweating, as he fiddled with the faulty microwave dish he just removed from the pole atop the truck. He felt the truck rock, then a warm, wet splat on the top of his head.

"Christ, what..." Jody's upward glance froze in shock as another splash of wet stuff hit him full in the face. He wiped his eyes and wished he hadn't.

Jody was a Global News Service engineer whose TV remote truck was parked in the half-circle driveway at the lobby of the Park Towers. He was trying to fix the dish he had taken off the mast, an extendible metal pole.

Jody raised the mast to thirty feet, so the other engineer inside the truck could see whether the problem with their test signal was in the mast cables. The mast elevated the microwave dish to send audio and video signals to the GNS receiver atop its building downtown.

The GNS news team was there to do a "live shot," a live remote broadcast from the party for Bren Forrest in the condo forty-six floors above.

Miller Andrews, the news cameraman working with Jody, was standing at the rear doors of the truck, getting a battery and a spare P2 digital memory card for his video camera. He also felt the truck shudder and looked up to see what it was.

"Oh God, oh God, Jody are you okay? Jesus, Jody, there's... oh God, look at that!"

Miller grabbed his camera and began to shoot video. Mentally he was on autopilot, the same way he reacted in tense situations before, in Fallujah a lifetime ago, in the big earthquake in Haiti and in other "oh crap" situations during his years as a TV news photographer.

With all his experience—the eternal Arab-Israeli carnage, a couple of plane crash aftermath scenes, the Mexican drug wars—Miller had never seen anything like what he saw when he looked at the roof of the TV truck.

Staring back at him, the eyes open in surprise and frozen in death, was a man, his arms outstretched, hands open as if anticipating a bear hug. The legs were spread-eagled, too, and Miller's shocked mind saw the whole picture as a sort of human windchime, suspended in air.

Then he saw why. The man was impaled on the mast atop the TV truck. He fell face down. The square metal cap on the top of the pole punctured his chest and the mast protruded about three feet out of his back.

Jody was trying to stand up on the roof, staggering, wiping the blood from his eyes.

Miller was dizzy for a moment as his video camera recorded the scene. His shock abated as he squinted through the viewfinder.

He zoomed his lens back to get a wider view, showing the entire body of the man, the mast holding him up there as blood oozed and dripped down the pole and puddled on the truck's roof.

GNS HEADQUARTERS

Max was standing by the domestic assignment desk, talking with a writer for the GNS live broadcast, when the phone rang next to him.

"News, Jackson speaking," said the writer. He listened, nodded and listened some more. Then hung up, his hand shaking.

"What, what?" said Max, exasperated at Jackson's silence.

"Holy shit," Yusef Jackson said.

"What is it?" Max asked again.

"Somebody just landed on the mast of our live truck."

"What do you mean, landed?" Max said.

"No shit! The tech called from the truck over at the Vaughn party, at Park Towers. He says the mast on top of the van was fully extended and a body just came outta nowhere and spiked itself on the mast!"

PARK TOWERS

Cassie opened the door of the news van with the station logo all over it before Daryl completely stopped. As her feet hit the pavement she saw lights go on around the Global News Service live truck. She turned on her cell and yelled into it as she ran.

A news crew from another Atlanta TV station, arriving to cover the party, also saw the GNS camera lights go on. The news photographer walked over quickly to where Miller was recording video.

"Chuck, Cassie here, we have to go live. Some guy just fell out of the building onto a TV truck. He's dead, I guess," she panted as she caught her breath next to Miller. Her own cameraman, Daryl, ran up behind her and began shooting video of the impaled body.

"Yeah, at the Vaughn's building, the big party. What do you mean we can't interrupt regular programming?" Cassandra shouted into the phone.

"For God's sake, Chuck, somebody falls out of the building where every VIP in town is attending a party and we can't take it live?"

Cassandra's voice rose as she caught her breath.

"Who is he? Whattaya mean who is he?" she snapped. "What the hell difference does it make who he is? He's a dead guy. Ever see a guy skewered on a TV truck mast, Chuck? It's a first, godammit, so let's go live in a coupla minutes.

"Oh for...geez, Chuck I don't know how... what's...just get us on, now!"

Cassandra's mocha complexion was reddening now, sweat trickling down her temples. Her black hair was matted with humidity and sweat from the heat of the July night and the run-around tension of the moment.

"Can you believe this jerk on the assignment desk?" she huffed to Daryl, as he continued to shoot the scene unfolding before him. "He says we normally don't report suicides, so Chuckie has to call the boss at home for permission to break in."

Daryl laughed but kept recording, walking backwards to get an extra wide shot and a pan down from the building to the speared body.

The security guard from the front desk of the building saw the two camera lights and sauntered out of the glass door into the driveway.

"What's up guys?"

"Up there," Miller motioned with his head.

The guard looked up, saw the body on the mast and saw Jody now sitting cross-legged on the roof of the truck, wiping blood off his face and clothes, silent, disbelief slowing his motion.

The security man looked sick. Miller thought he might collapse and shouted, "Call the cops."

The security man recovered and walked haltingly back into the lobby. At that point two police cars screamed to a stop out front. One officer made a call on his cell phone and the other began asking rapid-fire questions of the stunned security guard.

Another TV truck drove up with the blazing words "News9NOW Mobile Bureau," front, back and on both sides. The station had three of those video vans, but the promotions department renamed them mobile bureaus shortly after the station closed its real bureaus in the outlying small cities of Athens, Rome and Peachtree City. It saved money.

A reporter with salt and pepper hair—he added the pepper—jumped out of the truck and jogged to the officer on the cell phone.

The Channel 9 photographer went to where the others were shooting.

"Who's that?" he asked. The newsies all shrugged and kept recording.

"It can't be who I think it is, can it?" the cameraman asked. More shrugs.

A squad car arrived, then another, then an ambulance, lights flashing, and three uniformed officers rushed up.

A sergeant on a cell phone was heard saying, "Alert the chief."

"He's there, at the party? Go up and tell him."

"No, I don't want to go up there. Can't you text him?

"Damn. Stand by."

The sergeant directed a patrolman to put up some yellow crime scene tape and get the media back behind it.

Detective Jimmy Hagan slid his car behind one of the squad cars and walked over to talk with the sergeant. He then looked around, hoping to spot Cassie. He heard her first, talking animatedly on her cell. *I'll have to tease her about pushing that guy off the balcony just so she'd have a big crime story to report tonight. Nah, better not. She might push me outa bed instead.*

Jimmy walked into the lobby and to the bank of elevators. *If this turns out to be a homicide, it could be a long night for me. And Cassie too, but not with each other.*

At that moment, Sheila Belle, the GNS entertainment reporter who was there to do the live report on the festivities, walked from the ladies' room in the lobby out to the GNS truck.

"What's all the fuss about?" she asked Miller, a blank expression on her face. "Anything wrong with our signal?"

Miller adjusted his camera, then looked at Sheila.

"Oh no, the signal will be fine, as soon as we get the body off the mast."

Sheila looked up and shrieked, "My God, it's Cav Campbell!"

Even in the dark, punctuated by the camera lights and the flashing lights on the squad cars, Sheila knew the dead celebrity immediately.

His tan had not yet begun to turn death gray. Sheila had seen Campbell a dozen times with Bren Forrest. Now and then she would see something about him in the local alternate online newspaper, *The Riot*. Years earlier he was popping up on TMZ or Pop Tarts with some regularity, but not much lately.

Sheila choked back a gag and looked up at the mast again.

"It's Cav, it's our Cav, it's..."

She swallowed hard, brushed aside a strand of otherwise well-trained hair and turned to Miller.

"Does this mean we'll go live any minute?"

Ten feet away, Cassandra Page heard what Sheila said. She walked closer and realized Sheila was right.

She grabbed the phone again. *Chuck, pick up dammit*, she said to herself as the phone rang back at Channel 3.

"Chuck, Cassie here. We have the story of the year here, Chuckie, so I suggest we break in and go live now or else you're going to be under the viaduct with a sign saying 'Will produce TV shows for food,' get it?"

Chuck didn't respond, but Cassie could hear a lot of loud voices in the newsroom.

"Chuck, Chuck, listen. Cav Campbell, the movie star, Bren Forrest's boy toy, is hanging suspended over the driveway here on the mast of the GNS live truck. His fiancée is upstairs at a party with the mayor, the police chief and every other important person between here and the Antarctic. I'm, what? Call who? Hell, call the Milkman himself if you have to, but we need to go live now!"

Inside the GNS live truck, the engineer was on the phone with the writer at GNS headquarters downtown. It was his second call, a few minutes after the first.

"No shit. Sheila says it's Cav Campbell. Yeah, the Cav Campbell, honest to God. What? Did he fall?

"Hell, I don't know if he fell or jumped or what, but he must have been at the party for the boss. Yeah, our boss, Bren Forrest.

"Right. Sheila is here, yeah, yeah. But the dish is off the mast. We'll have to prop it up on the van roof and go with it.

"The picture may not be great, but we can't do... Jesus, no we can't put it back on the mast. There's a body there. Get somebody out here with a LiveU. Meantime, send us what you can see on your monitor with your cell phone. We need help out here!"

He pocketed the phone and yelled out the back of the truck toward Sheila.

"We're going live in five, grab this mic here, and your IFB!"

Sheila ran to the truck and clipped the little microphone onto the lapel of her black linen jacket, pulling a thread as she did. That never happened before.

Sheila was distraught. She had not put on her TV makeup yet and the humidity and heat made her hair a mess, she just knew it.

"I need to fix up," she said, as Miller handed her the IFB, the earpiece attached to a wire going to a small transmitter on her belt. It allowed her to hear what went on the air, plus instructions from the producer and director in the control room at GNS headquarters.

IFB is short for "interrupted feedback." Most reporters have more colorful names for it and for the off-air people who liked to shout orders through it at the on-camera reporters and anchors. To Sheila, however, the IFB was her substitute masters degree.

Her producers knew how little she knew about so much of what she covered. They often made her seem smarter than she was with timely information on the IFB.

Sheila did know, however, Cav Campbell died on TV, literally, and she had a worldwide scoop in the making.

GNS HEADQUARTERS

Max juggled phones at the GNS studio, struggling to keep things together, and analyze the information sputtering in from the Park Towers building. He barely noticed producer Ned Bastige at his desk, reading *Associated Press* news bulletins on his computer.

Realizing what happened, Bastige jerked upright in his chair, stood, walked to a row of empty desks and sat down in front of an idle computer.

He hit "Log In," then tapped, "NoBeeb@nwsuk.com."

"Password," the computer prompted him in the upper right corner.

"Hammer," he typed.

"Hammer, send second password," appeared on the screen.

"Mime," Ned typed, his fingers shaking.

"Password Invalid."

He went back and deleted the "M" and replaced it with a "T." "Time," it read.

"Hammer confirm action," popped up on his screen.

"Hammer confirms."

The machine hummed, the screen went gray, then lit up again a moment later.

Rows of gibberish type poured onto the screen, stopped for a few seconds, then more

"xoxpo8644h@xoewoeoro329L04oir9ekfkd6W*k,ju."

"Hammer Report."

Ned was sweating now.

"Hammer Down," he typed carefully.

"Repeat."

"Hammer Down," Ned typed again, his fingertips leaving moisture on the keyboard.

"Game Over," the screen read, then went dark.

Bastige pushed back from the computer and stood up. His armpits were wet and the small roll of fat over his belt was damp. He walked slowly past Max and Yusef, both of whom were yelling into telephones now. Eyes straight ahead, Ned walked out of the newsroom, down the hall and into the men's room.

In a stall, he pulled a scrap of copy paper from his wallet, tore it in two, then in two again, threw the pieces into the toilet and pushed the flush handle.

The water blurred the words "Hammer Down" as the paper bits swirled, then disappeared. Ned thought he ought to want to throw up, but he didn't feel sick. Fear maybe, but not sick.

4

ALDWYCH—LONDON

"It's finished," said the young man in horn-rimmed glasses. He stood up from his computer and turned to the older man behind him.

"Hammer says it's finished, completed, the message just came in," horn-rim said, nervous now, uncomfortable as always when talking with people other than via computer.

"That's ducky, Brian, make sure the girl's money is in Zurich on time."

The balding man smiled as he picked up his drink, Glenlivet on the rocks, and took a long swallow. His other hand went to the hair above his left ear. He smoothed it, then moved to the spreading bald spot on top. He touched it a hundred times a day, often without knowing it.

He was dressed like a flush, savvy business tycoon, or a cinematic exaggeration of one. His suspenders matched his maroon paisley tie. His shirt was Turnbull & Asser, French cuffs and spread collar, starched white against the French blue of the shirt.

Ian Phelps had rings on three fingers of his right hand, one with diamonds on white gold. The second, on his pinkie, was a ruby set in yellow gold, but cut flat rather than in a typical ruby oval. The third ring was solid gold with a Sterling silver emblem mounted on the top. It was in the shape of a satellite dish, facing upwards. It cost Phelps a fortune to have made and he never took it off.

"Call O'Reilly and tell him to bring the car around straightaway," Phelps said to Brian, who had turned back to his computer.

Phelps grabbed his suit jacket from the back of the black leather desk chair and strutted toward the door.

"Take tomorrow off, mate," he said to Brian over his shoulder as he pushed open the heavy oak door and walked to the elevator across the hallway.

Ian knew he did not have to worry about Brian not being there tomorrow. Brian Echols would be at work, at his computer. Brian worked virtually every day, usually twelve hours or more. He ate lunch at his console. He was a hacker whose greatest moments of emotion came while using his boss's computer system for things Phelps never knew about and might misunderstand.

Phelps's stride was almost jaunty. He hardly ever moved that way. His walking style, like his clothing, car and cash flow, was carefully planned and executed.

Tonight was different. Phelps was in the best mood he had been in for several months, ever since he decided to use drastic means to get Bren Forrest's attention. And her network.

"Snotty bitch," he said under his breath, smiling, but with spite, not mirth.

Phelps nurtured a roiling resentment of Bren Forrest ever since she created Global News Service fifteen years ago.

She grew up rich, married rich and had that satellite news idea handed to her without breaking a sweat. She could not have thought of that in a million years, but those horny bankers coughed up the bread and honey, hopin' for some round-the-world action with her, I'll wager.

Phelps knew Bren Forrest enjoyed a life of luxury. Her family was at the highest level of Atlanta society and her husband made his own fortune with radio and TV stations and a cable TV system that covered much of the South.

She was probably doing steeplechase and dressage in those stupid black costumes while I was getting grabbed by coppers on horseback for nickin' a few ciggies. Phelps shook off his private little envy tour as his office elevator swept him down twenty-one floors to the street.

Despite the late hour, a few Londoners were still out and about, flagging taxis at intersections, hoping the driver could find them an open club. London's cabbies know everything.

Phelps was in a buoyant mood. His Daimler eased to a stop at the curb in front of him and he opened the door before his driver could come around and do it.

"Beautiful night, eh, O'Reilly, me boy?" Phelps said with a grin as the driver pulled away from the curb.

"Yessir, boss, but you sure do put in the hours, you do," said O'Reilly, his eyes glancing at Phelps in the rearview mirror.

Phelps reached into his left front pants pocket and retrieved the private cell phone he never used for business. No one had the number he tapped into it. It rang five times.

"Yvonne, you up then?"

"Crikey, what time is it?" Her voice was thick with sleep.

"It's the best time of your life, my dear," he said. "I'll be there in twenty minutes, so fluff the pillows, if you get my drift."

Phelps pushed the end button and tossed the phone onto the seat beside him.

"O'Reilly, let's go to Ms. Tender's place and wait for me, mate. But first let's swing past the Beeb."

"Yessir, the Beeb it is, Guv," O'Reilly said, accelerating slightly.

One of these days or nights he was going to get up enough courage to ask Mr. Phelps why he always wanted to drive by Bush House, once a famed broadcast facility of the BBC, the British Broadcasting Company, but no longer. The network consolidated operations in another building, Broadcasting House, on Portland Place.

Phelps never liked that building either and often quoted George Orwell, who is said to have called the BBC at Broadcasting House, "A cross between a girl's school and a lunatic asylum."

Phelps must have requested that drive-by at least twice a week in the years O'Reilly had been driving for him. O'Reilly was reluctant to ask about all that. Maybe he would one day.

"One of these nights you must ring up my Missus and tell her I really am working this late," O'Reilly said with a nervous laugh as the car neared Bush House.

It was dark, which gave Phelps a rush of pleasure, loving the irony of seeing no lights on in a building that once housed the BBC World Service.

The BBC never sleeps my ass.

Phelps turned his attention to O'Reilly.

"How about a raise, say twenty quid a day, that'd keep her cake hole shut, eh?" Phelps said, pulling out his Dunhill lighter, filigreed gold with a satellite dish mounted on it, and fumbling with a packet of Silk Cut filters.

"Are you serious, sir?"

"Serious as a stroke," Phelps said, lighting his cigarette.

"That it would, sir, she'd clam up, she would," O'Reilly beamed, thinking how the extra cash would satisfy his wife for a while. Or maybe he would just endure his wife's tsk-tsk attitude and stash the extra money for his own rainy day.

"And another thing, O'Reilly, when you get home get out your passport and pack a bag. We're going to the States tomorrow."

PORCHESTER PLACE—LONDON

"Crazy bastard," Yvonne Tender said to her reflection in the bathroom mirror.

She was carefully applying a tiny strip of flesh-colored tape at the outside corner of her left eye, pulling the skin back from the eyeball.

The tape was from a large roll in her vanity cabinet. She used it whenever Phelps came over, so she had it handy.

Why doesn't he just find himself some Oriental bitch and be done with it? He's some kinda nut about this, but what the hell, it pays for the blow. And at least he hasn't hurt me much since I started the slant-eyed thing.

Yvonne cut off another piece of tape and affixed it near her right eye, pulling it back. She leaned in to the mirror to study the result.

She thought she looked more like preparation for plastic surgery than an Asian beauty, but she was used to it by now.

She applied a light coat of base makeup over the tape, to disguise it as much as possible. He'd know of course. Hell, it was his idea.

Her long hair, dyed coal black, hung straight off her shoulders, falling just below her waist. She would have preferred it shorter and easier to manage.

She put on bright red lipstick from a tube she kept only for Ian's visits. Then she removed two contact lenses from their case and popped them in. They were black, a world of shades darker than her natural hazel eyes. It took her a month to get used to them. The contacts were the first of the Asian-look items she always took off immediately after Ian left her place.

She arranged two lines of cocaine on the glass top dressing table and inhaled sharply through her nose. *That's great. Now, I'd better finish the look for this dope. Ha, dope for a dope.*

With the jade dress she was about to put on, Yvonne would look as Asian as anybody could whose zaftig figure looked more Hooters than Dim Sum.

Yvonne met Ian Phelps in a private club in London's West End, where she was a part-time hostess. His heavy tipping and barely disguised references to a supply of cocaine persuaded her to go out with him.

That led to a courtship smothered in coke that evolved into an expensive condo for her, clothing, a diamond ring with a gold satellite dish on it and no need to spend any more time fending off other Ian types at the club, men with less money and no drugs.

The chauffeur rolled the Daimler to a stop in the *porte-cochère* in front of the high-rise apartment building at 240 Porchester Place.

Phelps got out, nodded to O'Reilly at the wheel and walked up the four steps to the glass double doors. The gray-haired doorman saluted him with one finger from his sitting position at the front desk.

"Evenin', sir," he said, looking back at his racing form, not expecting an answer from the visitor he had seen many times before.

Ian knew a lot of foreigners lived in this building, including many aging Iranians who left Tehran with their wives and mistresses when the Ayatollah took over from the Shah. The apartments on the upper floors offered spectacular views south to Hyde Park and east along Oxford Street.

More than she's worth sometimes, Phelps thought.

Still, he never met an Asian woman who could do the amazing things with her tongue that Yvonne did, more impressive even than tying knots in cherry stems. And he never met another English girl who would indulge his Asian fantasies.

So, Phelps put Yvonne in this pricey apartment about eighteen months ago, a mutually satisfactory arrangement.

His wife, Ethel, was happy with her garden and her antiques at their townhouse in Belgravia, one of London's ritziest neighborhoods, made famous to the masses as the locale of the *Upstairs, Downstairs* TV series.

Ethel had only a live-in maid/housekeeper and a driver. She settled for that. At least they were there to chat with, especially important to Ethel during a lot of long evenings when her husband was elsewhere. She knew Phelps worked irregular hours and she learned early on not to question his schedule.

Ethel loved him once and now loved the stability of their peck-on-the-cheek marriage. He had married her, years ago, before his ambition and his appetites expanded. Ian was comfortable with Ethel as his housewife and Yvonne as his roll in the hay, or bamboo, as it were.

As Yvonne answered his knock, Ian went a little weak in the knees. He had seen her in the Asian getup a hundred times, but the adrenaline jump-start it sparked never failed.

"Good evening, Ian-San," Yvonne said with a small-mouthed semi-whisper. She bowed just the slightest bit, the way Ian insisted.

He smiled, stepped inside the apartment and took her in his arms.

"Where's the music, Hu Chi?" he asked.

She broke away gently and moved to the stereo cabinet by the window. "I have it right here, ready for you," she said, hoping her lapse in not having the Oriental lute music playing when he arrived would not provoke his anger.

"Hu Chi, Hu Chi, how many times must I remind you," he scolded. But his good mood over the news from Atlanta kept his temper in check.

Yvonne wondered how he came up with the name he called her, "Hu Chi." It didn't sound Japanese to her, Chinese maybe, or what, Vietnamese?

Phelps made it up the night he met her at the club.

"My Hu Chi girl. Yep, that'll be it, Hu Chi, ah, um, Hu Chi Coochie girl," he said, laughing with excitement.

Ian had never been to Asia, not even Hong Kong, where his company was part owner of a TV syndication service.

If he had to trace his fetish for sex with Asian women, it would have to be from a girl he knew in Manchester when he was sixteen. She was in his school, an exchange student to England from somewhere over there.

Her name was Wi or Woo or Shoo or something. It was not important to him, then or now. Her eyes, however, fascinated him. He took her out once, but she refused his advances, rebuffed his clumsy groping which ended their first date and would not go out with him again.

He hated that, desired her and vowed to have any Asian woman he ever wanted from then on. And he wanted every one he met.

Yvonne asked him, after she discovered his penchant for Asian girls, why he was attracted to her very un-Asian looks.

Ian slapped her then, on the cheek, twice.

"None of your business," he said in a menacing whisper. She never asked again.

The Oriental music plunked through the room, as Ian took off his jacket and tie and poured himself a Scotch at the small wet bar.

The glass in his hand bore the logo of his corporate empire, the satellite dish like the one on his ring. He could not resist putting his logo on everything and, in a sense, everybody.

He turned to Yvonne.

"Hu Chi, my dear, I have to go out of town for a few days."

"Going to the Olympics in America, are you?" she asked.

"Yes, if you have to know, I have business there."

The Chinese women's ping-pong team I'll wager, Yvonne thought, as she smiled and said something about missing him terribly.

It occurred to Phelps there would be a lot of Asian women in Atlanta for the games. And if they were not available, surely he could find an American girl who would fulfill his Asian fantasy for a fee.

"Switch the telly on, Hu Chi," he said. "Put on GNS, the news channel."

"Don't you own that?" she asked, as she bent to the TV set, the satin dress stretching over her rear end like snare on a drum.

"Not yet," Ian said to her, as he picked up the remote control and punched in the channel for GNS.

On the screen, a woman who looked to be too much meteorologist and not enough supermodel was giving the weather for Northern Europe.

"Don't they have hair and makeup people at that cheap-ass operation?" Phelps muttered, emptying his glass and pouring another Glenlivet.

"What's wrong with my hair and makeup?" Yvonne snapped back, turning to glare at Ian.

"Not you, Yvonne, I'm talking about the weather bimbo on GNS, one of my future employees."

Stung, but used to it, Yvonne sat on a dark leather couch and looked away, out the window toward Hyde Park, shrouded in the early morning darkness.

"Now, back to the news desk in Atlanta and Ethan Thomas," the weatherwoman said.

The anchorman filled the screen, aside a photo of the body on the TV mast.

"We are reporting on a tragedy in our own corporate family tonight," Thomas said, ad-libbing. "Here's the latest on the death of Hollywood star, Cav Campbell. He somehow fell or jumped or was pushed—we do not know which—from the forty-sixth floor of a luxury apartment building here in Atlanta..."

Ian flushed with pleasure. The news on TV, the scotch and Yvonne as Hu Chi were stirring his hormones.

She saw him smile, walked over and stood next to him, her hand moving through his thinning hair, touching his comb-over. He brushed her hand away.

"I know, I know, but you'll have to wait, my dear, one minute," he said, never taking his eyes off the TV.

"Mr. Campbell, fiancé of Bren Forrest, owner of GNS, was attending a party in Ms. Forrest's honor. Atlanta Police have sealed off the building..."

Phelps's smile became almost a sneer. Yvonne was frightened a little. He sometimes looked like that before he pushed her around. She moved away, but he turned, took her elbow and pulled her toward him.

"Hu Chi, it's happening. It's really happening. I will prevail, my dear."

With that, he squeezed her arm, hard, looked lustily into her tape-altered "Asian" eyes and pulled her toward the bedroom.

5

GNS HEADQUARTERS & PARK TOWERS—ATLANTA

"Standby, remote!"

Max Ippolito, the senior producer at GNS, was standing in the pit behind his director, holding a headset to his left ear.

"Jody, that picture quality sucks," he said to the engineer at the live truck in the driveway of the Vaughn's apartment high-rise building.

"Yeah, well, we never tried to go live with a body stuck on the mast before Max, ya know?" Jody was frustrated. He wanted to delay going live until the cops removed Cav Campbell's impaled body from the pole.

Ippolito overruled him, realizing if they waited for the police to do that, it could be hours. The GNS TV truck was evidence, key to the death of the fiancé of the woman who owned GNS. Police could and no doubt would impound it. Getting another live truck there, up and running, would take at least an hour.

He hoped the photog with the LiveU would get there faster, but figured the second truck would be needed for the long haul anyway.

Also, the LiveU system would give them the ability to use a second camera with its own first rate picture via a cellular video uplink. The LiveU, about the size of a large shoulder-strap backpack was a time, personnel and money saver.

Max decided to go for an immediate live report, body or no body.

The microwave dish was sitting on the roof of the live truck, connected and working. But because it was not up high on the extended mast, the picture was awful.

The image on the bank of monitors in front of Max and director Billy Olson was fuzzy with white electronic dots scurrying through it.

"We have snow," Jody said. "It's fuzzy leaving here." He was tweaking dials, turning the dish slowly a few degrees left, then right, hoping for a better picture.

Outside the live truck, Sheila Belle was standing with her back to the mast. On the monitors, Max could see her standing below Campbell's spread-eagle, speared corpse.

"Twenty seconds Jody, you too, Sheila, stand by."

She smoothed her shoulder-length blond hair and licked her lips so they would shine in the lights. She thought about her slightly disheveled looks, hoping the urgency of the story would make her reporting seem sincere.

Maybe I shouldn't smile off the top. But it's what people expect. They know my smile and they love it. Maybe a quick smile, then a serious look. Maybe...

Sheila's smile was an awesome thing, a product of years of daily, in-the-mirror practice.

In her bathroom at home, she had a life size head-and-shoulders photo of herself hanging next to the mirror, right over the toilet.

People who had been there often wondered whether the photo was for her daily smile alert or whether it was there to entertain men as they used the facilities.

"In ten seconds, Sheila," Billy said in her ear.

On the screen at that moment, GNS viewers saw the network logo and the bold, black words, "Breaking News."

"In five, Sheila, four, three, two..."

An announcer's voice, big, full of import: "GNS Breaking News. Reporting from Atlanta, GNS correspondent Sheila Belle."

"Take remote, cue her."

———

At the party in the penthouse, Police Chief Lutz was flushed, starting to sweat as he quizzed the sergeant in a noisy whisper.

"A body? Fell out of this building? Who, when?" The chief and the sergeant were near the front door.

The sergeant's cell phone vibrated. "Sarge, the TV types here have a hit on the jumper's ID," said an officer outside the building.

A few of the guests sidled closer to the chief, hoping to hear something about what was going on.

"Wait one," the sergeant said. He and the chief then moved into the library off the main foyer and closed the door.

"Go, whadaya have?" the sergeant asked the officer on the line, putting the cell phone on speaker.

"They say it's that actor, Campbell, Cav Campbell."

Chief Lutz looked faint, sweating more now.

"My God, he was here, at this party. I just saw him with Bren Forrest! He's her fiancé for God's sake."

"Standby, and keep your cell on vibrate until further notice."

The chief wanted to be somewhere else. He already could feel the heat that was about to focus on the Atlanta Police Department.

"I need to tell the mayor and get him to go get Ms. Forrest," the chief said to the sergeant. "Get this place sealed off, quietly!"

"Wait, how many men are with you down there now?"

"Sarge, five uniforms, two detectives and a million media. And, uh, GNS is on the air live. This is unreal."

"Go get the mayor in here, now!" the chief ordered the sergeant. "And Mr. Vaughn and the governor. Don't let anybody else know about this yet."

The mayor came in as the chief was turning on a small TV set on the bookshelf. Jerry Vaughn walked in next, followed by the mayor's security man, Ron Millstone. The sound and the snowy picture came up:

"We are live at a fashionable apartment building in Atlanta, where I have just identified the body of that man," Sheila said somberly, turning to point at the mast behind her, then back to the camera. "He is Hollywood star, Cav Campbell."

Sheila Belle was on the air live and loving it.

"It is one of the most horrible sights I have ever seen."

Miller, the cameraman, had a wide enough shot to show Campbell on the mast, looking like a still-life skydiver over Sheila's shoulder.

"Oh, Lord, lookit that," said the Mayor, "Oh, Lord, Lord, Lord..."

"Shhhhh, listen," said Jerry Vaughn.

"I knew this man, I interviewed this man many, many times on my regular show Hollywood Tonight. I liked this man and he liked me..."

"Jesus, tell her to just say what happened!" Max exploded into Billy's earpiece in the GNS control room. "I'm gonna kill her tomorrow, when I'm calm," Max said, "Tell her, Billy, now!"

Billy waved his arms like a preacher at a healing.

"Please, Sheila, describe what's going on there. Tell us what's happening right now, Sheila, now!"

He interrupted her rambling tale of when she last saw Cav Campbell at a Boys and Girls Club benefit in Atlanta, what Campbell said to her and how well they got along. She had slipped into her toothy, smiley-face demeanor.

"Well, uh, more on that later."

Now she was serious again, almost stern.

"Right now, here at the scene, this is a tragedy of tragic proportions," Sheila intoned.

Max groaned as she continued.

God, she's the tragedy of tragic proportions.

"I've not talked with police yet, but I can report they probably have not ruled out foul play here," Sheila said, with a dramatic tone she usually reserved for announcing the nominees for best actor.

"Jesus, can we get somebody else out there now?"

Max was in pain, watching Sheila's reporting on the death of the boss's boyfriend.

Sheila ran out of patter and was trying to interview a uniformed police officer standing near a TV news van.

"I knew Cav Campbell. Did you ever get to know him, officer?"

"Uh, no, ma'am," the pale, second-year man answered.

"What can you tell us about how this happened?'

"Uh, nothing, ma'am, and you'll have to move back from the TV truck now, ma'am," the officer said, repeating his orders from the sergeant.

"Thank you, officer, uh, B.W. Campbell," Sheila said, reading the name off the officer's nametag. "Well, what a coincidence, your name being Campbell and all. Our heart goes out to you." Max groaned louder.

"So, as you can see, ladies and gentlemen," she said, turning to the camera, "police officials are baffled about this shocking and tragically bizarre drama unfolding here in front of me."

———

"Baffled, my ass," griped Chief Lutz. "Somebody tossed him, is my guess."

"Oh, shut up, Chief, you don't have a clue and you know it," said the mayor in disgust. He could feel his Olympic glow fading fast in the chill of a scandal about to enshroud his town.

"Go get Reverend Smallwood," said the mayor to his security agent. "He was over at the bar last time I noticed.

"Then have him get Bren Forrest and bring her in here. And be careful not to cause a stir out there."

"We have to tell those people something," Chief Lutz said, nodding toward the party ongoing outside the room.

The mayor and Jerry Vaughn ignored him, riveted again to the TV as Sheila's cameraman zoomed to a close-up of Campbell on the mast.

"That, is, revolting, it's, uh, we, we just can't let Bren see this," Vaughn said. His six-foot-four-frame was sagging with distress.

He went out to the party and found his wife, Jan, talking with a couple of visiting dignitaries from France. Jan's facility with French, her charm and her looks were turning these Gallic egoists into Janophiles.

"Jan, the caterer needs you for just a minute, please," Jerry said, summoning a smile as he gently took Jan's elbow and guided her away from the Frenchmen.

He whispered in her ear as they moved toward the library.

"We have a crisis here."

As Cassandra Page clipped a lapel microphone onto her dress, she heard Chuck on the cell phone come back on the line from the assignment desk at Channel 3.

"Hey, Cassie, The Milkman says we can break in right after these next commercials. That'll be in three minutes."

"Well, let's get it done, Chuck. The other guys are here now and setting up."

Cassandra's mobile bureau was ready to go. A Channel 9 van, with "News9Now" splashed across the sides was about ready. A live truck from "NewsBuzz12" was just turning into the brick-paved drive in front of the apartment tower.

"Cassie, Art will be live in the Satellite News Center and he'll toss to you. We'll go to the video from the truck when you reference it."

"Hey, Chuck, we're not on satellite, we're eight blocks from the station for god's sake. Why're you putting Art in the control room?"

Cassie was irritated the anchorman, Art Toomey, would be on with her. She could handle this without him. She also thought Toomey was an idiot and she didn't think much of calling the control room the "NewsBlitz3 Satellite News Center."

The consultants thought it was catchy and sexy and would impress the viewers.

"Just do it, Cassie. Please, just do it. You know how it is. You're on in about two minutes." Chuck rang off.

Cassandra and her truck were back about a hundred feet from the mast where Cav Campbell remained, lifeless, bathed now in the lights from four TV crews.

Officers were taking large white sheets out of a police van, unfolding them, about to drape them over Campbell and the TV truck that held him aloft.

"Come on, come on, come on," Cassandra mumbled to herself, tapping her left foot nervously, worried the cops with the sheets would get to Campbell's corpse before her live shot did.

She won the race.

"This is a special report from NewsBlitz3," said the announcer's pre-recorded voice over a screen-filling graphic of the TV station's logo.

———

"The locals are up, at least Channel 3's just coming on," Billy Olson said to Max Ippolito, as they frowned at the bank of monitors on the wall of the GNS control room.

On the air, Sheila Belle was describing the scene from her privileged post a lot closer to the body on the mast than were the local stations.

"Now comes the grisly, gruesome, tragic task of solving this bizarre, shocking case," she told viewers, as though she actually said something.

"Billy, let's take a break and regroup," Max said. "Maybe we can get Ethan to the scene. He's at the party I think, but probably doesn't know what's going on."

Ethan Thomas was a journeyman anchor for GNS, there since startup. He had a knack for adlib situations and Max was confident Thomas could raise the level of this crisis coverage.

"Sheila, give 'em a 'We'll be right back, with ongoing live coverage, yadayadayada,' then throw to break, now," Billy said in her ear.

"All of America and movie lovers around the world huddle in horror as word of this tragedy spreads," Sheila said, wincing now, trying to make her voice deeper. "We'll take a break for just a moment. Please stay with us," she said, alternately frowning, pursing her lips, then spreading them in a mile-wide smile as the "stay with us" rolled off her tongue.

Sheila was pleased with herself.

"Any comment from downtown?" she asked Jody, as GNS did a ten second network identification slide and then a series of thirty-second commercials.

"Nope, they're real busy," Jody told her, deadpan, as he heard Max and Billy on his headset, swapping swear words about Sheila's performance.

In the control room, Max wondered what to do about Bren Forrest. He knew she was at the party, the honored guest. Should he page her?

No way. I can't tell her on the phone Campbell just did a nosedive. I'll get somebody to go over there. God, why me?

"This is Cassandra Page at the luxury apartment tower on Peachtree Street, where the biggest party of this pre-Olympics period has been touched by death tonight."

Behind Cassie, viewers could see the GNS truck and its unexpected baggage on the pole. They also could see three police officers, starting to climb to the roof of the truck, carrying those white sheets.

"A man who we believe is movie star, Cav Campbell, has died here. And yes, that is the body up there on the mast, the tower, of the TV truck belonging to the Global News Service."

"Don't touch it," the mayor snarled, as Chief Lutz reached to change the channel back to GNS.

The mayor had known Cassie Page for a couple of years. He thought she was as good as any of the local TV reporters, better than most and light-years ahead of Sheila Belle.

Jan Vaughn was staring at the TV, the disaster of the evening just sinking in. Her eyes got damp, but she tried not to cry.

"We don't have a positive identification yet, but the body looks like Mr. Campbell and he was known to be at a pre-Olympic party in this building tonight," Cassie said, her cameraman tightening his shot on her as she spoke.

There was a knock at the door. Reverend Smallwood entered, holding Bren Forrest lightly by the arm.

"What is it, what's going on here?" Bren asked as she saw the ashen-faced group before her.

Jan walked over to Bren Forrest and led her to a small two-seater couch against the wall opposite the bookshelves.

"So far, we have no idea how this happened, or why," Cassie was continuing, now voicing over video of the driveway scene shot earlier by her cameraman.

The mayor snapped off the TV set as Bren looked up at Jan.

"What is it?" she demanded, fear in her eyes, made stronger by the mist in Jan's.

"Ms. Forrest," Reverend Smallwood began, "Ms. Forrest, there's been a terrible accident..."

"Bren, dear, it's Cav," said Jan. The pastor and the others were relieved they didn't have to say any more.

6

ATLANTA

Lia did not enjoy a line of coke in a moving car, but it was better than no coke at all.

Some of the powder spilled off the magazine she held on her knees as she snorted through a rolled up dollar bill. She leaned back, her eyes closed.

"Come on, get on with it, get those things off," said the driver, looking at Lia through the rear view mirror of the black sedan.

He tossed a brown paper bag onto the back seat next to her.

"We don't have much time and don't forget the eyeglasses."

She opened the bag as the car lurched left onto the Interstate 85 on-ramp. It had been cruising just above the speed limit along Peachtree Road since it left the Park Towers a few minutes earlier.

The car picked up speed as it slid onto the highway, heading north. Lia didn't notice as she unzipped her black party dress and began the task of changing her appearance.

The scariest part of her job was behind her now. Not the killing. That was easy enough. Getting back into the Vaughn's place after her conspicuous exit was tricky. Getting out of there unnoticed after she tossed Campbell was the riskiest, she thought.

Leaving the party, then taking the employees' elevator back up to the kitchen entrance went smoothly. The kitchen door onto the hallway was unlocked, apparently for the busy catering staff's convenience. A wave and a wink were enough to get her past the only waiter she encountered in the kitchen. The sliding door to the balcony was unlatched.

She felt numb about pushing Campbell off the balcony to his death. She had killed before, but this time it was antiseptic, at least for her.

Besides he was a sleazy guy. He deserved it. No way he could survive that fall, right? What were we, forty, forty-five floors up?

No, Lia had no remorse about that. She never even heard the body hit the mast in her haste to get out of there.

The worst scare was on her way down in the service elevator. It suddenly stopped on the thirty-sixth floor. When the door opened, a guy with outsized eyeglasses and a big Dr. Seuss hat asked, "Going up, me-lady?"

Lia shook her head and pointed to the floor, then looked down.

"My, you're a shy one, ain'tcha," the cool cat in the hat said. "Oh, well, sorry you're not going to the party then."

As the elevator door closed, Lia thought she recognized that guy. *A rock singer maybe?* The thought vanished as she watched the light dance down the numbers as the elevator approached ground level.

When the door opened, she darted out to the right, ran through a back hallway and out the door by the lanai. Across the pool, in a driveway leading to a dumpster, she saw the car, motor purring.

She was in the back seat and being driven away within ten seconds.

As the car rolled out of the back entrance to the apartment building, Lia saw two police cars go by, slowly, then turn in the front gate, lights flashing, but no sirens.

Lia squirmed out of her tight dress and tossed it aside. In the bag she found a pair of khakis, a leather belt, a black cotton blouse and a pair of shoes, black flats.

Somebody's good at sizes, she thought, sliding into the khakis and buttoning up the blouse.

The driver slowed to fifty-five, hit his turn signal and moved the car toward the exit ramp marked "DeKalb Peachtree Airport."

Lia groped in the bag again and found a wig, sandy hair, cut short. It would make her look a little older.

Silly wig. Whoever saw a Korean with sandy hair? Must be a man who thought this up.

The glasses were tortoise shell, narrow rims, non-prescription lenses, slightly tinted.

Cool. Always wanted to wear glasses. Wish I had a mirror in here.

As she adjusted her wig, she saw a black purse on the seat, the kind with a braided leather shoulder strap. It had fallen out of the bag.

"What's with the purse?" she asked the driver.

"Take it with you. Leave yours, as is. Leave everything in there, even your cash. Everything."

She looked in the new purse and found lipstick, powder, a small packet of Kleenex, a small wallet with a Visa card and four hundred dollars in cash, all twenties.

"What about all my stuff?" she challenged the driver, a black man in his forties, big shoulders straining his black leather jacket. He looked back at her.

"Relax. Everything you need is on the plane. We'll be there in five minutes, ten tops." He turned left on the surface street. The runway lights glowed way off to the left.

Lia stuffed her black dress, her purse and her panty hose into the paper bag.

"Hey, don't forget your jewelry. All of it, in the bag, please. Watch, earrings, whatever." The driver spoke without looking back as he approached the entrance to the airport.

"Bullshit, my watch!" Lia was angry, not wanting to give up the diamond-ringed Rolex. It was a gift several years ago, in college, from a rich boy who introduced Lia to cocaine. They were together eighteen months. He spent his seemingly endless allowance on cocaine and gifts for Lia and she let him.

"Do it, ma'am, it's part of the deal, you have to do it." The driver was following orders to be polite to Lia, but firm if necessary.

She took off the watch and threw it into the bag.

"They better by God replace it," she seethed, straightening up and looking out the window as the car glided to a stop near a hangar.

The only lights were atop the towers, blinking red, and security lights above the hangar doors.

A business jet, twin engines humming, sat on the tarmac, white and shiny, the door open, stairs extended to the ground.

"Let's go, ma'am," the driver said, getting out and opening her door.

He looked her over quickly to make sure she bore or wore nothing of what she had on when she entered the car back in town.

Lia looked like a suburban housewife with her helmet-like wig and outlet mall clothes. She was not happy as she strode to the plane. A young man, blond, handsome and well built, wearing a white shirt with epaulets, appeared at the top of the stairs.

"Welcome aboard, miss," he said, smiling broadly.

"Thank you," she huffed. *Screw you*, she thought, climbing the steps and ducking into the cabin of the jet.

"Take any seat, Miss Lee," the blond man said. Lia looked around and saw the cabin configured for luxury business travel: Two rows of first-class seats, then a conference table with swivel chairs on four sides, a small bar to one side, a lavatory at the rear.

She sat in one of the spacious aisle seats and looked into the cockpit, as the blond man joined another crewmember who already was seated.

"You'll find everything you need in the side panel under the windows," the blond man said, as he closed the door to the cockpit.

Alone in the cabin, Lia flipped open the small wood-grain doors on the narrow cabinets under the windows. On form-fit shelves were bottles of Absolut, Bombay, Glenlivet and Jack Daniels Black, four glasses, a full ice bucket, small bottles of 7-Up, Perrier and a clear plastic bag full of white powder. Two hollow tubes, the size of small pencils, also were in the bag.

"Please, fasten your seat belt, Miss Lee, we'll be taking off now." It was the voice of the blond man on the intercom.

Lia ran two lines of coke and poured herself a glass of Perrier by the time the plane was off the runway and heading south through the night sky.

7

BUCKHEAD—ATLANTA

Traffic in Buckhead was a mess. Clumps of partying pedestrians spilled off the sidewalks into Bolling Way, walking from club to club, sweating in the hot July night, then shivering in the icy air conditioning of the bars. A policeman ticketed cars jammed into the "No Parking Any Time" spaces along East Paces Ferry Road.

It was a typical summer night in this hyperactive entertainment district, an alcohol-infused carnival of mostly heterosexuals, swarming, getting an early start on plans for their weekend cross-pollination.

This was Atlanta's one-stop social spot, Buckhead, a bit of Greenwich Village and Union Street with the pretensions of Coconut Grove and the gutters of Bourbon Street.

Harvey's had been at the vortex of Buckhead for a decade or more, catering to the jaunty and the jaded, mostly thirty-somethings and up. Nightwardly mobile Atlantans, from pre-prandial to any-port-in-a-storm, flocked to Harvey's.

It was a haven from the younger hormones that raged in bars up the street and in the head-banger clubs down the street.

The key keeper of that safe harbor feeling in Harvey's was Mick, a fortyish bartender who so clearly dominated the place that some newcomers assumed his name was Harvey.

An Amerasian woman slid through the three-deep crowd at the bar. She caught Mick's eye as she struggled to capture a place to plant an elbow and order a drink.

"Cosmo, please," she called, as Mick leaned in to hear her over the noise. He had not seen her here before. He would have remembered a girl who is that attractive.

The bar curved for thirty-five feet toward a dance floor in the back part of the building. The young woman was about halfway along the bar, standing in the middle of perhaps fifty people, many of whom noticed her striking appearance.

"Jim Beam, rocks," said a man who was jostling his way up next to her.

"One check?" Mick asked, glancing at the man, nodding toward the beauty next to him. Mick was hoping she was not with that guy whose Men's Wearhouse suit didn't do much to smooth his coarse appearance.

"Yeah, start a tab," the man said. He was 5' 10", muscular. Mick's first impression was the guy's neck was thicker than his head required for support. Mick wondered what the girl was doing with that guy. The bartender admired her profile as she turned to speak to "Neck."

"I don't think we can talk much business in here," she said with a nervous grin, feeling slightly uncomfortable with this man who walked into her office last week.

"Yeah, well it's fine. I just need some help with the real estate tax thing I told you about," he said, loud enough to be heard in a three-foot radius.

Neck told her his name was Leonard Cray, that he got her name from her accounting firm's branch office in Chicago. After his initial office visit, he insisted on meeting her at Harvey's, this night, exactly at this time.

Normally, she would not have agreed to that, but she was getting a little claustrophobic in her apartment lately and was pleased to have a night out. She heard Harvey's was cool and a lot safer than some bars in that area.

Because she was beautiful, going to singles bars was always a disappointment for her. Most men didn't have the guts to approach her until alcohol lowered their reserve and raised their chutzpah.

So, she agreed to meet Neck, a.k.a. Leonard Cray, at Harvey's. They arrived within a minute of each other. He was all business and that surprised her.

He was facing the bar, saying something about taxes, when she saw his face freeze, his mouth open.

"What is it?" she asked, as he looked past her at the TV set on the wall behind the bar. She turned and gasped at the image on the screen, a man's body speared on a pole on top of a truck.

A guy, two people down the bar, shouted, "Mick, turn it up. Mick, check it out. What the hell is that?"

Mick turned, saw the image on the silent screen, picked up the remote and increased the volume.

"This is Cassandra Page at a luxury apartment tower on Peachtree Road, where the biggest party of this pre-Olympic period has been touched by death tonight.

"A man who we think is movie star, Cav Campbell, has died here and yes, that is the body up there on the mast, the tower, atop the TV truck belonging to the Global News Service."

In the crowd along the bar, a glassy-eyed young guy with an Atlanta Braves cap on backwards said to no one in particular, "Wow, dude, is that a slasher movie or what?"

"Shhhhh. SSSHHHHH," bar patrons hissed as they strained to hear the audio on the TV.

"Geez, Mick, did you see that? That's just south of here, isn't it?" It was the guy two people down from where the Amerasian girl was standing with Neck, staring at the TV.

"I guess so, looks like that ritzy high rise down Peachtree."

Mick had a glass in one hand, an olive in the other, suspended in mid-mix. People at the bar were getting quiet now, a chain reaction of elbow nudges as they absorbed the image on live TV of a man impaled on a TV news truck.

"See if it's on GNS," the man waiting for his martini said to Mick. The bartender put the olive in the glass and changed the channel to the news network.

Ethan Thomas was at the anchor desk. A large still picture of the body on the mast was suspended over his shoulder.

"We are reporting on a tragedy in our own corporate family tonight," Thomas said, ad-libbing. "The latest we have on the death of Hollywood star, Cav Campbell, is this: He somehow fell or jumped or was pushed—we do not know which—from the forty-sixth floor of a luxury apartment building here in Atlanta.

"Mr. Campbell, fiancé of Bren Forrest, owner of GNS, was attending a party in Ms. Forrest's honor. Atlanta Police have sealed off the building..."

Everybody in the bar who could see the TV was watching now.

"How horrible. How can they show that on television?" the Amerasian girl asked her companion.

"Shit, they'll show anything these days," said Neck, draining his drink and lifting the glass to show Mick he wanted another.

"Not me, thanks," she said to him sarcastically, when he failed to ask whether she wanted another drink. The one she already had was warming her throat and loosening her tongue.

"You really are all business, aren't you?" she said to Neck. He ignored her remark, looking past her at the TV.

"...to our Washington bureau for reaction from our nation's capital," Thomas said.

On the screen, an anchor in Washington was talking. His lips were moving but no sounds came from the TV. After about ten seconds of that, Thomas appeared again from the Atlanta studio.

"We seem to be having audio difficulties..."

"Go back to Channel 3," somebody said to Mick, who already was punching the remote.

"Let's go, now," said Neck, chugging his second drink.

"Sure, why not?" The girl was irritated now, eager to see more of the drama unfolding on television and she had tired quickly of Neck. He was a dud and she was ready to go home.

A commercial played on TV and the noise resumed in the bar.

As Neck paid the bill, cash, two twenties on the bar, the trio started playing again. Amidst the noise, Mick leaned across as the girl picked up her purse.

"Come see us again," he said. "By the way, what's your name?"

"What? I can't hear you with the music," she smiled.

Neck took her elbow and began to pull her gently but firmly away from the bar.

"I said what's your name?" Mick repeated.

"Tia," she said, her voice barely audible. "Tia Lee."

Neck was moving her away from the bar now, toward the door.

Mick shook his head, cupped his ear and smiled." Well, Mia, come back and see us."

8

PARK TOWERS—ATLANTA

"Friends, we have a tragedy on our hands and we have to deal with it."

Chief Lutz was talking to the assembled party guests after he tapped on a glass to get their attention.

Bren Forrest was still in the library in as much seclusion as Jan Vaughn could arrange. The governor had ordered Ron Millstone to guard that door, giving Bren some privacy while police questioned the guests.

"Mr. Cav Campbell has fallen or jumped to his death from this apartment tonight," Chief Lutz said, his voice as dramatic as he could make it.

He appeared almost to enjoy the instant reaction; gasps from the guests, followed by murmurs of "Oh, no… can't be true, How could it happen? My God, it must be a joke, But I just saw him, Oh, poor Bren," and so on.

The chief felt for a moment the way some journalists do, a brief, warm wave of temporary superiority, as in, "I know something you don't know and I'm about to tell you some of it." The wave passed and he flexed his jaw muscles a bit to show determination.

"Please, please friends," the chief went on, "Our investigation is urgent and we must insist on your cooperation."

He was, in his own mind, an inch taller by now, warming to his role and forgetting to ask the mayor to speak as he was told.

"The chief means to say," the mayor broke in, walking over to stand next to the chief at the piano, "our officers must get statements from each of you, so we hope you'll understand and be patient."

Jerry Vaughn emerged from the library at that moment and stepped between the two men who were almost jostling each other for the job of spokesman.

"Ladies and gentlemen, we beg your indulgence as police try to figure out what happened here tonight."

He had their attention.

"Chief Lutz, why don't you turn this over to the detective now," Vaughn said.

"Yes, of course. Friends, homicide Detective James Hagan and his men want to talk to each of you. So, if you would just take a seat, we'll get this over with in a hurry."

The chief bowed a bit, shook Jerry Vaughn's reluctant hand and walked back to the small library where Jan Vaughn was consoling Bren Forrest.

"All right then folks, let's start with whoever saw Mr. Campbell in the past half hour or so," Detective Hagan said. He was underwhelmed by the crowd of celebrities and power brokers, but unnerved a bit by the challenge of finding out what happened to Cav Campbell.

The police chief and the mayor made it clear he must solve the case before the Olympics, just three days away.

Jimmy Hagan, a slender six-footer with reddish, almost copper colored hair and blue-green eyes, had been a detective for seven years, in homicide the past three, having worked his way up from patrolman. At thirty-seven, he was the first and only member of his family to be a cop. Most of his relatives were on the other side of the law or indifferent to it.

Hagan grew up in Cabbagetown, an enclave of poor Appalachian whites east of downtown Atlanta. He was a hell-raising teenager, the son of a drunk who destroyed his liver and died in his mid-forties. Jimmy was twelve at the time. After that, his mother mostly whimpered herself to sleep every evening, leaving Jimmy to fend for himself.

"Come on now, ladies and gentlemen, you all know, uh, knew who Mr. Campbell was, so who talked to him tonight?"

Nothing. No hands went up, nobody spoke up.

"Well, then, let's do it this way," Hagan sighed.

He pointed at a clump of people on the long, bottle green leather couch. "You four, please go into the bedroom, through that door, with Detective Perez."

"Over here," he gestured toward several people still standing around the piano, "you all please go with Detective Monroe into the kitchen."

As his designated questionees moved slowly as ordered, Hagan pointed at his own chest.

"You five folks here, come with me, please. The rest, please stay seated and we'll get to you just as soon as we can. Thanks very much."

Hagan took his group to a guest bedroom, loosened his tie and opened a small notebook. It had a beige cover and the words "Reporter's Note Book" on the cover. Hagan had a supply of these, given to him by his girlfriend, Cassandra Page of Channel 3. Most reporters in America used them, furnished by their TV stations or newspapers.

Some company in Virginia was getting rich off those things. Hagan taped his business card over the word "Reporter's" on the cover, not ever wanting to be mistaken for a media person.

"Your name, please?" he asked a middle-aged woman in a silvery floor-length dress. A nickel-sized ruby on a white gold chain around her neck was her only jewelry.

"Martha Daley. Mardy to most people," she replied, standing on one foot, then the other. "And this is my husband, Malcolm."

Mardy was a sixty-three-year-old woman who looked fifteen years younger and knew it. Her hair was honey with streaks of silver put back in to add a "don't dismiss me" attitude.

The Daleys probably had more money than anybody else at the party. They owned DDD, Daley Daily Delivery, Inc.

"We want to help, officer, uh, Detective, but can we be assured the media won't show us in all this?"

It was Malcolm Daley at his most naive.

In 1972, Malcolm Daley was twenty-three years old, an unemployed ex-postal clerk. He was fired from the post office in

Jackson, Tennessee, for demanding pay raises be awarded for merit, not just seniority.

One night in a bar, he bragged he could deliver packages better and faster than the US Mail.

A buddy who thought it was liquor talking bet him three hundred dollars he couldn't do it. Daley started with only a thousand dollars, borrowed in bits and pieces from his aunt, his uncle and his girlfriend's father.

He marked off a zone in the downtown business district and blitzed the block with pamphlets promising faster and cheaper delivery in central-west Tennessee than merchants could get with the US Mail.

Within two years, DDD had three trucks and was winning the delivery battle in Jackson.

He collected the bar bet and used it to pay back his girlfriend's dad. Six months later, he and the girlfriend, Mardy, were married.

In the late nineties, Malcolm and Mardy swallowed up a smaller delivery company and moved the firm into an expansive new headquarters complex in Atlanta.

On this night of unexpected turmoil, Daley Daily Delivery was the largest package delivery company in the country. Having the Olympics in Atlanta gave his corporation a huge boost to its image as well as its bottom line. The distinctive "Triple D" trucks seemed to be everywhere and pretty much were.

So in the Olympic spirit, as Daley called it, DDD bought a lot of TV commercial airtime for this week, broadcasting what insiders call "image spots." These thirty-second commercials feature high-toned messages of smiling faces of people from every racial and cultural group in the world waving at the newly painted fleet of DDD trucks rolling through the Streets of Atlanta.

The image DDD was developing was of a prosperous, civic-minded firm, welcoming the world back to beautiful Atlanta. Now, Daley was despondent.

We're spending all this money to create an image of happy people sending happy stuff to other happy people via Daley Daily Delivery and what comes along and craps all over our efforts?

Unbelievable. A famous guy does a header out of an Olympics party.

Goodbye to DDD's image of world class good guys, hello non-stop TV showing the new image of Atlanta, a guy speared on a TV pole-thing. Un-fucking-believable.

"I'm sorry, Detective, would you repeat your question?"

"Did you talk with Mr. Campbell tonight? Jimmy Hagan again asked the Daleys.

"Yes, I did, early on," Mardy said, almost in a whisper. "He was with Bren Forrest, of course."

"I was there, too," Malcolm Daley added. "We didn't talk about much, just the party, the GNS anniversary coming up, that sort of thing."

"How was his demeanor? I mean was he nervous or sulky or what?"

"He was his usual arrogant self," came a man's voice from the couch. It was Clarence Justice, a society hanger-on who had two lame claims to fame and bored people with them regularly.

Hagan looked at him, slouched in the corner of the three-seater. *He resembles somebody, some TV guy, hmmm, the guy who was on that show with Kathie Lee. The short guy, big talker. I can see him, always telling stories about nothing. God, who is that guy?*

"Your name, sir?" Hagan asked, pushing his private Name-That-Star game aside for a moment.

"Friends call me Regis, or just Reej," said Clarence Justice. "Can't figure out why, can you?" He said it with a satisfied smile that reminded Hagan of one of those old actors who had late onset career booms pitching gold on TV.

Regis. Regis Philbin. That's who this turd looks like. Only fatter and with smaller teeth. Yeah, that's it.

"Well, Mr. Reej, I don't know why they call you that, but could you give me your real name please?"

The other two people on the couch moved away from Clarence as his smile spread.

"Justice, Clarence Justice, you probably heard of my son, the ballplayer," he said, laughing with anticipation at the expected reaction from the cop.

Asshole. He should be so lucky.

Nobody in the room laughed. Hagan ignored the reference to David Justice, the black, one-time star outfielder for the Atlanta Braves. Hagan stared at the white, puffy man in front of him.

"Well, Mr. Justice, why do you say Mr. Campbell was arrogant tonight?"

"Hell, he always is. May he rest in peace, of course," Justice answered in an unctuous manner he used when nobody around would buy his Regis Philbin/David Justice routines.

"What did he say to you specifically?"

"Nothin' much. Just hey, how ya doin', you know."

"Again, what was the arrogant part?" Hagan asked, frowning, not taking notes, realizing Justice was resentful Campbell actually had been in movies and on TV and didn't just vaguely look like someone who had.

"Geez, I'm sorry I brought it up," said Justice, uncrossing his legs and brushing some sort of small debris off the lapel of his dark brown, double-breasted suit.

"What was he doing when you saw him last?"

"He was talking with Bren Forrest, and Jan, uh Mrs. Vaughn, and one of the games hostesses, the Oriental gal, ya know? But she left, I think."

Hagan was taking notes now, hoping these people would have more to offer.

"Then what?" he asked.

"That's it," said Justice, crossing his legs again, left ankle on right knee, his beige socks stopping short of a patch of leg hair below his cuff.

"I went back to the bar, that's all. Period. Zip. Nada. The End."

Hagan stared for a moment.

"Tell you what, though," Justice added in a wink-wink sort of whisper, "I'd trade in Kathie Lee for that Chinese broad in a heartbeat. She was hot, man, like that green pasty stuff they put on sushi, ya know, whattaya callit, uh, Mesabe? Yeah, she's a firecracker."

"Well, thank you, Mr. Regis," Jimmy said with a straight face. "We may want to talk with you again later on."

Justice stood abruptly and stalked out of the room.

"Don't pay any attention to him. He's a crank, but he's harmless," said Mardy Daley.

She told Hagan Justice earned a living by going to parties with a blowzy, flashy woman who tried, unsuccessfully, to look like Kathie Lee in her prime.

Their act for hire mainly was pretending to interview party guests, a la Regis and Kathie Lee. They also often slipped in old classic movie dialogue. They seemed to think their wrenching rendition of, "Frankly my dear, I don't give a damn" or, "After all, tomorrow is another day," was cutting edge.

Still, some hostesses around town thought they were good icebreakers at parties and less likely than palm readers or organ grinders to steal the flatware.

"Is Kathie Lee, I mean the woman, his partner, here?" Hagan asked.

"Probably, but she'll be at the bar, if any place," Mardy said.

Hagan wrote down the names and phone numbers of the other couple on the couch, a county commissioner and her husband from the northern suburbs of Atlanta, and told them he would be in touch.

"So, thank you all," he said, handing his card to the commissioner and to Mardy Daley. "Show this to the officer at the door and he will let you out. And if you think of anything more, please call me at that number."

Hagan walked out first, hoping to spot Kathie Lee's double at the bar. He was intercepted by Detective Perez.

"Chief wants us in there now," he whispered, pointing at the door to the small library.

"Perez, have you seen Kathie Lee anywhere?" Hagan asked as they walked toward the door. Perez shook his head.

"Not since I was seven," Perez said with a grin. "Maybe she's down in the lobby putting her hand prints in cement, thanking her imaginary fans. But I'll check the guest list. Maybe Clark Gable will be on there, too."

9

CHANNEL 3 NEWSROOM

By ten o'clock, Channel 3's news director called in extra people for what could turn out to be all-night live coverage.

Channel 3's promotion department, called "Creative Services," also was at work shortly after the first live report on Cav Campbell's demise.

"Hey, man, we really need that video now," snapped Annie Block, the number two person in Creative Services.

She was in one of the small video editing suites along one wall of the TV news department. All reports, or packages as most TV people call them, were produced and edited on computers in these rooms, connected electronically to studio control rooms elsewhere in the building.

Annie, a short, slight woman of twenty-nine, leaned over a man sitting hunched over a laptop. "Really, bro, I need the video card with footage from the Park Towers," she said to Ben Hinske, one of the station's veteran shooters and editors.

He cringed at the "bro" coming from Annie, the only white woman in town with cornrow hair. She had an affected wannabe black accent she always used when talking with African-Americans.

She didn't know Ben and most of the other black employees laughed behind her back.

"When she quits, we'll have to hire a black person to keep the quota," Ben once joked to the news director about Annie.

Ben and Annie were watching the video of Cassie's most recent on-air report, what TV people call a "live shot," from in front of the building where Cav Campbell landed on the mast of the GNS news truck.

"Listen, sister," Ben said, the irony lost on her, "nobody gets this until I finish the edit for TV Score, period."

TV Score was the syndicated news feed Channel 3 received several times a day from its network. A TV Score editor called Channel 3 and pleaded for a quick news story on the Campbell death to send to other stations around the country. Ben was giving it first priority.

"Yo, Ben-man, listen, I need to get a promo done like now, ya know? Just a thirty second job, Ben, just a quickie saying NewsBlitz3 is on the story, ya know what I'm sayin', man?"

"Promo my ass. Geez, we've only done one live shot and you want a promo on the air already? Get out of here, Annie, please! I'll Airdrop it to your desktop soon as I can."

Annie didn't budge.

"Man, you know what's gonna shake if Channel 9 gets their promos on before I do, know what I'm sayin'?"

"Gets *it*s promos on, not *their* promos, for God's sake. *Its* promos, Annie, singular. Now, get out of here. You can have it in five minutes. Now beat it."

She pulled the sliding door shut behind her so hard she broke a nail.

About forty feet away, at the assignment desk, Chuck was on the phone with Cassie at the scene.

"Cass, can we do another live shot in about six minutes?"

"Hang on, Chuck, I think we're getting a positive ID on Campbell now."

Chuck could hear his reporter shouting at someone outside the apartment building.

"Chuck, let's go for it. The cop here says it definitely is Cav Campbell."

"Well, we need to wait for the next commercial break in this show. But hey, Cassie, the eleven o'clock producer wants you to record a couple bumps and teases for the show. Can you do that?"

"What, promos, now? Damn, Chuck, let's get the live shot on first. Gimme a one-minute standby, I want to see what's going on over there."

Chuck put the phone on the desk, knowing he was dismissed.

"Hi, Chuckster, what's going on?" It was Annie, talking white.

"Like you don't know, Annie," Chuck said. He was a white guy, extremely white with freckles and fair hair, thirty-five, sleeves rolled up, shirt wrinkled but all-cotton, an almost yuppie who broke into the news business before the days when the promotions and marketing people made most of the decisions.

"Chuckie, can you get Cassie to feed me a promo, now? I need it. Like immediately.

"Yeah, sure, after her next live shot. Wait a minute."

Chuck turned to the summer intern sitting at his left.

"Call Carl at home, get him down there now."

The intern, a sophomore beauty from the University of Missouri, blushed.

"Mr. Charles, you mean call Mr. Dayton, our political reporter, at home, at this hour?"

Chuck blinked, wondering whether she was serious, realized she was, then said in a quiet voice that grew a bit louder with each phrase, "Call Mr. Dayton now, Sydney," he insisted, using the "Mr." in mockery.

"Call him at home or in his car or at his girlfriend's apartment or in the men's room at the bus station, wherever, but find him."

"But, Mr. Charles, he is the political reporter and he may not like being sent to this, uh, event," she said with a weak smile.

Chuck knew she was right. Carl earlier asked to cover the big party at the Vaughn's condo, knowing every politico in the south would be there. The news director turned him down, saying it was not a political story, insisting that covering it like politics would "slow down the shows." This generation of TV managers tended to call newscasts "shows."

Annie saw an opening.

"Maybe he'll do the promo before he gets too busy down there," she said to Chuck. "Thanks Chuck-o, I owe you one."

Annie walked back to Ben's edit room.

"Yo, bro, no prob man, Carl's gonna do a promo. That mofo will do the 'live, team coverage' thing, cool?" Annie was back to black. Ben ignored her.

At the assignment desk, the intern was nervous. She heard what Annie said to Ben.

"So, Mr. Charles," she asked, twisting a strand of hair with her fingers, "You want me to call Mr. Dayton and ask him to go down there and do a promo, is that right? Is that really what you want?"

Chuck looked at the two young women; Annie, the promotion producer and Sydney, the college girl with the looks of a cheerleader but with a career potential of, maybe, Pia Zadora. He shook his head and waved them both away.

"Annie, what's a mofo?" Sydney asked.

"Shee-it, girl," Annie said, "I mean, Sydney, dear, "they're all around you and you don't even know it."

—

Cassie ran across the driveway to where the police set up a command post by the front door.

"Hey, guys, I'm going with this positive ID. It's solid, cold, right?"

A patrolman who heard Cassie's question began talking into his cell phone. Cassie waited, hearing snippets.

"Detective...media wants...confirm...back...?"

The other voice crackled through static and Cassie recognized it as Jimmy.

"...confirm...know how it...talk to 'em in....Cassie...?"

She edged closer.

"The detective says yes, it's solid, it's Mr. Campbell. You're Cassandra Page, right, miss?"

"Yes, is that Detective Hagan up there? Can I talk with him?"

"No, ma'am, not now, but he says he'll have a news conference in a half-hour."

Cassie shouted into her cell phone as she rushed back to where her video truck was ready for another live shot.

"Chuck, here it is. Police confirm the body on the mast is Cav Campbell. Obviously, he was at that party, so let's go."

"Cassie, can we call this exclusive, the ID?"

"I don't know yet, but I don't think so. I mean GNS identified the body earlier, just not confirmed. Let's just get it on and be done with it."

Annie walked by the assignment desk, heard Chuck say, "...this exclusive..." and ran to a phone at a nearby desk.

It rang five times before a woman's voice came on:

"Hey, Lisa, it's Annie, we have an exclusive here. We need to do an extra thirty second promo spot and a couple of ten second promos, too."

Lisa, the promotions director for Channel 3, brightened.

"Sure, Annie, and call it, let's see, call it, yes! Call it 'Cav Campbell's Final Role: Movie Star Murder in Buckhead!'"

"Well, uh Lisa, I'm not sure it was murder, ya know?"

"Like he jumped?" Lisa snorted. "No way, do it and get it on now. Besides, it's just a promo. It doesn't have to be true!"

Annie hung up and rushed up to Chuck on the assignment desk.

"Pleeease, pleeeease, just twenty seconds of video, that's all I need until Carl feeds his promo, Chuck. I can do the rest with graphics, pleeeease, Chuckster!"

A writer ran by the desk with the video card the editor, Ben Hinske, just handed him.

"We need to feed this to TV Score now, Chuck," the writer shouted as he headed toward the room where feeds were handled. "What's the slug on this story?"

"Movie Star Murder in Buckhead," shouted Annie as she ran after him, hoping to get the video in a few seconds.

"Bullshit," Chuck hollered at the writer. "Just call it 'Cav Campbell Death.' Period."

Sydney had her phone to her right ear. Her face was turning the color of fresh blood.

"But, but I'm just passing along... but Mr. Dayton, Mr. Charles says you have go down there..."

Chuck looked up as Sydney listened.

"...yes, yes, that's the place, but...well, he said..." She stopped talking, held the phone away from her ear as though it was toxic and then hung up.

"Was that Dayton?" Carl asked.

"Yes."

"Is he on his way?"

"I don't know. All he said was if I could find someone in the news department who had an opposable thumb, to have them call him at home."

"Jesus Christ, forget it," Chuck grunted.

Sydney looked dejected.

"Mr. Charles, what's an opposable thumb?"

———

"One minute, Cassie, standby. Plug in your earpiece, please."

Cassie was standing in front of the GNS truck. White sheets hung from a large frame hastily erected around the mast.

Behind it, police and two employees from the medical examiner's office were trying to figure out how to get Campbell's body off the pole.

They decided not to try to pull him off from the top. It would tear up the body, not to mention the mast.

So, they brought in chainsaws, with the idea of cutting through the corpse to the pole, then separating the body.

Cassie could hear the voice of the anchorman, Art Toomey, in the Satellite News Center.

"...and police have surrounded the building..."

"Ten seconds, Cassie, stand by."

The sound of the saw could be heard in the background.

"Five, four..."

"...so let's go live to Cassandra Page at the scene. Cassandra."

BBBBRRRRRAAANNNNNNGGGGGGG

The sound of dueling chainsaws drowned out Cassie's words.

Viewers saw her, with the white-draped TV truck in the background. Her lips were moving, but all they could hear was the chainsaw.

Max Ippolito was watching the Channel 3 report from the control room at GNS.

"Holy shit, look at that!" he said to an assistant. "They ought to kill that picture. They can't show that for God's sake."

Max and everyone else, however, watched…fascinated, the way passersby often react to a car wreck.

Behind Cassie, police lights created silhouettes of the chainsaw men at work. Cassie never looked back, so she didn't realize it.

Her cameraman was concentrating on her, straining to hear her voice, so he did not really notice either.

But more than a hundred fifty thousand viewers in the NewsBlitz3 coverage area saw a muted reporter, drowned out by the buzzing of chainsaws clearly visible in silhouette, cutting the body from the mast.

At Channel 3, the news director and the station manager were in the newsroom, watching the row of TV monitors along the wall. With them were Annie, the promotions producer, and Chuck, the assignment manager.

"Off, get it off, we can't show that!" shouted Chuck as he turned to call the control room.

"Why not, it's riveting," shouted Annie above the din of the saws.

"Tell 'em to zoom in past Cassie, get a close-up of those sheets," hollered the news director to Chuck.

"Riveting? Riveting?" asked Chuck, incredulous. "Are you joking? Rivets would be better. They're chainsaws for Christ's sake."

"I guess it's better taste with those sheets there, ya think?" said the station manager. It was the first time tonight he had spoken to Chuck, who was livid.

"No, why not just remove the sheets and maybe some blood would splatter on our camera! Hey, that'd be great, right?"

Chuck was losing it, shouting now at his bosses.

"Yeah, that's the ticket, shoot through the blood, sure, why not, it's the same color as our station logo! Terrific."

Chuck slumped against the desk, almost whimpering now.

"You people have lost your minds. Me, too," he said.

Nobody heard him.

Cassie was shouting into her lapel microphone now, trying to hear herself over the chainsaws.

"...and behind me, the authorities are dealing with this crisis, or trying to." At that point, she turned around and saw the tableau of silhouetted chainsaws hacking and BRRAAANNNGGing away at what was left of Cav Campbell.

"Oh, my Lord, we, we..."

In her ear, Cassie heard the director, "Step aside Cass, we're in on a close-up now, honest to God we are."

"Kill her mic, kill it!" the news director hollered to Chuck, who just handed him the phone and walked out of the newsroom toward the water cooler in the hallway.

Cassie's cameraman gave her a "cut" signal, the hand across the throat, fingers together.

She turned back to watch what her audience was seeing and started to cry, mostly out of anger.

10

PARK TOWERS, BUCKHEAD—ATLANTA

"That is the most disgusting thing I have ever seen on TV," said Chief Lutz, a shimmering river of sweat sliding off his upper lip, down the creases at the corners of his mouth.

He was in the small library off the foyer in the Vaughn's apartment. He stared at the paper-thin TV as Detectives Hagan and Perez walked in, closing the door behind them.

On the screen, he could see the chainsaws in silhouette behind the sheets police had hastily put up around Campbell's body.

"Jesus, can't we turn that off?" asked Perez.

"Wait, there's Cassie, uh, Cassandra Whatzername," said Hagan, catching himself.

The camera pulled back from the close-up to reveal Cassie standing there, apparently stunned. Her mouth opened and a second later, she began to speak, clearly upset.

"Unfortunately, we have shown you the effort by police to get Mr. Campbell's body off the mast of the TV truck. It's a shocking sight to all of us here.

"All we know now is police plan a news conference in a few minutes and we'll carry it live here on NewsBlitz3."

Hagan could tell Cassie was shaken, almost shaking. He had never seen her that discomposed on the air.

"For now, let's go back to Art Toomey in the studio, I mean, in the Satellite News Center," Cassie said.

"God, that really stinks," said Detective Laurie Monroe, turning away from the TV.

"You wanted to see us now, Chief?"

"Yes, let's compare notes. We must meet with the news folks in about ten minutes, so let's see what we know so far," the Chief said, his posture improving, his speech calm, belying all the perspiration on his face.

Hagan went first, summarizing his session, followed by Perez, then Monroe. Then Hagan spoke again.

"One other thing. That loony tunes who thinks he's Regis Philbin said he saw Campbell talking with an Asian woman. Which of you took her statement?"

Monroe shrugged and looked at Perez, who shook his head.

"Yeah, one lady I talked to said she saw Campbell and Mrs. Vaughn and Ms. Forrest with an Asian girl," Perez said. "But she says the girl left the party some time ago."

"Yeah, that's what the let's-pretend-Regis said, too," said Hagan. "Who is she, the girl?"

"Another man said he saw her leave," Detective Monroe added. "Said she was gorgeous, thinks she was some Olympics employee, that's all he said."

Chief Lutz interrupted, visibly upset now.

"Is that it? Is that all we have, that some beautiful woman talked with Campbell, then left the party?"

"Chief, we have eight more people out there to interview, including one British rock star who lives in this building, so let me go see what he and the others have to say." Hagan was trying to keep the Chief from losing his temper.

"Go ahead, but make it fast," said Lutz. "I have to meet the jackals of the press in ten minutes."

Hagan walked out, glad to be away from the Chief's imminent emotional meltdown.

Sitting at the piano, cruising the upper keys with his right hand, was the rock star, who called himself Bexx. He wore a large top hat, à la Dr. Seuss, and sequined sunglasses, jeans and penny loafers, no socks. He glanced up as Hagan approached.

"Cop, right?"

"Yeah, cop." Hagan answered, trying to keep a snap out of his voice. "Rock star, right?"

Bexx laughed. "Yeah, but no drugs, not even one toke over the line, officer."

Hagan smiled and asked the singer where he lived.

"Downstairs, ten floors below, and of course in London and in Maui."

"Of course," Hagan made a note.

"Do you know Mr. Campbell or did you see him here tonight?"

"Well, I know who he is, but we never saw him. I was a little late arriving because I was watching Mayberry on TBS. Love that old show and I really love that Barney Fife, don't you, officer?"

"My kinda cop," said Hagan. "Now, Mr. Bexx, by any chance did you see an attractive Asian woman here tonight?"

Bexx looked down, thoughtful, and riffed the keys. Then he smacked the top of the piano with his left hand.

"Blimey, I saw a girl like that on the service lift at my floor, I did."

"When exactly was that?"

"While I was coming up here. I always use the service one. Avoid the crowds, autographs and all, you understand?

"I pushed the button and the lift stopped on thirty-six, going down. This beauty was standing there, startled to see me, I think. Sort of a deer caught in the headlights.

"I asked whether she was goin' up. She didn't say a word, just pointed down and shook her head.

"Then she poked the button again, and the door closed. I had to wait for the lift to go all the way down, then back up. Musta taken five minutes."

"Had you ever seen this woman before?"

"No, but I'd like to see her again. A beauty, she was, killer body, great face, she must be a model, somethin'."

"How old was she?"

"Dunno, twenty-one, twenty-two, maybe twenty-three or so. Tall too, taller than me without my lifts, I'll wager."

Hagan noticed Bexx's' shoes under the piano, the stack heels reminiscent of something from the Seventies. He smiled and closed his notebook.

"If you ever see that woman again, please let me know," said Hagan, handing Bexx his card.

"Well, Detective, truth is, I don't see people. People see me, if you know what I mean." Hagan knew. He saw how the public fawned over even a local "celebrity" such as Cassie Page when they were out for lunch or dinner.

"I understand, Mr. Bexx. Thanks for your help. By the way is Bexx your first name or last name or what?

"It's my name, that's all, just Bexx. Less is more, right, mate?"

As Hagan headed toward the library, he turned back to Bexx at the piano.

"By the way, I must ask you. Do you write the words or the music?"

Bexx smiled, brought both hands to the keyboard and pounded out the opening chords of his most famous song, about a movie goddess who died young.

"The music, mate, the music," he said with a grin.

11

PARK TOWERS, BUCKHEAD—ATLANTA

Jan Vaughn was standing over Bren Forrest, who lay on her back on Jan's king-sized bed in the Vaughn's opulent master bedroom.

The drapes were drawn, muted burgundy and forest green striped fabric, with a black lining that kept out any light. This night, they kept out the world, the glow of the city skyline that Jan usually loved to look at before drifting off. The Vaughn's live-in maid, a short, slender woman from El Salvador, stood tentatively a few steps from the bed.

Bren was lying with her arms folded over her stomach. A dark washcloth, cool and wet, covered her forehead. Her bangs, usually brushed slightly to one side, were damp, curling at the ends, matted at her temples. Her eyes were closed and puffy, her nose red from crying, cheeks streaked from tears she swiped at occasionally with the tissue crushed in her left hand.

Her breath was even now, but she was wide-awake.

Twice she tried to rise up, to ask in anguish what happened to Cav. Each time, Jan gently pushed her back to a resting position, her head on the pillow.

"Shhh, Bren, not now, just try to rest, shhhhh, just relax, sweetie," Jan whispered.

She gestured at the maid, giving a cupped, hand-to-mouth motion indicating she wanted water for Bren. The maid nodded and almost ran out the door, obviously relieved to be away from her boss and the grieving woman she was trying to comfort.

"Jan, please, please talk to me," Bren said, her voice harsh and halting. "They said he went off the balcony, do they...I mean is it...was it..." She choked back a sob and rose up on one elbow.

"Jan, please," a searching, pleading look in her eyes, "please, you're my friend, tell me the truth, Jan!" Bren's voice was stronger now, or at least louder.

"Honey, they don't know, the police I mean. They're all over the place, trying to find out what happened. "

Jan touched the washcloth, stroking Bren's forehead with it, then her cheeks.

The knock at the door was the maid, back with a glass of water.

"Yes, come in, yes, bring it over here," she said. The maid glided to the bedside, handed Jan the glass and backed away, not wanting to touch the mourning Ms. Forrest.

Bren took a small sip of the water, then lay back on the bed and sighed deeply.

"How could he fall off that balcony, Jan, it's at least waist high, the concrete railing, isn't it? Don't they have to make them so people don't fall off, Jan? Don't they?"

"Shhhhhh, Bren, take it easy, darlin', yes, they make 'em that high for safety, but nobody knows what happened. Somehow, he fell off and, and..."

"Did he suffer, Jan?" Bren sobbed loudly again, a new wave of grief rising in her mind, in her heaving chest.

Jan bit her lip and squeezed her eyes, fighting back tears herself.

"No, Bren, honey, I'm sure he didn't even know what happened."

"He doesn't handle pain very well," Bren said, suddenly calm for a moment. "No, he doesn't do well with little hurts, you know, like paper cuts and all, he howls and complains and wants to see a doctor. I mean it's embarrassing sometimes, Jan."

Bren was silent for a moment. "So, I hope there's no pain because it would be horrible for him, the fear and all, he wouldn't like that, no he wouldn't, not one bit, no, no..."

Jan didn't respond, waiting, letting Bren vent, her stamina spent, her mind reeling in an effort to grasp the fact her fiancé just fell forty-six stories to his death.

Bren slumped slightly and stopped rambling. She closed her eyes and seemed to doze a bit, her lips parted in an unintentional sliver of a smile.

"Try to sleep, darlin', try to sleep now," Jan whispered, backing away and turning toward the maid, who held open the bedroom door.

"Turn off the light on the dresser and stay here with her," Jan told the maid, who shuddered at the thought. "Let me know immediately when she wakes up," Jan said softly, then left the room, closing the door behind her.

In the living room, Jerry Vaughn was sitting in a grey, upholstered club chair, talking quietly with one of his business partners and with Mardy Daley, who had stayed behind with an offer to help.

The crowd was gone now, released by police after the questioning. Officers escorted them out the back door of the maintenance area, behind the lobby. Reporters who swarmed the front of the building did not see the guests leave.

Clarence Justice, however, declined to slip away. He rounded up his Kathie Lee partner, and walked around the building to the gathered throng of media people.

Now, almost two hours after Campbell's death, the body was removed, the area cordoned off, and the press was corralled into a media pen of sorts about a hundred feet from the front door.

The reporters were antsy, especially the TV people, whose eleven o'clock newscasts were just minutes away. Camera lights were popping on and off as the photographers shot video of the general scene, pictures to go with the reporters' narration — once they finished showing the good stuff: the body, the removal of it through the sheets, that sort of thing.

Chief Lutz was in the lobby in a makeshift command post behind the reception desk. Jimmy Hagan was there, sitting on the corner of the desk, talking softly into a cell phone.

The chief promised a news conference, but he wanted to make sure it was carried by all the stations, so he waited until eleven o'clock, when the stations' newscasts were on live.

Lutz did not often get to be the lead story on the local TV news, much less on GNS. He was in a spot, or on the spot, not sure which yet.

Much of the past forty-five minutes he spent getting blistered by the mayor, who reminded Lutz whose ass was on the line if the case was not solved before the Olympics began in three days.

The chairman of the Olympics committee, the leader of the city council and other officials had been calling him at the command post with such supportive comments as, "We're behind you a thousand percent, Chief," and "It's up to you now, we're all counting on you!"

Lutz decided if he was going to take the heat, he also would take the publicity. He had a plan how to deflect blame, if it should come to that.

12

PARK TOWERS, BUCKHEAD—ATLANTA

At ten fifty-nine at night, a barrage of TV lights went on in the designated press area.

"Yes, I hear you," said Cassandra Page, her left hand pressed against her ear so she could hear the director back at the TV station through her IFB earpiece.

"One minute, Cassie, you're up live at the top, right after the open."

The director, a relative newcomer to Channel 3, was nervous as he started to give Cassie a countdown to the top of the show.

"Art goes first, then tosses to you, forty-five seconds now. Standby."

Reporters for the other local stations assumed similar positions, not more than fifteen or twenty feet from each other. The news babble was about to begin.

Cassie's colleague at Channel 3, political reporter Carl Dayton, stood about six feet from her, also wired with his earpiece and his microphone. He would have the second report in the newscast and would have only about eight seconds to get into position when Cassie finished her lead story.

"Carl, you hear me? Mic test, please, Carl," the director was in Carl Dayton's ear, loud and clear.

"I hear ya and we're ready here, mic check one-two-three, check, check. And listen, when the chief comes out, I grab him, right?"

Cassie heard that and barked into her microphone to the control room, "Hey, no way, man, the chief's mine, guys, you know that!"

She glared across at Dayton, who turned away and talked into his microphone again.

"Look, it's a natural. Cassie does the lead, tosses to me, I get the chief live and we move on, what's wrong with that?"

The novice director turned to the producer of the newscast, who sat at his left in the control room.

"Hey, deal with these ego-freaks, will ya? Fifteen seconds to air." Then, on his headset, he said, "Standby show-open, standby studio."

He saw Art Toomey on camera one, massaging his mustache, then touching the knot in his tie, then his right temple.

Toomey's wavy black hair, graying at the temples, was part nature, part the skill of his long-time hair cutter, Geoffrey. Art had more hair than brains and a cleft chin viewers actually mentioned in some surveys. Some thought it was sexy. A few winced at the survey question. One respondent asked, "What's he keep in that chin hole anyway?"

Art came to Channel 3 five years ago from San Antonio, Texas, where he angered Hispanic viewers by trying to over-accent any Spanish-language words he had to say.

Any word with an "r" in it became a trill-orgy in Art's mouth. Burrito became "Burrrreeeeeto," sounding like a drunken Scotsman in a Mexican bordello.

Art, forty-six, knew he and local TV news made a fine fit. He was a news director's dream, an anchor who would read anything written for him. He also was an actor, eager to sob his way through sad news stories and smile through the warm and fuzzy ones. An even slightly upbeat story provoked a giddy giggle from Art, everybody's good-news newsman. A TV news consultant once told Art to draw happy faces on his scripts if the story was upbeat, sad faces for the so-called tragedies. Since then, Art was successful at aping the little faces on his copy.

Sometimes Art would say something on the air that made the behind-the-scenes staffers convulse with laughter. For example, while reading a story about a murder in New York City, Art read, with a somber face, "A man walking his dog was shot to death three times…"

Art continued, while all the off camera staff who heard it put their hands over their faces to keep from laughing out loud.

Another time, Art said on the air about a bank robbery in St. Louis, "Police are looking for three men in ski masks." He apparently did not consider the likelihood the robbers would have ditched the masks as soon as they scrambled into their getaway car.

The "Art-ism" for which he is best known, probably, was when he reported a story about a scientific breakthrough. "Scientists have discovered a new orgasm." Even Art laughed at that and quickly said, "I mean organism. Organism."

In Atlanta, the big time for Art, he decided he would sound worldlier if he could adapt his news reading to fit the stories about other languages or cultures.

Whenever Art read a story about Britain or British people, he affected a British accent and used the word "lift" for elevator and "flat" for apartment. He would say "bonnet" for the hood of a car, "brolly" or "bumbershoot" for umbrella and "chips" for fried potatoes.

It puzzled all but the most pretentious viewers and infuriated his news director. Other on-air people at the station thought it was hilarious.

The bosses ordered Art to knock it off. However, when he read a story one night about an event in Birmingham, Alabama, Art insisted on calling it "Birming-um," the British way of saying it. He did it three times. Some viewers called to complain, some just to laugh.

Art Toomey was popular anyway, because he accepted every speaking engagement he could find, including visiting elementary schools at naptime to share juice and blankies with the kiddies.

"He must love this town," viewers often said in surveys, "and he loves the little people!"

Cassie thought he was a fool, but stifled her resentment. She had no time for that now.

"Ready open, standby camera one, standby Cassie, sound up," said the director. He was less nervous now, dealing with details of production instead of on-air egos.

On the pre-recorded opening video, an F-15 jet zoomed through the picture. Trumpets heralded the flyover and viewers heard the swelling sound of violins and watched a laser trace of the Atlanta skyline appear, lights dancing, sparkling.

The announcer's voice boomed in: "This is NewsBlitz3, Nightside Edition."

The voice ended, the jet plane swooped in again, contrails blooming to form a "Channel 3" in the night sky.

"Fade it, cue Art," said the director.

"Good Evening, Georgia, our top story tonight: A hometown movie star plunges to a gruesome end here in Atlanta and the world is riveted on the death scene at this hour."

Toomey looked somber, his voice pitched down as far as it would go. He leaned into the camera, head slightly turned. He had learned how not to blink while reading a sad story. He had to learn, because blinking interrupted his concentration.

"Standby, Cassie, ten seconds," the director said.

In the lobby of the Vaughn's building, Chief Lutz was watching Channel 3.

"Let's wait a minute, then we go out there. Is there a place set up for my news conference?"

"Yes, Chief," said a uniformed aide. "It's about ten feet in front of the rank of reporters. All the stations have mics on one stand and lights are ready, so just walk up and I'll let you know when they're ready to go live."

"While we're waiting," Chief Lutz said, "I need an update from the people running our social media on this story. An hourly update. Get Sergeant Randle on the Facebook stuff and make sure Sergeant Teller is keeping the Twitter thing up to speed."

The chief's interest in social media was partly to put the Atlanta PD's spin on the investigation, but mostly to make sure he knew what the Twitter and Facebook hordes were saying about him.

The city of Atlanta employed fourteen PR people at a cost to the taxpayers of more than a million dollars a year. Cynics observed the city officials must be incompetent if it took that many flacks to put up a good front.

Cassie tensed slightly, listening to the anchorman's voice in her ear.

"...not known whether he jumped or fell or was, well, pushed," Art intoned. "For more on this shocking and bizarre tragedy, our Cassandra Page joins us live, at Park Towers in Buckhead. Cassandra, it must be a sad scene there right now."

"Take remote one, cue Cassie," the director said.

"Art, the big question here right now is," Cassie began, ignoring his comment about the mood at the apartment building, "how this happened. Police Chief Lutz will give us the latest in a moment, but first, let's retrace what happened."

"Video up, go Cassie, voice over, go," said the director.

On the screen, viewers saw a close-up of Cav Campbell's body, impaled on the mast of the TV truck. Cassie described it without emotion, then talked about how Campbell, fiancé of Bren Forrest, was at the party of the year on the forty-sixth floor. She reported police had questioned the party guests.

She was looking at notes in her "Reporter's Notebook." Doing live reports, she often used notes rather than a word-for-word script. Many reporters could not do that smoothly.

More video played, showing file pictures of Campbell and Bren at a recent charity event, then showing a clip of his latest, last film, Party House IV.

—

In the Park Towers lobby, Chief Lutz was ready.

"Let's go, let's go, now," he said and strode toward the door, moving across the pavement toward the designated site for the news conference.

His aide ran ahead, telling TV crews to hit the lights and get ready if they wanted to go live. They did.

Carl Dayton rushed over to the microphone stand, positioning himself to get in the first question.

"Wrap it, Cassie, wrap it now and toss to Art. Standby, Carl. Standby, camera one. You're on, Cassie!"

Her mind was whirling. She wanted to stay with it, to walk over to where Chief Lutz was standing, his uniform medals, buttons and brass sparkling in the TV lights. She wanted to walk over and question the chief.

Cassie knew Carl Dayton would have done it, but she also knew she would foul up the director if she did. They were expecting her to throw it back to Art in the studio.

"I see Police Chief Lutz is about to have a news conference here, right behind me, so as I go over there, Art, back to you."

"Thank you, Cassandra," Art baritoned.

Art read a short item about who was at the party besides Campbell. The chief's public relations woman was relieved, in that it gave the TV camera people time to line up their shots for the news conference.

"Now, Atlanta Police Chief Lutz is about to talk to our reporters at the scene," Art told his viewers. "Let's go live to NewBlitz3 Political Reporter, Carl Dayton."

"Thanks, Art. Here at this luxurious high-rise condo building, the movers and shakers of Atlanta and the state have become part of a world-headline event, the death of Cav Campbell."

Carl could not resist starting like that, rather than turning immediately to the police chief. It was the break Cassie needed.

She walked directly to the right side of Chief Lutz, forcing photographers from the competing TV stations to zoom into tight close-up shots to keep Cassie out of their pictures.

As a result, people watching two of the three other stations could see only the chief's lips, nose, eyes and the bill of his cap.

By the time the stations superimposed their "fonts," the identifying words in the lower third of the screen, the words "News9NOW" and "NewsBuzz12" obliterated the chief's mouth and nose.

"Chief Lutz, how did Mr. Campbell die?" Cassie asked.

"It is my unpleasant task to tell you that, at approximately eight forty-five this evening, Mr. Cavanaugh Campbell fell from the forty-sixth floor of this building, while attending a party in honor of Ms. Brenda Forrest, president of the Global News Service."

Shouted questions from five reporters peppered the Chief, but he ignored them, continuing the statement he had rehearsed. "We are investigating details of Mr. Campbell's death and will give them to you as soon as we know more."

"Chief, Chief, Carl Dayton, NewsBlitz3," Dayton yelled, his anger over Cassie's first-question coup showing in his face, "Do you have any suspects? Is this a case of murder?"

Other reporters leaned in, shouting over each other.

"Why is Homicide Division on this one?"

"Where's Bren Forrest?"

"Is there a suicide note?"

"Was he alive when he hit the mast?"

Cassie was closest to the chief, so he answered her first.

"Homicide is leading the investigation because we have not ruled out foul play here," Lutz said. "Detective James Hagan is in immediate charge and I have confidence he and his people will provide the facts we need in this case."

Lutz thereby planted the seed of his own off-the-hook ploy. If this turned into a debacle that dampened Atlanta's orgy of Olympic boosterism, Lutz could lay the blame on Hagan.

"Please direct your specific questions to Detective Hagan now," the chief told the media. "I must get back to my office. Thank you, ladies and gentlemen." Lutz did an almost military about-face and walked in a semi-march to his waiting unmarked car.

13

NORTH ATLANTA

Sheamus Cross was sitting up in bed at his sprawling ranch house north of Atlanta on the banks of the Chattahoochee River. He turned on the late TV news and was fully prepared to fall asleep as soon as the weatherman stopped droning on about troughs and isobars and finally delivered the five-day forecast more or less in English.

But Cross was wide awake in an eye blink when the anchorman began the newscast with information that shocked everybody who saw it: "A hometown movie star plunges to a gruesome end here in Atlanta and the world is riveted on the death scene at this hour."

A barrage of conflicting thoughts filled Sheamus's brain.

What actor? Hometown? What star lives here? I know Julia Roberts grew up here but...wait...Jane Fonda maybe? She was here a lot when she was married to Ted Turner, uh, when, I don't know.

What about that actress who bought Braselton, that town north of here, the whole town, paid twenty million for it. Kim Basinger, I think. Well, whichever one it is, this thing will trump everything. Aw geez, now I have to tear up my prep for tomorrow's show and get busy on this story.

Sheamus was the hottest radio talk show host in town, with a quick wit and a devilish sense of humor that left everybody laughing, everyone but the butts of his ridicule. He spent several hours earlier that evening working on some "bits" for his eight am to noon show the next day on WNAG AM, the material mostly aimed at lampooning the Atlanta Olympic Games.

Pre-program preparation was a key to Sheamus's ratings success, that and his penchant for hating political correctness. His detractors often mocked his first name by calling him, "Sheamus on you, Cross," or another favorite, "Have you no Sheamus, Cross?"

Just that morning, he infuriated Chief Lutz and some members of the city council with what he called, "a simple solution to Atlanta's homeless problem."

"Here's what we do," Sheamus told his listeners during the morning rush hour. "We rent a bunch of railroad cars and hook them all together in one corner of the train yard. We furnish them with nice cots, blankets and pillows, clean portable toilets, and three tasty, nutritious meals the first two days. We pick up all the homeless people we can find and offer them free use of the boxcar 'residences.'

"Then, late the second night, while the contented homeless folks are slumbering in their comfy quarters on wheels, we hook up an engine to the train cars, these sort of rolling motels, and ship them by rail to Toledo.

"Shazam, no more homeless problem during the Olympics. Great, eh?"

The calls poured into the radio station from outraged listeners. "Cross, you are shameless!" And even more from his fans, "Hey, Famous Sheamus, why not make room on the train for all the politicians too? Then you go get under the train!"

Sheamus knew his boxcar bit that created such an uproar when it aired would be forgotten by the time Atlantans awakened the next morning. He knew he'd have no trouble getting listeners to call in about Cav Campbell's death, full of rumors, speculation, lots of B.S. and a few gems of wisdom as well. The trick was to get the balance right and to leave them laughing by the time the show ended every weekday at noon. Good luck doing that tomorrow.

This thing, this bizarre story of an actor falling out of a tall building will be national news. What if it's a suicide, or even more shocking, a murder? It could even upstage coverage of the start of the Olympics on Friday night. Hilarious.

Sheamus made one decision before he clicked off the TV.

I need to find Jimmy Hagan first thing and get plugged in.

The cop and the radio talker met a couple of years before when Sheamus received some death threats from an irate listener. It was a cat lover who believed Sheamus's elaborately produced farce of a program, on which he pretended to throw cats out of a low-flying airplane, 'just to see if they really do always land on their feet.'

The 'event' included sound effects of Sheamus saying "happy landing" each time he pretended to hurl a yowling kitten to earth without a parachute.

Most listeners realized it was another of Sheamus's stunts, but one woman, who police later said had at least two dozen cats in her smelly, one bedroom apartment, thought Sheamus was a crazed cat killer. She wrote and signed her name to threatening notes to the radio station.

"I am going to see you burn in hell, where hellcats will chew you to pieces," one note read. Another said, "Don't even buy any green bananas, Cross, because you are sure to die a horrible death by the weekend."

Sheamus laughed off the threats, but the station manager asked police to check out the sender anyway. Jimmy Hagan, then a sergeant, interviewed Sheamus, copied the woman's name and address off her threatening notes and went to her place.

One whiff when she opened the door made him ask her to step outside for a chat. After a check showed she had no criminal record, Jimmy gave her a stern warning.

"Ma'am, if you ever send another threatening note, we will take away all your cats and give them to Mr. Cross for safe-keeping." She was not heard from again.

Remembering all that, Sheamus stayed in occasional touch with Hagan. Now it was time to see him again, tomorrow if possible. He set both his bedside alarm clock and a clock radio for four a.m.

14

BUCKHEAD, VIRGINIA HIGHLANDS—ATLANTA

"Listen, I need to talk some business, so let's go to your place, all right?"

Leonard Cray was direct, unsmiling. Tia thought his approach was the most disagreeable she ever encountered from a guy on the make.

She tripped slightly on the curb in front of Harvey's as she looked at Leonard, who she now could not stop thinking of as "Neck." She was surprised at his matter-of-fact suggestion.

It was not a suggestion. And he did not take her arm as she stumbled.

"Can we just schedule a meeting in the office tomorrow?" she asked, knowing the answer would be no.

"Sorry, no can do. So, where's your car, which lot?"

"I came by cab," Tia told him. She usually called taxis for evenings out. Tia took the drunk driving laws seriously, even though she seldom had more than two drinks in an evening.

She once saw a TV news special about the drunk tank at the Atlanta City Jail. It was a nightmare of winos and dopers crowded into small, communal cells with government green walls. It was guys throwing up and hunkering down, a lot of fetal positioning. She also remembered a couple of women in a nearby cell, hair matted and stringy with puce highlights, lipstick smudged, eyes glazed.

Tia swore she never would get a DUI. She remembered the drug and drinking haze her sister Lia waded through in college. Tia feared if one twin was one way, the other was a drunk or an addict in waiting.

Tonight, however, Tia wished she had used her car.

"So, I'll drive you, no big deal. Car's over there, under the street light," Neck said, pointing to a midnight-green Buick Enclave, several years old, parked in a tow-away zone.

"I'd rather we do business tomorrow, Leonard, if that suits you. I am tired and a little shook up by that movie star's death on TV, so can we call it a night?"

He opened her side door and motioned her into the passenger seat.

"Hang on a minute." Leonard closed her door then went to the back of the car, opened the trunk and peered in, closed the trunk and slid into the driver's seat.

He started the car, did a U-turn on the street in front of Harvey's and headed north, seeming to know where he was going.

"Oh, yeah, uh, where do you live?"

"Take a right here, on Piedmont."

Neck slowed, made the turn, sped up a little and then had to brake at a stop sign two blocks down. He continued on, turning left on Morningside Drive. One right turn later he pulled over.

"How did you know to turn there?" Tia was nervous now.

"Well, you sorta nodded that way, didn't you?"

Tia was silent.

"So, is it this apartment house here?"

"Yes, thanks for the ride."

Neck parked and was out of the car before Tia could get her car door open.

"Let me help you, it's kinda dark here."

"Thanks, but I can run in by myself, really."

"I'll walk you up, ya never know any more." Neck opened the trunk of the car and took out a thick attaché case.

Tia shrugged at what she assumed was paperwork and walked up the steps to the third floor landing, Neck right behind her.

She put the key into the lock on the second try, turned the knob and pushed the kick plate with her foot. As the door swung open, Neck stepped in so close behind her she could feel his breath on her hair.

"Leonard, please, I don't..." Her words died in her throat as he put his hand over her mouth.

"Shhh, keep quiet now, missy, just keep quiet and move!" He shoved her toward a low-slung couch in the small living room. She half fell and half sat down. As she looked up at him, he took a short step to the couch, leaned over and slapped Tia twice, hard.

She started to scream and he slapped her again, stopping the noise. He pulled a washcloth from his back, left trouser pocket and shoved it into her mouth.

Tia struggled to stand up. Neck pushed her back onto the couch. Her eyes, wide with fear, grew wider as she watched him open the case and take out a black dress, with silver threads in the straps and at the neckline and hem.

"Put this on, now."

Tia shook her head, and tried to say something through the gag. He slapped her again, harder.

"Just do it, now, dammit, now." Neck was impatient.

Tia guessed the dress was some sort of foreplay toy for Neck. She turned her face into the pillow of the couch and began to cry. He grabbed her by the shoulders, pulled her up to a weak-kneed standing position and pushed his face into hers.

"Put on this dress and the pantyhose or I will cut your throat as you stand here!"

He shoved her back onto the couch and threw the clothing in her lap. He pulled a pair of black high heels from the case and tossed them on the floor.

"Put on the shoes too, now."

Tia's hands trembled and she sobbed through the gag as she unbuttoned the ivory silk blouse she was wearing and unzipped her navy skirt.

This is it. I'm going to be raped here.

Her mind was clear, even as her body shook with fear. She kicked off her skirt and reached for the dress.

"The hose, goddammit, the pantyhose first," he said, turning away as she picked up the pantyhose, gathered them down to the toes and struggled into them.

He rummaged through the attaché case, finding a small black purse, gold drop earrings and a woman's Rolex watch, ringed with small diamonds.

Tia had the pantyhose on now and was standing in front of the couch, pulling the dress down over her hips. She tried to speak again, but nothing intelligible made it past the washcloth in her mouth.

She reached to pull it out. Neck growled, walked over and slapped her again before it came out. Tia was hysterical now, the clear thoughts of a few moments ago jumbled into terror.

Maybe if I just run, or, no, maybe I should just submit and then he won't hurt...no, oh, Jesus, help me!

"Here, put on the watch and shit."

He thrust the jewelry at her. One of the earrings fell between the cushions on the couch. Tia put the watch on her right wrist and the one earring on her right ear.

Neck threw the purse at her, hitting her in the stomach.

"Hang on to that."

She picked up the purse and clutched it to her chest.

"Stand up." She did, her knees weak, her lips quivering.

"Please, don't hurt me," she tried to say, but Neck heard only a muffled sound behind the cloth in her mouth. It didn't matter, anyway.

He walked around behind her and as he did, she turned to watch him.

"Now, rub your hands. Do it."

She stared at him, fear and puzzlement in her eyes.

"Bwhaa..." she tried to say, the cloth still in her mouth.

"Just rub yourself all over, squirm around in that dress, ya know, like ya love the feel of it."

Neck stared. Tia began to rub herself.

"More, I want your smell in that dress, bitch, don't you get it?"

She rubbed faster, fingers fumbling, shaking.

"Yeah, that's it, faster, faster."

He said it deadpan, no emotion now, no interest. That scared Tia even more. She realized it was not a turn-on for Neck.

She turned her back to him now, sobbing, her eyes downcast.

She felt hot. Bubbles of sweat ran in rivulets under her arms, down the sides of the little black dress.

She could hear nothing, see nothing, feel everything.

She thought of her sister, of her parents, of Neck, somewhere behind her in this room that now seemed like a coffin.

The washcloth felt like a pillow in her mouth. Tia reached again to pull it out. Neck grabbed her wrist, twisted it behind her back. A bolt of pain shot up her arm, into her shoulder.

"Move," he hissed, pushing her toward the hallway, toward the bathroom.

"In there," he said as he pushed her again. She lurched into the small bathroom, her heels slipping on the tile.

Neck pulled open the shower curtain that hung over the tub and turned on the water, low level, letting it run.

"Now, take all that stuff off. All of it. Put it on the toilet seat there."

Tia kicked off the shoes, struggled out of the dress, pulling it over her head.

"Fold it up, neat like." She did, trembling, fear in her eyes.

"Come on, goddammit, the pantyhose, the jewelry, all off, on the toilet, hurry!" She squirmed out of the pantyhose, took off the earring and the watch and put it all on top of the folded dress.

"In the shower, go on, in the shower." He shoved her. She stumbled as she stepped into the tub, shivering, her arms folded over her breasts.

"Face the wall and hold still."

He grabbed her head from behind, his hands open, one on each side, covering her ears. She cried out, the sound muffled by the gag.

Neck snapped her head sharply to the right, then back to the left. A sound like tree branches breaking filled the room.

Tia was dead before the second snap.

She slumped against him. He eased her to the bottom of the tub, propping her twisted neck so it lay on the lip of the tub.

He pulled out the gag, then stepped back, reached up, turned up the showerhead and felt the spray until it was warm. He pulled the shower curtain closed, wiping a few drops of water from his sleeve, then walked out of the bathroom and the apartment.

15

MARCO ISLAND, FLORIDA

Lia was about as high as the plane and coming down about as fast as the jet swooped over the beach at Keewaydin Island and continued down the coast toward Marco Island.

She had no idea where she was. The few streetlights she could see on the ground gave no clue. Lia was about to touch down at a place she had never been, the southwestern Gulf Coast of Florida. Hardly anybody knew she was there.

The pilot had flown secret trips before.

After gaining speed and altitude over Atlanta, he headed south toward Valdosta, Georgia, then out over the Gulf of Mexico.

He flipped on the intercom to the passenger compartment.

"Ma'am, when we get to our destination, you'll be able to see some interesting things on the ground as we're landing."

Soon after, the plane skirted Naples and the pilot contacted Marco Island's executive airport on 122.8, the Common Traffic Advisory Frequency. He knew from experience the Marco Island facility was an uncontrolled airport, deserted at night.

Circling once to check for activity, the pilot clicked his Unicom five times. The ground lit up as the automatic runway lighting system came on at low intensity.

"Please, check your seat belt, ma'am, we are about to land." The pilot's voice over the intercom sounded like a Delta pilot, folksy, with an affected southern drawl.

Lia doubted he was Southern. She noticed with some irritation most pilots used that Southern thing, even guys from New Jersey or Seattle.

She once asked a pilot about it on an overnight flight. He spent a lot of time with the passengers on that flight, especially the beautiful Amerasian girl in 12c.

"Well darlin','the truth is most pilots want to sound like Chuck Yeager, the pilot's pilot. He could have been an astronaut, I gather, but he didn't need the NASA bullshit, uh, I mean the rigmarole, ya know?"

Lia had listened politely and coyly resisted the proposition the pilot worked into the conversation. That was just a year ago, but she could not remember that pilot's face. All she recalled was his comment about the southern drawl.

Now, as Lia was sobering up, she was restless.

Ned Bastige told her she would be set up in a safe place, a resort area, with money and time to spend until it was safe for her to return to Atlanta.

What that was and how long it would be, she had no idea.

"Where are we?" she shouted toward the cockpit.

"We have almost a full moon tonight so watch the edge of the runway, just off it.

"You may see some movement in the shallow water. It probably will be a nest of crocodiles or a bunch of alligators. They're just part of the wildlife down there.

"When we land, watch when I turn the plane and shine the lights on the water."

Lia wasn't particularly interested, until they landed. Then she saw what the pilot was talking about. Crocodile experts call it "eye shine." The crocs' eyes glowed orange, bright and piercing. She stared for maybe a minute, then yelled at the pilot.

"What the hell are you doing, trying to scare me to death? Well, it's working so get me the hell out of here, now!"

"See, ma'am, those crocs have like little mirrors at the back of their eyes, so when light strikes their eyes, it bounces back to the source and that makes the critters' night vision twice as good."

He was in full condescending voice now, part Chuck Yeager, part patronizing third grade teacher talk.

"Don't worry, ma'am, we're taxiing as far as possible from the critters and there'll be a car to meet you. I just wanted to give you something to write home about."

Wait 'til she hears this. Could be a turn on. Wouldn't be the first time, I'll bet.

"You can tell your friends you and I landed in the midst of a bunch of American crocodiles. Most people know we have alligators, but not crocodiles. We do, though, something like a couple thousand of them in southern Florida."

"Are you drunk up there?" Lia asked loudly. *Jesus, I'm at the mercy of either a stoned pilot or a swamp full of crocodiles or both.*

The intercom came on again.

"One more thing, ma'am. Most of what you see as land around here really is a dense cover of mangrove trees in swampy water. Don't go alone into the mangroves. There's a saying down here: 'If the gators and crocs don't get you, the mangroves will.' And then there are the pythons, those huge snakes that apparently love this part of the world now. They also eat mammals, will swallow them whole, including us."

She reached for the baggie of coke. *Where the hell am I? Better get some answers soon, and a new Rolex, too, goddammit.*

The plane eased to a stop on the runway, then turned onto the tarmac. Through the window, Lia saw a small frame building, unlighted. She saw a few other small jets parked in a line by the office and a chain link fence along the perimeter. A dark sedan rolled quietly to the side of the plane. The doors of the car and the plane opened at the same time and the pilot extended the folding steps.

The runway lights went off automatically as Lia went down the steps and toward the car.

"Greetings, ma'am, we're in a hurry. Please get into the car."

The driver was some Caribbean nationality, Haitian maybe. Lia didn't know, didn't care.

"Where are we going? I insist you tell me," she said to the driver.

"The Wavecrest, ma'am, on the beach. It's very nice. Now please, get in the car."

Lia slid into the back seat. A small canvas tote was on the seat against the far window.

"You'll find some things you'll need in that bag," the driver said over his right shoulder as he drove through the automatic gate. His headlights showed a narrow, blacktop road, bordered by a dense mangrove forest no more than fifteen feet back from the pavement.

"What's the name of this place? Is it a town or an island or what?"

"Marco Island, ma'am. A town on an island. We're just off the island now, but we'll cross the bridge in a minute and be there."

Lia ignored the view in the headlights and poked through the tote bag at her side. In it, she found a woven belt and a small, basket style purse.

In it she saw cash and feathered the bills with her thumb. Four hundred in fifties.

That makes eight hundred in cash. Cheap bastards, better do better than that.

The car was on an incline now and Lia could see the lights of the bridge on both sides. It was a twin span, brightly lighted. Off to her right, the Marco River shone in the moonlight, an expanse of relatively shallow water less than half a mile across. A marina with a lot of empty slips was on the right, some two-story houses on the left.

The road leveled as the bridge met the island. In the median was a huge American flag, lighted and unfurled. At its base was a large sign bearing the words, "Welcome to Marco Island."

"Up yours," Lia said to herself, as the driver headed slowly west toward the Gulf of Mexico. There was no traffic at this hour, but the traffic lights were on day schedule, so Lia's driver had to stop twice along the way.

In a few minutes the car was moving parallel to the beach. Lia lowered the window and could hear the surf off to her right, growing louder as the driver turned into the courtyard driveway of a beachfront high-rise apartment building.

Lia opened the door and stepped out as the car stopped. The driver opened the building's large glass doors with a key. She walked into the lobby, expensively decorated with Florida style wicker and cane settees and game tables with chairs. Sculptures of pelicans and herons in bronze were on pedestals along the walls.

"To your left, the elevators," the driver said.

The ding-ding of the elevator and the lighted panel showed she was on the twelfth floor as the door opened.

"Right, second door," the driver said, walking next to her, carrying the tote.

He opened the door to 1202 and stood aside as Lia walked in.

The place was beautiful, a gray marble floor in the foyer leading to a living room with ten-foot high sliding glass doors to a balcony with a panoramic view of the beach and the Gulf of Mexico.

Off to the right were double doors, leading to a master bedroom. She walked in, tossed her purse, well, somebody's purse, onto the king-sized bed and went into the bathroom on the right. It was almost as big as the bedroom, with a spa tub, separate shower, toilet room with bidet, all in marble, with granite counter tops.

Throwing open the sliding closet door, Lia saw eight or ten garments hanging in the closet. Built-in drawers revealed several swim suits, underwear, T-shirts, blouses, cotton pullovers and other casual clothes.

"I could get used to this," Lia said to the driver, who was filling a small ice bucket from the icemaker built into the wet bar in the living room.

"Any food and drink in the place?" she asked, as she walked through a swinging bar door into the kitchen.

"You could survive a hurricane with what's in this apartment, miss," the driver said. "I am leaving now, but I will be back tomorrow morning at nine to see if you need anything. Oh, may I have your cell phone, please?" It didn't sound much like a question.

"Why?" Lia asked. "I need it."

"Sorry, but the boss says no email, no texting, no Tweeting, no LinkedIn, no Facebook. Hand it over. Thank you. If you must make a call, use the phone there, on the counter. But, no long distance calls, period.

"And keep to yourself," he added, not sounding like somebody's servant anymore.

16

CHANNEL 3—ATLANTA

"Child survives tornado by hanging upside down in a tree. That story is coming up on NewsBlitz3."

The anchorwoman read the "tease" with that sincere look anchors use.

"What the hell does that mean?"

It was the news director, watching the morning newscast with staffers gathered at the oblong table in the Channel 3 conference room.

"Did the kid see the tornado coming, decide the safest place was in a tree, upside down, then climb up there to survive? Geez."

"Oh, yeah, I see what you mean," said the morning news producer, Rita Runner.

"I guess I could have written it differently, huh," Rita said with a frown. Then she brightened, smiled and said, "But, hey, it got your attention, right guys?"

"Well, we could tell the weather anchors to put that in their next reports on what to do in a tornado," said Cassandra Page. "You know, like, "If you see a tornado coming, have your children go hang upside down in a tree and they'll be fine."

Cassie barely smiled as she said it, exhausted from the previous night's work on the Cav Campbell death. She resented having to be at work this early for an eight o'clock emergency staff meeting, called by The Milkman.

Nobody else reacted to Cassie's sarcasm. The news director ignored it too, picking up a yellow pad of notes.

"We need to get busy. The Milkman will be along shortly, but we can start without him. We have this major national story on our hands and we want to wrap ourselves in it and make it our own."

The news director was wearing a madras short-sleeve shirt and khakis from The Breech or The Knuckle or some such trendy place. He wore loafers with no socks. He had five madras shirts, three with short sleeves, and kept them on their own shelf in his closet at home. He had worn a madras shirt at every casual Channel 3 function since he arrived there two years earlier. Only the most observant employees noticed they were all different. Most just thought he owned one madras shirt and wore it all the time.

The no socks thing began with a now-departed anchorman who hated socks and never wore them. The news director always thought that was cool, but feared the disapproval of the Milkman and other superiors, so he took a chance and came to work sock free only on special occasions. This was one of them.

"Cassie, we want you back at the crime scene for the noon newscast, plus cut-ins at least four times in the afternoon, then at six and eleven, of course."

Cassie frowned. She didn't get home until almost two o'clock that morning after the station's exhaustive coverage of what staffers took to calling, "The Great Impalement."

Jimmy had been in bed for a half hour or so and woke up just enough to give her a groggy hug. He'd be up and out before Cassie.

"Why can't Dave do the noon live shot?" Cassie asked to nobody in particular at that morning meeting. "He's doin' them now for the morning show and that'd give me some time to do some reporting, find out what's going on."

As the news director started to nod affirmatively to Cassie at the end of the table, the Creative Services producer, Annie Block, broke in.

"Hey, girl, we need yo bad self on the air all the time with this thing, know what ah'm sayin'?"

Cassie frowned at Annie's "I be yo sistuh" routine.

"Annie, knock it off, for God's sake. I just thought it would be nice to actually be a reporter on this story. I know it's a new concept to some people."

Cassie wished she hadn't said that, but Annie irritated her sometimes. So did the news director, who usually did what the promotions department wanted done.

"Annie's right you know, Cassie," he said. "You have done such a great job out there, I think we need our number one reporter on every show for a few days, you know, show the flag, that sort of thing, right?"

"Well, then who's going to homicide headquarters, then call the people who were at the party and do all the legwork?"

"The assignment desk can make some calls," said the news director, "and we'll get an intern to help out. It'll work. So why don't you just check the news web sites, the relevant tweets and Facebook and all that and then head down to Park Towers. Thanks Cassie, you'll be great."

She stood, frowned and walked out of the conference room, knowing she had been dismissed. Cassie and the other reporters often complained the writers, producers and managers seldom asked for the reporters' input. Not that they had to ask. Some of the reporters went around inputting most of the day, mostly to people who did not care and paid no attention.

With Cassie gone, the assistant news director asked Rita Runner what she planned for her newscasts.

"Vell, ah muftly dvorless brang wiff grallus vchep," Rita answered, her mouth full of the better part of two Heath bars.

"Rita, for God's sake, please," said the news director.

Rita was the only producer at Channel 3 who never had to worry about other people using her workstation when she was not there.

Debris from her two-fisted, at-the-desk eating frenzies littered the area. Week-old popcorn left butter and salt smudges on the desktop. Chocolate from a room temperature Rolo stained the handset of her desk phone. Chunks from a sucked-on jawbreaker were visible on top of her video monitor.

Rita once dripped some yogurt on her sweater. Rather than wiping it off with a napkin—she had none—she lifted up her sweater and licked off the yogurt. Four other writers and producers who saw that had to leave the room.

Nobody ever touched Rita's computer keyboard. It was a mini landfill of dropped and dribbled food and drink.

After repeated slobberings of some Nutty Buddies, Rita's keyboard letters "a" and "s" stuck together permanently so every time she typed "USA" it came out on the script "UASAS." One anchor who read it on the air that way a couple of times generated complaints from irate viewers who accused him of saying, "You asses."

Recently the letters "t" and "r" began to merge as well, because of the daily dripping of instant cocoa between the two keys. That was especially disconcerting, because the most popular word in local TV newscasts was "tragedy." Whenever Rita wrote "tragic" or "tragedy," which was a dozen or so times for each newscast, it came out "trrtagedy" or "trrtagic." Last Halloween was tough for anchors reading Rita's copy because there were a lot of "trrtick" or "trrteat" phrases in the newscast.

Rita Runner was on a short leash. The news bosses knew she was not very good, but they were reluctant to fire her because she was a minority.

They found out about Rita's alleged ethnicity the previous summer, shortly after Rita did. She told her colleagues at work she was about one sixty-fourth Calusa Indian and used that to claim minority status.

In recent weeks, Rita had taken to wearing Native American clothing, regularly soiled by bits of food, mostly dark blue and brown things of indeterminate origin. She prowled costume shops and theatrical supply houses, hoping to find some Indian headdresses. When she did find one here or there, sales clerks were reluctant to let her try them on, fearing they'd get stuck.

One day Rita overheard a couple of news writers whispering about her and her clothing. "As if her outfits aren't bad enough, it's disgusting with all those food stains…"

Rita made a point to tell them her Calusa ancestors didn't wear much clothing because of the warm climate of their homeland in

Southwest Florida.

"So if you don't like what I wear or how I wear it, maybe I should just 'go native,' so to speak."

That pretty much cooled the conversation.

Rita began taking language lessons. She could not find a single Calusa language teacher in town, perhaps because there were no known descendants of that warlike tribe still alive.

When Rita used Google to get to Wikipedia, she learned most or all of the tribes in southern Florida, the Calusa, Tequesta, Mayaimi and Tocobago, probably spoke dialects of a common language.

So Rita began studying Cherokee instead.

She loved to leave little messages in other people's computers, brief, positive reinforcement picker-uppers. Trouble was, she wrote them in Cherokee, which irritated some co-workers.

One reporter asked her about it.

"Hey, Rita, what the hell is this message, what's it say?" he said, loud enough for all in the newsroom to hear.

She smiled and touched the feather she had stuck in her sticky hair. "It means 'May the great bear of the mountains leave your honey alone,'" Rita said. "I know you have children and I thought it was a reassuring Cherokee saying."

The newsroom grew quiet. Writers and producers stared at their computer screens, trying not to laugh, hoping the reporter on the spot would.

"Well, Rita, that's very nice. My kids, Fighting Pillow and Spending Fool, will love it."

Rita laughed, reached for a handful of Grape-Nuts out of the box on her desk and said, "Hey great, I can take a joke, and that's a good one."

This morning, the newsroom had no time for jokes about or from Rita.

The managing editor stood up from the conference table and stepped to the large, white wall board to write which reporters and photographers will be covering what stories and what stories will go in what newscasts.

"Well, we could do three live shots at noon, five at six, and we'll see about the eleven o'clock show," he said, trying not to watch Rita as the candy in her mouth threatened to make an explosive exit.

"So, one goes to Cassie at the apartment building, one to homicide, send, uh, Daryl there," said the news director. "Hold the other cameras in reserve for now."

"Hey, here's an idea," Rita said, intelligible now with no food in her mouth. "How about we get Deirdre to do a package comparing the dangers of impalement with, say, being shot through with an arrow?"

The news director, wishing Rita had kept her mouth full of food, grimaced and shuffled some papers.

"Not bad, Rita, not bad, but we can do better, don't you think?" Annie asked, seeing thirty-second promos in her head. "We need a three part NewsBlitz3 Special. Yeah, that's it." *Using Deirdre Dawson, the medical and health reporter on this story was a good idea,* Annie thought. "Why don't we get Deirdre on the conference call and kick around some ideas?" She suggested to the news director.

He shrugged his shoulders, as if to say, sure why not.

Deirdre Dawson was ambitious, good at her job and not tactful. She knew the difference between news and hype and insisted on sharing her views with all who would listen. She never learned or maybe never tried to learn the difference between a handshake and a right hook.

On the conference call, Annie was animated talking to Deirdre.

"Hey, Deirdre, here's your chance for an Emmy, darlin'. We need you to do a three-parter, right away, right now."

The news director interrupted Annie.

"Deirdre, Cav Campbell died of a puncture wound, one of the all-time puncture wounds, right? So let's do something on the dangers of puncture wounds, you know, how to avoid them, what to do if you have one, that sort of thing."

Deirdre was silent for about five seconds. Then she exploded.

"Are you out of your minds? You want a series on puncture wounds and how to avoid them? How about we say, first rule is, never fall from a high-rise building onto a TV truck. Wait, what about rule number two, that Cav Campbell was a professional so viewers should not try that at home?"

"Deirdre, please, just listen..." but she cut off the news director with another outburst.

"Wait, yep here's what we do. We'll use one report on the place of puncture wounds in world history, with emphasis on their role in the development of Atlanta. Yeah, I'll speculate on what if General Sherman stepped on a nail right before he set fire to Atlanta, okay, boss?"

Annie butted in, scooting closer to the speakerphone.

"You're the medical reporter and you have to do this, that's it. Make part one the general stuff, use plenty of the Campbell video, you know, the difference between impalement and, say, say, uh, an arrow through the chest..." She went on to describe the series she thought would be a ratings blockbuster. Deirdre was silent, cursing under her breath, knowing she would have to do it or be in big trouble.

"I'll be there in forty-five minutes," Deirdre said to the gathering in a calm, quiet voice. "Tell security to let me in the back door of the asylum. I don't want any real people seeing my car out front. Ta-ta!" She hung up.

The news director then ran down a list of possible stories relating to the death of Cav Campbell.

"Hey, we don't know whether it's murder or not, right?" It was the assistant assignment manager. Others at the table ignored him and went on talking about story ideas.

"Where's Bren Forrest right now, anybody know?"

"Who's going to get to her for reaction?"

"Bet she's under police escort 'til they figure out whether Campbell jumped or was pushed."

"Anybody been in the Vaughn condo? Anybody ever seen that balcony they say he flew off of?"

"Why not anchor all the newscasts from the Vaughn place, you know, in the front drive there?"

"We need somebody at GNS for a report on reaction within the network and about their coverage and all."

"Yeah, and don't forget they're doing a live hour at ten tonight, so we'll go to it live, at least for her speech, right?"

"Wait, will she go ahead with it? And where is she?"

"Police haven't said. They're being real assholes about info on this thing."

At that point Annie spoke up. "One promo is running now, as you know, and we will want to do a new one, image stuff each day, plus the topicals for each show. But, dudes, this story can help us get back some of the Olympics audience we're gonna lose to GNS next coupla weeks, so go out and get us some ratings points, 'kay?"

The news people at the table were quiet, digesting Annie's approach to the story. All but Rita.

"Hey, you give me the horses and we'll ride this sucker into Nielson heaven!"

"Rita, um, we want to give you some help," the news director said. "I know you don't normally produce four shows a day, so I'm putting Glenn on with you as a producer for the six and eleven o'clock newscasts today and tomorrow."

Rita suspected Glenn was not coming in to help, but to make sure she didn't screw things up. She could tell the news director's remark was not a question.

"Sure, I can always use another body," she said, stabbing at a box of Cocoa Puffs with a clenched fist, reaching in, grabbing a huge handful and stuffing it into her mouth.

The door opened and The Milkman lumbered in to the sounds of chairs scraping. His employees made motions to rise, but he waved them down.

"Mornin', ya'll. It's a grim day that's for certain, but I knew you'd want me to be here with you," the Milkman said. His voice boomed through the room, as it boomed everywhere he went.

Some of the news staffers nodded, some mumbled "Good morning, sir," "Yessir," and similar greetings. None looked at him directly, hoping to avoid any sort of personal contact with the man who owned this TV station and two others—one in Austin, Texas and the other in Charleston, South Carolina.

"Mr. Hampton, we are just starting and thank you for coming," the news director said, moving his chair aside so The Milkman could sit at the head of the table.

He wore a blue and yellow windbreaker with a golden eagle embroidered on the left front. The matching pants of the jogging suit were the same blue with yellow piping. His baseball cap bore the same eagle logo and colors.

The Milkman had several great passions in life and all were in evidence this day.

First was his alma mater, Georgia Southern University in Statesboro, whose colors and Eagle mascot adorned most of his ties, socks, casual clothing and the dashboards of his Mercedes and his Dodge Ram truck.

Another passion was food and drink, evident in the triple X sized jogging suit he needed to encase the bulk he had accumulated on his five-foot, nine-inch tall body.

Being there in the newsroom on this big news day reflected The Milkman's third love, hanging around the newsrooms of his three TV stations, especially this one in Atlanta, the largest in the Hampton Group.

"Well, folks, we have a tiger by the tail on this one, I'd say," he drawled, his cow eyes intense.

He pulled a blue and yellow oversized handkerchief from his back pocket and wiped his face, tilting his Eagles cap back on his head.

"Yessiree, a tiger, a real tiger, yessir."

The news director waited, knowing The Milkman was not finished.

"Where's our chopper now?" he asked.

"On the pad at the moment, sir," the news director said, knowing the toys of the TV news trade fascinated The Milkman.

"And the satellite truck, where's it at?"

"We've moved it to the scene of the crime, so to speak, so our other two stations can feed their reports from there," the news director replied.

"Good. Now I need someone to take me down there."

"You want to go there, to the apartment where Campbell was killed?"

"Hell, yes, that's the action ain't it? Let's get movin', boy," the Milkman said, showing some impatience.

"Well, sir. We really..." the news director began, but The Milkman cut him off with a wave of his beefy hand.

"Hey, boy, they don't call me The Milkman for nothin'," Hampton said, still waving his hand as though he were making a patriotic speech.

He loved his nickname, not because it referred to the fortune he made in the dairy business, but because of his successful plunge into the sexy, high-powered world of television. He thought the moniker "Milkman" had some swagger to it.

Harold Hampton thought "The Milkman" sounded gangster-like, not unlike "Larry The Torch" or "Bugsy," as in Bugsy Siegel. What the Milkman didn't know was how much Benjamin Siegel disliked his nickname, reportedly called that because of his volatile nature and quick temper.

Hampton thought being called The Milkman added a swashbuckler aura to his persona. He was the only person on earth who thought that.

The Milkman stood up, walked to the door and said, "Well, let's go. Can we land the chopper there?"

"Sir, it's only an eight minute drive and there's no chopper pad at that building," said the news director, almost in a whisper. This day was going to hell in a hurry.

"Well then, call security and have the guard drive me down there. Is Cassandra Page there? Quite a gal, that one. I'll get her to show me around."

The Milkman walked out, his jogging suit swishing loudly where his thighs met as he walked. A producer at the table laughed, picturing Cassie coping with The Milkman outside the Vaughn apartment building.

The Milkman was a news reporter wannabe. His proudest accomplishment at Channel Three was coming up with the name, "NewsBlitz3," a year ago.

"Hell, that Eyewitness News is old crap, Action News, too. Let's get some oomph into our product," he told the department heads when he announced they would be NewsBlitzers from then on.

The Milkman's other brilliant idea never came to fruition. He wanted to use a jazzy version of his dairy's musical jingle as the signature music for NewsBlitz3.

All his junior executives met without the Milkman present and agreed it was a stupid idea. They noted the jingle on the Hampton Dairy commercials was sung by a Howdy Doody type voice, "Hampton Makes Every Meal a Holiday," and so on.

Seeing a rebellion in the works, The Milkman backed down and agreed to a compromise. They would use the jingle music as the news theme, but would get the Ray Conniff Singers to record it with a vocal sound but no words. When nobody could find out whatever became of the Ray Conniff Singers, the staff abandoned the idea and The Milkman never brought it up again.

"Okay, back to business," the news director said to his troops around the table.

The discussion centered on specific assignments of reporters and photographers for the various live shots and packages, live reports by people in the field and the pre-packaged video stories they would send in to run during the next newscast.

"Boss, how are we planning to treat the GNS special tonight?"

The assignment manager needed to know whether they could and would take sections of it live in a direct feed from GNS. If so, Channel 3 would not have to devote its own resources to covering it.

"Jim, call GNS, get a hold of Ippolito there, the senior producer, and see if we can get a direct feed.

"Get Cassie to find out where Bren Forrest is now and whether she'll be making her speech on the anniversary special, or what, Jesus, if she does it could be dynamite.

"Wanda, call homicide and see if they're having a news conference anytime before six. We want it live.

"Oh, and warn Cassie on the cell phone The Milkman is on his way."

17

ATLANTA

"Hi. We can't take your call right now, but if you'll leave the day and time you called and a brief message, we'll get back to you."

Mae McIntosh listened a second longer, then talked to the machine on her daughter's phone.

"Tia, this is your Mother. I guess you're in the shower. I just wanted to remind you of our lunch today, dear. I'll be at the jewelry counter at Saks by eleven. "Let's eat there in the mall, if you don't mind. With that awful business down Peachtree, you know, that actor? Well, I don't want to go anywhere near there, with the police and all. See you soon, love-love."

The digital display on the answering machine showed the time, 9:34 a.m.

—

"I'm sorry, but you can't speak with anyone here right now." It was a police sergeant on the phone in the library at the Vaughn's apartment. "Yes, I am to refer all press calls to homicide headquarters. So, no comment. "Look pal, I don't know any more than you do and you can't talk to anybody here, so how about just going through channels."

The sergeant hung up the phone and walked out to the foyer, where Jimmy Hagan was talking with Jerry Vaughn.

Vaughn rubbed the bridge of his nose with his thumb and forefinger, his head down, eyes closed.

"How'd she sleep?" the detective asked.

"Fitfully, you know, off and on. She asked for Jan once, but the sedatives helped."

Fitful didn't come close. For Bren, it was a terrifying jumble of horror, shock and nausea as her mind and nervous system battled the frenzy that ebbed and flowed through her consciousness.

That can't be Cav who fell off the Vaughn's condo balcony. He'd never do that accidentally, yet who in the world would want to harm him? Cav! Cav! Come back now, Cav, and tell me this was just a stupid mistake. It wasn't you. It was some drunk at the party, right, Cav? Right? Talk to me, Cav.

Dreaming, dozing, slipping in and out of sleep, Bren's thoughts and feelings lurched from reason to fantasy. One second, although it seemed like hours, Cav would appear, laughing, taking Bren's hand. "Darling, it's a practical joke, that's all," she heard him say in a remote part of her being, but his voice was muffled, almost distant.

Then she'd find herself waving a sad goodbye to Cav as he slipped away, replaced in her dream state by jumbles of sensory input. Some of it was benign, her upbringing as part of a wealthy Atlanta family.

She had enjoyed a worry-free childhood; the best schools, an active life full of good grades, good friends, an athletic ability that showed itself in her lacrosse playing, her equestrian trophies and her prowess as a competitive swimmer. Being a beauty was a plus as well.

College was an adventure. Born and raised in Atlanta, Bren most of all wanted to go somewhere other than in the south, some place with new names and faces. She had a wide choice of options, but decided on Bryn Mawr College near Philadelphia, where she majored in economics and political science.

Her friends in Atlanta teased Bren about going to Bryn Mawr, suggesting she did so mainly because the exclusive school's most famous alumna was actress Katharine Hepburn. They were on target.

By the time Bren enrolled at Bryn Mawr in 1987, she had seen every one of Hepburn's movies.

Guess Who's Coming to Dinner had a major impact on her and so did *The Lion in Winter*, which she saw at least four times. Enthralled by Hepburn's portrayal of Queen Eleanor of Aquitaine, King Henry

II's estranged wife, Bren was able to recite her idol's dialogue word for word.

"She is so strong, on and off screen," Bren would tell her Bryn Mawr classmates. She scoffed at Hollywood gossips and tongue-cluckers who whispered about Hepburn's private life and Bren admired her heroine's independence and toughness. She especially enjoyed Hepburn's resistance to the press and her reputation as a role model for many "modern women" in her day.

All of that swirled in Bren's feverish nightmares, calmed a bit by the Bryn Mawr memories, jolting painfully in a few seconds by the image that made her cry out in her sleep. It was one she dreamed about for years, seared into her brain specifically since 1995, when her life changed forever, the first time.

—

"Sir, we need to talk to her," Hagan said softly, checking at his watch. It was nine- thirty-five in the morning. "My men are getting nowhere fast and we need whatever she can give us this morning."

Vaughn looked toward the closed door of the bedroom where Bren Forrest spent the night. Jan was in there with her now. She and Jerry slept a few hours in the second guest bedroom. The maid stayed in the room with Bren all night, dozing in the side chair. A uniformed policeman was on watch in the hallway outside the apartment. He didn't dare doze, knowing Detective Hagan and Chief Lutz were in and out of the apartment.

"I'll check with Jan."

Jerry knocked lightly, then went into the bedroom.

"Hi, Jerry." It was Bren, propped up on one elbow, hair flattened against her head, eyes red, nose sniffly.

He walked to the bed and took her outstretched hand, holding it in both of his.

"Good morning, Bren, did you sleep at all?"

"A little I think, thanks to Jan and you, too, Jerry."

Jan walked in and joined Jerry on the edge of the bed.

"I ordered some coffee, Bren, or do you want tea?" Jan asked.

"Coffee's fine, a little milk maybe," Bren said, scooting herself to a sitting position against the upholstered headboard. Her face felt puffy, her skin dry and tight. She resisted the impulse to look into a mirror and focused on her lap, then squared her shoulders a little and looked straight at the Vaughns, these two good friends who were hurting for her.

"Tell me the truth, everything, now, please," she said to the Vaughns.

"Bren, the police really need to talk with you. They still don't know what happened, how Cav fell, who..." Jerry stopped, then said slowly, "and they want to ask you some questions. Can you do that?"

Bren sighed heavily and closed her eyes tightly. A tear squeezed out of her right eye and rolled down her cheek. She said nothing for a moment, then, "Yes, but I don't know what to say."

"Can I bring Detective Hagan in now?" Jerry asked.

A knock on the door brought the maid in with coffee, three cups, cream and sugar on a rattan tray, the morning paper folded in the slot on the side.

Jerry grabbed the paper before Bren saw it.

"Please, Jerry, let's get it over with," Bren said.

—

Forty-six stories below, Cassie heard a ruckus at the police crime scene barrier. She was standing at the front door of the Vaughn's apartment tower, talking with a reporter for the *Atlanta Journal-Constitution*.

"What's all that about?" she wondered aloud, as they heard a man's voice, yelling at a female police officer at the barricade.

As Cassie and the newspaper reporter walked toward the noise, her cell phone rang in her purse.

"Page here," she answered.

"Well, when is he coming? It's almost ten o'clock now. Oh geez, I think he's already here. Must run," she said and hung up.

Cassie realized the noisy man yelling at the officer was the Milkman.

"Young lady, I own Channel 3 and I want to see my people, ya heah?"

"Sir, do you have press credentials?" the officer asked, unimpressed with the large man in the blue and yellow jogging suit.

"I don't need credentials, little girl, I own the station, so let me through now!"

"Sir, without a press pass you cannot..."

Cassie rushed up and interrupted the woman in uniform.

"Officer, this is Mr. Milk...I mean Mr. Hampton and he does own Channel 3 and he is my boss, so can you let him in this once, please?"

The officer looked at Cassie, whom she'd seen many times on TV, then frowned at the hulking, red-faced man in the jogging suit.

"Okay, Miss Page, I'll allow it," she said without expression. She then leaned in and whispered in Cassie's ear:

"But tell this redneck bastard if he calls me 'little girl' again I will shove my weapon up his ass and pull the trigger, just to kill that eagle on his silly hat."

Cassie stifled a laugh, said thanks and turned to The Milkman.

"Sir, come with me," she said, and walked The Milkman toward the wide driveway that circled in front of the lobby of the building.

—

"A Death in the GNS Family" read the big block letters on the screen. The announcer's voice boomed in as somber music faded to the background.

"This is a special report from GNS: 'A Death in the GNS Family.' Now, from GNS headquarters in Atlanta, here are Ethan Thomas and Amanda Grace."

The anchors faced the camera, then each other. The director in the control room switched to a single shot, a close up of the woman anchor and she began to read off the teleprompter.

"It's ten a.m. here in the East, seven a.m. Pacific time, and at this hour, police have not yet determined whether actor Cav Campbell jumped or fell or was pushed from the forty-sixth floor of an apartment tower here in Atlanta last night."

"Mr. Campbell was the fiancé of Ms. Brenda Forrest, the chair and CEO of this network, GNS."

—

Max Ippolito was in his office adjacent to the GNS newsroom. He and his producers had the story under control so far, but he was worried about the hour-long, live special scheduled for ten o'clock this evening. It was scheduled as a celebration of the fifteenth anniversary of GNS.

Now, Max had to transform it into a combination anniversary observance and tribute to Cav Campbell.

His biggest problem was Bren Forrest. She was scheduled to make a major speech as the climax of the anniversary celebration. Now, Max had a sensational headline story on his hands, involving his boss.

Should she make the speech? Will she? What might she say? Do we go live or record it ahead of time? Can she get through it without breaking down?

Max knew the program, if it happened, might be the biggest ratings winner in the history of GNS. He also knew if it was his wife, there would be no way in hell he would share his grief with a world of TV watchers.

He grabbed his phone and called the national news assignment desk.

"What's the phone number at the Vaughn place? I need to talk with Ms. Forrest and I guess she's still there."

He scratched the number on his desk calendar, hit the handset button and punched in the number.

"Vaughn residence, Sergeant Reed speaking."

Max identified himself and said he needed to speak with Ms. Forrest.

The officer checked the list of five names on a small index card Detective Hagan gave him.

"Sorry, sir, you're not on the list of authorized calls to Ms. Forrest."

Max thought about that for a moment.

"Then let me leave an urgent message for her, please. Please take it down."

The sergeant grunted a "yes" and wrote on a pad as Max dictated.

"So sorry, but must talk about live show tonight. Most urgent. Call Max at GNS."

In the bedroom, Jimmy Hagan was standing near the window as Bren sipped more coffee and talked, coherent but rambling.

"Detective, I don't know what happened. All I know is I left Cav talking with one of the Olympic volunteers over near the balcony as we went over to hear that country singer, uh, Jake something.

"Cav liked that music sometimes, me too, but not as much as other music, you know? We never danced. He said the press would take unflattering pictures if we did that, so we never danced. I can't believe he's dead and we never even danced!"

Her voice rose almost to a shout and she cried, sobbed, for at least forty-five seconds. Jan consoled her, arm around Bren's shoulders.

Jimmy Hagan stared out the window, his eyes burning with fatigue and frustration, hoping she would stop crying, knowing it probably was good for her.

"I'm, I, I'm sorry, Detective, I really am. I don't know, I don't know, I don't know. Did he jump? Was there a note?"

She wasn't really asking for answers from Hagan. In a way, she was asking herself, hoping to pull some answers from inside her pounding brain.

"Ma'am, was he upset or angry about anything, do you know?"

She shook her head, saying nothing, looking down at the soggy tissue she had twisted into a wet ball.

"Did you know the woman he was talking to at all?"

"No, just met her here, last night. Do you know her? Is she, did she, does, uh, well, why do you ask about her?"

Hagan disregarded the slightly accusing look in her eye, the way her jaw jutted, the harshness in her voice.

"Ma'am, we only know she was a volunteer, name of Lee, Lia Lee, and she left the party at least fifteen or twenty minutes before Mr. Campbell fell, or, uh, passed away."

"Well, find her and demand some answers, for God's sake!" Bren cried, hugged herself as though she were cold and then slumped in the bed and sobbed, afraid of what she didn't know about what happened to Campbell.

18

PHIPPS PLAZA—ATLANTA

Mae McIntosh fumed about the long red light at the entrance to Phipps Plaza mall. She was on edge this morning, not sure why.

When the light changed to green, Mae made the right turn a bit too fast, guiding her 2009 Volvo sedan toward the ramp that led to the covered parking under the shopping center.

The dip where the driveway met the ramp was designed for about ten miles an hour. Mae was going twenty-five and the jolt jarred her just enough to convince her to slow down a bit. The clock on the dashboard showed eleven o'clock straight up as Mae pulled into a parking slot not far from the elevator up to the mall. *Tia will be there by now. She's never late, unless that traffic light delayed her too.*

Mae stepped off the elevator and walked to the mall entrance to Saks. She walked past display cases showing accessories, purses and scarves, leading to the jewelry department. Mae expected to see Tia at the counter, trying on a bracelet or admiring the fourteen-carat gold pieces "on sale."

Seeing Tia, as Mae did almost weekly, made her miss Lia even more. Mae had not seen her other daughter for more than a year. She knew Lia worked at GNS, had heard she was still using drugs and worried she might never come home again.

Lia and Tia were identical twins. They were born two years after Mae and Ralph McIntosh married in Seoul, South Korea, where Mae's father was a consultant to a Korean electronics corporation. His primary job was to help the firm increase its market share in the U.S. and Canada.

Ralph met Mae Lee at a holiday party his company hosted for its parts suppliers. Mae's father's company made innards for smart phones. Mae and Ralph were engaged within ten months and married four months after that. Ralph soon was transferred back to the U.S., to his firm's field office in Atlanta, his hometown.

From infancy, Tia was the "good" sister, Lia, the troublemaker. Their beauty smoothed their way through the social spider web of high school, but Lia always stayed out later and often had teacher trouble.

Lia also was smarter than Tia. She did her homework better, faster and earned higher grades. Lia was known by some of the other kids at school as "The Angler," and it had nothing to do with fishing.

Lia always seemed to have an angle, a shortcut, a way to slide over obstacles and get what she wanted. Those who made the mistake of getting in her way often seemed to relent or slink away or sometimes call in sick for a few days.

The biggest battle the girls ever had with their parents was in their junior year of high school.

They were the only Amerasian students at the high school in the suburban town of Alpharetta, north of Atlanta. At that time, they were Lia and Tia McIntosh, daughters of Ralph McIntosh and his Korean-born wife, Mae Lee.

Lia came home one afternoon and announced to her astonished parents she no longer would be called McIntosh. From that moment on, she was Lia Lee, using her mother's maiden name.

Ralph was angry when he realized Lia was not joking.

"We are half-Korean and proud of it, Lia said, as Tia nodded in acquiescence. "We don't look like people named McIntosh and that's it," Lia told her parents.

"Like hell it is," their father erupted, pounding on the dining room table. "You're half American, Scottish-American I might point out, way back there somewhere. And in this country, you use your father's name, period."

"I am now Lia Lee and there's nothing you can do about it," Lia snapped, and walked out of the room and up the stairs to her bedroom.

"Daddy, I think Lia's right," Tia said softly, her father steaming, his face red.

"We can't look the way we do and not recognize our Asian heritage. We want to do this Dad, please?"

Mae just sat there, confused, feeling pleasure at her daughters' desires, anxiety at her husband's reaction.

"Tell 'em, Mae, tell 'em they can't do this," Ralph demanded.

"Dear, I'm as American as you are now," Mae responded, trying to calm her husband. "But if the girls want to, uh, celebrate the Korean half, what's wrong with that? How about they hyphenate their names?"

"What the hell is that, you want some cockamamie names like, like what?"

Tia jumped in. "Daddy, how about we call ourselves Tia Lee-McIntosh and the same for Lia?" Tia smiled now, thinking her idea brilliant.

"Ralph, would that be acceptable to you?" Mae asked, hopeful.

Ralph said nothing for about ten seconds. Then he smiled a small smile, and said softly, "Well, maybe if it were McIntosh-Lee, maybe..."

"That's a deal, Daddy, yes!" Tia said, hugging her father around the neck. She ran up the stairs to tell Lia, who was not impressed.

"That's bullshit, Tia, and you know it."

"Sure, but why not cool it for now, take the hyphen thing and then let it evolve?"

"Well, tell him whatever you want. He'll believe it, 'cause he wants to. But I will be Lia Lee, period, whenever he's not around."

The McIntosh-Lee name stuck through high school, but when the twins started college, they filled out all their forms with the single last name, Lee.

Their official status as minorities helped Lia get a financial scholarship to Georgia State University at its urban campus in downtown Atlanta. She agreed to go there only if she and Tia could get an apartment in town and not have to live at home in the suburbs.

Ralph and Mae agreed, reluctantly, assuming Tia would be a sobering influence on Lia. They were wrong.

In college, Lia partied through four years of a drug haze and graduated with a two-point-five average. She eeked out a degree in communications.

Tia moved out of their shared apartment late in their freshman year, unwilling to join Lia's lifestyle and sick of having to tiptoe around it. She studied hard, enjoyed aerobics and spent most of her time in the gym or the library.

Tia graduated with honors and a business degree. By that time, the twins drifted apart and seldom saw each other. Tia went home often, but Lia did so less and less. By her senior year, she saw Ralph and Mae only at Christmas, preferring her in-town friends, her cocaine and using her beauty to acquire plenty of both.

Lia also flirted her way into landing an internship at Global News Service.

She laughed to herself when she won the prized position over other applicants. They had higher grade point averages, she was sure, but she had other "attributes."

She was smart enough to do well enough on the job. Of course she enjoyed generous amounts of coaching and extra attention from helpful male superiors who thought she had "potential."

After Lia began working at GNS as an intern, she seldom went home to Alpharetta. "The press of work," she told her parents.

She never saw Tia, who landed a job with a major accounting firm in Atlanta. Tia also worked part-time as an aerobics instructor at a health club.

Mae cherished her frequent lunch and shopping visits with Tia. Phipps Plaza was a convenient place to meet, just off a key expressway that poured several hundred thousand suburbanites into Atlanta every day.

Tia was not there when Mae walked up to the first jewelry counter at Saks. It was ten minutes after eleven o'clock now and Mae was curious.

"May I help you find something, ma'am?" The sales clerk was smiling, expectant.

"Oh, no thank you. I am just meeting someone here," Mae said.

"Miss, by the way have you seen a young woman, Asian, long hair?"

The sales clerk scrunched her eyes in thought.

"No, I don't think so, but we've been busy this morning, especially with the Olympics jewelry in the counter just over there. But no, I don't think so.

"Wait, we had some people in from Pakistan, I think, or was it India, oh, I don't know, but that's over there in Asia, isn't it?"

Mae Lee smiled.

"No, I mean Korean-Asian, not, well, you know. It's my daughter. She sorta looks like me."

"Oh, I'm so sorry," the clerk said. "I didn't mean that you look like those, I mean, I don't think you all, oh, I don't know." Her lower lip quivered and her effort at trying to say the right thing evaporated in embarrassment.

"It's fine, really," Mae said, "but please excuse me. I have to make a call. My daughter is never late and I want to call her place."

The clerk looked relieved at having avoided more chit-chat and Mae tapped in Tia's home phone number.

"Hi. We can't take your call right now, but if you'll leave the day and time you called and a brief message, we'll get back to you."

"Damn," Mae muttered as she listened again to Tia's recording. She knew it was irrational to be angry or to worry over Tia being, what, twenty minutes late now?

Mae then tried Tia's cell. No answer. She left a message and continued to worry.

She never, ever is late, never. Car trouble? What could it be?

VIRGINIA HIGHLANDS—ATLANTA

"Mr. Ranger, this is Jamie in 202. I'm hearing water running in the pipes from inside the walls, I think. It's been going on for hours now, ever since I woke up. Is there a leak somewhere or what? Do you know?"

The apartment manager didn't need this while he was trying to do the maintenance records for the boss, due the next day.

"Hey, I haven't noticed any problem. You leakin' somewhere?"

"No, no leak that I know of, for sure not in my apartment. It just seems like the people above us have been running their shower or toilet or whatever for a long time. It's annoying, all that noise. Can you check it out?"

"What, in 302, the Oriental girl?" *Sure, any chance I get to see her up close is a day-maker. Hell yes, I'll check her out.* "Yeah, sure, I'll get to it before lunch."

"Well, how about, say, now? It's a pain, and all that rushing water makes me want to, like, go to the john, ya know?"

"Geez, just turn up the radio, pal, and I'll check on it soon."

The manager hung up and went to his dresser. He brushed his hands through his thinning hair, sucked in his stomach, tucked in the tail of his faded plaid shirt and smiled at the mirror.

GNS HEADQUARTERS

"May I speak to Mr. Ippolito, please? This is Jerry Vaughn."

The desk assistant answered the phone at GNS, put his hand over the mouthpiece and hollered across the newsroom.

"Hey, Max, it's some guy named Vaughn for you."

Max grabbed the phone.

"Yes, sir, Mr. Vaughn, Max Ippolito here. Is Ms. Forrest with you?"

"She is and she asked me to return your call. She cannot talk with you right now but wanted you to know about tonight, the program."

Max said nothing as Vaughn continued.

"Against my better judgment, Bren, Ms. Forrest, asked me to tell you she will take part in your program and will speak live."

Max scribbled on a yellow legal pad and held it up for the assistant producer sitting next to him to read.

"And she said to tell you, quote, 'give me ten or twelve minutes in the last segment, plus at least one bump tease,' unquote. Does that make sense to you, Mr. Ippolito?"

"Yessir, it does. And, how's she doing?"

"She's resting and the police are still here. Detective Hagan of Atlanta P.D. wants to ask you a few questions. Can you hold please?"

Max said yes and pushed the mute button on the phone.

"Jenny, get Ned Bastige in here now and tell him to format the show to put in Ms. Forrest for the last two segments. Tell him to get file video of Campbell and her together. And tell him to kill the bunting on the podium and get some black cloth instead. Now."

Max turned back to the phone.

"Hello?"

"Hello, Mr. Ippolito? This is Detective Hagan, Homicide. Can you give me a few minutes?"

19

GNS HEADQUARTERS

"The entertainment community is shocked and grieving over the untimely, tragic, dramatic death of Cav Campbell, and all of Hollywood is asking how it happened."

Sheila Belle was on the air again, in spite of Max Ippolito's disgust at her breathless, toothsome style. GNS was non-stop live on the story of Campbell's death.

After covering the latest developments and replaying the removal of the body from the TV mast several times, the producer called on Sheila to give the perspective of Campbell as a celebrity.

"Why, I've had, well, it must be literally a million phone calls from friends in Hollywood, asking me the inside story. And I can report to you, without hesitation at this time, that police so far have not decided whether Mr. Campbell's death was an accident. That is confirmed. That is, I have confirmed they don't know yet. I mean, we definitely know we don't yet know and that's confirmed." Sheila flashed her 'I am a celebrity too' smile, her teeth peroxide white, dazzling inside her collagen-enhanced red lips. "But here's the latest butt-scuttle from around town," she said with a conspiratorial tone, leaning in closer to the camera. "Word is that Cav was despondent in recent weeks over the failure of his last few films and TV projects..."

"Butt-scuttle? Did she say 'butt-scuttle'? Dammit, this isn't the Real Hip Hop Network for chrissake! It's not even Entertainment Tonight! What the hell is butt-scuttle anyway?" It was Max, shouting now at the TV sets around the GNS newsroom, all showing close ups of Sheila's perfectly made up face.

"I think it sort of means cool, inside information nobody else knows," said a production assistant who was standing with two other women at a shelf of battery chargers in a corner.

This was the part of Sheila's report the studio crewmembers were waiting for, the juice, the inside stuff. The butt-scuttle. Sheila disappointed them, however, by pouting again, her version of being somber, and summarizing the scene as she understood it.

"The extremely tragic nature of this bizarre accident, or incident, whatever, is casting a poll at this hour on all of Atlanta, the nation and the world," she said, turning her smile into a pout, as close as she could get to her intended appearance of mourning.

"A poll? Cast a poll? Did she really say that? Puh-puh-puh-pole?" Max was stuttering in anger now. He turned his back on the monitors, shook his head, walked toward his small office and slammed the door.

VIRGINIA HIGHLANDS

Ollie Ranger didn't catch Sheila's poll-pall mistake. He was watching GNS on the small TV on the card table he used as a desk in his tiny office at the apartment building he managed in the Virginia-Highlands neighborhood of Atlanta. He was focused on Sheila's face, her cheekbones, her slightly too long eyelashes. *Wonder where she lives? I wonder if I could get her in here someday soon.*

That reminded Ollie he promised to check on the running water noise in apartment 302. A chance to have a chat with the "hot" girl up there would be even better than watching "that Sheila babe" on the news.

Ollie was out of breath by the time he walked up to the third floor. The elevator, surprise, surprise, was out of order, again.

He put his hand on the door of apartment 302, breathing heavily, then dropped his cigarette and stepped on it. He sucked in his gut and pulled his belt up a bit. It wouldn't go up very far. He welcomed excuses to visit that "Oriental gal," as he referred to her to his wife, Dorothy. Even so, Ollie wasn't sure of the girl's name.

Tree or Pea, Knee maybe. Kia? Somethin' like that. What a number. Wish she was friendlier, kinda standoffish, stuck-up I guess, but Lord knows why. Just a Chinee or Jap is my guess. Maybe a half-and-half. Who knows? No matter, would I like some of that!

Ollie had been the manager of the place for eight years. A few single women were his tenants during that time. He was careful not to stare at them too much in an obvious way, but he watched whenever he could get away with it. They were all about his granddaughter's age, twenty-something. *But what the hell, nothing wrong with lookin'.*

His wife was ill most days and stayed indoors, except to go to the doctor a couple of times a month.

Ollie took good care of the tenants he liked, especially the young ladies. The tenants tolerated him and gave him enough Jim Beam at Christmas to keep him happy.

He knocked on the door of 302, then again, then twice more. No answer. The electric buzzer was hanging loose a bit. He pushed it and heard it buzz inside. Still, no answer. Ollie put his ear to the door, listening for the sound of running water that the guy below had complained about.

Nothing.

"Hello in there, anybody home?" Ollie shouted, knocking louder this time. Quiet.

He grinned to himself as he separated his passkey from the ring on his belt loop, put it in the lock and turned the key. *Good, no chain on, maybe she's asleep. In the shower? Awright!*

Ollie pushed the door open and stuck his head inside the living room, dim because the window blinds were drawn.

"Hello, miss, you here?" He spoke softly now, hoping she would not hear him. "Hello, hello-o," he whispered, as he moved across the living room, looking first into the L-shaped dining extension off the main room, then into the galley kitchen.

No radio on, no TV, not even any ambient sound.

Then, as he moved toward the hallway, he heard the sound of water running behind the closed door to the bathroom on his right. *Geez, if I walk in there and she's naked in the shower, she'll scream and it'll be my ass. So, if I knock, speak up and then open it, she'll be warned, but still be naked and I'll get a peek before she can cover up.*

He turned the knob and pushed the door open a few inches. "Hello, miss, hello uh, ma'am, you here?" Ollie could not see clearly because of the steam, everywhere, a coat of moisture on the floor, the sink.

The black dress, damp now, lay folded on the toilet seat, pantyhose crumpled on top. An earring and a pair of dressy heels were on the floor. A watch lay on the pantyhose. To Ollie's left, the shower curtain, Dodger blue with white piping, was pulled shut.

Must be a hundred 'n fifty in here.

"Miss, you here?" He shouted now, sensing she was not in the room, backing out as he repeated his loud question. He went back through the hallway to the bedroom and walked in. Midday light beams pierced the curtains, creating little spotlights on the un-messed bedspread. Nobody there.

A door at the end of the hallway, just outside the bedroom, was closed. Ollie turned the knob slowly, then yanked the door open. Just towels and sheets, a six-pack of toilet tissue on one shelf, a couple of bars of deodorant soap, some Q-Tips.

He shouted now to the apartment as a whole. "Hey, anybody here, helloooooo!" Nothing, not even an echo.

Steam now was rolling out of the opened bathroom door.

Better turn the damn thing off. Hate to see her water bill this month.

He went back into the bathroom, pulled open the shower curtain and saw Tia in the tub, as he always hoped he would someday; her lovely body, naked.

Then it hit him. She was dead.

20

GNS HEADQUARTERS

Max Ippolito recognized Jimmy Hagan immediately. He had seen him on many local TV newscasts telling reporters about a victim, discussing motives or loot taken during a homicide or maybe an update on suspects in custody.

Detective Hagan was the designated sound-bite man for Atlanta Police Homicide. As such, he was a regular on TV, especially on the eleven o'clock nighttime newscasts which offered a blotter full of violence committed between seven and about ten forty-five.

Max was impressed that Hagan managed to give the TV guys what they wanted; zippy snippets of information, usually in chunks of about twelve seconds, without giving away anything the police wanted to keep to themselves.

Ippolito stood and walked forward as he watched Hagan following the twenty-something female intern who had met him at the GNS lobby and escorted him into the main newsroom on the twelfth floor.

"Detective, I'm Max Ippolito, nice to meet you."

"Same here, Max. Is there somewhere we can talk?"

The main newsroom wasn't noisy, just the tap-tap-tap of a score or more computer keyboards. But Hagan didn't want all those news people hearing his chat with the GNS senior producer.

The two men walked toward the back of the room, away from the U-shaped assignment desk up front. Max pushed open a glass and chrome door to his office, also walled in glass and metal. The newsies could see in, but they could not hear.

Max sat on the edge of his desk and turned down the sound on a TV monitor at one corner, tuned to News Blitz3.

"Wait, can I hear that?" Hagan asked, noticing Cassandra Page was on live from the driveway area in front of the Vaughn's building.

"Police have questioned the guests at the party, but one of the people who was seen talking to Cav Campbell there has not been located. Sources tell me she is one of the official Olympics hostesses who left the party some time before Campbell's death.

"Police also believe Campbell either was murdered or committed suicide. Investigators who did a fine-tooth comb inspection of the balcony are known to believe no one could have fallen over the four-foot concrete railing by accident. Now, let's go to..."

Hagan waved at the TV, indicating he didn't need to hear any more.

"Is she making that up or what?" Max asked the detective. "If not, she's cultivated some pretty good sources in your shop," he grinned to Hagan.

"Well, I'm no expert, but she seems better than most of the reporters in town," Hagan said with a frown. "I don't think she makes up stuff and she's been doin' body bag stories a long time."

Max turned down the volume and smiled at Hagan.

"So, what's on your mind, Detective?"

"Call me Jimmy," Hagan said, leaning against the glass wall. "We want to talk with the girl that Cassie, uh, Cassandra Page was talking about, the one who'd been talkin' to Campbell at the party. We hear she was an intern here at GNS."

Ippolito grimaced.

"Geez, that's all we need, another connection to this damn thing. What's her name?"

Hagan told him and described what little he knew about Lia and her actions at the party.

"She's Asian?" Max picked up the phone and poked at the buttons. Hagan nodded, as Max asked someone at the other end whether Lia Lee was working and if so, to send her over.

Hagan, watching the TV, saw video of Cav Campbell, file video of him with Bren Forrest at some party in Hollywood a while back. Campbell had an aura of success, tanned and handsome. Bren looked in love.

"Okay, see if you can find her."

Max hung up the phone and turned to Hagan.

"She was scheduled in early today but didn't show up. And at home her answering service is picking up, but they'll try again. She won't be working here much now until after the Olympics, with her hostess duties and all."

"Thanks. Do you know her or much about her?"

"Nope, neither. I have heard one of our producers, Ned Bastige, dates an Asian girl. May be her. Not sure I've ever seen her."

Hagan rolled his eyes.

"From what I hear, you'd remember. They say she's gorgeous."

Max smiled, walked around to his chair and sat down, motioning Jimmy to a straight-backed chair a few feet away.

"Ya know, Jimmy, don't quote me because it sounds sexist, but we get two types of women trying to work here at GNS. First, the beauties, knockout gorgeous, some dumb, some not, who crave careers in TV. They all want to be anchors or star reporters, although some would rather be Katie Couric or Megyn Kelly than anything and they see this as a way to that."

Hagan laughed.

Sounds like Cassie talking about some of the super ambitious women in local news.

"Then you have your furry-legged feminists, all squinty-eyed and sharp-nosed, who want to come in here and use GNS to tell the world what sexist pigs all the men are."

"Nothing in between the Tens and the Zeroes?"

"Oh sure, but we could use a dozen more. Like Cassandra Page. She has a great face, and smart, too, it seems. She'd do well here, but probably makes more money over at Channel 3."

Hagan grinned, saying nothing.

"So, do you know her, Detective? I mean, is she caught up in celebrity bullshit or what?"

"Yeah, we've met, but no, I don't think she's a glory hog. She seems pretty levelheaded, the little I've dealt with her on the street. I mean on cases, you know. She covers a lot of crime-related news."

Ippolito's phone buzzed. It was the supervisor of interns, letting him know they tried again and failed to reach Lia Lee.

Hagan motioned to him to hold on a minute.

"Barbara, hang on a sec, please. What, Jimmy?"

"Get me her home phone. And her cell."

"Barb, give me Ms. Lee's phone numbers, please, and her address, too. No address? Well, the numbers then."

He scribbled them on a yellow sticky note, thanked the woman on the phone and hung up.

"No address on her records, but here's the number."

"Thanks, that'll save me some time," he said, folding the note into his jacket pocket.

"How about that producer, Ned something, who you say may be dating the Lee girl? He here?"

Max told Jimmy Ned Bastige was at lunch but would be back in an hour or so for a production meeting on plans for the special program tonight.

"Well, Max, I appreciate it. I might check in on the Bastige guy later on. And let me know if you catch up with the girl."

"You do the same. And, Detective, next time you run into Cassandra Page, tell her I said I wouldn't mind if she stopped by for an interview, real informal, you know?"

"Sure, of course, but I don't see her often," said Hagan, as they walked out into the newsroom and headed toward the hallway exit.

"By the way, Max, how about that Sheila whatsitz, the show-biz reporter. Is she for real?"

Ippolito hesitated, obviously trying to suppress a smile, and said with as much irony as he could muster, "She is a valuable member of the GNS team and we're pleased to have her with us. And, she shaves her legs."

Their laughter rippled through the newsroom as Hagan said good-bye and walked toward the elevator.

21

ATLANTA

Riding the elevator to the GNS lobby, Jimmy thought about how or whether he would tell Cassie about Max's opinion of her work and his overture toward having her "stop by for an interview."

Jimmy knew Cassie was annoyed almost daily with the lame, shallow things local TV news can produce. But she'd never been a job jumper, as far as he knew. *It would have to be something special for her to make a change. She's at the top-rated station in town already. And would it be smart to go from her prominent role there to the news assembly line that GNS could be? No, she'd probably just shrug it off.*

Cassie Page made it to major market TV news through the back door, so to speak, the back door of her parents' restaurant in Galveston, Texas. Before she turned thirteen, Cassie was helping her mom and dad in the Opera House Diner, a breakfast-lunch favorite in a busy commercial area of the city, so named because it was just two blocks from the historic Grand 1894 Opera House.

She did everything but cook, often working before school prepping for the early crowd, then helping clean up and close up after the long-lunch patrons went back to their jobs. To pass time while working, she daydreamed about being a celebrity chef one day, or maybe a big deal restaurant owner.

Cassie's family owned the diner as long as she could remember. Their clientele was diverse racially, being in a business district where people pretty much mingled, on the job and in the bars and restaurants, if not always in their churches and neighborhoods.

Being African American was not on Cassie's list of things to worry about. She had no animus toward whites or Hispanics and didn't expect any from them.

She breezed through high school with an A-minus average and made straight B's in her first year at the University of Texas at Austin. She could have done better, but she had to work to help her parents pay for college.

So, she scored a forty-hour a week job as a server at Shorthorn's, a popular bar and grill near the Capitol, a hangout for print and broadcast journalists. It made sense because she assumed she'd be in the restaurant business one day. She soon realized majoring in business was boring, as tedious as cleaning pots and pans in her parents' restaurant kitchen. Cassie wanted to be out front. A friend, also a server at Shorthorn's, told Cassie over a beer after work one night that she ought to be a restaurant critic.

"You know so much about restaurants, why not write about the ones here in Austin?"

Within a week, Cassie scored a job interview with the editor of *The Daily Texan*, the student-run newspaper at UT.

After reading her resume, the editor looked up and smiled.

"What do you want to do here at *The Daily Texan*, Ms. Page, cook lunch for the staff every day?"

She stared at him stony-faced, then said calmly, "Well, not every day, but if I did cook for you, I'd recommend you hire a food taster."

She stood up and walked to the door.

"Wait, wait, I was just kidding, really I was. Sit down and let's talk."

"I'll stand," Cassie said. "If I want to leave again, it'll just save time."

"Whatever. So. What?"

"I'd like to write about food and restaurants, you know, trends, cooking tricks and yes, I'd like to write reviews, too."

"We have a food critic as you must know, but she is a senior, so, reviews it is then. We'll work out your schedule, pay and all that. It's not much…"

"Excuse me, but one more thing. You do pay for meals I consume at the places I review, right?"

"Um, yes and…"

"Oh, and for a companion, too? I mean if I always dine alone they'll catch on real quick that I'm a critic."

The editor sighed. "All right, but go easy on the foie gras and caviar, as in never. Deal?"

"Deal."

Within six months or so, Cassie realized she enjoyed the writing part of her job more than the food part, especially seeing her byline under the column title, *The Food Page.*

In her junior year, still working part time at Shorthorn's, Cassie met a young man at the bar, a recent hire at KJGZ TV in Austin, owned by Harold Hampton, "The Milkman."

Cassie's new friend was just a year out of Southern Methodist University, fresh from a brief stretch reporting news at a small Dallas radio station.

For Cassie, hanging out with him and his media pals was an eye opener. As she told him one night, "When you cover a story, you usually get to tell it yourself on the air. That has to be more fun than writing it in a newspaper."

"Cassie, you may have to learn to lighten up a little and loosen up a little," he said, "but you have the brains and the looks and God knows you have the ambition gene."

"Yep, if it's TV, it's for me," she said, already a little lighter and a little looser.

Cassie shoehorned two TV-101 type courses into her senior schedule and even before graduation was contacting the Austin TV stations, hoping for at least an entry-level job.

"Ms. Page, you have been coming around forever, volunteering to help, begging for a chance," said the weekend assignment editor at KJGZ one day. "You don't take no for an answer. So, will you take yes for an answer and take a job as a writer and fill-in reporter? If so, it's yours."

"Yes, absolutely. I…"

"Right. Now get out of my office and get to work."

Cassie was a natural, especially on a deadline or in a flood or a fire. She relished covering crime news that had good guys and bad guys, clearly labeled, two-minute TV dramas she nicknamed "G and E" stuff. Good and Evil.

With local TV being the mother lode of G and E news coverage, Cassie quickly shed the "fill in" label. Some weeks she was getting more face time on the station's newscasts than some of the anchors.

The anchor people noticed and weren't thrilled. The suits, including the station's owner, were impressed. The Milkman saw video of her coverage of a convenience store robbery-homicide in Austin and phoned the general manager of his station in Atlanta, NewsBlitz3.

"There's a gal here in our Austin news department you might wanna take a gander at, pal. She's ready for a major market."

In the Milkman's world, the phrase, "You might wanna take a gander at" meant, approximately, "How soon can you sign her up? This weekend would be good."

Cassie was out of Austin and in Atlanta, on the air at NewsBlitz3 within three weeks.

22

DELTA FLIGHT—LONDON TO MIAMI

Ian Phelps was the only passenger in first class who had not put his chair back to the most relaxed position. He sat almost erect, watching the on-board video of news from GNS. It was hours old, however, the same thing Phelps saw live at Yvonne's place in London the night before.

"Mr. Campbell, fiancé of Bren Forrest, owner of GNS, was attending a party in Ms. Forrest's honor. Atlanta Police have sealed off the building..."

The anchorman droned on, Phelps listening with one ear, actually one earpiece. The other had slipped down his cheek and he had not reinserted it. He watched, grinning, sipping his single malt Scotch, enjoying the glow from the success of his plan.

Phelps hit the flight attendant call button.

"Sweetie, another Glenlivet, please, and are we on schedule to arrive in Miami on time?"

"I'll check for you, sir, but I think so." She went forward and Phelps turned back to his drink.

He ordered a large sedan to meet him at Miami International to take him to Marco Island. It was a two-hour drive across the state to the Gulf Coast.

I can deal from there, get the GNS partners locked up, get it signed at the games, then I'm gone. Sure, I have to deal with Bastige and the girl somehow. Hmm, I'd better check her out on Marco Island first. That has possibilities.

Ian Phelps was on the verge of getting the communications empire he craved for a decade. He also would have, by acquiring GNS, the jumbo TV presence around the world he needed to compete with and beat the BBC's global television reach.

Bastards, little slimy bastards!

Phelps hated the BBC since his own inability to progress there in his early twenties, when he joined the network as a sales associate. He assumed he would set the world on fire while rocketing up the Beeb's corporate ladder and into the highest ranks of network executives.

His first evaluation by his thirty-four-year-old boss was an indication he'd never get his wish.

"Mr. Phelps, you are a bright young man, but your people skills do not seem to give you much hope of a successful future with us," the boss said.

"Why the hell not? I mean, for what reason, sir?" Phelps snapped in response.

"Well, there's a good example, isn't there?" said the boss. He launched into a litany of Phelps's shortcomings; his superiority complex, his low tolerance for women in the business and his take-no-prisoners attitude toward the competition. Phelps's superiors at the Beeb were unanimous in their opinion that this hotheaded plebe must go.

The BBC was a gentlemen's operation. Its corporate culture was weighted with quietude and careful speech. Oh, people stabbed others in the back, make no mistake, but they used small knives and almost no bravado.

By the end of his first year there, Phelps believed he could count on two things shaping his career in the future. First, he'd never be fired. The BBC hardly ever fired anyone. Second, he'd be stuck forever as a salesman in the network's Northern Ireland office.

Phelps was never patient, which is what kept him from being pecked to death at the BBC. He quit with a flourish of flaming swear words and a good nose-thumbing to boot.

To his work associates, he pledged to see them again on the field of corporate combat. Under his breath, he wished them all dead and swore to see to it himself if he could.

Phelps soon signed on with On Air Europe, a fledgling satellite service, delivering music videos and rip-and-read news headlines to no more than a hundred thirty thousand satellite dish and cable viewers in Ireland, the Netherlands and Belgium.

The BBC, at that point, had not made as big a commitment to satellites or international television at that time. Phelps thought that might be the British broadcaster's Achilles heel.

After cultivating several key clients of On Air Europe, Phelps quit the company and formed his own venture, World Video, Ltd., made up of three small, almost bankrupt TV services, in Bavaria, Luxemburg and Belgium. He then hired away several of On Air Europe's best managers and their advertisers.

World Video made money in its first year. Within five years, he added lucrative channels in France and the Netherlands. He cracked the Spanish market, then Portugal and planned to move into Italy and Switzerland. Britain was a lockout, however.

Pressure from the BBC and Phelps's old firm, Air Europe, kept the regulatory agencies in Whitehall from allowing World Video to sell its satellite dishes in Britain. Stumped, Phelps realized he would have to buy or gain control of a system already licensed to serve British viewers.

The one to have was obvious, Global News Service. Its satellite footprint was growing daily in Europe, especially Britain, where the GNS English-only service had no language barriers. Phelps approached the cable TV partners of Bren Forrest, hoping their willingness to sell GNS would convince Ms. Forrest to do the same.

Now, as Phelps headed to the U.S., the partners were ready to deal, but Ms. Forrest was not convinced. Phelps needed a jolt, a blockbuster event to turn her around.

Then came the crap from Cav Campbell, Bren Forrest's cokehead fiancé. His threat to expose Phelps's drug dealing and money laundering was the impetus Phelps needed. It became clear Campbell had to be removed. That doing it also might push Bren Forrest into getting out of GNS was too delicious a coincidence for Phelps to pass up.

Arranging the murder of Cav Campbell was a first step, not one Phelps planned from the start, but one he believed was required by the urgency of his mission. Phelps felt good about Campbell's death and the way he made it happen. *Fuck with me, will he! That has-been could've still been breathing if he had paid his dope debts. Trying to short my people on the stuff he sold in Los Angeles, Atlanta and elsewhere. Geez, what an idiot.*

And that business about exposing me to Forrest and her goddam partners at GNS. No way they need to know about the money laundering. GNS is a natural for expanding the coke business. Bet they'd do it, too, if they thought they could get away with it.

Campbell, that sonofabitch, he deserved to go off that building. And what a landing! God, I wish I could've seen that in person. The girl is good. Wonder if she'd rather do that for a living. Naw, she just wants to be on TV, wants to be famous on GNS.

Wonder if she's as good on camera as she was on the balcony!

He smiled, then reclined the airplane seat more and closed his eyes, still thinking about the girl he sent to Marco to hide out.

We'll play hide and seek, heh heh. She'll hide…

Phelps dozed lightly, his head nodding to the left. The flight attendant noticed and took the drink on the tray out of his curled hand. She made a mental note to tell the balding man in 2A when he wakes up he would, in fact, get to Miami on schedule.

23

VIRGINIA HIGHLANDS—ATLANTA

Detective Hagan parked his unmarked car at the curb under the shade trees on Amsterdam Avenue. He knew he was going to see a body, apparently that of Lia Lee, the girl they had been trying to find in connection with the Cav Campbell investigation. The dispatcher reached Hagan as he was driving up Peachtree Street from GNS, heading toward the Vaughn's place. What a difference a few miles and a zip code can make.

He checked the name he had scribbled on a sticky note and put on the dashboard, a Mr. Ranger, the apartment manager.

Meet him at the entrance to the building, the dispatcher said.

"I didn't touch a thing, not one thing, officer."

It was Ollie, looking nervous, rocking on the balls of his feet, back and forth, back and forth, as Jimmy walked up.

"Well, that's good, Mr. uh, is it Ranger? Ollie Ranger?"

"Yessir, Ollie Ranger. Been the manager here for a coon's age and she was just layin' there, all peaceful like, no blood, just quiet. She wasn't breathing neither, I could tell right away, so I didn't touch nothin'. I just called 9-1-1, ya know, right quick."

"I'm Detective Hagan, Homicide Division. You want to show me up there now please?"

Ranger waved his hand, like brushing a cobweb away from his face and backed up a couple of steps.

"Oh, no sir, I surely don't want to do that. You can't miss it, number 302, top-a the stairs," he said, short of breath, pointing up at the top floor.

Hagan took the stairs two at a time, puzzled by the death of Lia Lee, wondering how it was tied to Cav Campbell's death. The uniformed officer outside the door nodded.

"J.L. Palmer, sir. Nobody's in there but the victim. The medical examiner is on the way."

The door to the apartment was ajar. Hagan stepped in, quickly inspected the living room and headed for the bathroom.

He knew at once her neck was snapped. The rakish angle of her head, bent like that on the side of the tub, made the cause of death seem obvious. This was no bathtub accident.

She was beautiful and shapely. Hagan felt as though he should cover up her naked body, but he knew enough about fiber evidence not to sully the murder scene with a blanket or a towel.

He touched her shoulder and realized rigor mortis was doing its thing. She had been dead several hours, probably more.

Hagan saw the dress and the underwear folded on the toilet seat and made a mental note.

As he started to back out of the bathroom, the phone rang. He stopped, seeing the answering machine by the bed. On the fourth ring, it answered.

"Hi. We can't take your call right now, but if you'll leave the day and time you called and a brief message, we'll get back to you. Thanks for calling."

"Dear, where are you? I'm at Phipps. You're very late and I am starting to worry. Are you there? Hello? Well, call me at home when you get this message. I can't wait here any longer. Please call. Bye, honey. Your mother loves you," the voice said with a chuckle, "even though you stood me up."

Hagan, who had been stepping slowly toward the phone, picked up the handset with a handkerchief.

"Hello. Who is this please?" he said.

"What? What? Who is this? Who are you? Where is my daughter?" Hagan could hear the fear in the woman's voice.

"This is Detective James Hagan, Atlanta Police. Ma'am is this your daughter's..."

"Police? Police? What's happened, what's going on there?"

Hagan tried to calm her, asked where she was and said he would send a squad car for her immediately.

"There's been some trouble here, ma'am, and we need you to be here, so please, just sit down and try to relax. An officer will be there momentarily."

"But officer, what is, I mean is she hurt? Where is she? I want to speak to my daughter!"

"One minute please, hold on, ma'am." He covered the phone with his hand and shouted to the officer at the door.

"Palmer, in here, now! Get a car over to this address on the double. Bring the lady there here and do not tell her anything. And hurry."

Hagan turned back to the phone.

"Officer Palmer will be there in a few minutes, ma'am, and I will be waiting for you here."

He hung up, feeling guilty, but knowing he had to get the mother there to identify her daughter's body before she went to pieces.

24

PARK TOWERS

"I must go to work, Jan, I really do. There's no way I cannot appear on the anniversary show tonight. That's it."

Bren was dressed, sitting in an ivory colored armchair in the sunroom of the Vaughns' condo. Her half-empty teacup was on a glass-top side table. A piece of toast, one bite taken, was on a paper napkin.

"Jerry says a policeman out in the foyer is assigned to stay with you for now, Bren, you know, just for, for, safekeeping," Jan Vaughn said softly.

"It's dumb, isn't it? Do they really think somebody wants to kill me too? Isn't that far-fetched, Jan?"

"Honey, I don't know, but he'll drive you home or..."

"No, I want to go to the office. I've so much to do, all these calls, these messages, the speech tonight. I have to do something. I want to get busy."

Jerry walked in from the living room, carrying a cup of coffee from the Nespresso machine on the granite pass-through counter to the kitchen.

"Bren, the police have ruled out an accident," he said gently.

"They say he either killed himself, jumping off, that is, or someone pushed him. I'm sorry, but I know you want to know what is going on, so..."

"Yes, Jerry, thank you, but I just can't believe he would take his own life. I mean, we had so much to live for, so much happening."

She choked up a little, her eyes moist, still red from the ordeal of the past night and morning.

"No, someone killed him, no question, not a doubt in my mind. If it wasn't an accident, then someone did it."

She gripped the arm of the chair, her hand turning white, a vein standing out on the left side of her neck. She swayed a little as if she might be about to pass out.

"I must lie down. It's just too much," she said with a sob. "But I have to make that speech tonight, so could you please wake me in an hour or so. I..." She faltered, first her words caught in her throat, then her right knee buckled. Jerry leaped from his chair, threw his arms around Bren's waist and slowly walked her into the bedroom.

Jan fluffed a pillow and they helped Bren lie down.

"Just an hour, I just need an hour and I'll be ready," Bren said, in a halting way that meant she was a long way from feeling ready.

Jerry adjusted the window curtains to darken the room. Jan leaned over and kissed Bren lightly on the forehead. Her friend clearly was afraid to go to sleep and have those horrible dreams again, but she also feared if she didn't rest she'd never make it to or through her speech on live television that evening.

The nightmares began as though they had just taken a lunch break from heartbreak.

The rush of images, colors, smiles and tears permeated her being. There she was, her wedding day, walking up the aisle of the church on her father's arm, Bren Harding, a twenty-four-year-old beauty, radiant against the background of the Cathedral of St. Philip.

It was her church home since childhood and her parents' house of worship since they were children. It was a landmark on Peachtree Road near the heart of the Buckhead neighborhood for decades after operating at several other locations since it was established in 1846.

In her dream's eye, Bren's mother, Marcie, blew her a kiss from her reserved pew in the front row. Then her about-to-be-husband, Whit, swooshed into view and also blew her a kiss from his place with the groomsmen near the altar. She had never seen any other groom do that, blow a kiss to the bride in mid-procession, but she loved it. Bren once told Whit she thought his name must be short for "whimsy," because of his playful nature.

"Maybe it's short for 'witty,'" he retorted, pretending to be miffed.

Bren smiled amidst her fitful sleep, the dream time-traveling back to when she and Whit met.

"The situation of our meeting was beastly," Bren liked to say, usually getting a puzzled reaction.

She referred to a charity event she was chairing in her role as a volunteer for Friends of Zoo Atlanta. It was a good match. She was still a student at Bryn Mawr College, but already was exploring possible ways to do something good for animals. The Friends of Zoo Atlanta seemed about right. She knew the people there and shared their commitment to improving and expanding Zoo Atlanta.

After she graduated, her trust fund allowed her to do volunteer work full-time. Her life-long love of horses easily morphed into a career supporting animal conservation.

Her efforts to help the zoo thrive began to get local media attention.

As one local TV producer explained to his staff, "Here's a gift to TV news, a park full of cute and scary wild animals, represented to us media types by a bright, brainy beauty, get it? This is the ultimate petting zoo and I want her and her four-legged friends on our newscasts a lot. Let's make the zoo and Bren Harding ours."

Bren and Whit knew about each other before they knew each other. It seemed to him she was on local TV more than Animal Planet. And as Bren trolled the treasuries of rich Atlantans, raising money for the zoo, Whit Harding's name was on the A list.

Whit decided it would be good business, as well as good citizenship, for his company's TV, radio and cable systems to become a major financial supporter of the zoo and even the Atlanta Humane Society, which was founded in 1873.

Whit phoned the zoo, introduced himself to Bren and asked if they could meet to discuss their mutual interest—animal welfare.

"I'd like that Mr. Forrest," she told him. "But here's a thought. Perhaps you could attend our fund-raiser reception, on Thursday, in the Egyptian Ballroom at the Fox Theater. We could chat there."

"That would be great Ms. Harding. Shall I wear a red pocket kerchief so you can identify me?"

"Mr. Forrest, you could wear a gorilla costume and I'd know who you are. See you then, bye now," Bren said with a laugh and rang off.

At seven o'clock Thursday evening, Bren was chatting with a gathering of guests near a champagne fountain in the Egyptian Ballroom. She heard a slight commotion at the main entrance, more of a rustling, really. What she saw was a gorilla entering the party.

She laughed out loud, strode over to the simian costumed human and said so others could hear, "Welcome, Mr. Forrest, do you come in peace?"

From behind a nearby pillar in the ballroom, Whit Forrest emerged, walked to the gorilla guy, removed the headpiece of the costume and said, "Ms. Harding, may I present my company treasurer, Mr. Paul Primate, who comes bearing a contribution to your fund-raiser."

For the rest of their lives together, Bren and Whit counted their anniversaries from that "Girl Meets Gorilla" moment. On their first official date, ten days later, Whit arrived at Bren's door not with flowers, but carrying a gift-wrapped snowy paperweight with a lowland gorilla in it, above the words, "Have a gorillie good time at Zoo Atlanta."

Many of their dates while they were falling in love involved animals of some sort—riding horses on a Sunday afternoon, watching any and every movie ever made that featured animals, from *National Velvet* to *Free Willy*, from *Old Yeller* to *Flipper* and many in-between. Blockbuster was their go-to hangout place.

They rented a lot of old westerns, but for the steeds, not the leads. Roy Rogers was cool, but Trigger was a bigger thrill for Bren and Whit. They thought Silver was the star, not The Lone Ranger or Tonto. They loved to watch Gene Autry's horse, Champion, and even enjoyed the singing cowboy's dog, Rebel. Without a doubt, Bren and Whit were the world champions of animals-in-movies trivia. How many Lassies were there? They knew.

What was the name of Rin Tin Tin's owner in the TV series back in the 1950s? It was Rusty, of course, the brave orphan who was adopted by troops at Fort Apache in Arizona.

Remember Dale Evans? What was the name of her horse? Bren answered first, "Buttermilk," but Whit recouped his losses by naming Buttermilk's hair coat color—nope, not buttermilk. It was buckskin.

Bren was smiling in her sleep at that point, as the dreamy retelling of some the best days of her life emerged.

The one hesitation she ever had about having a life with Whit Forrest was resolved fairly quickly the first time she mentioned the issue to her parents.

"As you know, Whit is ten years older than I am, Mom, Dad. Any thoughts on that?"

"Are you having some?" her mother asked gently. Before she could answer, her father spoke up.

"Bren, you're a grownup, right? You can vote, drink, drive, well, you know what I mean. Honey, you're over eighteen so your age and Whit's are nobody's business but yours.

"Besides, if he's self-conscious about being ten years older than you, tell him you'll just lie about your age."

Bren laughed, her mom smiled, only a little but ruefully, and her dad gave her a big hug.

"Just ask your mother, honey. I have nine years on her and she still has to hustle to keep up with me."

—

Dreams are fickle, fearsome things that can be relentless liars and torrid truth tellers. Bren's nimble mind always had headlined events, real and imaginary, that careened from heavenly to hellacious. So it was as she slept, tossing off the duvet as she saw again her parents' blessing of her marriage to Whit. It was an omen of good things to come. If only that chapter of Bren's life could have ended there.

On May tenth, 1995, Bren arranged for Whit and her to have a quiet, romantic dinner at one of their favorite restaurants, Nikolai's Roof, on the top floor of the Hilton Hotel downtown. She told Whit she really wanted to go there to celebrate their second wedding anniversary. She checked to see what item was designated for that one, as in silver for the twenty-fifth, gold for the fiftieth and so forth.

When she told him the second anniversary was "cotton," he laughed. "Wow, I'll have to get you a really terrific, uh, T-shirt, yeah, a nice cotton T-shirt as a second anniversary gift. It'll be memorable. I'll have it custom made with writing on the front. How about, 'I have the world's greatest husband!'"

She was having the last laugh, however, because she had another major reason to celebrate that night. She was going to make the announcement to Whit over dinner and drinks at their favorite place. Well, Whit would have champagne, but Bren would stick with sparkling water.

She couldn't recall the name of her favorite water, but knew Nikolai's would have it if she reminded them it came from a spring somewhere in Tennessee. That would be her beverage of choice for the next nine months or so.

Bren thought a lot about how to tell Whit they were going to have a baby. They discussed having children in general terms and he always was enthusiastic. His first marriage was childless and he said a few times if Bren wanted children he'd be thrilled.

They agreed to just relax and see what might happen.

Bren decided to tell Whit the good news as soon as they were seated at a table that offered a panoramic view of downtown Atlanta's skyline. That way they could talk about her big news all through dinner.

The red and gold ambience of the restaurant was a perfect setting, a warm, inviting reflection of the Russian-French menu.

When Whit ordered their favorite champagne, Bren said, "Honey, I'd like some sparkling water, too, please, that one from Tennessee if they still have it."

The waiter popped the cork, using a linen napkin to keep it from flying across the room. Whit tasted the bubbly, nodded and the waiter started to pour it into Bren's champagne flute.

"None for me right now, thanks," she told the server with a smile, "just some water please."

Whit glanced at her with a raised eyebrow. She returned the eyebrow-up look and said nothing until the waiter left.

"No champagne on our anniversary?" Whit asked. "Is my cotton T-shirt gift not hilarious enough?"

She grinned and reached for his hand across the table. "I have a joint gift for us to share, sweetheart. I brought it with me, but I won't be able to give it to you for a while."

"Is it a horse, Bren? No, wait. Ha, I know it. Is it the team of Clydesdales I always wanted?" he asked with a laugh. That explains your no alcohol tonight. You're saving room for the wagon full of Budweiser that comes with the horses."

Bren was laughing so hard and feeling so happy she had tears in her eyes.

"I'm so sorry, Whit, I did try to get the Clydesdales for you, but their owners said those beautiful beasts don't play well with others and would never get along with my sophisticated, refined dressage horses."

Whit made an exaggerated frownie face. "I am deeply saddened, Bren, but I guess we'll just have to leave the horseplay to us, if you know I mean."

"That's not a problem, at least for a while," she said. "I went to see Doctor Drake today."

"Who's Doctor Drake?"

"She's a specialist recommended to me by our primary care doctor, you know, Maggie Darst."

Whit stared at Bren, not knowing whether to be happy or afraid.

"She's an OB-GYN, sweetheart, and she says we're going to have a baby."

Whit kept on staring for a couple of seconds, then picked up a menu.

"That's excellent," he said in a fake nonchalant tone. "Now, what do you feel like having for dinner, Big Mama?"

—

Dinner was delicious, Bren and Whit agreed, as they tipped the parking attendant who brought their car. Well, Whit's car to be exact, a classic beauty—a yellow, 1974 Mercedes Benz 450 SL, a convertible with a removable hard top.

He didn't drive that cool car as often as he wanted that spring and summer. He was reluctant to leave it with any parking lot attendant he didn't know personally. Also he didn't want to seem too flashy. It was bright yellow for goodness sake.

His anniversary dinner with Bren warranted flashing the Merc, however, even more so now, he thought, as he eased the car through downtown, heading north toward their home in Tuxedo Park.

"So, Bren, honey, if it's a girl you wanna name her Mercedes? You know, after this wonderful car?" She knew he was joking, or was pretty sure anyway, so she played along, sitting as close to Whit as the bucket seats would allow.

"Sure, why not? Mercedes is good, but I was sort of leaning toward naming her, um, Volkswagen Beetle."

Whit was quiet for a moment. Then, "But you said you don't know the baby's gender yet, right?"

"Right, but if it's a boy," she said, smiling, "we could name him Benz."

—

"Gosh, Whit, this is so much fun, I've not been paying attention, but we're almost home and it's only just ten o'clock. I'm so pumped up by the baby and our anniversary and all, I'm not sure I'll be able to go to sleep for a while."

"Now look here, young lady, you must get your rest," Whit answered with a laugh. "You are sleeping for two now, don't forget. Little Mercedes Benz needs his or her rest as well."

It was the last thing Whit Forrest ever said.

As he put on his signal to make a turn onto Tuxedo Road, a car with only its parking lights on filled Whit's entire field of vision. Bren heard it for less than a second, then saw the grill of the speeding car crash into the driver's side door of Whit's car.

The noise was deafening, a flash of light, screaming metal, Whit's door window shattering, a wall of metal striking Whit's door, pushing it into his head. A piece of the doorframe sheered off and hit Whit's face, flattening his nose. The impact of the collision rocked the Mercedes off the pavement, its two left wheels rising four or five feet in the air, then slamming down.

Bren reached, screamed, clawed, trying somehow to push away from the crash scene, but it surrounded her with loud noise and withering pain. She lost consciousness, as Whit had a second or two before.

Two cars slowed on West Paces Ferry. One of the drivers tapped the brakes, but kept going past the crash scene. The other car stopped. The driver and his female companion walked over to the wreckage. Just then a man came out of one of the big houses on the road, wearing a bathrobe.

He saw the people who had stopped at the scene.

"How's it look over there?"

"Bad," said the man, now leaning in, closer to the wreckage of the Mercedes. I see a man and woman in this yellow car, and they're not moving.

"Can you phone for help?" his companion asked the neighbor.

"I just did. Called 9-1-1. They asked if anybody was alive. Jesus."

—

"It looks like a T-bone, a bad one," said the EMT on his radio. We have three people, all unconscious, major injuries. The one guy, white male, the one who must have crashed into the smaller car, is not responsive and I'm not getting a pulse.

"Another white male, apparently the driver of the small yellow car, is breathing, but not well. We're getting him out of the car, but it's a slow go. We put a neck brace on him 'cause his head was hanging to one side. He's banged up, his nose and cheekbones fractured. Also, his pupils are uneven and non-reactive. Doing CPR and will continue in the truck.

"The white female in that small car, passenger side, apparently has a low cervical fracture, C-four or five, I think. We put her in a brace. She has cuts and contusions, lots of broken glass in the car. She's breathing, but it's shallow. Wait one. We're loading them both now. Hang on."

Bren moaned, semi-conscious, as they lifted her into the ambulance truck and put an oxygen mask on her. The two EMTs then gingerly placed Whit on a gurney and hefted it into the ambulance.

"Grady Trauma, they're both in the truck now and we're en route to your ER.

In the second ambulance, an EMT was giving CPR to the man they pulled from behind the wheel of the car that T-boned Whit and Bren. He was not responsive, his face and neck badly cut up. They did all the right things as the ambulance sped to the Grady Hospital ER.

Police on the scene also knew he was dead. Their first report to headquarters was succinct. "White male, no ID and no driver's license on the body. Approximate age, twenty-five or so. The car is totaled. We estimate it was moving about fifty miles an hour when it collided with the Mercedes. No skid marks visible. We've made photos of the wreckage showing four empty beer cans and a fifth of, uh, bourbon I guess, about two-thirds empty. Looks like they'd been on the passenger seat or the floor on the right side of the sedan, the car that crashed into the smaller car.

"No eyewitnesses found yet, but a neighbor heard the crash and phoned it in."

The EMT working on Whit saw he was slipping away, his breathing labored and irregular. His face seemed to be turning blue. The EMT strapped a device on Whit's face that forced air into his lungs and then let the air out. As he worked, he said to the EMT working on Bren, "This guy's heart rate is slowing and getting weaker. And weaker.

He knew his patient was gone, but he kept at it.

"Shit, I think we lost him," the EMT said softly, as the truck neared the Emergency Room ambulance entrance at Grady.

—

"This patient is DOA," the ER physician said to the others in the room during triage. "His external injuries are bad, but probably not the cause of death. Could have been a rapidly developing subdural, but we'll know for sure soon."

Bren was stirring, still moaning, in the trauma center at Grady. After X-rays and an MRI, doctors confirmed the EMT's observation she was, at least temporarily, paralyzed from the waist down, a result of her fractured spine.

The doctors also discovered Bren had been about six weeks pregnant. But abdominal injuries in the crash caused internal bleeding, and she miscarried.

—

Until Bren's mother and father arrived at the hospital, they knew only Bren and Whit were in an accident. A receptionist led them to a room set aside for doctors and nurses to meet with loved ones of patients.

"Mr. and Mrs. Harding, I'm Doctor Ridell. I'm very sorry for the loss of your son- in-law. He was hit directly in the head and shoulder by a speeding car. That caused a severe concussion with massive bleeding into his brain, causing it to shut down. He never regained consciousness and almost surely felt no pain. I'm so sorry."

The Hardings clung to each other in grief, speechless for a moment.

"What about our daughter?" Bren's mother asked, trying not to pass out, leaning against her husband, her heart pounding with fear.

"She has serious injuries, with some paralysis from the waist down, but we think it is temporary and reversible. She will survive."

Bren's mother burst into tears, partially in relief. "Oh, thank the Lord," she said, taking the doctor's hand.

"But she is badly injured and will take a long time to get well. We'll take good care of her here and I know you'll do the same when she can go home. I can't say for sure when that will be, but probably three to four weeks."

The doctor decided Mrs. Harding might not be able to take the other horrible reality of Bren's condition. The doctor led her to a couch and suggested she sit. A nurse hovered nearby.

"Mr. Harding, may I speak to you privately?" Bren's dad nodded and they walked a few steps down the hall. "I don't want to upset Mrs. Harding any further right now, but I must inform you both that while treating your daughter for abdominal bleeding, we discovered she was six to seven weeks pregnant. The trauma of her injuries caused a miscarriage."

Bren's father put his right hand on the wall to steady himself. He rubbed his eyes with the palm of his left hand, forcing back tears. "I think I'd better tell her myself," he said to the doctor. "Maybe when we get home and she's lying down."

"I'll get something to calm her, to take before she goes to sleep," the doctor replied, handing Bren's father his card, urging them to phone him at any time. "If you feel well enough to drive home, Mr. Harding, you should go. There's nothing you can do here tonight. You can call my office tomorrow and we'll tell you everything we know about Mrs. Forrest's situation."

Bren's dad coughed and cleared his throat, trying to keep his composure. "Will she be able to, I mean, how much can...well, will she walk again?"

25

PARK TOWERS

The Vaughns' housekeeper eased open the bedroom door and approached Jan to tell her, "Mrs. Forrest is awake ma'am."

A few minutes later, Bren came out, still attaching her left earring, heading toward the door to the apartment. She was more restless than rested, with a determined grimace on her face. If she were a boxer, her expression would indicate it was time to stop strutting through the crowd and get into the ring.

At the door, Bren turned back to the Vaughns and embraced them in a group hug.

"Thank you, my dear friends, but I must go now. I'm going to work and write the speech I will make on TV tonight. It'll be live and I think it will make news. I will offer a huge reward for Cav's killer. We will find whoever did it. We will."

As Jan and Jerry escorted her out, Bren summoned the security man at the elevator.

"Young man, please call my driver downstairs and tell him I'm on my way. I need to get to GNS immediately."

"She's back, Jerry," Jan said, as they walked back into their home.

"I think you're right. She's still hurting, though, and she's angry. I sort of wish she'd record her speech ahead of time rather than going on live."

GNS HEADQUARTERS

"Mr. Ippolito, this is Bren Forrest. I am returning your call of this morning."

Max was surprised to hear her voice on the phone. He stood up at his desk.

"Yes, ma'am, Ms. Forrest, I am so sorry for what happened. How are you doing?"

"Well enough now, Max. It is Max, isn't it?"

"Yes, and I am glad to hear you're holding up. Ma'am, I need to get some direction from you on what you want to do with this live special tonight. It was supposed to be a celebration, but..."

"Yes, yes, I know the problem. Tell you what, Max, meet me at the assignment desk in fifteen minutes and we'll go over it. Get your people together. There's no time to waste."

Max gulped and looked out at the newsroom. Maybe fifty people were on hand, dealing with both routine news and pre-Olympic events, including the death of Cav Campbell.

"Oh, and, Max, is there anything new from police on Cav, I mean, Mr. Campbell's death?"

—

Bren had not been in the main newsroom for at least six months and that was just fine with most of the troops at GNS. She was nice enough, but a distraction, slowing the work, increasing the tension.

When she walked in that day, nobody made direct eye contact until she walked over to the assignment desk and greeted Max, who was standing stiffly.

She turned, almost three-hundred-sixty degrees, her eyes sweeping the room.

"My friends and associates, I just want to say thank you for all your work in this difficult time."

As she began to speak, the computer keyboards stopped clicking, the monitors went mute and the earphones came off those who were listening to raw video of news coverage.

"Tonight at ten o'clock, we will go on with our live, one-hour anniversary celebration, as scheduled. But it also will be a tribute to Mr. Campbell as well as to GNS." She teared up, but quickly dabbed at her eyes with a tissue and continued speaking. "I will make a speech

I hope will make you proud. I also hope it will make the people of America want to help us catch the killer of Mr. Campbell.

"And about that, I want to urge you to ignore any rumors or idle talk Mr. Campbell may have taken his own life. I know him, knew him, and I know that is not true. The police say it was no accident, that he did not somehow just fall from that balcony. And if that's true, it leaves only one possibility. Someone pushed Mr. Campbell to his death.

"I am going to make a recorded comment to that effect, which you are free to air on your hourly newscasts from now until the special this evening. Also, your reports may include, without quotation, it's believed on the special program, GNS and its president will be announcing a substantial reward for the capture of the killer. You can help us by doing your jobs as well as you always do them. Now, please, back to work and thank you."

The room was silent but for the coughing noises of people determined not to cry. Some other employees were weeping. Bren was dry-eyed. Max was dumbfounded, wondering whether there was any possible chance the past ten minutes somehow had been recorded on video or someone's cellphone.

Two women at the international news desk stood and began to applaud slowly. Another desk assistant, a boy just out of Emerson College, joined them. Then another, and another. As Bren Forrest walked over to Max and slipped her arm through his, leading him to his office for a private talk, the newsroom was delivering a standing ovation.

It seemed slightly out of place, sort of the way applause does in church. It died as Max closed his office door. Bren sat on the front edge of a chair across from Max's desk.

"Now, Max, let's plan the best goddam show in TV history."

26

VIRGINIA HIGHLANDS—ATLANTA

Detective Hagan used his pocket-handkerchief to push the on-off button on the TV remote in the living room of Tia Lee's apartment. It was a long shot, but he wanted to find out what channel she may have been watching before she was killed. The set burst to life, the sound too loud, a few seconds into an afternoon news update on Channel 3.

"...special one-hour edition of NewsBlitz3. Good Afternoon, I'm Art Toomey. We begin our complete, comprehensive, live Team3 coverage of the death of actor Cav Campbell with a report from Atlanta Police homicide headquarters. Our Cassandra Page joins us live. Cassandra..."

"The late word here is Campbell, the fiancé of Global News Service owner Bren Forrest, did not fall out of that building by accident. As you know, he plunged forty-six stories to his death last night and was impaled on the mast, the pole atop a TV remote truck.

"It happened during a major pre-Olympics party at the penthouse home of philanthropist and Olympics official Jerry Vaughn...."

Hagan pushed the volume-down button, realizing Cassie had nothing new. *Won't be long, though. I'll have to let her know about this body now, before the police public information office releases it.*

Hagan was waiting for Mae McIntosh to arrive with the uniformed officer. Normally, he would have the body transported to the morgue and then have the next of kin come in to identify it. But it seemed more decent, somehow, more humane, to have the mother come here, in private.

He went into the bathroom, took the plastic shower curtain from its rings on the pole and draped it over the body in the tub.

No fibers on that. No way they can say we tainted this crime scene.

As he walked back into the living room, Officer Palmer came in, his hand on Mae McIntosh's arm.

"Ma'am, I'm Detective Hagan." She nodded, numb with fear. "I'm sorry to tell you that a woman who I think is your daughter is, has been, is dead."

She sagged slightly. Palmer clutched her with both hands to hold her up. He led her to a chair. As she sat, Hagan turned off the TV.

"Oh, Lord, oh no," she said, almost in a whisper. "How, how, how?" Tears trickled as she looked up at Hagan, who was silent. "She's never, ever late for our lunch dates. Never. I just knew something was wrong, but..."

Hagan sat down in a chair next to her.

"Ma'am, can I ask, are you, will you help us? We want to know why she died. Can you identify her for us?"

She nodded, then asked, "Was it an accident, what, how..."

"We don't know, but if you can come with me for just a minute, we'll take you right home."

"I must phone my husband, I must. But what happened? Please tell me, what happened?"

Hagan helped her to her feet and led her toward the bathroom, Palmer walking ahead, opening the bathroom door.

"Mrs. McIntosh, we think she died of a broken neck, either by accident or..."

She shuddered, fear in her eyes.

"An accident, then, yes, of course, a terrible accident."

Then she saw the shower curtain covering part of the tub.

"Is that her under there, oh no, please, please, no!"

Hagan had to get this over with.

"Palmer, please," Hagan said, nodding to the top of the shower curtain.

The officer lifted it slowly, revealing the girl's head and shoulders. The face was turned away slightly, the neck at that ugly angle.

Mae sobbed, shaking, getting heavier in Hagan's arms as she stared at her dead daughter.

"Is this your daughter?" Hagan whispered.

She nodded, her body almost convulsing.

"Yes, yes, dear God, yes. How could she fall like that?"

Palmer put the shower curtain back in place. Hagan turned Mae toward the door and out of the bathroom.

She lay on the couch. Palmer fetched a dishcloth from the kitchen, put cold water on it and folded it on her forehead. Eyes closed, her hands clenched, she lay there crying, mumbling something in Korean.

Hagan motioned Palmer out to the balcony, told him to find out when the coroner would arrive and to notify forensics. The two men went back inside.

"Mrs. McIntosh, I must ask you, I know it's hard, but I have to do my job."

She turned slightly, opened her eyes. "Yes, Detective, anything."

"Ma'am, do you know anyone who might have wanted to hurt your daughter?"

"No, of course not, she was, was wonderful, kept to herself mostly, just..."

"Well, ma'am, please think about that, it would be helpful to us. Also, where can we reach Mr. McIntosh?"

"I think he's playing golf with some other men from his office."

"Do you, uh, get along with your husband?"

She seemed puzzled.

"I mean, should we tell him what happened or be with you when you do? See what I mean?" Hagan was as gentle as he could be with this grieving woman.

"Oh, yes, of course. He loves her so much, you know. Never any trouble, oh God, what is happening to us?"

Hagan asked Mae the name of the golf course after deciding to find McIntosh and have him taken to homicide headquarters rather than here to the apartment.

He called his office and told two officers to go to the Ansley Golf Club on Montgomery Ferry Road and find Ralph McIntosh. They could check his tee time at the pro shop to figure out approximately what hole he'd be on.

Mae sat up on the couch as Hagan hung up the phone.

"Detective, could somebody really have done this? Why? Why?"

"I don't know that, Mrs. McIntosh, but we're going to find out."

Hagan went into the bedroom, closed the door and called the private number of Police Chief Lutz.

"Lutz here."

"Sir, Hagan here. We have another body and I think it's the girl we're looking for, the Asian girl people saw talking with Campbell at the party."

Lutz wiped the back of his hand across a line of sweat forming on his upper lip.

"Somebody do her?"

"Yessir, snapped her neck. Seems professional to me. I think we have two murders on our hands, Chief, and we need to get the word out."

The chief wiped his mouth again, then said in a low voice, "Detective, we will do no such thing. If we tell the public Campbell was murdered before we are absolutely positive, it'll start a shit storm. You hear me, Hagan? Say nothing until the ME does an autopsy, nothing, period."

Hagan fumed, knowing Lutz was afraid of the mayor and the others climbing up his back and down his throat. "I hear you, Chief. So, what are you going to tell 'em?"

"Nothing for now, you know, investigation underway on Campbell, nothing on the dead girl 'till I tell you. That's it. Stay in touch."

Hung up on, Hagan redialed. When he heard Cassie's answering message, he entered his number as a callback and hit "call ended."

Four minutes later, Cassie called.

"Hi, Jimmy here. You can report the last person seen with Campbell Tuesday night has been found dead in her apartment in Virginia Highlands. No attribution, nothing. And you cannot use the address, babe, just this for now. It's my ass if you connect me to this. The chief is belching bile, he's so scared. See you tonight."

He hung up fast, uncharacteristically. He had to and Cassie knew it.

27

ATLANTA POLICE HEADQUARTERS

"No sign of forced entry. The clothes she'd been wearing were folded neatly, her jewelry there, no sign of theft." Hagan was reading and partly paraphrasing the medical examiner's report to Chief Lutz on the phone. "The neck was broken, a pro, no doubt about it. No hand prints on her head or neck, no prints anywhere, nothing."

Lutz grunted a volley of questions.

"What about ID? Are we sure this is the girl who was talking to Campbell at the party? What's her name? Husband? Boyfriend? Other suspects? How about that apartment manager? Is he a nut or what? What the hell, Detective, what do we have?"

Lutz saw the image on NewsBlitz3 change from a commercial to Cassandra Page, live outside homicide headquarters.

"Hang on a minute, Hagan," he said, and pushed the volume control on the remote.

"NewsBlitz3 has just learned police have found the body of a young woman who is thought to be one of, perhaps the last person, to see Cav Campbell alive. "Sources tell us she was a guest at the party last night at the Vaughn penthouse. Other guests have reported seeing her talking with Campbell at one point in the evening. We do not know whether authorities believe the two deaths are connected..."

Chief Lutz exploded into the phone.

"Shit, Jimmy, that broad on Channel 3 found out about the girl. Who leaked it Jimmy... I'll have his head on a goddam plate!"

Hagan shook his head, then said, "Jesus, Chief, I don't know how these people get this stuff so fast. It's like they're flies on the damn walls. And there's no chance Ms. Page will tell us any time soon, if ever."

"Screw her then, ya know? Just try to keep the lid on over there. And anybody asking about that report gets a big fat 'no comment,' period."

I can handle both those orders, Hagan thought.

"Right, Chief. And, I guess we can treat the Campbell case officially as a homicide now, right, Chief?"

"Goddammit, yes, YES! DammitDammitDammitDammitDammit. Crap!" The chief ended the call, worried about his future.

—

"No comment and that's all we have to say at this point." Hagan's face was shiny with perspiration in the camera lights in the media room at homicide headquarters.

A mid-afternoon thunderstorm was dousing Atlanta, forcing the reporters inside for the briefing. Shouted questions came in a jumble from the reporters who heard about Cassie's exclusive on the death of the girl.

She stood near the rear of the pack, trying not to appear smug, wondering how she could get some kind of acknowledgment from Jimmy the girl's death meant Campbell obviously was murdered.

"Come on, Detective, we need to know something!"

"Geez, Jimmy, this is big stuff and you know it. Give us what you have."

"Detective, do you have a dead girl or not? You can't keep a death secret!"

A reporter for the *Atlanta Journal-Constitution* spoke up, "Detective Hagan, we're reporting in tomorrow's paper some of the people at the party say the girl they saw with Campbell was an Asian or Amerasian, that she apparently worked for the Olympics committee. Can you confirm that?"

The TV reporters tensed, sensing big news.

The truth getting out might help bring someone else forward with information, Hagan thought. *Or it could cost me my job.*

"Sorry, Murray, but I can't comment on that. We will let you know what we know, as soon as we know it, for sure." *There. That's a seven second sound bite the TV guys can use, but I didn't say anything.*

"When, Jimmy, when can we get something? The network wants it, too. You know you'll be a household word in a week!"

Jimmy smiled at the reporter's attempt at bribing him with celebrity status. "Yeah, Keith, but I'd be an unemployed celebrity, and that's off the record," he said with a grin.

That broke the tension.

"Next briefing, six tonight. Chief Lutz," he told them. The camera lights snapped off and reporters began to call their offices.

Cassie lingered for just a moment, knowing better than to go up to Jimmy at that moment. She called the station, confirmed her next live update and told the cameraman she would take the video card back to the station herself. "I have to run back there anyway."

She drove first to a small Mexican restaurant on Ponce de Leon Avenue, which the locals pronounced Ponts-duh-LEE-ahn. Cassie and Jimmy had met there just once before for lunch. It was a cop hangout, so they thought it unwise to be seen there together. Today, she wanted to phone Jimmy and to grab a burrito to go.

"Jimmy, Cassie," she said, standing in the back service hall, near the ladies room.

"Hey, what's up?"

"Just checkin' in. You did well there, my man, proud of you."

"Don't try this at home, you know, I am a professional," he kidded.

"Jimmy, are you guys treating Campbell's death as a murder case now?"

"Hmmmm, interesting speculation on your part. Is there a source for that?"

She loved his teasing, but needed to be sure about this. "Hope to have one, right about now."

"No problem," he said, "but I have to run. I'd check with the Olympics people. The young woman was a hostess there. Same rules, you slip up, it's my ass. Bye."

"Love it and you, too. Bye."

Cassie ended the connection slowly, chewing on how best to use her next exclusive. She knew if she popped this stuff on the six o'clock news or in a special live break-in, she'd drive the city officials nuts trying to find the leak.

That was appealing, but the chance they might figure on Jimmy and nail him, that was scary. She needed something independent of her favorite detective. He said she was an Olympics hostess.

I'd better get to Olympics headquarters. Nope, getting this recording back to the newsroom comes first. Wait, no, it comes second. First, that burrito, green chili and cheese, but no meat.

—

"And now, our newest, hottest game here on the Sheamus Cross Show, all the rage around town right now. We call it, 'Which Way to Go.'"

That's the first thing Jimmy heard when he flipped on his car radio on the way to Olympics committee headquarters. Jimmy knew the voice as that of the often annoying, never dull talk show host. *Oh yeah, I never returned Cross's phone call. Maybe later today, at least to see if he knows anything I don't know. Wonder what this new bit is he's doing. Hope he's picking on somebody besides the cops this time.*

"Here's how 'Which Way to Go' works, folks," Sheamus went on. "I throw out a challenge and you can phone in your answer. Warning—it's not for weenies. Our challenges today are ripped from the headlines, as they say.

"Number one: Which Way to Go: You can slide naked down a forty foot razor blade into a pit of hungry pythons. Or, you can fall off the penthouse balcony of a forty-six story building and be impaled on the mast of a TV news truck. You choose which way to go."

Jimmy was stunned. *I knew Cross was gross and outrageous, but this rips it.* He turned up the volume on the radio.

"Our first caller is Joe from Marietta. Which way to go, Joe?"

"Hey there, Sheamus, how you doin'?"

"Don't waste my time, Joe from Marietta, choose or lose."

"Well, answer me this, Sheamus, is the razor blade very sharp or real dull?"

"Joe, I'm sure it is very dull, yet still a lot sharper than you. Now get off my phone. Okay, next challenge in the 'Which Way to Go' game. On a skydiving adventure, your parachute doesn't open and you plummet into a pack of ravenous hyenas. Or, you can fall off the penthouse balcony of a forty-six story building and be impaled on the mast of a TV news van. You choose, which way to go."

"Next caller, Shadow from Snellville, if that's your real name. Go."

"Hello there, Mister Cross, sir," the caller said in a low, slow, smoky voice. "I'd take my chances with the hyenas." Then the voice changed into a creepy cackle. "Unless the head hyena was you, Sheamus, you schmuck."

Sheamus hung up and said to his listeners, "Who—was—that? What—was—that? Like I said folks, ripped from the headlines, or more accurately, impaled on the TV news, literally. Who knows, maybe that last caller did it.

"I tell you what, folks, we'll demand some answers and we'll get them here on the Sheamus In The Morning show. Memo to Police Chief Lutz: I'll be at the big airline shindig at the Marriott tomorrow night and I'll have a few choice questions for you, Chief. See you there, pal.

"Friends, stay tuned to WNAG News Radio, because as our friends in the TV news nuthouse always say, 'When news breaks out, it's news to us.'"

28

OLYMPIC COMMITTEE HEADQUARTERS

Jimmy Hagan wanted to get to the Olympics people about Lia Lee before Cassie showed up. He knew it wouldn't take her long to get what she needed.

"Detective, welcome. Dan Handleman, I'm public relations," the man said, with a touch of motivational speaker and a firm, double pump handshake. He was in the lobby of the Olympics committee headquarters building downtown to meet Hagan at the reception desk. "Nasty business. Any news on what happened to Cav Campbell?" His words echoed across the marble expanse of the lobby.

"Well, we need to talk to more people about that. That's why I'm here, as I mentioned on the phone. Can we go somewhere and talk?"

"Let's walk outside. No curious ears there." Handleman loosened his tie. He left his suit jacket in his office, an acknowledgment July in Atlanta can be a beast of heat and humidity.

As they stepped onto the steamy sidewalk on Harris Street, Handleman turned to Hagan. "Detective, we have a big problem here. This Campbell thing is getting worldwide attention. If ya'll don't solve it before the games begin, the foreign press'll be on your ass as well as ours."

"They're already here, some, aren't they?" Jimmy asked, knowing newsies from all over were here or on their way.

"You bet, and some of these European guys, especially the British tabloid papers, make our local folks look like Edward R. Murrow by comparison," Handleman said. His shirt was now stuck to his body in patches of sweat.

Hagan had briefed Handleman on the phone about his interest in Lia Lee. For the moment, he left out the fact she was dead. "So, what can you give me on the girl, uh, the woman, Lia Lee, Mr. Handleman?"

"Dan, please call me Dan. Well, I checked her out. She's one of our hostesses. We have seventy-five, you know. She works at GNS, low-level, maybe an intern. I'm not sure. She was chosen for the job because she speaks at least two languages and, well, from the picture in her file, she is a gorgeous girl, don't you think?"

Hagan flashed back to the naked body in the tub.

"Yes, I gather she is. You have any details on her family or friends, maybe some references in her job application?"

"Well, I'll check further. I know her parents live around here somewhere. She listed their home as her address on the application to be a hostess for the games.

"References, I don't recall. But like I said, her language skills and her appearance were about all she needed."

They were three-fourths of their way around the block that surrounded the building. Hagan picked up the pace, knowing he had all he would get from Handleman. As they reached the double glass doors to the office building, Handleman stopped and put his hand on Hagan's forearm as he reached to open the door.

"Detective, I have to do some serious damage control here, if this girl is involved in any way with the Campbell thing. So, lay it out, please. Do I have a problem here?"

"Yep, I think so, Dan, I think so."

Handleman's hand shook slightly as he released Hagan's arm.

"So, why can't you just question her about the party, about Campbell and all that?"

"I can't question her, Dan."

"What is it? What, did she, I mean was she involved, in his... No way, right? I mean she probably even knows Bren Forrest, working there and all." Handleman was sweating more than the weather demanded.

"I don't know yet, Dan, but we can't ask her. She's, uh, out of pocket. We need to know whether she knew Campbell. We need to know more about her private life."

"Well, I'm trying to help, but you have to help me, too."

"Sure, Dan, sure. Thanks. Call me if her file turns up anything more."

Hagan walked to his car, half a block down in a no parking zone. Handleman rushed through the glass doors, across the marble floor of the lobby and into an elevator. As he pushed the button for the twelfth floor, Cassie Page walked into the elevator, smiled at Handleman and shook his hand.

"Can you spare a minute, Dan? Hey, you are soaked through. Been outside all day?"

"Cassie, this is not a good time. I mean you didn't call or anything, so please, give me a break for now."

"All I need is confirmation Lee was, is, a hostess for the Olympics. I know it's true, just need you to confirm it."

The elevator stopped at twelve. As the door opened, Handleman shook his head.

"No way I can comment on that, Cassie, no way."

He stepped out and turned toward his office door down the hall.

"Hey, Dan, I know she worked for you. I know she was at the party. And I know she's dead, so give it up will you?"

Handleman stopped. As Cassie caught up to him, she saw his face was pale.

"She's dead?" he asked, in a near whisper. "What do you mean she's dead?"

"Well, that's what my sources tell me. They found her dead in her apartment this morning. You didn't know, Dan? Oh, dear. Oh well, you didn't hear it from me."

It worked.

"She was one of the hostesses, yes, you already knew that." He turned and went into his office, not looking back.

Cassie pushed the elevator button, already thinking about her live shot at six.

29

ANSLEY GOLF CLUB—ATLANTA

Ralph McIntosh was at the top of his backswing with a driver when he heard someone call his name.

Irritated, he stopped and turned to his left. A police officer stood forty feet away, under a dogwood tree, hugging the shade it offered.

"Mr. McIntosh, are you Ralph McIntosh?"

"Yes, what is it?" He was as upset about losing his concentration as he was curious about the cop.

The other men in his foursome, all sales and marketing people, moved closer to the policeman.

"Sir, may I have a moment? It's important, Mr. McIntosh."

Ralph stashed his club in his golf bag on the cart and walked over to the tree. "What is it, officer?"

The policeman walked to within two feet of McIntosh, steering him away from the others with an arm on his elbow. "Sir, there's been an accident and I need you to come with me to our station."

"Is it Mae, my wife, is she all right? What happened, what is it?"

"No, sir, it's your daughter. She's been hurt, an accident, and we need you to come right away."

"My daughter? Which one? Lia or Tia? What happened, where, who?" His face reddened, his voice trembled with emotion.

"Which one? I didn't know you had two daughters, sir, so please, just come with me right away."

McIntosh turned to his friends, who knew something was wrong. "I, I have to go with the policeman, something's happened at home, to Lia, or Tia, I don't now. Sorry, but I...you know, now." He turned abruptly and almost jogged to the golf cart the policeman had used to get to the tee.

They rolled up toward the putting green on Montgomery Ferry Road, across the street from the Ansley Clubhouse. Another officer was sitting in a squad car parked on the street.

"Officer, please, please tell me what happened, where, when, please."

"Sir, all I know is, one of your daughters was in an accident at her apartment on Amsterdam."

"Oh, God, it's Tia," McIntosh said, now rubbing his chin with his hand, nervous, scared.

"Tia, sir?"

"Yeah, Tia lives in Virginia Highlands, he said, shaking his head, his eyes moist.

"And the other one, the other daughter?"

"Lia, you mean, Tia's twin. We don't see her much. She lives in the Ponce area somewhere, used to be kind of hippy stuff. Not sure about now. Listen, can't we go any faster? I'm sick, I'm about to faint, I think," McIntosh said.

The officer hit the siren switch and accelerated, dodging cars driven by people whose radios or CDs were up so loud they never heard the siren.

He picked up the police radio microphone on the dashboard and called homicide.

"... and tell Detective Hagan Mr. McIntosh is in route. Mr. McIntosh is the father of Tia Lee, that's Tia—Tango India Alpha—Tia. And her twin, Lia—Lima India Alpha—Lia. Make sure he gets that exact message."

—

At homicide headquarters, Jimmy Hagan was waiting with Mae McIntosh in a private room the police used to question victims or relatives of victims. It had light green leather lounge chairs, a coffee table of Goodwill quality and a card table with four uncomfortable matching chairs. A small TV was on a metal stand in the corner next to a drab two-seater couch, showing its age with a built-in ashtray in the right side armrest.

On the otherwise empty ashtray was a fold-over table card that read, "If we see you smoking, we will assume you are on fire and will take appropriate measures."

Mae sat on one of the leather chairs, sipping coffee in a plastic cup. She was watching the TV without seeing much of it. A woman officer sat on one of the card-table chairs, also watching the TV, tuned to NewsBlitz3. Art Toomey was on the air live.

"NewsBlitz3 has learned a hostess for the Olympics here next week has been found dead in an apartment in Virginia Highlands. Our sources say the young woman was at the party where actor Cav Campbell fell to his death Friday night.

"We also have learned the woman, Lia Lee, was among the last persons to see Campbell alive. Atlanta Police will not comment on these reports. Homicide Detective Jimmy Hagan talked briefly with reporters earlier today."

Up came video of Hagan at the "no comment" news conference. As he spoke on the video, Mae asked Jimmy to turn up the sound.

"When was that, Detective?" she asked, distractedly.

"About half an hour ago, while the officer was taking you home and then bringing you here."

"Where's my husband? Is he coming here? She talked slowly, as though she were on a sedative. "Does Ralph know about Tia?"

"Yes, Mrs. McIntosh, I think so. An officer is bringing him here now. And, Ma'am, did you say your daughter's name is Tia? Not Lia?"

Before she could answer, a young detective, Diego Mendoza, knocked twice, then flung open the door.

"Jimmy, you need to hear this. Out here, please."

A minute later, Jimmy walked back into the interview room. Mrs. McIntosh sat quietly, watching the TV, dabbing at her now dry eyes with a wadded Kleenex.

"Mrs. McIntosh, do you have two daughters?"

"Yes, of course," she said, starting to cry again. "I did, I mean, Tia is dead, isn't she?" she sobbed, head down. "They're so different, those girls. How they could be so different, yet be twins? They were close as children, but then Lia changed, acting out, wilder and wilder and she didn't come home much. Drugs, you know, I think it's drugs or drink, I don't know and she'd never talk about it, but I think she's involved with drugs somehow. Oh, my God."

Jimmy sat on the arm of the leather couch and put his hand on her shoulder as she rambled.

"I always thought Lia would be in trouble, get hurt, you know, but never Tia. She was a homebody, she loved us, came over all the time, not like Lia. Oh God, Detective, why Tia?"

Jesus, twins, like some cheap mystery novel, goddam twins. Easy mistake, yep, anybody would've done it. Lutz is gonna crap, then dump on me big time. And Cassie, she will look silly as hell.

He broke his rule and called Cassie's cell phone. When she picked up, Hagan told her quickly of the screw-up, that the dead girl was Tia Lee, the sister of the girl they were looking for, the Olympics hostess.

"Jimmy, Jesus wha..?"

"No time now. Just kill it, go with the right one. Her name is Tia Lee, an accountant, American father. And Cassie, listen, if there's any way to make us seem less foolish on this, I'll owe you."

"Jimmy, I'm the one who looks stupid. You can just 'no comment' the thing to death. But guess what," she said with a smile he could hear, "I'll always know, and you'll pay privately for, oh, a long, long time." She clicked off before he could respond.

"...and that's the up-to-the-minute information on the Cav Campbell investigation. We'll have complete, live NewsBlitz3 Team Coverage at six. Now, here's Jamie Whittaker with a preview of her weather report at six. Jamie."

"Art, the swelter continues and it looks like it will get steamier tomorrow. I'll have details at six, but here's a hint. There'll be lots of dew tomorrow morning on your car and your lawn if you leave them out overnight."

Jimmy shook his head. *Moron. Where do they get these people?*

He turned back to Mae, who was staring at the TV, her mind numbed, her face a blank, her world upside down.

"Mrs. McIntosh. Ma'am, Mrs. McIntosh, do you want some more coffee or something?"

She didn't answer, staring at the TV. Art Toomey was saying good-bye for now.

"You know what, Detective, that man on TV, Art something, he dyes his hair. I'm sure he dyes his hair because a couple of years ago it was grayer than it is now."

Jimmy nodded, saying nothing.

"Why do they do that on TV, Detective? Do you dye your hair? You're on TV sometimes, but no, of course not, you're too young. How old are you, Detective? Too old for my daughter, I guess. She was twenty-four, you know, Tia, that is. Lia too. But actually Tia was a couple of minutes older..."

Her words were running together. She was mumbling now, unintelligible.

The young detective knocked again and opened the door.

"Jimmy, the chief's office called. He wants you down there, now."

Hagan nodded, stood, patted Mae's shoulder and motioned with his other hand for the female officer to come sit next to her.

30

GNS HEADQUARTERS

The atrium at GNS headquarters in downtown Atlanta was jammed. The guest list for the live anniversary TV special had been trimmed and re-trimmed to make the event fit into the courtyard at the lobby level.

Cav Campbell's bizarre death morphed what was planned to be an upbeat birthday gala for the all-news channel, of little interest to competing networks, into a melodrama nobody could ignore. The executives at GNS maintained a somber demeanor befitting the mixture of mourning and murder in their midst. They all sensed, however, the TV show would be a viewing audience record-setter, perhaps with higher ratings than the opening ceremonies of the Olympics two days later.

A score or more of TV news cameras teetered on a scaffold cobbled up overnight on one side of the atrium. Media swarmed the place, from pundits to paparazzi. By nine forty-five, fifteen minutes before the GNS special was to begin, the courtyard, even with its fourteen-story open space, was stifling, the air stale, humidity and collective blood pressure rising.

Ficus trees and some large palms adorned the back of the stage to hide the fast-food restaurants and souvenir shops that lined the walls of the lobby.

In front of the foliage, padded folding chairs were lined up in a chevron pattern, four rows deep on either side of the center podium. The chairs were full of VIP guests; the mayors of Atlanta, Marietta, Savannah and other Georgia cities, the governor of Georgia and those of three neighboring states, various military commanders, most members of Georgia's congressional delegations and other local and regional bigwigs.

On the floor level, another three hundred chairs were set up, now mostly filled with GNS employees not involved in the program. Many came from their offices and news facilities on the upper levels, having been pressed into action to cover the breaking news earlier in the day.

Far back on the right, down a wide expanse leading to the athletic club and restaurant, the award-winning Georgia Tech Band was warming up and tuning up, creating a jumble of discordant sounds, forcing the people in the seats to talk louder to be heard.

On the left, next to an office supply store, a small banquet table had been squeezed in for the print media. Because their view of the show was limited, two flat screen TVs were suspended above the reporters' table so they could follow the action. A dozen or so reporters shared the table, pecking away at their laptops.

On a six-by-ten foot platform, about four feet off the floor, between the audience and the TV cameras, the co-anchors of the GNS special were in place.

Max had intended to do a replica of the first anchor set used on GNS's first day on the air way back when, but it appeared old, not quaint, more relic than retro, so he settled for a modern set with a glass top on Lucite legs.

The anchors, Ethan Thomas and Amanda Grace, had not been at GNS from the start, anyway. They were the premier anchors right now, their hair, teeth and teleprompter-reading skills familiar to the American public. Usually, it wasn't obvious their knowledge of issues and current events was spotty.

Ethan and Amanda got along with each other fairly well for short bursts, but had little to do with each other when not on the set doing the news. Even there, most of their conversation was in present tense and would have ended anyway if the two-minute commercial breaks had been any longer.

Loyalties among people who worked on their prime time newscast were divided. The Ethanites thought the Amandians were as phony as she was. Those loyal to Amanda felt Ethan was a snob, a know-it-all who didn't.

Ethan was reading over his paper script, underlining words and phrases he wanted to emphasize even though it was all on the prompter. Amanda's eyes were darting around the room, spotting celebrities, winking at co-workers, holding her hands over her ears in mock pain at the noise of the crowded room.

TV photographers on the scaffolding, fiddling with their gear, also noticed the din, as everybody buzzed about the sensations of the moment.

"Ya know, with all this hot air and the real trees in the atrium, we could create our own eco-system in here," said an audio tech from NBC to an engineer from Univision.

"So, will it rain in here then?" the Spanish language network tech asked.

"Why not? When Bren Forrest talks, there won't be a dry eye in here anyway," answered NBC.

"Twelve minutes to air, twelve minutes," said Max Ippolito quietly into the microphone in his headset.

Max was in the back of the main control room at GNS. He had ordered up six live cameras for this show and was checking their shots on the bank of monitors. Satisfied, he turned to the director, Billy Olson. "We have, what, five stationary cameras on tripods, right"

"Yes, and one of them will stay close up on Ms. Forrest nonstop so we'll have a tight shot of her, no matter what."

"Great, yes, fine," Max said, distracted. Bren Forrest was in her office, the door closed, virtually the entire afternoon, going over her speech, making some notes in the margins.

She asked Max to give her the last segment of the show, about ten minutes. He knew she would take more, deserved more, so he blocked out extra time.

His other major change from the show's pre-impalement format was to order Sheila Belle to record her retrospective, "The Life and Times of Cav Campbell," ahead of time with no live open or close. Max's blood pressure went down just thinking about how he arranged to keep Sheila out of live, ad-lib situations in the next hour.

He formatted the program to open with a live helicopter shot of GNS headquarters. The anchors would voice-over that shot. Then Max would show video of the first moments of GNS, when the anchors' first words were, "Welcome to the Global News Service now on the air. Here's what's happening."

Then would come a wide shot of the atrium, then a cut to Ethan and Amanda and the show would be underway.

"Simple, clean. I like it," Max said to Billy.

The show was designed for TV, not for the audience in the atrium. Big screen monitors on three sides would give them a chance to see what the TV audience saw, old clips of GNS's early days, a quick reel of bloopers and foul-ups for levity, endorsements and congratulations on video from various world and national leaders, that sort of thing.

"Ned, remember, no commercials at the end," Max said to his least favorite producer, Ned Bastige. "When Ms. Forrest finishes, she wants the band to play two numbers. You have 'em listed there. Then, to black for three seconds, then show the credits over wide shots around the atrium with regular theme music. Clear?"

Bastige nodded, checking the last two pages of his show rundown sheet.

"And, Ned, don't forget. Kill the commercial selling downloads of the special. We'll run it an extra time or two in the next hour but not at the end of this show."

Bastige nodded again, not speaking. His mind was only partly on this program. He had not heard yet from Lia. Guess she made it to Florida. She knows she shouldn't call here, but, dammit, she could just call and then hang up! Bastige's last hit was wearing off. It was earlier in the afternoon and now he was a few minutes from air and had no time for another line.

—

Outside the GNS building, a Delta Air Lines billboard blinked the time and temperature: "9:57pm, 88 degrees F."

Lined up like birds on a wire on the parking deck attached to GNS were reporters for the local stations. Ten yards away were their live trucks. Joining them were satellite trucks from the big three networks, CBS, NBC and ABC.

Lack of a breeze protected their correspondents' sprayed hairdos. Every TV reporter who ever did a live report in an outdoor setting feared the inevitable bad hair days. That does not include reporters who stand outside amidst historic hurricanes, blowing hair and everything else hither and yon. Some think it makes them look fearless in case a network executive tunes in and says to an underling, "Get me that lunatic before he's swallowed up by an epic wave."

Critics loved to use hair spray as a symbol of the shallowness of TV news, but it was not a fair criticism. Honest viewers would admit in any contest between a reporter's hair blowing all over the screen and the reporter's words and pictures, silly hair wins every time.

This airless, sweltering evening was, at least, not a bad hair day.

Cassandra Page was second from the left in the line of local reporters, about six feet from the others. She could hardly wait to have them overhear her first few lines, about the dead girl, the correct dead girl, but she knew she'd catch flack from the others when she had to correct her earlier "source" report.

So far, the police had said only, "no comment."

"Minute-n'-a-half, Cassie, standby." It was the director, talking on the IFB in her ear.

"Art starts here, throws to you right away, then when your piece finishes, you toss to Carl Dayton at the McIntosh house. Cassie, what's your cue for the video?" the director asked, so he'd know just when to bring up that portion of her report.

"Uh, it'll be, 'police aren't saying much, publicly, at least.'"

"That works. One minute."

"Stand by chopper shot, one minute."

Ned Bastige watched as the director talked into the microphone to the photographer in the helicopter hovering over the GNS building.

Billy Olson pushed another mic button on the control panel.

"Stand by, Ethan, Amanda, less than a minute now. Remember, you're voice-over the chopper, keep it short, no chat."

31

GNS HEADQUARTERS—ATLANTA

Bren Forrest sat back from the computer keyboard in her condo on an upper floor of the GNS building. Her left leg was stiff from sitting there, tinkering with her speech yet another time, crossing out a sentence here and there, crying a little, typing a little.

She noticed the low-grade pain in her thigh, as she often did ever since that horrific car crash on what should have been one of the best days she'd ever experienced. The real pain was the memory of losing the love of her life, her beloved husband Whit. She stared off, daydreaming, seeing Whit fleetingly at their wedding, then in his favorite yellow Mercedes. Time warped and Cav's image poured into her. The tragedy of Whit's death twenty-one years ago in a flash morphed into Cav Campbell's gruesome fate when a killer pushed him off that balcony.

How odd, Bren thought, *that those two life crises would meld. After all, I never even met Cav until nineteen years after I lost Whit. Why do I seem to always have both of them with me, one on each shoulder? Maybe it makes the intense, endless recovery from my own near death a bit easier to handle.*

Somehow Cav came along at the right time and he was, it was, it felt, so, um, so appropriate. Sounds weird to call him that, don't mean to diminish our love, but he and I sort of just fit. He was handsome and self confident, never seemed to feel threatened by my long hours, frequent business travel and all that, just the opposite. He was just what I needed, entertaining, fun and charming.

Oh, and he never seemed to have an ounce of jealousy or resentment over Whit, who even in death has always been a major force in my life. It was just, well, yes, that's the word—appropriate.

Her mind flashed back in an instant to that time when pain and grief were so strong that happiness and normality were, at best, suppressed longings having little to do with her daily life. Until the day her doctor walked into her room and said he had good news.

"Mrs. Forrest, I'm pleased to tell you we've stabilized your spinal fracture to the point where you can now advance your recovery."

"Sounds good, doctor, but please call me Bren. And what's the good news?"

"You'll be wearing a halo for a six or eight weeks."

"A halo? Really? A halo like…"

"It's a medical device," the doctor said, hurriedly interrupting Bren's question. "Here is a photo of it and before you say anything, believe me, it is crucial to your recovery."

Bren didn't know whether to laugh or cry or try to crawl out of the hospital. What she was staring at was photo of a contraption that fastens on the head with pins inserted on the outer skull. Vertical bars secure the halo to a vest worn by the patient. The halo prevents the head and neck from moving during recovery from a neck injury. It is worn virtually every minute of every day.

"Doctor, seriously, two months in this? Does anybody ever do this?"

"Yes, because without it you will never be able to walk or stand correctly and your horse riding days will be gone forever."

"I don't know, I just don't know," Bren said with almost a whimper.

A nurse walked into the room with a girl, maybe seven or eight years old. She was smiling. And wearing a halo.

"Clarice, I'd like you to meet Mrs. Forrest. Ma'am, this is Clarice. Tell the lady how long you've been wearing your halo hat.

"I dunno," the child said. "Are you going to wear one, too?"

Point made, Bren thought. *If this child can do it…*

Three weeks later, after rigorous rehab work that exhausted Bren's body but improved her emotional outlook somewhat, the Hardings drove Bren to their home. They had prepared a suite for her with a sitting room, spacious, airy and bright, off the bedroom. A private nurse would live in separate quarters in the house.

It was a good fix for Bren, who dreaded going back to the house where she and Whit had lived and loved. The pall over the house was palpable. Bren's emotional rock bottom was scraping her soul, sure to leave mental scars. Even when she tried to rally, her head and her heart were not in it.

I wonder whether I'll ever smile again. I can't find anything, not one single thing to be pleased about. And happy? Probably never. I know I should thank God for sparing my life, but I just can't, not right now. Life without Whit? Without the tiny life inside me?

The days dragged on, but one afternoon a small bright spot emerged, the day she was allowed to take off the halo. It was exhilarating, like a life's passage in a small way. And that was an emotion she had not thought possible since the crash. But because of the crash, she would have in her body forever, a rod to support her left femur, fractured in the accident. The rod extended from hip to knee.

"Bren, if you ever get tired of people asking about your injuries, just tell them you're walking with the help of a Nazi Doctor from World War II."

"What? A Nazi? What on earth…"

"Well, he may not have been a Nazi himself," the doctor said with a laugh. "But a version of the rod, or nail as some call it, like the one in your thigh was developed by a Dr. Gerhard Kunschner, who served with Hitler's forces on the Eastern Front. If the story is true, The British and American troops noticed German troops were able to return to battle within a few months of incurring broken legs, but our troops were often out of action for good. So, from Kunschner's work evolved the use of rods. Yours, by the way, is made of stainless steel."

"Well, Doctor Ridell," Bren said, her eyes squinted and smiling, "did you learn all about that in medical school?"

"No," he said. "It was in a TV documentary not long ago, a show about battle injuries in World War II."

"Well," Bren said slowly, I guess the rod is a lifetime souvenir of my personal battle."

———

There. No more changes. I just hope I can get through this speech without a lot of tears. That was important to Bren, because she knew TV news loves it when people cry on camera. *If I speak well for nine minutes and cry for thirty seconds, the tears will lead every local newscast for forty-eight hours, unless I cry again after that.*

Bren stood as the announcer on the GNS monitor on the desk said, "Our regularly scheduled program, GNS Evening News, will not be seen tonight, so we can bring you this special GNS program."

When the wide shot from the helicopter of the GNS tower filled the screen, Bren emailed the script to Max, who would make sure it was put on prompter. Then she hit the "Print" command. The laser printer started to spit out the final version of her speech as she went toward her private bathroom to repair her makeup.

32

MIAMI

Ian Phelps walked into the airline lounge at Miami International, intending to hit the bathroom and then have a drink at a concourse bar before he met his car for the drive to Marco Island. The GNS logo that filled the TV screen next to the bar caught his eye.

"Our regularly scheduled program, GNS Evening News, will not be seen tonight, so we can bring you this special GNS program."

"Bartender, could you turn that up there, the TV, and get me a Glenlivet, no ice. There's a good fellow."

On the screen, Phelps saw a swooping, wide view of downtown Atlanta from a helicopter. He could see the heat waves shimmering off the concrete and steel of the city.

"On this July night, the Global News Service enters its sixteenth year of informing the world." It was Ethan's voice, rich and full, words he had practiced a dozen times in the past twenty minutes.

"Tonight," said Amanda, as the helicopter moved north for a close-up of the GNS neon sign on top of the building, "a special one-hour report on the world today and a look at the world since GNS began dominating non-stop twenty-four hour news seven days a week."

"Take camera two, sound up!" Billy Olson said into his headset microphone.

Up came video of the first moments of GNS on its inaugural broadcast on that equally hot day in Atlanta, fifteen years ago. Two of the original anchor people, Walker Hartman and Lois Davidson, smiled nervously and welcomed the few viewers watching the nascent network.

"Welcome to the Global News Service, I'm Lois Davidson."

"And I'm Walker Hartman. Now here's the news."

That simple opening came after hours of hand wringing and navel contemplation by the executives of GNS about how to begin what they assumed was their history making all-news channel.

Some wanted something profound. "A Window on the World" was one of the suggestions. Others argued for a catchy slogan, such as "All the News, All the Time," but it seemed a goal that might take some time to reach.

The bosses, led by Bren Forrest, decided just to do the news. That dictate led to the simple, "Now, here's the news." It was almost too grand a promise, in those early days.

—

"Take three, cue announcer," Billy said and the wide shot of the atrium filled the screen. GNS had aged electronically from zero to fifteen in a nano-second.

"Now, live from GNS Center in Atlanta, Georgia, the United States of America, here are GNS news anchors Amanda Grace and Ethan Thomas."

Ethan was furious, having heard Amanda's name announced first. He fumed at the announcer, a big-voiced broadcaster who was not involved in news programming as such. The announcer had ad-libbed, reversing the anchors' names on his script. He considered Ethan a pompous ass. He realized he could just say it was a mistake if anybody asked. He knew Ethan would ask and hoped he would look petty by doing so.

ATLANTA

At that moment, Art Toomey began the NewsBlitz3 special report and was throwing to Cassandra Page, outside the GNS building.

Cassie had the story of the day and she figured no one else did. The others didn't have it when she was wrong and probably never caught up with the correct information, either.

"Yes, Art, the eyes of the world are on Atlanta at this moment, even before the Olympic Games begin.

"As we watch Global News Service deal with this story of death and possible murder in its own family, we have breaking news to report at this hour."

In the GNS control room, Max could see Cassie and the other local stations' newscasts on the several wall monitors. As the "Breaking News" sign went up on the screen below Cassie's head and shoulders, Max reacted.

"Josh, turn up Channel 3 audio please."

"...at this hour. NewsBlitz3 has learned the body found in a Virginia Highlands apartment today is not that of an Olympics hostess who attended the party where Cav Campbell died Tuesday night. According to our reliable sources, the dead woman, whose name has not been released, is in fact a twin of the young woman police want to question regarding Mr. Campbell's death. Police aren't saying much, publicly, at least."

Up came the video report Cassie prepared earlier. It showed a photo of Lia Cassie coerced from the Olympics public relations man, Dan Handleman.

Max grabbed a phone and called his boss, the senior executive vice president of GNS.

"You hear the Channel 3 report? Yeah, cops found a dead girl, twin of our intern, Lia Lee. They thought it was her, at first. Now they really want to find Lia. What do you want us to do with it? Should we quote Channel 3 and do an anchor piece or put one of our reporters on it or what?"

The answer, as Max expected, was to do both. If the story didn't involve GNS and Bren Forrest, he would not have bothered to ask his boss. Max had authority to make such decisions, but on this one, he wanted backup.

—

In the atrium, Jimmy Hagan stood at the back of the platform, behind the VIPs. He could see Chief Lutz from where he stood. He noticed Mardy Daley in the third row, her husband absent for some reason. Jimmy decided to talk with Mrs. Daley after the show, recalling she was among the people who talked with Cav Campbell and with Lia Lee at the Vaughn's party. He turned to look at the anchor desk as Ethan Thomas and Amanda Grace began to welcome the viewing audience.

"We begin with what we hope we do best here at GNS," Ethan said, "that is, bring you the news from around the world, live."

"So, we want to touch base with many of our international bureaus," Amanda picked up.

The scriptwriter was careful to call the bureaus "international" and not "foreign." Bren Forrest herself banned the word, "foreign," from being used on GNS. The idea was if GNS was to be truly a worldwide service, it had to moderate the perception it was an American news service designed for American viewers. Using the word "foreign" narrowed the focus, Bren thought, and subtly alienated viewers in other countries.

The banishment of "foreign," however, was taken to absurd lengths by a couple of mid-level producers, who wanted to set a fifty-dollar fine for any on-air person who said the word "foreign."

Cynics in the newsroom tried to find devious ways to make fun of the ban. A GNS sports anchor won that contest, hands down. One night, while showing highlights of that day's major league baseball games, he showed video of a pitcher calling time out to remove something from his eye.

Said the sportscaster without irony, "Schultz had to call the trainer out to the mound, to help remove an international object from his eye."

He was reprimanded, but the language police in the newsroom cooled it after that. Still, the word "foreign" rarely was heard on GNS these days.

"First, to London and Dorian Mayfield, Dorrie?"

Berlin, Paris, Beijing and other news centers followed in order, with GNS reporters each doing two-minute reports on the top news in their regions.

Jimmy was fidgety, hoping to hear soon from the men he sent to try to find where Lia Lee lived. Her father told police Lia lived somewhere in the Ponce de Leon area. The GNS personnel office had a photo of her, but no address other than her parents' home.

Officers with her photo on their cell phones were on the streets now, talking to apartment managers, showing the picture to shopkeepers, bartenders, anybody who might have seen the beautiful Amerasian girl in the neighborhood.

Hagan also figured Ned Bastige had some answers, but Bastige refused to spend any time with police until the news special he was producing was over. Jimmy acquiesced, not wanting to be blamed later if the special program went awry with Bastige not there.

"Thank you, Corva Pommering, for your live update from Rome," Ethan said, turning back to his close-up camera. "The impact of GNS has been significant on the men and women who make the news. And some of them are with us now. So, let's begin in Washington and at the White House. Ladies and gentlemen, the Presi..."

A dozen cell phone ringtones came to life at that moment, echoing through the fourteen-story atrium, drowning out the anchors' voices on the speakers in the building.

The mayor, the police chief, Jimmy Hagan and other law enforcement people reached to mute their phones. Just then, a second wave of electronic noise ricocheted through the room, as phones sounded on the belts of most of the TV photographers in the building.

Ethan stopped in mid-word, looked side to side, flustered.

Jimmy looked at his phone and saw the "missed call" number of the homicide division. Chief Lutz had called as well. The mayor's press secretary was calling his boss. The managers of every newsroom in town, except NewsBlitz3, were calling their people to catch up on the Tia Lee story Cassie just aired.

The message was essentially the same to all those who responded: About Channel 3's report, get it confirmed or denied and let us know ASAP.

Hagan stepped behind the VIP platform and called his office to get an update. It wasn't much. Somebody at Tia's apartment building had seen her coming in Tuesday night with a guy, a wrestler maybe, body-builder type, but nobody could identify the guy and nobody saw anything unusual about it.

On Ponce de Leon Avenue, a convenience store manager recognized Lia's photo. He said she came in there sometimes, usually walking, no car. He assumed she lived nearby.

Hagan's office also told him about Cassie's report. Hagan told his sergeant to call a news briefing at homicide for eleven-thirty that night. He gave instructions to have the picture of Lia photo emailed to every police officer and to all the media people at the briefing.

"One other thing, Jimmy," the sergeant said, "a bartender in Buckhead called to say that he saw the girl's photo on the news. Says she was in his bar Tuesday night when the news came over of Cav Campbell going off the balcony. The bartender's name is Mick, at Harvey's."

"I know the place, yeah, so did he say it was Lia or the dead girl?"

"He's not sure, thought she said her name was Mia. Said she was in with a rough-looking guy. Didn't seem to like him much. He said the guy's neck was so big it's a wonder he could breathe. Says he and the girl left in a hurry."

Chief Lutz was still in his seat on the platform, hunched over his cell phone, listening to his aide in a panic.

"Chief, that Page woman has it all, even a picture of the dead girl, or one of 'em, not sure which. Anyway, we've had a million calls here in the past five minutes, including the mayor's people, ya know?"

"Listen now," Lutz whispered coarsely into the phone, trying to talk toward his armpit so the people on either side could not hear him. "Get a hold of Hagan and tell him to call a news conference in an hour or so, at homicide. I want Hagan to deal with this.

"And get out the paperwork on this Lia Lee. And her photo. I want her found. Send it to Florida, South Carolina, the whole southeast. Now!"

Lutz closed the cell phone and looked around. He saw Jimmy in the corner on his phone. Hagan noticed the chief trying to catch his eye, but turned away. The mayor was raising his eyebrows at the chief, trying unsuccessfully to get his attention.

MIAMI

Ian Phelps drained his glass and held it up to the airline lounge bartender with an impatient gesture. His eyes never left the TV set.

Come on, cut the bullshit and get to it. I want to hear you tell us the news, you bastards. Tell us how your cheap-shit actor tried to hustle me, how he fell off the building for it, eh? Tell about the mystery of the second death, eh? Tell how your fancy Ms. Forrest is about to sell out to somebody who can deal with the real world out there! Tell it for goddsake. I have a car waiting for me!

GLOBAL NEWS SERVICE

The President, the Vice President, the Speaker of the House and the Majority leader of the Senate made their obligatory video congratulations to GNS. Producer Ned Bastige was into his second commercial break, on schedule.

The phone rang next to Max Ippolito, at the rear of the control room.

"Mr. Ippolito, Max, this is Bren Forrest. I am about to leave my office for the atrium. Do you have any news I should know?"

"Well, ma'am, you've heard about the body they found, the girl, and that it's not the one at the party. Yeah, yes, she has a twin, and it was her.

"No, we don't have it confirmed, but we are putting together a special live piece now for the bottom of the hour, quoting Channel 3 here and trying to get confirmation from Atlanta police."

"Max, go ahead and air it as you must. Is there, I mean, do you have a story about Cav, about his life and his career? A look back, sort of."

"Yes, ma'am, it will air before you go on, I mean, if that's all right with you..."

"Yes, yes, yes," she interrupted, "of course, just keep getting the news on, Max. Don't stop, even if you have to go past the hour, keep on going."

"Of course, yes, that's our plan."

"Now, what time do I go on, exactly?"

"We're just about on schedule, maybe thirty seconds over now, so I would say—hold on a second—Ned, give me an exact time for when we do the intro of Ms. Forrest. Okay. Ms. Forrest, we intro you at forty past the hour. Plan is for Jerry Vaughn and the mayor to escort you to the podium, applause, applause, then your speech. And when you finish, you'll get a standing ovation, the band will play, we fade to black. The anchor will do the proper bye-bye as a voice over. Is that acceptable to you?

"Sure, whatever, but if I go long, it's not a problem?"

Max chuckled slightly.

"Ms. Forrest, it's your network. You talk, we'll cover it."

"You're very nice, Max, a nice man, but you know what I mean. Thank you, Max."

———

Out of the commercial break, Ethan read a brief introduction to a "life and times" video report about Cav Campbell, narrated by Sheila Belle. It had soaring music, lots of video dissolves of various still photos of Campbell's public activities, accompanied by Sheila's swooning style of instant hero-worship narrative. It chronicled Campbell's career with brief clips of several movies, ending with a seven-second shot of him in his last film, the unlamented Party House IV.

Then came home-movie type video of Campbell and Bren Forrest, at benefits, on a friend's yacht, at an Atlanta Braves baseball game, at the Emmy awards ceremony and other events. The report was short on praise and testimonials. GNS had only a few hours to stitch it together, much of it with video fed by satellite from the Los Angeles bureau.

Sheila ended the piece with a paragraph she had not shown the producer in advance of recording her report. It was her personal comment and she didn't want to share it with her bosses ahead of time.

"Tonight, America has lost a legend, but has gained one, as well. Mr. Campbell was a legend in his own time. Now, he is even more of a legend in death. The death of a legend. The legend is dead. And even though he died, the legend lives on, in another time, another place, another plane of legendary existence." Her voice choked with emotion. She had recorded the next line three times before it sounded just right to her.

"You gave us good times, then someone gave you a bad time. We'll miss you, the nation will miss you, the world will miss you. Good-bye, Cav Campbell, good-bye and good luck."

In the GNS control room, an eternity of silence exploded into groans and a few laughs.

"Oh, my God, she is insane," said the director, Billy Olson.

"Jesus, didn't anybody see that first?" Max screamed at Ned Bastige, whose face turned the color of beets.

"Get off my back, goddammit," Bastige said through his clenched teeth. "Talk to the idiot reporter, for chrissake, if you don't like it!"

MIAMI

At the airport lounge in Miami, Phelps laughed out loud, startling the bartender who was mixing a drink for another patron.

"That was downright touching, eh mate? A legend, eh? Hey, you silly bitch," Phelps shouted at the TV with a grin. "Bennie Hill is a legend, John-fucking-Wayne is a legend, but Cav Campbell? What a yutz, what a cock-up, what a crock!"

Phelps was still laughing, buzzed by the three Glenlivets he had consumed in the past twenty minutes. Others in the lounge looked the other way or laughed nervously, not wanting to irritate this man who obviously enjoyed yelling at the television.

"Bottoms up, mate, one for the road please, kind sir," he said to the bartender. "I must make my way to another part of your fine state. Good night, sir, and God Bless the U-S of A."

33

MARCO ISLAND, FLORIDA

The July sun was still hot, even approaching sunset, as it moved slowly toward the western horizon. About eight-thirty, the ball of fire would ooze slowly into the Gulf of Mexico.

People watching from along the beach on Marco Island would stand still briefly, soaking up the moment, knowing they'd never see another sunset exactly like that one. Then, most of the sunset worshipers would turn their backs on the gulf and walk slowly through the sand to the hotels and condos on the beach. Some would head to their parked cars.

Locals on Marco knew many of the people who left the beach right after the sun set were not familiar with the often spectacular colors and cloud textures that fill the sky in what the sunset savvy called the "afterglow." Some island residents developed a proprietary attitude toward the afterglow, not telling visitors about its beauty and snickering as the uninitiated trudged off the sand sans afterglow magic.

Lia stood in front of the sliding door onto her condo balcony. At that moment, GNS began airing a promotional announcement for a feature on the life of Cav Campbell. It would be broadcast in about a half hour, with a fuller report in the network's ten o'clock special.

The short promo captured Lia's attention. It felt weird seeing Campbell in various life situations on the video, knowing she put an end to all that less than twenty-four hours earlier. *Oh, well, guess at least he died looking good, never had to put up with getting old, fat and nasty. Guess I'll watch the big show and see what happens.*

She went out to the balcony of the ninth floor apartment and looked left and then right. The surf was calm, the breeze renewing. She daydreamed a little.

Lia already knew a bit about Campbell's career. She knew he was an actor, a "ladies' man." Ned Bastige had briefed her on the basics two nights before the hit. Lia was not aware, nor did she care at the time, about Campbell's early movies.

The deal was clear to her. Push him off the balcony and she would be guaranteed all the cocaine she could use and a contract for a news anchor job. At least two-hundred-thousand dollars a year to start, courtesy of the soon-to-be new owner of GNS. Some British TV guy, is all she knew.

Lia didn't particularly enjoy killing. She didn't dislike it either. It was like, say, washing the car. It had no moral distinction. You did it when it needed doing. She did it for what it would bring her, just as she had done once while in middle school, at a summer camp in the North Carolina mountains.

The counselors told them not to try the rock climbing range without supervision, but Tia had done it the day before with no problem. Lia wanted to prove she was as good an athlete as Tia. She also wanted Holly out of her life.

Holly was Tia's friend and Lia's rival for the affections of her boyfriend that summer, Normie Lattimore.

Normie thought Lia was great looking, but Holly was too and she had "great jugs," as Normie and his pals called them. Lia was not developed much at the time.

Lia told Holly several times to please stay away from Normie, but Holly just giggled, thrust out her greatest assets and walked away. Lia then began to ingratiate herself with Holly, turning her from an enemy into what Holly thought was a budding friendship.

Tia was thrilled her often stubborn and sometimes vengeful sister had changed her attitude, pleased her sister and her friend were friends now.

So, when Lia laughingly challenged Holly to a race on the rock-climbing course, Holly agreed. "Great, Lia, we'll both show Tia we can do it too, right? It'll be a hoot."

They set out late one afternoon, during quiet time, before supper. Lia offered to go first to find the handholds. As they moved up the course, Lia hated every minute, every small scratch on her leg, every inch of progress. Holly was having fun, but out of breath, every inhale a gasp.

About seventy feet up, Holly slipped once and screamed. Lia laughed. "Come on, Holly, get with it, come on, come on."

Holly reached for the next hold, grabbed it, then brought up one leg and her other hand. As she was moving, Lia straightened from her hunched-over position, dropped one leg sharply and stomped on Holly's right hand.

She screamed as she fell backward, tumbling, bumping, slamming into the rocky slope as she plummeted toward the ground.

Lia did not smile or frown. Without a sound, she began slowly to retrace her path down the rocks. At the bottom, Holly lay unconscious in the clearing. She was a mass of bloody cuts and gashes.

Lia walked to her, furious to see the girl was breathing, her ample chest heaving. Lia saw that as Holly mocking her for having bested Lia for Normie's attention.

Next to Holly's left leg was a rock the size of a softball, rough and jagged. Lia did not hesitate. She stooped, grunting as she picked up the rock and smashed it across the top of Holly's skull. She did it again, and a third time, careful not to get any blood on her khaki hiking shorts and her olive green Banana Republic shirt.

Lia smiled when Holly's chest stopped moving up and down. Lia sat on the ground nearby, looking at the dead girl's face. She sat there motionless for maybe fifteen minutes. She thought she ought to feel guilty or at least afraid of what would happen when the counselors found out. She felt nothing, no joy, no pain. Her thoughts ran to how Normie would react, how she, Lia, would show her grief at the funeral, what she would wear to it. Lia's only worry was whether this would cut camp short or end it altogether for this summer.

Lia didn't think about that incident much. It was about as meaningful in her memories of her childhood as maybe getting a big zit before the prom, maybe not even that important.

She had a clearer memory of getting into trouble for setting fire to two neighborhood cats. She was about eleven then and her mother was furious. Mae McIntosh never cared much for cats. Her relatives in South Korea even ate them sometimes, when Mae was a child. But Mae gleaned an American child in a suburb of Atlanta who set fire to cats was not just having growing pains.

Her husband waved it away as a prank gone too far and convinced Mae not to talk about it with the school psychologist.

Lia was ordered to apologize to the people down the street whose cats she torched with one of those barbeque friction lighters. She even conjured up a tear, saying it was a horrible accident.

The lady put her arms around the sniffling Lia and comforted her. Lia took the cookie she was offered, did an almost curtsy and walked home. It was not fun, not awful. The worse part, she thought, was pretending to care. The best part was the chocolate chip cookie.

—

As the sun melted into the gulf, Lia 's thoughts returned to her present situation. *I wonder how long they'll want me to stay here. Wouldn't mind a long visit, but I have to get back by the time the Olympics start or I'll lose my hostess job. It's a perfect cover, Ned said. That prick. Can I trust him on this?*

She went to the wet bar off the living room and opened a bottle of Perrier. She filled a glass from the ice maker under the bar, poured in the fizzing water and padded back to the sliding door, opened it and walked out into the soft twilight.

Lia sat down on a patio chair, moving to keep her leg off the metal frame, still warm from the sun. She drank most of her Perrier in one long swallow, like the ones those models do in the Coke commercials on TV. Some of it dripped off her chin onto her chest, cool and wet, giving her a small sunset shiver.

Guess Ned was right. I should be outta pocket for a while, but I'll bet the cops want to talk to everybody at that party, so maybe...screw it. I know they'll have a million questions, but I'll show up with my great alibi. I'm covered.

Why did I come here? Hmmm, I was upset? Too upset to be around there? But how did I get here? I don't have a private plane, can't afford that. Better ask Ned about this. They must have it figured out.

She leaned back, closed her eyes and rubbed the bottom of the cold, sweating glass on her forehead. *I could learn to like this place. Maybe after I get the news job, I'll buy me a small condo on this beach. And Ned promised a guy from Capri-something, near here, will show up tomorrow with some snow.*

Lia dozed, her head turned toward the sun. She could not hear the GNS anchors telling their worldwide audience of the latest developments in the investigation into the death of Cav Campbell.

34

ATLANTA & SOUTHWEST FLORIDA

"Let's go back to Cassandra Page now, live outside GNS Headquarters," Art Toomey said to the NewsBlitz3 TV audience. "What's the latest from there, Cassie?"

"Art, GNS has just reported to its worldwide audience our exclusive story here on NewsBlitz3, on the death of the sister of an Olympics hostess, who police would like to, um, interview as they call it. They want to know about her conversation last night with Cav Campbell, not long before he plunged to his death."

Cassie was thrilled GNS quoted her report, which the network had been unable to nail down independently by the time the special went on. But she was angry with her bosses at the station for their decision not to carry Bren Forrest's speech live. She argued for it, expecting some high drama. The Channel 3 news director said "no way" to Cassie, and then he called the show producers together to explain his reasoning.

"She'll drag on forever," he told his producers, "and if she cries, we'll turn the video around and air it right, anyway."

On the air, Cassie was showing video from earlier in the GNS celebration, mostly shots of the celebrities and officials who filled the atrium.

"In a few minutes, we expect Bren Forrest, the owner of GNS, to speak during the network's special report. We don't know for sure what she'll say, but unconfirmed reports circulating here say she will offer a major reward for information leading to the killer of Cav Campbell."

As Cassie finished her live tag, with a promise of an update later in that hour of news, the anchorman, Art Toomey, burst in with a question. She knew he would.

Toomey thought asking questions of the reporters in the field made him look smart, concerned, caring. Trouble was, Art usually did not listen to much of what the reporter said. He usually busied himself during field reports by telling the generally underpaid studio crew about his latest travels or new luxury car or some other reflection of his high-income lifestyle. The behind the scenes staffers in the studio and control room usually just nodded and smiled or shook their heads and frowned, whatever Art's self-indulgences seemed to require.

"Well, Cassandra," Art said to the camera, "what about these wire reports that Bren Forrest will offer a major reward in the death of Cav Campbell?"

The director in the control room punched up Cassie's camera and her face filled the screen.

"Art, as I just said, we've been hearing that here, but it is not confirmed," Cassie responded, a hint of annoyed impatience in her voice.

The anchorman ignored the sarcasm and plowed ahead.

"So, how much will the reward be, Cassandra?"

"We do not know that, Art, because we don't even know for sure whether there will be a reward, Art, and that's all from here for now." Cassie was through talking with the anchorman and made that clear to him and the viewers.

—

At GNS headquarters, Billy Olson said briskly to his technical director, "Take four, the ID slide, and cue announcer."

"We continue now with this GNS Special Report. Here again, Amanda Grace and Ethan Thomas."

"Take three, cue 'em."

"Ladies and Gentlemen, friends of GNS around the world, here is the creator and owner of the Global News Service, Ms. Bren Forrest."

———

Static scrambled and scratched the sound on the car radio, as Ian Phelps's driver, O'Reilly, fiddled with the dial, trying to make the news report audible.

What O'Reilly and his boss could make out amidst the interference on the AM radio band was:

"...and police now are intensifying ...woman ... sister found murd ... reward for ... GNS headquarters in Atlanta...rain will be gone ... mostly sunny..."

The radio station in Miami was fading and crackling as the black sedan headed west across the Everglades on U.S. 41, also known as the Tamiami Trail.

"Geez, Paddy, let me do it!" The bulky man in the front passenger seat reached over and brushed the driver's hand off the radio buttons. He was Jax, the bodyguard whom Phelps hired several months earlier. He went everywhere Phelps went these days, except for those late night visits to Yvonne Tender's flat in London.

Jax and Paddy O'Reilly didn't like each other. Phelps was reminded of that when Jax called Paddy by his first name.

Paddy O'Reilly preferred the last name only. He recalled his father's days in Northern Ireland, when a man named Paddy could get himself killed in the Protestant neighborhoods. Paddy was a name only Roman Catholics used, a nickname for Patrick, the name many Irish Catholics had, in honor of the saint who saved their land.

Billy, short for William, as in William of Orange, was the Protestant counterpart to Paddy. After a couple of beatings and a lot of threats in the early eighties, Paddy O'Reilly Sr. insisted his limo clients call him Billy when they were in the Protestant areas of Belfast.

Eventually it became easier and safer to be known only as O'Reilly. Paddy Jr. adopted that rule himself when he moved to London and drove for his cousin's gypsy cab company.

A few months later, an ad in the *Daily Mail* caught O'Reilly's eye. Phelps's company placed the ad, looking for an experienced chauffeur. Phelps offered him the job and O'Reilly had been driving for Ian Phelps ever since.

Jax and O'Reilly disliked each other instantly, but Jax showed it more. He never understood why the boss liked O'Reilly, joked with him and sometimes drank with him, yet ordered Jax around like he was some truant kid.

What, with me having 'is life in me 'ands and all, you'da thought ee'd be kissing me bum, you would. Still, 'e pays me great and all, and it's easy work and all, so I'll keep the bloody job and get Mr. High-and-Bloody-Mighty Patrick O'Reilly some fine day, I will.

The car radio crackled again, as O'Reilly sped past an Indian village on the highway. The only part of the village visible from the road was a gas station and souvenir shop, empty of tourists this particular summer evening.

This two-hundred-sixty-four mile road was named Tamiami Trail because it ran from Tampa to Miami. Construction began in 1915 and it was opened officially in 1928. It cut through the Everglades and was the northern border of Everglades National Park.

Even more common along the Trail than the Indian villages were the alligators and snakes, including pythons. Once in a while, drivers on the Trail would see a Florida black bear or an elusive Florida panther.

Phelps was not interested in the wildlife. He was focused on the car radio.

"Try another station, Jax," Phelps said.

Jax hit the "scan" button. At the third stop, a news reader was saying, "This is GNS Radio for Southwest Florida, WGNS in Naples. We go live now to Atlanta, for GNS simulcast coverage of its fifteenth anniversary observance. GNS owner Bren Forrest is about to speak at GNS headquarters. We now join the broadcast in progress."

"Damn, it's her," Phelps said almost to himself, as he heard Bren Forrest's voice. Apparently she just started her speech.

35

ATLANTA—SOUTH FLORIDA

"Thank you, thank you, please, please...thank you very much," Bren was saying as the waves of applause washed over the podium where she stood. She motioned for the audience to take their seats, but most of them remained standing, clapping, smiling, showing heartfelt concern for her grief and admiration for her being there after what happened.

"Camera three, get closer, there, hold it there, standby three," said Max in his headset to the director. By now, Max had taken over control of the program from the line producer, Ned Bastige. Ned was furious, but Max didn't give a damn.

"She's choking up a little, take three now, three!"

Bren's face filled the screen, her hair perfect, her smile fixed, her eyes showing the strain of the past twenty hours. She dropped her arms and gripped the rostrum.

"Friends of Global News Service, friends, thank you so much for your kind reception," Bren said. As she spoke, the applause waned and the people began shuffling into their seats.

"Get a waist up, camera two, standby two, and one, camera one standby your high-and-wide shot. Take one, Billy."

The TV audience saw the entire atrium, the widest shot Max could get.

"This is one of the happiest days of my life, and, one of the saddest," Bren said. The room was still.

"Ready two, take two," Max said, more quietly than he had spoken until that moment.

The shot of Bren was from dead center. The TV showed her head and chin thrust forward, her shoulders straight in the black dress, no jewelry except small diamond stud earrings.

"She looks great. God, how does she do it?" Jan Vaughn whispered to Jerry in the VIP section behind and to the left of the podium.

"Billy, she's just amazing," Max whispered in his headset to his director.

———

On Marco Island, Lia came in from the balcony as Bren began to speak. She went to the ice maker, put two cubes in a napkin and rubbed the back of her neck, then plopped onto the living room couch to watch Bren Forrest on TV.

Lia's only emotion was amusement as she watched the fiancée of the man Lia dispatched. *This is great, I'm on the beach and the bitch doesn't have a clue. She doesn't know what I know.*

———

"To all of you who have worked so hard to make GNS what it is, words cannot express my gratitude."

Somebody near the back of the hall began chanting, "Bren, Bren, Bren..."

"To the many of you who said it would never work, we have enjoyed proving you wrong."

That was followed by laughter and extended applause. Bren smiled.

"To the few of you who actively have tried to make us fail, you have our condolences."

More laughter, louder now. Bren had broken the tension, allowed her audience to get off the emotional roller coaster she had been on.

———

Ian Phelps powered down the rear window of the car and snorted with contempt.

"Whistling through the graveyard, she is, right, O'Reilly?"

The driver nodded as he adjusted the rear view mirror so he could see Phelps. He was going seventy-five miles an hour now, about as fast as that stretch of the Tamiami Trail would allow.

—

"GNS is alive and well and will continue to inform the world as best it can. On the day we began our service, fifteen years ago, I said we would stay on the air until the end of the world. There's no reason now, fifteen years later, to modify that pledge."

The applause was loud and long.

Max changed camera shots to get a close-up of the governor and his wife clapping, a shot of a woman trying to move the hands of the toddler in her arms in a clapping motion, a wide shot of the press horde in the back on the scaffolding.

"But we have a crisis in our GNS family. I refer, of course, to the death of my beloved, Cav Campbell."

Not a word, not a sneeze or a cough, not a scrape of a chair leg. Max took a close-up.

"I am here to tell you this evening Cav did not jump off the balcony last night. He did not fall off by accident, either."

The tension was palpable.

"Someone killed Cav Campbell."

A loud murmur swirled up from the audience, then died as the people heard their own involuntary reactions join with the others.

"Yes, there is no doubt in my mind someone killed him. And it probably was an enemy of mine, not his. Because, Cav had no enemies that I know of, none. His fans loved him. He hurt no one. Yes, you can be sure whoever killed Cav did it somehow because of me. No one has told me this. The authorities have no suspects and say they're not even sure it was murder. But I know. I know it in my heart."

"Wish to hell she'd tell me who did it then," Jimmy Hagan whispered to nobody, as he watched Bren from his position off to the side of the stage. *Why the hell did she say that on TV? She doesn't know jack about what happened or why. Does she? I mean, how could she? We really need to talk to her again. Christ.*

His thoughts turned to Cassie, who was out there with the other local reporters, sweating in the hot, sultry night, watching Bren on a large screen TV set up by GNS for the news people stuck outside.

"God, we should be live with this," Cassie fumed, talking to her cameraman, who nodded and took a long pull on the small bottle of water tucked into his camera tripod.

She pressed her earpiece with a finger to hear the NewsBlitz3 weatherman talking about an occluded front somewhere in Alabama. Cassie yanked the IFB out of her ear and turned back to the big screen, now showing a close-up of Bren, her eyes blazing, anger oozing from her demeanor.

"Our police and the other authorities are doing what they can, but I need your help, friends, all of you watching, I need your help."

Max saw camera three trained on a medium shot of Chief Lutz, squirming a bit in his seat, trying for once in his life to look shorter. Max decided not to take the shot. Bren was too hot all by herself.

—

Lia sat up on the couch, impressed by the fire in Bren's eyes. *Not bad, lady, not bad at all. You are good. I think I'll enjoy anchoring on your network one day soon. Wonder if you'll be around to watch me!*

—

"So this evening, I am announcing a five-hundred-thousand dollar reward for information leading to the prosecution and conviction of the person or persons responsible for the death of Mr. Cav Campbell."

The audience gasped, then burst into applause and shouts of approval, a spontaneous outpouring of support, ignoring whether it was appropriate.

"Bren, Bren, Bren…" the chant spread bouncing off the walls of the atrium

"Jesus, here we go," Cassie said to the cameraman. "Tony, tell 'em need to do a live update, now, tell 'em Tony."

"Half-a-mill..." Jimmy Hagan said out loud, catching himself in mid-sentence.

Chief Lutz grimaced, then applauded politely, still in his seat. *Goddamit, now we'll have five thousand calls a night. Every nut in the country will have spotted the killer for sure at their nearest convenience store.* The chief tried to get Detective Hagan's attention, but Jimmy turned away and was on his cell phone to the office.

———

Lia let out a whoop and a laugh of surprise anybody within a hundred yards up or down the beach could have heard. *Half a million dollars, for me? Wow... Hi, my name is Lia Lee and I'm worth half-a-million bucks at the moment. Yes!*

She enjoyed the moment, the surge of adrenaline, the feeling of power. The twinge of fear that invaded her euphoria was about Ned Bastige. *I wonder if he'd cave for that much? Nah, they'd nail him too then. Unless he could cut a deal, get immunity by naming me.*

Her thoughts tailed off to a jumble, as the impact of Bren's shocker on the audience in Atlanta waned. Lia watched as Bren continued.

———

"I know it is a lot of money, but our stockholders need not fear. It is my money, not that of GNS. Now, if our producer will put up the number on your screen, here is an eight-hundred number, a toll-free number you can call with information about the murder of Cav Campbell. Write it down and please, please," her voice faltered, choked a bit before she continued. "Please, call if you know anything. Anything at all might be helpful."

Chief Lutz sat up again, relaxing a bit as he realized many of the crank calls would go to that toll-free number, rather than to police headquarters.

"If anyone calls homicide, give 'em that number, the one on the screen," Jimmy Hagan was phoning his sergeant in his office. "Then, I'll coordinate with the GNS people for any leads."

Cassie was ready. NewsBlitz3, at that point, decided to take Bren's speech live.

The news director, in his office at Channel 3, was screaming into the phone to the producer, Rita Runner, in the control room downstairs. "Go now, now, take it now, Rita! Tell Art to throw it to Cassie down there right now!"

"Lriggrmh, Bosh, choo ghotuh," Rita responded, trying to swallow a large handful of M&Ms as she talked into the phone.

"What, what did you say? Oh, just do it," the news director barked.

"Arth, Arthie gho bhabeh, tosh ta Chashee now," Rita spewed into her headset, candy spraying on the desk, bits falling onto the floor.

The anchorman put his hand to his earpiece and raised the other in a sort of stop sign motion.

"Ladies and Gentlemen, I am being told of new developments in my ear right now."

He affected a studious look just to the right of the camera, as though he were deep in thought. Inside he was roiling because he could not understand what Rita was saying.

The director saved him, jumping onto the intercom, telling Art to go live immediately to Cassie downtown.

"Yes, I am told we are going live now, to Cassie, downtown. Cassie what do you have for us?"

"Art, Bren Forrest, the owner of GNS, has just offered a half-a-million dollar reward for the killer of her fiancé, Cav Campbell. And she claims someone did murder him, an enemy of hers. Let's listen to her speaking now at GNS headquarters."

Bren was calm now, the audience quiet again as she folded her arms across her chest and looked straight into the close-up camera.

"We will catch the killer. GNS will not rest, I will not rest, until this person, or these people get what is coming to them. Justice demands it. Our laws, our decency, our way of life demand it. I am in a state of profound grief at this moment and my life sometimes seems not worth living. But I know Cav would want me to be tough, to keep going.

"So, I warn the killers. You will be caught. You will be punished. And if there is any justice in this world, you will die for your crimes."

Dead silence in the room. Bren stood motionless. Her arms stayed folded, so tight it seemed they might block her breathing. She didn't blink. She didn't move. She just stared, contempt in her eyes, resolve in her body language.

Whatever amusement Lia felt earlier watching the TV coverage slipped away as she sat on the couch in the Marco condo. Bren's body language and resolute facial expression seemed to pierce the TV screen and send a chill through Lia's body.

—

A shiver of dread ran through Chief Lutz. Suddenly he was overwhelmed by the pressure he was under to solve these crimes.

A rush of respect for Bren Forrest filled Jimmy Hagan's senses as he turned back from his call and stared up at Bren on the stage.

—

"Turn that shit off, now!" Ian Phelps growled at the men in the front seat of his Town Car. O'Reilly beat Jax to the radio dial and switched it off, just as the awe in the audience gave way to a stampede of applause and cheering.

Silly old cow. She's all talk. Outta her league, she is. Cow. Stupid bitch. Phelps reached for the bottle of Glenlivet in the sidewall of the car door and poured himself three fingers in a crystal glass on the shelf. No ice. He drained the glass in two swallows, then shuddered as the car sped toward Marco Island.

36

HARVEY'S BAR—ATLANTA

Harvey's was so deserted nobody even booed when the piano man tried his best to sing "People, people who need people…" Usually that song brought a round of derision from the crowd at the trendy bar in Buckhead. It was a tradition.

At one-thirty in the morning, only three of the cocktail tables were in use. Seven people were at the bar, which left forty barstools vacant. The customers were mellow, apparently concerned with personal matters of the moment, uninterested in Streisand's proposals to solve the world's problems by just being "people."

Cassie Page sat in one of the black leather banquettes that lined the wall opposite the bar. Jimmy was in the men's room. This was their first "date" in several weeks, a chance to be together, alone, not in the apartment they shared.

She sipped her drink and tried to remember the last time she was in this bar, one of Atlanta's most popular among media people. That took her mind to when she met Jimmy, in the line of duty.

Cassie was doing a "Special Report." That was Channel 3-speak for a three-part series of stories on a single subject. Her special that month was called, without embarrassment, "Is God Punishing Us?"

She was required to string together video of every hurricane, flood, forest fire, ferry sinking, battle atrocity and grisly murder in the previous five years. Then she was to interview cops and clergy, professors and pedestrians about their views on why all these things happened. One of the policemen she called was the man in charge of the city homicide squad, Detective James Hagan.

They met for a chilidog and a giant Coke at the Varsity, a grease pit landmark near Georgia Tech University that sold tons of great-tasting food that clogged arteries without regard to race, creed, color or gender.

Jimmy Hagan laughed out loud, almost choking on an onion ring, when Cassie explained her series. "You're calling it, 'Is God Punishing Us?'" he snorted, Coke almost coming out of his nose. "You're kidding, right?"

Cassie was not amused. She argued against doing the series, but the promotions people convinced the news director "Is God Punishing Us?" would be a blockbuster ratings winner. Cassie remembered the conversation in the boss's office that day.

"Look, Cassie, it'll be great," said the news director. "Great video, some sound from real people on the street, experts arguing over why it's all happening. What more could you ask for?"

"Seems to me we're missing the number one interview subject here," she responded, unable to hide the sarcasm.

"Who?"

"God, who else?"

The boss shrugged his shoulders and the promotion director, Lisa, standing impatiently by the door, tossed her head in disgust. She originally wanted the series to climax in part three with an interview with actor George Burns as God. She was livid when several newsroom people laughed their heads off as they told her Burns died twenty years ago.

The series survived, however, and Cassie, having lost the argument against hosting the report, went to work on it, including this cop she just met.

"No, I am not kidding, Detective," she said to Hagan. She nibbled on an onion ring and looked annoyed at him. "You have seen so much horrible stuff in your job. All you have to do is tell me about the worst of it. We'll get video to illustrate it. Then you can give the world your view on why things are so bad sometimes."

He stifled another laugh, looking at Cassie carefully now, admiring her smooth, mahogany skin, her intelligent eyes and her ability to look sexy while angry or irritated.

"All right! I'll do it, but only if you promise you won't edit me into stupid little sound bites. Deal?"

"Deal." She smiled, a big, "yes" smile.

"And, one other condition," he said. "You have to call me Jimmy, off the air, I mean."

Cassie groaned. Before she could speak, he jumped in.

"I know, I know, it's a dumb thing to say, sexist too probably, right? I just meant I wanted to call you something other than Miss Page and..."

"Okay, Jimmy it is, Jimmy. And I'm Cassandra."

She grinned, opened her eyes a bit, leaned forward and said, "And maybe if you're very nice and a wonderful interview, later you can call me Cassie."

They laughed together, ate the onion rings and the hot dogs and had the best half-hour either of them had enjoyed with someone else in months.

"...No more hunger or thirst..." the singer in Harvey's continued, his work on the keyboard better than his vocal effort.

Cassie toyed with an Old Fashioned. It was a drink so far out of fashion in her circles she ordered it sometimes just to surprise her friends. She also liked the fruit. Cassie wasn't much of a drinker. She used it as stress relief and this night had been stressful enough for a sidecar full of Old Fashioneds.

Jimmy slid into the banquette and picked up his drink, a Molson Ice, a bottle, no glass.

They agreed to meet at Harvey's, knowing they'd both be up and on the case early the next day. They just didn't want to go home yet. "Home" was a one-bedroom apartment in Midtown, a newish place near Piedmont Park.

By day, the park was safe for in-line skaters, Lycra-clad hard bodies and businessmen and women on lunch break. At night, the park became fair game for "urban outdoorsmen," as Hagan called homeless men, plus prostitutes of various sexual orientations and late-night dog-walkers, apparently oblivious to the park's day and night vicissitudes.

Cassie and Jimmy chose their living location because it was only a ten-minute drive from Channel 3's studios and not much more than that to homicide headquarters.

Location, location, location was an easy concept when it came to real estate. Location, when it meant proximity to another soul, that is, living in the same place, took a little longer to become second nature.

They still were at the stage of taking turns in the bathroom and having separate accounts for household expenses. They didn't even put both their cell phone accounts on a "family plan."

Now and then Cassie would tease Jimmy by holding up her state-of-the-art, super smart cell phone provided by the TV station. Management's theory was if the station gave key employees free cell phones, they'd never have an excuse for not being in touch.

Jimmy's Atlanta PD-issued cell phone was, by comparison to Cassie's, paleontological.

Other household adjustments were progressing with minimal disruption.

By now, Cassie knew Jimmy could not stand the taste of baking soda toothpaste. She forgave him for that. Hagan realized and learned to deal with Cassie's occasional snoring when she slept on her back.

"Still thinking about Campbell?" Jimmy asked Cassie as he slid across the booth and took her free hand. She grinned.

"No, in fact I was thinking about that series I did, 'Is God Punishing Us?' Remember that?"

"What I remember most is the conclusion, the answer 'News Blitz3' came up with to the question about God and punishment."

She laughed out loud now.

"Yeah, pretty good huh? 'Is God Punishing Us? We're not sure.' The bosses thought it was great! Jesus, are they out of it sometimes."

She sipped her drink again, more this time, her eyes flashing a smile at Jimmy over the glass at her lips. Those eyes, black, shiny, sexy, had helped Cassie get her TV jobs and gave Jimmy a thrill the first time he managed to get close to her.

Cassie knew she had great eyes. Sometimes in the mirror she would try that quick, back-and-forth thing actors do in movie close-ups, that darting eyes thing as they face each other, almost close enough to cause their eyes to cross.

She never really learned how to do that, but she thought it was fun and funny. Once, in their apartment, she noticed Jimmy watching her try it, and they both collapsed in giggles that led to a half-hour of smiley lovemaking.

Eventually it became their signal. At a dull party, if either of them walked up close and did the eye-darting thing, the other would know it was time to get out of there.

At dinner, or almost anywhere, if one of them did the back-and-forth eye dance, the other would know it was time to make love.

Cassie even did it on the air once, the eye thing, that is, at the end of a studio on-set close-up shot. Hagan missed it. He was in the bathroom at the time. The newscast producer saw it and, after the show, asked her whether she was having trouble with her eyes. Cassie laughed and hurried home.

"Regrets, I've had a few..." the piano player sang, working hard not to feel bad about being ignored.

Cassie looked at Jimmy and he put down his beer. "You wanna talk about the case?"

"No, babe, I do not. I do not, not, not wanna talk about the case."

Cassie smiled, her eyes narrowing. "You having eye trouble, lady?" he grinned, pulling her slightly closer.

"I'm having you-trouble, boy, and what are you gonna do about it?"

The piano man interrupted them with a loud, lonely ending to his version of "My Way."

Jimmy ignored the music, and moved his face to within lash-batting distance. "What I'm gonna do about it is, make your eyes light up and your body say howdy," he said, sliding into the twang he grew up hearing in Cabbagetown.

"Suh, it's make yo stomach say howdy, not yo body," she said, in her best Southern, smoky voice. "But I'll take yo Shoo Flah Pah any 'ol time I can get it, not to mention yo apple pan dowdy."

Hagan put down his beer bottle and did a cartoon-like lip-licking thing.

She stood, picking up her small black leather purse.

"Let's go, Jimmy, we have six hours until I have to be at work. With luck, we can even get a couple hours sleep."

37

CABBAGETOWN—ATLANTA

As Jimmy and Cassie drove in their separate cars from Harvey's toward their apartment, Jimmy thought about the pressure to solve the crimes as the Olympics opening day loomed.

How many twenty-hour days would this case require? One thing for sure, there is no way I'll make Sunday dinner with Mom. Bone-tired now, Jimmy's thoughts turned to his most recent Sunday with his mom, three weeks ago. There had been a month of Sundays reminding him of his roots.

That Sunday was typical. He drove to Carroll Street and his old family home in Cabbagetown, passing a small grocery store with the shingle hanging slightly off center, "Little's Grill & Gro, Since 1929."

As a kid, Jimmy spent too many hours loafing with his friends in front of that place. It was his getaway from all the noise and nastiness his father created at home.

He drove past the Salvation Army mission, a squat, concrete block building, part church, part soup kitchen. It was not there when Jimmy was growing up. Cabbagetown didn't need the Salvation Army back then.

The mill buildings, old brick, musty, six-stories high, were on the left, graffiti covering the lower walls. An urban artist spray-painted "Cabbagetown" in five-foot high letters, a three-color splash of pride in a neighborhood where some of the houses could have used that spray-paint. Jimmy noticed two new developers' signs in front of the old mill building: "Loft Properties and Offices Available."

The yuppies are coming, probably change the name to Meadow Sweet Trace Vista Knoll blah blah blah. Wait'll they lose the tires on their Beamers the first week, they'll head for the burbs so fast it'll look like a fire drill here.

Right on Tennelle Street, Jimmy saw a spotless Harley on the small front porch of a frame house. It was one of those shotgun homes the company had scattered on the streets east of the mill.

Right on Savannah, Jimmy now was on his street. He was going back years for every block he drove deeper into the mountain folk community that was his childhood home, his heritage. A few of the shotgun houses were spruced up with paint and flowers. The frame exteriors ran to colonial colors, a sort of low-rent Williamsburg look, the military blue, the burgundy, some with Victorian trim. *Good try. Maybe this place really could come back. Naw, they're rotten on the inside, too many generations of coal stoves and whisky stains.*

The flowers in the patch between sidewalk and street were annuals, impatiens, vinca, salvia. Crepe myrtles planted fifty feet apart several years before, were in bloom, purple and pink. The flowers helped hide the cracks in the sidewalks and the broken pickets on the short fences around the ramshackle houses that had not been fixed up.

Jimmy parked the dark blue sedan in front of 164 Savannah Street, his mother's home, his house, the house he was born in. The house seemed so big when he toddled, so small when he rebelled, so smelly when his drunken father raged and stumbled and threw up on the linoleum in the bathroom.

The house was white when the Fulton Bag and Cotton Mills built it and two dozen more like it in 1889, two years after the mill opened on this flatiron shaped parcel of land off Memorial Drive, east of downtown Atlanta.

The company builders who put up these houses called them "shotgun" homes, because, "You could fire a shotgun through the front door and hit the back door." The rooms were one behind the other, living room, bedroom, kitchen and bath, all the width of the house, nineteen feet.

Jimmy Hagan's great grandfather, Byrd William Hagan, was born in 1895 in Rabun County, Georgia, in the lower reaches of the Appalachian Mountains. When B.W. was two years old, his parents went to a meeting at the Full Gospel Church outside of town and signed up to go to Atlanta to work in a new mill there.

Jacob Elsis, a German immigrant, had moved his textile business from Cartersville to Atlanta and had sent his people into the North Georgia mountains to find cheap, unskilled labor. He wanted hard working, God-fearing people who could be counted on to do their jobs and to establish a close-knit community.

They were insular and inward looking, mostly ignoring the changes swirling around them in greater Atlanta. These Appalachian whites, mostly descended from settlers who came to America from England, Ireland and Scotland, had no skills and little education. So, they willingly learned the menial jobs Jacob Elsis needed doing to run his mill.

Jimmy was the third generation of the Hagan family to be born and raised in Cabbagetown. He grew up thinking it normal for the men and women to work together in the mill and for the kids to work there, too, as early as eight or nine years of age.

He also thought everybody's neighborhood smelled like cabbage. Legend was, that's why they called it Cabbagetown, because of that smell. Cabbage was a staple the women could put on to cook in the morning, put in a full day's work in the mill, then come home and have the mainstay of the evening meal ready to eat.

Jimmy didn't look forward to having his monthly dinner with his mother. She spoke little, fussed a lot. She cooked almost nothing anymore, eating mostly frozen dinners, sometimes barely heating them.

So, to make sure she and he ate right, Jimmy always brought the food. That day, he had a roast chicken, fresh sourdough rye bread and coleslaw from an upscale grocery in Buckhead. The in-town, slimmed-down version of the huge farmer's markets in the suburbs was Jimmy's primary source of meals.

The air-conditioner whined and rattled in the window next to the front door as Jimmy rang the bell, turned the knob and walked in.

"Mom, you didn't lock the door again," he said in a loud voice as he walked through the living room toward the kitchen. He knew she would be there, sitting at the "kitchenette," as she always called it.

She would be in her Sunday housecoat, listening to the radio, a table model Philco, at least sixty, maybe seventy years old, black Bakelite with AM only. She would be listening to Reverend Roy, a radio preacher who yelled a lot and asked for money at the end of the half-hour. Jimmy urged his Mother not to send cash to radio Roy, but he knew she did, usually a ten-dollar bill, with a note asking the preacher to "pray for my son, the policeman."

Jimmy had not heard Roy ever actually do that, but his Mother insisted he did, at least once a month, exhorting God to "hold safe in your hands, the brave and God-fearing officer who keeps us safe from the devil-inspired hordes that run wild in the streets."

His mother said radio Roy never mentioned him by name. "Getting your name mentioned must cost at least twenty-five bucks," Jimmy told her.

The Hagans were Roman Catholics all the way back to Ireland, of course. But the mountain people evolved their faith to suit their needs. Jimmy retained his religion in principle, but seldom went to Mass.

His mother's Sunday morning allegiance to Reverend Roy's Pentecostal radio harangue was her own religious comfort zone, as she slipped toward senility.

"Morning, Mom, how're you doin'?"

She looked up, smiled, waved Jimmy to the other chair at the table and put her finger to her pursed lips in a sign to be quiet.

"He may pray for you today, Jimmy, it's about the right day for it." She turned back to the radio. She stared at the radio as she listened.

Jimmy put the bags of food on the counter and sat down across from his mother, feeling guilty he was wondering how soon he could get out of there.

"I brought dinner, Mom, the roast chicken you like, see?" He opened the bags, retrieved two plates from the cupboard and put the dinner on the table. He pulled out two paper napkins from the red plastic caddie that sat on the table, next to the toaster and the glass salt and pepper shakers.

"Want a Coke, Mom?"

She nodded, still watching the radio, as Reverend Roy talked about a prayer cloth his followers could get by mail for a small contribution, twenty-nine dollars suggested.

Jimmy watched her, recalling the long hours she put in at the mill, with most of the other adults and teenagers who lived in Cabbagetown back then.

He remembered how she insisted he stay in high school when others were dropping out to work full-time in the mill. His dad, unless he was drunk, didn't give a damn what Jimmy did. With a snootful, however, he would rant at his son, "You worthless piece of shit" and demand he get a full-time job "to pay your freight around this house."

Jimmy's mother always kept the lid on until the old man sobered up and forgot about his kid again.

Jimmy went to school mostly with black kids from the projects. Because of that, or in spite of it, Jimmy was one of the few unbigoted white men to come out of Cabbagetown. He had a few black friends, fewer white ones from his neighborhood.

He did three years in the Army after high school. He learned to shoot a rifle in basic training, then wrangled an assignment as a clerk-typist for his advanced training. Knowing how to type a letter and to write a coherent sentence vaulted Jimmy to the rank of Spec-4, then Spec-5, a sergeant of sorts. Jimmy found his comfort zone when he was assigned to a military police unit. He loved police work and his next step was clear, an honorable discharge at the end of his tour and application to the Atlanta Police Academy.

He was not the smartest cadet, but was in the top ten percent of his class. His rise in the department was steady, not spectacular. He applied for detective twice before he made it, and it took three efforts to get into the homicide division. Jimmy's break came when the ranking officer in homicide somehow riled the chief, something about his politics, and was reassigned to Hartsfield Airport.

Hartsfield was one of the world's busiest airports, but for a promotion-minded cop, airport duty was a career move akin to being a school crossing guard.

Jimmy won the promotion. His ability to get along with and get respect from the black officers was a key to his advancement.

"Listen, Jimmy, it's you, it's you," his mom said, shushing him again.

"...keeps us safe from the devil-inspired hordes that run wild in the streets."

Jimmy smiled at the pleasure he saw on his mother's face.

He reached over and stroked her hair, tied in a bun, still as long as it was when she was married.

"That's great, Mom, thanks for the prayer. Let's have dinner now, Mom."

38

PARK TOWERS, NEWSBLITZ3—ATLANTA

"There's no bloody place to really show this story," the cameraman from London complained as he set up his tripod on the sidewalk.

He could get a good wide shot of the Vaughn's apartment building, where Cav Campbell fell to his death, but that was about it. Police and private security teamed to keep the media people well away from the entrance, crammed into a roped-off area out near the Peachtree Road driveway entrance.

The British TV crew was just one of about forty that had arrived in town by now.

The reporters lined up in their limited space to do their on camera "stand-ups." Their elbows almost touched as they told their live audiences or their camera recorders the latest on the Campbell death.

It was always news time somewhere in the world, so the carnival of communications continued non-stop, at the Vaughn's building, at homicide headquarters, outside GNS and near the Olympic stadium downtown.

Even before her scheduled live report at noon, Cassie already had an argument in the newsroom over her coverage for the day. It started about ten o'clock with Rita Runner, the producer.

"Hey, Cassie, we need you live at noon at St. Carpaccio's, showing everybody praying for Bren Forrest to find Campbell's killer, you know the bit."

Cassie was surprised she could understand Rita, who usually had wads of food in her mouth. She was not surprised the food-obsessed producer would get the name of the cathedral wrong, calling it "St. Carpaccio's" instead of St. Ignacio's.

"Well, I don't know, Rita," Cassie began, hoping to avoid a fight. "I think maybe I should actually cover the story, at the cop shop, the search for the hostess, Lia Lee, don't you think?"

Rita wiped her hands on the tail of her T-shirt. The words on the front, smudged by earlier hand wiping, read: "'Pocahontas Pisses Me Off." It was a shirt she acquired recently when some Native Americans held a noisy protest outside a movie theater showing the latest sequel to the Disney *Pocahontas* movie.

The Indians hadn't liked the original animated cartoon treatment of one of their historic role models and detested the sequels. They boycotted the new film and called it racist. Rita attended the demonstration. She marched around, shouting a slogan in the Cherokee language. Nobody at the rally spoke Calusa, Rita's Indian language of choice.

The demonstration was a watershed for Rita, who took to signing all her memos at work, "yours in Native American unity..."

The news director told her she could not take part in any future demonstrations. She told him that was a restriction of her freedom of expression, so he backed down, fearing an Indian protest outside Channel 3 someday, with Rita up front.

Since that incident, Rita wore the Pocahontas T-shirt to work at least two days a week. It carried the stains of a thousand Heath Bars, the encrustations of a million Fruit Loops.

Cassie could not look at the shirt as she talked to Rita. "So, let me do the noon report from homicide headquarters, all right?"

"Gee, Cassie, I really want the prayer angle."

"What is the prayer angle exactly, Rita? You mean people go to church on Sunday? What's that? And how will I know who's praying for Bren Forrest and who's praying for rain? Should we put wireless microphones on all the folks going in?"

"Well, we don't have that many microphones but maybe on a couple of people, great idea!"

Cassie shook her head and walked toward the assignment desk. "Who else is working this story today, Harry?" she asked the intern sitting at the desk, listening to police radio scanners.

"Hey, Ms. Page, well..."

"Never mind, I see the names on the board there," Cassie said and turned back to Rita. "You have three other reporters now, so put one of them at the church, hell, put 'em in the pulpit for all I care, put a mic on the statues if you want, but I want to go to homicide and track the search for the girl."

Rita knew she would lose the battle, so she gave in. "You know, Angie really should do the church coverage for us. I just remembered, she goes to church several times a week, so she'll be perfect," Rita said to Cassie.

"Rita, I think Angie is a born-again, you know, an evangelical, uh, fundamental Christian thing, the hands-in-the-air stuff, isn't she?"

"So, what's your point?"

Cassie suppressed a grin, knowing she had won, not wanting to blow it. "Oh, nothing. She'll be great. Tell her to get some emotion into the piece. She'll have 'em crying in the aisles," Cassie said, walking toward the door to the parking lot.

Rita went back to her desk, grabbed a bag of marshmallows from the center drawer and stuffed six into her mouth. Comforted, she thought about how to organize the coverage on the noon newscast.

I'll open with Angie at the church, give her a couple of minutes at least. Then, Glenn at the stadium, Jerry doing the angle on minorities in the world press corps coming to town, then, let's see, a couple of items for pacing, promo the six o'clock show, then, right before the commercial break, I'll go live to Cassie at homicide. A minute fifteen, max. The bitch'll wish she'd gone to the church.

Rita liked her plan, especially the put-down of Cassandra Page. Rita smiled with pleasure. Several dribbly marshmallows popped out of her mouth and added to the tapestry of her T-shirt.

39

ATLANTA

"Look, there's nothing to indicate suicide, nothing, so forget that, your honor, sir. "

Chief Lutz was on his cell phone, talking to the mayor. He was parked outside the Marriott Marquis Hotel downtown and about to attend a dinner inside. One of the dozens of pre-Olympics events around town he looked forward to before the Cav Campbell death.

"Chief, here's the deal. Bren Forrest tells the world Campbell was waxed, and you have no comment? For God's sake, Chief, get out there and tell the people what's going on!"

Lutz squirmed, sweating in his dress white uniform as the air conditioner blasted comfort through the car. He took off his cap, gold braid making the bill too heavy, and tossed it onto the seat next to him.

"Are you sure you don't want to handle the news conference yourself, sir?" *Bastard's scared shitless of this thing. He'll hang me out to dry until it's solved, then jump in.*

"No, no, it is a police matter officially and I don't want to Bigfoot my chief of police. It's not my style, as you know. But get off your ass, Chief, or someone up here is gonna kick it, hard."

"Is that all, Mr. Mayor?"

"No, it's not. Fill me in."

"Well, we searched Campbell's things at Ms. Forrest's place. No diary, no pills, no weapons, no dirty pictures, nothing. Clean. And Ms. Forrest can't help much."

"Well, how'd she decide he was murdered then?" the mayor asked, frustration in his voice.

"It's in her head, she just believes it and so do we at this point. Just have no idea who."

"What about the girl, that Asian girl at the party. Find her yet?"

"No, but we ought to get some leads now that her sister was found dead, murdered for sure. Obviously related to the Campbell thing, if the Asian girl was involved."

"Chief, that's a helluva stretch. What else do you have now?"

"That's our best right now, and we're on it. Hagan's running it and we're rousting all the snitches. We'll find her, Mayor, and see what she's all about."

The mayor chuckled.

"Hey, I saw what she's about! Amazing! By the way, Chief, where are you?"

"I'm outside the Marriott, the dinner, you know, the airline sponsor's deal. Just a touch and go, then back to the office."

"Well I'm inside the dinner, Chief. They patched you through. Get off the damn phone and walk a hundred feet and we can talk in here." The phone went dead.

Chief Lutz wiped his face with a hip pocket handkerchief, squirted a blast of Binaca in his mouth and climbed out of the car.

The Marriott Marquis was an imposing presence in downtown Atlanta for two reasons. One was the way it seemed to snare most of the city's major events and thus often had celebrity guests from the worlds of politics, sports, mass media and show business.

The hotel also was imposing literally, dubbed by local wags as the "Pregnant Building," because of its bulging base and large atrium.

To get to the head table in the main ballroom, where Lutz knew he'd find the mayor, he had to weave through fifty or so round tables for eight, mostly full already, guests of this party thrown by the airline that paid forty-million dollars to be the "Official Airline of the Olympics."

Ten or more similar events were going on around town as corporations jockeyed for the most attention, best press coverage or at least the hottest "A" list of invitees who actually showed up.

The airline party probably won. The mayor was way down the dais, outranked by five governors, six or eight US senators and a few army generals, plus he was outsparkled by a gaggle of local, national and international media celebrities.

Jerry Vaughn was whispering with the mayor at the left side of the head table.

"It's a gut feeling, that's all, Mr. Mayor. Bren just knows, or at least hopes in her heart, Campbell didn't take a dive. You know, Bren really thinks that hostess is involved, the Asian girl. She really does. You think? Or do you know anything?"

"Jerry, we don't have a damn clue right now," the mayor whispered, close to Vaughn's ear, his hand covering his mouth from the eight hundred others in the room, all involved in their own noisy conversations. "But the girl is a possibility. Her sister was murdered, as you know, and all the stuff, clothes, jewelry, all matched with what the hostess had on at your place, so, hell, I don't know."

Jerry kept his tight smile fixed, turning to nod to an acquaintance who greeted him, then another hello to a guest who shook his hand as he passed.

Chief Lutz was pressing his way through the seated crowd, easing around chairs at the tables placed too close together. He was trying his best to avoid having conversations involving more than a "Hi there, how are ya?" with anybody in the ballroom. He especially was wary of local heavyweights from politics and news media.

It was self-defense strategy, because none of those people were talking about how cool it was for Atlanta to be hosting the Olympics again. Locals and visitors alike, from ambassadors and potentates down to the restroom attendants, were whispering, buzzing, musing and sometimes pontificating about Cav Campbell's demise.

The separate conversations had the same theme. They all agreed the story of the movie star who was impaled on a TV news van was one for the annals of Atlanta and the world, ranking up there with the suspicious death of Michael Jackson, the OJ Simpson case and the Charles Manson slaughters.

Chief Lutz decided at every Olympiad from then on, some sage or hack or cable news talking head would find a way to bring up the "The Great Olympic Impalement." He just hoped his name was not part of the lore of this sensational crime that happened in his town, on his watch.

As the chief tried to reach the head table near the podium, his way was blocked by a cluster of autograph seekers around the prominent sports broadcaster, Chip Caray.

Caray spotted Chief Lutz and laughed to himself, recalling a similar situation at the first Atlanta Olympics, when Chip's father and grandfather had been alive. Harry, the patriarch, had a Hall of Fame career as an announcer for, among other teams, the St. Louis Cardinals, Chicago White Sox and Chicago Cubs. Harry's son Skip, Chip's father, also was hugely popular as a long-time announcer for the Atlanta Braves.

Chip, too, was a natural broadcaster. His first big league gig was announcing games of the Orlando Magic of the NBA. He later signed a contract to do Major League Baseball on Fox Sports.

"Hello, Chief Lutz, it's been a while," Chip said, "Nice to see you. And congratulations. The last time we met you had just been promoted to Deputy Police Chief."

Chip tried not to chuckle as he recalled that previous meeting where Lutz pushed through the crowd around the three Caray men and stuck out his hand.

"Mr. Caray, a real pleasure," he said to Harry Caray, who looked up from signing his name. "I'm the deputy chief of police here, welcome to Atlanta. Glad to have you here, love your work, 'Holy Cow,' you know? Great, terrific, good to see you."

Harry started to speak, but Lutz turned to the man seated at Harry's left. "And, Chip, it's a pleasure to meet you, too," Lutz said, pumping the man's hand.

"No, I'm Skip, the Braves announcer," Skip said, without a smile.

This dork in a comic opera uniform is the deputy chief of police? No wonder criminals roam the streets at will.

"Oh, sorry there, Skip, of course, you and Ernie make a great team, love your work."

"Ernie retired two years ago," Skip said deadpan, referring to his former partner, Ernie Johnson, Senior. "His son, Ernie, Junior, is on TBS Sports," Skip added with a go away tone in his voice.

"Yes, of course," Lutz said, turning to the young man on Skip's left.

"Ernie, great to see you too," Lutz said, taking the man's hand.

"No, I'm Chip, Skip's my dad, Harry's my grandfather," Chip Caray said, laughing.

"Chip, Chip, yes, Chip, I see the resemblance in the eyes, sure do. I mean, you all three wear glasses and all. Anyway, Chip, Skip, Harry, have a great time in our town, and give my best to Ernie, both of 'em." Chip watched Chief Lutz and his two-man security detail jostling their way toward the mayor and Jerry Vaughn at the head table.

I wonder whether this Chief Lutz is any smarter now than he seemed at that first meeting when he was only a deputy chief, Chip thought.

Jerry Vaughn looked up as Chief Lutz approached. "Hello, Chief, just talking with the mayor here about the Campbell thing. How's it going?"

"Making some progress now, Mr. Vaughn, yes, we are making some progress." Lutz glanced at the mayor, wondering what he had told Vaughn.

"Chief," Jerry said in a quiet voice, "I don't know anything about police work. I wonder whether your people have talked with any of Ms. Forrest's business partners in GNS?

"Oh, I don't mean as suspects, of course," he added, as the chief seemed surprised. "But they may have some background information or some insights that, if put into context, could be helpful."

Chief Lutz reacted carefully.

"Mr. Vaughn, I cannot imagine they would be involved in such a thing."

"No, Chief, what I'm saying is Ms. Forrest believes, well, you heard her say on TV whoever killed Campbell must be an enemy of hers. So, her partners might have something, some little thing that might help you, that's all."

Jerry stared at the chief, wondering whether this chat was a waste of time.

"Good idea, Jerry," the mayor said, with a look at Lutz that said, "Get on it, now."

As Lutz and his security men turned toward another part of the room, a microphone appeared in front of his face, with a sign on it, WNAG News Radio, larger than the mic itself. It was Sheamus Cross, reaching around as he approached the chief from behind.

"Hello, Chief Lutz, have you caught the killer yet?

"Who the hell are you?" the chief snapped, "and get out of my face." With that, his bodyguard cops stepped between Sheamus and the chief.

"Like you don't know me, right, Chief? Me? That's a good one, Chief. So, how about it, any news on Cav Campbell's sky dive?"

The security cops kept pushing Sheamus slowly away from the chief.

"Come on, Chief, tell the truth while you still have your job." Two more pushes by the chief's men and Sheamus was out of earshot.

At that moment, the lights in the ballroom dimmed and images of jetliners soaring through sunny skies loomed from the big TV screens in the four corners of the room.

Familiar music from the airline's commercials filled the room, all violins and harps and timpani swells.

40

MARCO ISLAND

The *BeebKiller* moved at just above idle speed as it rumbled smoothly through Big Marco Pass, a "no wake" zone.

"How about a grouper sandwich at the Snook Inn, boys?" Ian shouted from the back of his Grady-White boat.

O'Reilly, at the wheel, nodded. Jax, next to him, shrugged. O'Reilly watched the channel markers carefully. At low tide, the sides of the pass could be as shallow as a foot or two. He adjusted slightly, moving the boat away from Hideaway Beach on his right.

The white sand beach was almost deserted at Hideaway, the exclusive private development on the northern tip of Marco Island. Phelps's was one of the few boats in the water on this Thursday in July, slow season on Marco.

The Snook Inn was crowded, however, as the *BeebKiller* grooved into the dock at the restaurant. O'Reilly was as good a boatman as he was a chauffeur. He'd had lots of practice since Phelps built the house on Marco Island and bought the boat to go with it.

Phelps tried to get to Marco Island at least once every two or three months. As time and caution allowed, he tried to combine a little pleasure, the boating and fishing, with business, drug smuggling. He established a connection with two fishing captains on the Isles of Capri, a village on the mainland just across the pass from Marco Island.

The charter boat captains knew the thousands of tiny mangrove islands along the Gulf Coast, great places for small boats to sneak in with drugs dropped from small planes or from ships way out in the gulf. They'd been smuggling marijuana for years but gladly switched to cocaine in the deals Phelps set up.

"Why waste time on wacky backy when a little blow is the way to go?" he said to his fellow entrepreneurs.

He kept the two captains happy with more money than they could make fishing, yet scored the coke cheap enough to make huge profits when it moved through his system.

The Cayman Islands became his money laundry via three offshore companies he established with those cooperative Caribbean bankers.

So, Marco was ideal, a peaceful, mostly upper-class town with just enough yuppies and families to keep it from being a total Sun City drowse. His wife had been there once and would not return. She hated Florida, feared the sun, loathed fish and fishing.

That suited Phelps, because Marco Island met his needs even better without the wife.

Growing as it was, Marco had a daily stream of pickup trucks carrying construction workers and sub-contractors on and off the island. New people came and went, so Phelps's couriers never worried about someone asking a deputy sheriff about "that new guy in town."

Phelps himself drew little attention. Marco attracted a lot of European vacationers, mostly Britons and Germans. Virtually everybody else on Marco came from the US or Canada.

They fled years of up-to-the-hips snow and crime and traffic to live on Marco, where most of the homes were on the water. Many residents never locked their car doors, probably a mistake these days, and some didn't even bother to lock the doors to their houses, a mistake for sure.

Phelps was careful to build his house in a good part of the island, but not the most expensive. He bought property on Liberty Drive, a house positioned to have the "play" areas, pool, lanai and boat dock, facing west on a small bay. Sunsets were everything.

For what he paid for the lot and the house, he could have had a luxury condo in one of the high-rises along the beach. But he wanted privacy, without condo managers or prying eyes in the elevators. He didn't want people badgering him to stop in the recreation room for bingo night.

The house provided Phelps with his own pool, sun deck and Jacuzzi, a dock for the *BeebKiller* and two extra bedrooms for his men.

The office he installed off the screened lanai gave him state of the art hi-tech communications with his office in London, on-line connections to anywhere else.

The kitchen was large, all white, with a well-stocked pantry and refrigerator. But Phelps didn't cook much. He preferred to patronize several of Marco's casual restaurants. His favorite was the Snook Inn.

The Snook Inn was built in the early 1960s when there wasn't much else on the island. Over the years the owners expanded the restaurant and tore down the fifteen-unit motel. By the time Ian Phelps discovered the Snook, it epitomized life on Marco, with casual waterfront dining, a lively bar and music by guitar players who knew every Jimmy Buffett song by heart and every Zac Brown hit as well.

Seated at a picnic-style table next to the chickee hut bar overlooking the boat slips, Phelps smiled at the waitress and ordered Bloody Marys for himself, O'Reilly and Jax.

"You must be new here, young lady. I don't recall seeing you here before." She smiled, blue eyes intensified by her deep tan.

"Yes, just been here two weeks. You local?"

"No, but I do have a little place here, come as often as I can."

"Good," she smiled and went to order the drinks at the U-shaped bar under the big chickee hut.

"What's 'Bee-B-Killer' mean, sir?" the waitress asked as she brought the drinks to the table. She noticed the three men as they docked the boat.

"What's 'at dearie?" Phelps asked.

"Your boat, a beauty by the way, the name, 'Bee-B-Killer.' What's it mean?"

"No, it's not 'Bee-B-Killer,' luv, it's *BeebKiller*, Beeb, rhymes with, uh, geez nothing rhymes with Beeb, does it? Anyway, Beeb is slang for the BBC, the British goddam Broadcasting Company. That's a Beeb."

"And you're a beeb killer? Ohhh, I don't think we have any of those around here, you may be the only one, love," she said, smiling, teasing Phelps, imitating his accent.

"It only takes one when that one is me, me darlin'. And what's your name then?" Phelps said, noticing the waitress was in good shape for her age, probably thirty-five or so. He envied her tan and enjoyed leering at her body, slim, leggy in cutoff jeans and a Snook Inn tropical shirt. *Hmmm, wonder how she'd look a bit more Asian, the eyes I mean. Worth sorting out at some point.*

"Liz, me darlin'," she teased. "Anyway, nice boat. Now, can I get you gentlemen somethin' to eat?"

They ordered and Phelps said to Liz as she wrote, "Liz, luv, how about you join us on the *BeebKiller* this evening and I'll tell you the whole story about its name?"

"Mr. Killer, or can I call you Beeb? I can't make it tonight, but gimme a rain check, 'cause I'd like that. How long are you here for?"

"Leaving soon, I'm afraid. But I'll be back. I have my house here, you see," Phelps said with a grin. "And you, Liz, me lovely, you can call me Killer."

41

MARCO ISLAND

"In Atlanta, police have released a photograph of a woman they want to question in the death of actor Cav Campbell."

The picture on the TV screen jolted Ian Phelps at first. He had forgotten how beautiful she was, how lovely she was even in that trans-Atlantic still photo his Atlanta people showed him during a teleconference two months ago.

The ABC News anchor was leading his newscast with the Cav Campbell story, talking about how the pre-Olympics murder case had official Atlanta in turmoil.

"She is identified as Lia Lee, a hostess for the Olympic games that begin this weekend in Atlanta."

Phelps rattled the ice in his glass, then drained the last of the Glenlivet, watching the TV over the rim of the glass. He never put ice in his scotch except when he was in Florida. Or, on the way there. It just seemed the thing to do there.

"Lee reportedly was among the last to see Campbell alive. Moreover, her twin sister was found dead yesterday, and police first thought it was this woman."

Phelps smiled and refilled his drink. *So far, so good, as planned. Using the other girl, the twin was genius, throwing them off, giving us time. And boy is that Lia babe smashing. I've a mind to get me some of that before I head to Atlanta. No, shouldn't mix business with pleasure till it's over, then...*

Phelps had arranged Lia's flight to Marco Island, to the condo on the beach. He knew it was about a five-minute drive from his house. He reached for his phone, then grabbed the remote control when the face of the anchorman replaced the picture of Lia on the screen. Hoping to see her on one of the other networks, Phelps began changing channels. CBS was showing video of a violent clash somewhere in the Middle East. Zap to NBC, where a female anchor was talking to her White House correspondent about politics and new polls showing the president's job satisfaction rating plummeting.

Back on ABC, Phelps was startled to see video of Bren Forrest talking with reporters gathered on a sidewalk outside of GNS headquarters.

"... and sources say Bren Forrest has given police the names of other people she wants them to talk to about Campbell's death. We asked her about that this afternoon."

A close-up shot of Bren popped up as her sound bite ran. "Well, they are not suspects, of course, not in the least. The police simply asked for names of my business partners in GNS, and I supplied them. Don't make something out of this that isn't there, I implore you."

Phelps slammed his glass on the countertop and picked up his cell phone. After he tapped in the fourteen-digit number, he heard the familiar ring of the British telephone system.

"Make the Georgia contact on the uplink now," he said, when a male voice answered. "I need to know whether my name has come up in the Campbell thing, from Forrest or anybody else. Do it now, mate, and call me at the Marco house. Oh, and get me the phone number for the condo here when you call back. Yes, the Marco condo, the Wavecrest I think it is."

He hung up and looked out of the sliding glass doors at the bay. Three pelicans swooped low, their wings still, cruising six inches above the water, fishing for dinner. *Funny buggers, those pelicans. So beautiful in flight, so ungainly when they land. I wonder how they taste. Probably not as good as bald eagles, I'd wager.*

Phelps loved shocking people or pretending to with his creepy sense of what's funny. He stared at the water for three or four minutes.

Someday, when I get this thing finished, when the BBC sodders are sorry second-raters, I may buy this island, or a good chunk of it. I'll have my own bloody pelicans and my own bald eagles,

I will. Who knows, maybe I'll invite Bren Forrest down for a weekend.

The chirping phone interrupted his reverie.

"Phelps. Yes, Jim, where are you calling from? Right, go ahead."

It was Jim Jenkins, owner of the nation's fifth largest cable system, which owned fourteen percent of Global News Service.

"Ian, the cops are asking a million questions about our takeover effort." He waited, expecting Phelps to respond, but he didn't. "God knows I don't know what that has to do with the Campbell thing, but they seem intense as hell about this. Is there something I need to know here, Ian?"

"What do you mean, something you don't know? About my effort to buy the place, about Campbell's death, what?"

"Hell, I don't know, Ian, but they wanna know who wants Bren to sell, who doesn't, even who our stockholders are. They even asked me if I had any silent partners. Sniffing pretty close to home here, don't you think?"

Phelps could hear the fear, the nerves, in Jenkins' voice. He could not see Jenkins was fiddling with the gold lighter Phelps gave him six months before, eighteen karat, with the Phelps diamond satellite logo on it. He clicked it on, off, open, shut, tapped it on the table, then shoved it back into the pocket of his suit jacket.

Jenkins was calling from his hotel suite in the Buckhead section of Atlanta. He had arrived that morning and was greeted with a message from Atlanta Police, requesting the interview that occupied a good chunk of the afternoon.

"So, what did you tell 'em, mate?"

"Nothing much, Ian. Your name never came up, but everybody in the business knows you've tried to get GNS, so somebody is bound to mention you somewhere, somehow. I can smell it a mile away."

"Bloody hell," Phelps said, mostly to himself. "Well, good lad there, Jim, thanks for handling it so well. If they want to talk to me, fine, I just want her company. I'll be in Atlanta by tomorrow night. Tell me you'll have Forrest turned around by then."

"We're on it, Ian, the others are, too, but man, the heat is on and she's tougher than ever. Her guy's death seems to have strengthened her resolve. Just what we need now."

"Jim, you have to deflate that stock a couple of points, that's all. Then all the partners will lean hard on her to sell at the premium I'm offering. How can she refuse? I mean all that money, all this trouble?"

"Hey, Jim, she'll cave. She's has to be upset and ready to get the hell out by now, eh?"

"Just the opposite, Ian. I'd like to find the sonofabitch who killed Campbell and push him off that damn balcony too, ya know?

"And, Ian, do you think that girl, the Chinese or whatever, think she's involved? Cops would like to find her."

"What girl is that?"

"Man, when you hit the island you really do chill. Turn on the TV, Ian, you'll see her. Some sort of Olympics hostess. She was flirting with Campbell at the party where he bought it. She's a ten, too, a knockout. Check it out, Ian."

Phelps said he had another call and told Jenkins he'd see him the next day, at Jenkins' hotel suite.

O'Reilly shuffled into the kitchen as Phelps pocketed the phone.

"Boss, mind if I call me ball and chain? She gets mad if I don't check in."

Phelps nodded and waved at the cordless landline phone in the living room.

"Use line three, case I get another call on one," he said.

He was thinking about whether he should go to Atlanta now, tonight, and make sure things didn't fall apart, when his cell phone rang.

"Go ahead," he said, not waiting for a greeting.

"Sir, Hammer says your name has not come up in news coverage of that business and he's heard nothing in private."

"All right, thanks for that. And what's the condo phone number here? What? Good. G'night then."

"Oh, sir, one other thing. Hammer says one of his people was busted in the GNS parking lot last night, selling crack. Hammer says he has it under control."

Phelps started to speak, then stopped and hung up. *Shit, these dumb little bastards will be the end of me yet. But that girl, she's a smart one, she is. Think I'll just stop by and introduce myself. That ought to pick up my spirits, yes it will.*

Lia was stoned when the voice on the phone identified himself as "your benefactor." She had not met the man behind the plans for her future. She only knew Ned Bastige said he was from Europe.

"Well, sir, it is a pleasure to meet you by phone," she said sharply, her words brittled by the cocaine.

"I sort of thought we could meet tonight, in person I mean. I'm here on Marco for a few hours and would love to come by and say hello."

Lia agreed and Phelps said he'd be along in an hour or so.

ATLANTA POLICE HEADQUARTERS

Drug squad detectives knew they would get what they wanted from Paulie Sklaw, the GNS studio camera technician they busted for selling coke to the anchorman in the parking lot.

"Wake up, guys, we can plaster your names all over the media tomorrow, and you, Smithson, it'd just about ruin you, right?"

The anchorman was sweating, his tie loose, his spray-caked hair in disarray on his bowed head.

"No kidding," he said. "If you put me in the Internet zoo, the tweeters will go nuts with it. I won't even be able to get a job at a low power AM radio station in Guam, damn straight."

"And you, Sklaw, you're going down, too, right? But if you help us, you know, give us the people selling to you, we might make this whole nightmare just go away, so whaddaythink?"

Smithson saw a glimmer of a future and grabbed it.

"Hey, I'm with you, Detective, but uh, can I be sure your bosses will go along?" He had seen similar conversations in grimy precinct interview rooms on TV cop dramas.

"Mr. Smithson, I promise nothing, but if you give it up, I can assure you the people of Atlanta and their police department will be grateful. "You're not an addict, right? Not a pusher, right? Just a get-along guy, yes? So give us your supplier and you walk. No charges, no court, just a warning to stay out of trouble. Cool?"

"Wait a minute, Smitty, you can't..."

"The hell I can't. He's a prick and you know it, Sklaw."

Smithson tucked in his chin and seemed to focus on his necktie. "His name is Ned Bastige. He's a producer at GNS. He sends trainees and others out to move the coke, but he's the one, no doubt about it."

Sklaw glared at Smithson. The anchorman, stood up, brushed at his shoulders and rotated his neck as if to loosen up.

"Can I go now, Detective?"

"Just leave your phone number with the clerk and you're outta here."

"Why my number? I thought I was free and clear," Smithson said, frowning.

"Hey, Smitty, no sweat, just routine. You're our favorite TV person, right after that Sheila Belle gal. Now there's a piece of work, 'eh Smitty?"

The detective was smiling as the anchorman walked out.

"Mr. Sklaw, you can leave, too, if you just help us find Mr. Bastige and maybe show us how he does business."

MARCO ISLAND

"Let me out here," Phelps said to O'Reilly, in the circle drive of the Wavecrest condo building. He could hear the waves on the other side of the beachfront building, a gentle lapping, barely a surf.

"Jax, you stay with the car, too."

Jax grumbled something unintelligible, displeased he'd be sitting in a parked car in the dark for several hours with O'Reilly while his boss was up there, getting his jollies.

O'Reilly shrugged. It was his job.

"Lia, hello, I'm Ian," Phelps said, putting out his hand as Lia opened the door. She wore white denim short shorts and a gauzy white cotton pullover with large armholes and a long shirttail.

Her beauty astonished Phelps and Lia could feel his admiration as she smiled and stood aside for him to enter the apartment.

Any thoughts Phelps had about keeping their relationship businesslike dissolved as he set the bottle of Glenlivet on the wet bar and saw her in the mirror, behind him.

She seemed jumpy, nervous maybe. Phelps turned, closed the distance between them and touched her long, black hair. "You have a great future in this business, Miss Lee, or can I call you Lia?"

"Oh, wow, sure call me Lia. I mean that's my name, isn't it? And that part about my future? Great, terrific, glad to hear it, what makes you say so?" She spoke fast, words tumbling together.

"Well, I..." Phelps began to answer, but she plowed on.

"Oh, where are my manners, Mr. Phelps, I mean, Ian, it is Ian, right? Can I get you a drink? I mean, of course you brought your own and it's a good thing, too, because I don't have any scotch, but..."

Phelps knew it was the cocaine speeding up her system, combined with some nervousness. The coke more than the jitters, he assumed. He leaned in and kissed her softly on the lips, then walked to the couch and sat, legs spread, kicking off his loafers. "A scotch would be grand, Lia, just grand."

She almost ran to the bar, not eight feet away, filled the rocks glass with ice, tumbled it full of scotch and lurched toward the couch. As he reached up for the glass, she tripped and the scotch cascaded onto Phelps, soaking his shirt and his lap. She fell onto the couch next to him, laughing.

His initial flash of anger gave way as the momentum of her fall pushed her against his left side.

"Oh, I'm sorry, Ian, Mr. Phelps, uh, Mr. Ian, so sorry," she giggled, wiping at his wet shirt with the tail of her shirt.

He held her wrist and guided her hand between his legs, smiling now, staring at her, aroused by the touch of her hand and the look of her face.

She stroked him gently, widening her eyes, drops of sweat forming at her temples now, her head spinning. Phelps lay back as she touched the tab on his fly, then pulled it down a couple of inches. He reached inside her flimsy pullover and cupped her right breast in his hand.

Lia smiled, remembering through her hyper haze what she had done to the last man whose zipper she opened.

———

Phelps returned to consciousness, hearing the rustling of clothing, the sound of change jingling in a pocket. Disoriented amidst the rumpled sheets and the pillows in odd places, he sat up slowly.

Lia didn't see him wake up. She was going through the pockets of his trousers that had been on the floor at the foot of the bed. She had awakened about fifteen minutes earlier, drained by the drugs, a bit nauseous. She slipped on a light silk robe and went into the bathroom. A glance at the digital clock radio told her the sun would be up before long.

That sonofabitch, mean little bastard, actually slapped me when I wanted to do it straight. I'll show the fucker. Job or no job, he can't treat me like that. I should ice him, is what I ought to do. No, that'll get me in deep shit. Nope, I'll just make him pay without him even knowing it.

She tip-toed out of the bathroom and picked up Phelps's khakis. In his billfold, she saw four fifty-pound notes and three twenty-dollar bills. At the bottom of the pocket was a gold Dunhill lighter with the diamond studded Phelps satellite logo on the side.

Lia was putting the lighter and the cash into the pocket of her robe when Ian saw what she was doing.

"Bloody hell, what are you up to, you bitch!"

He jumped out of the bed and reached for Lia, grabbing her by the hair, pulling her to the bed. He yanked so hard she fell on her back.

"Thieving little whore," he hissed, slapping her hard on the left cheek, then on the right.

Lia brought her knee up as hard as she could, catching Phelps in the crotch, doubling him over in pain.

He hit the floor, swearing, holding himself.

Lia ran from the room, slamming the door behind her. Fully awake and sober now, she ran down the hallway toward the elevator, not knowing where the emergency stairs were.

In the bedroom, Phelps crawled to the night table and picked up his phone. He punched in the number for O'Reilly's cell phone, which was on the seat next to him in the car out front.

"O'Reilly, trouble. Get the girl who's running out of here, now. Get her and stop her. Shit, put Jax on."

"Here, boss."

"Jax, the Asian girl. She can ruin this whole thing, mate, so make sure she doesn't, you understand? Stop her, for good."

"Righto, boss. She's history."

O'Reilly pointed to the lobby.

"There she is, Jax, running toward the front door, there. What'll we do with her?"

Lia didn't know what hit her as she swung open the door and rushed out on to the concrete walkway. Jax chopped her hard on the back of the neck with his right hand. She dropped, unconscious.

O'Reilly ran to where she lay.

"Jesus Jax, now what?"

Jax smiled. "The boss said to wax her, so we wax her. Jax picked her up quickly and carried Lia around the side of the building, where it was dark. He squinted and frowned, trying to decide what to do with her.

At the beach side of the building, five chickee umbrellas lined the sand, their silhouettes barely visible in the little moonlight that filtered through the cloud cover.

"O'Reilly, get over here. I need you," Jax said in a coarse whisper. "Grab her feet. We'll toss her up there, on top of that straw thing, the thatched whatever. They won't find her unless a plane flies over real low."

Jax thought it was the smartest idea he'd had in a while. He'd seen those chickee huts, at the Snook Inn, at the hotels, along the beach. Phelps said Seminole Indians wove them from palm leaves and fronds.

"Is she dead?" O'Reilly asked. Before Jax could answer, Lia stirred, moaning.

Jax pulled a ten-inch knife from a holster under his left armpit. He pulled her head up by her hair and slit her throat with one fast motion.

"She is now."

O'Reilly gulped and averted his eyes.

"Come on, old son, give us a hand here, we should toss her up on that cheechee-roof thing and get out of here."

O'Reilly at her feet, Jax with his arms under hers, they hoisted Lia's body up and onto the slightly sloping top of the chickee's umbrella-shaped thatched roof.

The two men reached the car as Phelps was coming out the front door of the building.

"Let's go, now, to the house, fast."

42

ATLANTA

About the time Phelps was having Lia in the manner that made her so angry, Atlanta narcotics detectives were having an easy enough time with Ned Bastige.

"Sure, come on in, what can I do for you?" Ned said casually when the detective rang the bell at his condo in the Morningside area of in-town Atlanta. He showed them to a couch, offered beer or soft drinks, sat on a desk chair and smiled.

"Mr. Bastige, we can do this the easy way if you like. You seem like a smart man."

Ned's smile fell into a frown. His large, black eyebrows curved down. His widow's peak of thick, black hair seemed to darken and move south on his forehead.

"Do what the easy way? What are you talking about?"

"You've been dealing drugs at GNS. We know it, and you know we know it, and we want to know your source, now, with no fuss, no B.S."

"Mind if I smoke?" Ned asked, his hand trembling a bit as he reached into his shirt pocket.

The lead detective shook his head with a thin smile. "Not if you tell us what we need to know."

"I really have no idea what you are talking about, gentlemen. I do not deal drugs. I have no source." He lit the cigarette with a version of the Phelps lighter, the cheaper model he gave to his employees, chrome with a gold-filled satellite, the Phelps logo.

"We have two people who'll name you in court, a seller and a customer. No shit, Ned, they're going to fry you. And there's other stuff too, just icing on this cake, get it?"

Ned seemed stunned, stared at them, silent.

"Like I said, Bastige, we can talk like grownups here. You tell us what we need, and we'll see to it that you still have a career."

"But if you don't give it up right now," the other detective broke in, his first words to Bastige, "we'll throw your dope-dealing ass in jail with some guys who'll give you a nickname and a couple of nights that'll make you walk funny for a month. You understand me?"

Ned went pale, his dark hair and eyes looking even blacker against his blood-drained face. "I don't, I mean, what do you mean give it up, exactly?"

"What I mean is," the first detective said softly, "you tell us names and places, your contact, the guy with the coke, the crack, whatever. You give us a list of your worker-bees and their customers. Now, Mr. Bastige, right-goddam now."

"Christ, I wanna help, but I don't know anything. I don't!"

The second detective shook his head slowly, stood up and walked to the front windows. He eased the Venetian blinds back and peeked out to the front sidewalk. The neighborhood was asleep.

"Ned, don't be a schmuck," he said, still gazing out the window. "Don't make us roar up here in five minutes with three squad cars, lights and sirens on, disturbing your neighbors, who will look out their windows and see you being led away in cuffs."

"Yeah, Ned, and don't make us show up with a couple of uniforms at GNS tomorrow, asking lots of questions about you, talking about drugs, talking about you and drugs."

Ned had his head in his hands now, stifling a sob.

"Ned, Ned, Ned, you make us do that, you're out of a job in three hours, out of a career in a week, in jail for three months waiting for trial."

The detective who was sitting, stood and walked over to Ned, putting his hands on Ned's slumped shoulder. "So, come on, now, boy. Who's supplying you? Who are you working for?"

Ned sat up in the chair, his cheeks streaked with tears. "Man, I do not know. I do not know his name, I swear to God I don't. He's somebody on the other end of a computer, honest."

"That's more like it. Ned, you're doing great, now let's chat a bit more."

"That's it, man, really. I just contact this Internet address and go from there, ya know?"

"Where is he, Ned, where's the computer you contact?"

"Have no idea, really no idea, but..." Both detectives were standing in front of Ned now, staring down at him.

"But what, what?"

"Maybe in Europe or somewhere else outta the country, maybe, not sure."

"More, Ned, more. Why do you think it's foreign?"

"Well, I know sometimes he goes to Florida, or somebody who works for him, I think, is in Florida. Same with overseas, whatever."

"Why do you think that?"

"I can't prove it, but, but a couple of times a guy has called my cell phone asking for the 'boss' and when I say, 'Who's calling,' thinking they mean my boss here at GNS, the person on the phone says, 'Is this area code 239' and then the number, and I say, 'You have the number right but the wrong area code. This is 404'."

"So what, what's that tell you?" the detective asked.

"Both times the guy hangs up in a hurry. So the last time, I looked up the area code they wanted, 239, and that's in Florida somewhere."

Bastige was pouring out words now, spilling so fast the cops had to ask him to slow down.

"Where exactly in Florida?"

"San Marco or Marcos Isles or something like that, Marco Island maybe. One time, after the last time that happened, I dialed my cell number, but with the 239 area code instead of my real one here, and the woman who answered said it was a marina on Marcos Island Florida and asked who was calling. That scared me so I hung up.

"Jesus, guys, that's all I know. Please, please let me get outta this thing. I've told you everything!"

"Ned, we need that phone number. Write it down for us."

Ned went to a desk in a niche off the kitchen and wrote on a piece of paper, handing it to the first detective, who read it.

"You know what, Ned? If I were you I'd be changing my cell phone number faster than Usain Bolt," said the other detective.

"I will, I swear. Now can I go, please?"

"In a minute. So, Ned, who's buyin'?"

"I can't do that, man, innocent people..."

The second detective grabbed Ned's shirt collar and tugged on it.

"Hey, wake up, man, if we don't shut down this thing, get your guy and scare the shit out of your customers, we'll be back at your candy store in six months with the same problem, just different names, get it? Now, give me five names for starters. On paper."

Ned wrote, scribbled mostly, the names of five people who bought drugs from him or his lackeys at GNS. He handed over the list.

"Hey, some familiar names on here," the second detective said with a smile.

"Now, the world of sports," the detective said in a fake, announcer voice, mimicking the TV sportscaster whose name was on the paper. "Yeah, your scores and highlights are right here, pal," he said with a laugh.

There was one other name on the list he recognized.

"Holy shit," he said, erasing the grin, gesturing to his partner. "Well, well, check this out. Boy, Jimmy Hagan's going to owe us big time. I mean big freakin' time!"

43

MARCO ISLAND

"Now, honey, have you noticed those penguins flying up there? You won't see that many of them back in Springfield," the thirty-something mother was saying to her six-year-old son. They were walking along the beach of Marco Island at eight o'clock in the morning, earlier than the boy or his father trailing behind wanted to be up and out. The mom, Lorene, had insisted.

"We'll never get one of the chickee things, Gary," she said over her shoulder to her husband. "You know what I mean, the thatched-top, umbrella things those Indians make. They'll all be taken and we'll boil in the sun. Come on, Gary."

The boy looked up at the birds as his mom pointed to the sky. They were pelicans, of course, not penguins, but Lorene was anxious, in a hurry, taking quick little steps, guiding her family through the sand.

Lorene had never seen a pelican or a penguin, except on the Discovery Channel. That, plus her euphoria on this Marco morning brought about the confusion. She had to plead with Gary to make this trip. He wanted to go fishing in Minnesota, but Lorene nagged him into a beach trip in mid-summer.

This was day one of what she promised Gary and the boy would be four fun-filled days and three glorious nights on Marco Island. Her son didn't know the difference. Her husband didn't care. He plodded along, a small cooler full of Dr. Pepper in one hand and a copy of Tom Williams' newest thriller in the other. Gary just wanted a place to lie down and read his book.

Lorene saw a vacant chickee umbrella and hustled her son over to it. She threw down her beach towel and told the boy to sit on it. She turned back to her husband and waved him over.

"Here, Gary, here's our place, make yourself comfortable, babe."

Gary shuffled over, plopped his cooler and his book onto the sand, took the beach towel from over his shoulder and spread it.

His wife sat down next to him, almost snuggling, which irritated Gary, who didn't want to be on the beach this early anyway. He wiggled himself a foot or so away from her and lay on his side, up on one elbow, facing toward the water.

Lorene slathered sunscreen number fifty on the boy as he squirmed and frowned, then on her own arms, legs and shoulders.

"Here's the sun stuff, hon, it's number fifty, good protection," she said to Gary's back.

Gary shrugged and spoke without turning. "Christ, that stuff will take color out of your skin."

She ignored him, lay back on her towel and propped open her own paperback book, *The Voracious Vampire: 666 Recipes to Please Your Favorite Neck Biter*. Lorene was very late to the vampire craze, which had come and gone some years ago. She just started reading that genre the winter before. When her friends asked why then, she usually said, "Some things in literature transcend time and place."

The little boy ran to the water's edge and began an attempt at a sand castle where the tide began to ebb, leaving packed, wet sand to play with.

Lorene, sliding off her towel from the slathered sun lotion, opened her book and tried to lose herself in the world of a vampire chef, famous in some circles, known as "The sexy chef with blood on his incisors."

Drip. Plop. Drip.

The paragraph she was reading was blotted out by a Rorschach blob of red. She blinked and read the next line. Splat. The next drop was larger, followed in a split second by another drop that dribbled slowly down the page, adding a multimedia effect to the book.

She touched the viscous liquid and smelled it. Nothing. She touched the stuff on her finger with the tip of her tongue.

"Oh, my God, Gary, my God, Gary, Gary, what is this?" She was almost screaming now, staring at the blood on her finger, wondering whose blood she just put into her mouth.

Gary looked over, reluctant to leave the funeral scene he was reading, the bagpipe-loving cop mourning the murder of his friend.

"What is what?"

She scrambled to him, finger in the air.

"This, is it blood, Gary? I mean I'm reading this vampire recipe book and all of sudden there's blood on the page."

Gary stood up and saw the red splotches on the book and now on the beach towel. Just then a drop fell past his face onto the sand. On the roof of the chickee, another droplet was forming on the end of a frond, about to break free and fall to the sand.

"Honey, I think ..." he started to say, when blood dripping from another frond tattooed a four-dot pattern on his forehead.

"Jesus Christ, it's blood!" he sputtered, wiping his face, smearing it down his cheek. "Something is on this roof, bleeding through it." Gary scrambled out from under the chickee hut, backed off a few feet and peered up. Nothing. He backed off farther, then a bit more. A shape, a something seemed to be on the roof.

"Get out of there, now," he shouted to his wife and son. "I'm going to call somebody. You two get over to that hotel, and wait there."

Mom and the boy scrambled out from under the chickee hut, dragging towels and other stuff as they went. She left her vampire book where it lay, bloody, barely read.

A blast of air-conditioned cold struck Lorene as she opened the glass door of the hotel's beach entrance. She saw a young man in an island-style bellman's uniform, khaki shorts, white shirt and burgundy flip flops with gold trim, walking toward her.

"What is it ma'am, may I help you?"

"Yes, there's something on one of the chickee things out there, something dripping blood. What? No, I'm serious. My husband is over there calling 9-11 now. Is there anybody you can call? It's horrible."

The bellhop blinked, started to smile but stopped.

"Dripping blood?"

"Yes, young man, blood! Now, what are you going to do about it?"

"Are you a guest of the hotel, ma'am?"

"No, I am not a guest, but my husband is out there getting bloody from something or somebody on your chickee roof and..."

Lorene stopped, spying a house phone on a marble topped table in the middle of the lobby. She rushed over, grabbed the phone and punched zero.

"Hotel operator. What room are you trying to dial, please?"

"Um, um, I need the manager's office. Hurry please."

"One moment please."

Lorene heard the phone ringing at the other end. She shifted her weight to her other foot on the fifth ring. On the tenth ring her face was getting crimson.

"I'm sorry, ma'am, but no one answers in the manager's office. Would you like to leave a message?"

"What the hell, leave a message? Are you nuts? Yes, I have a message. Tell the manager to get out here and do something. There's a bloody something out there, bleeding on me and my husband, just tell 'em that."

As she was slamming down the phone, he could hear the operator saying, "Madam, I will give you the voice mail for..."

Lorene ran out of the lobby door, and saw Gary standing in the sand, fifteen feet from the chickee umbrella, staring up at the roof.

To his right, Gary heard an engine roaring, getting closer. A white police car was heading toward him, lights flashing, no siren.

Gary looked at Lorene. She was pale with fear, her eyes moist, her hands trembling as she clutched their child.

44

SOUTHWEST FLORIDA

Lia's lifeless body was draped across the top of the chickee like a throw rug. Her face, eyes open, staring at him, was the first thing the Marco policeman saw as he climbed to the top rung of a ten-foot ladder he'd borrowed from the hotel next door.

He had seen dead fish that way, even a shark once, beached in death, staring at the people who gathered to watch.

"Oh, shit, the people," officer Franco Mazzone said to himself, as he stared at the body, then down at the dozen or so tourists standing around the chickee.

The blood was coagulating at Lia's throat now, but there still was so much of it, soaking through the thatch, still dripping slowly from three places onto the sand.

Two women tugged on their children, pulling them away, but others were coming, attracted by the police van.

Mazzone punched in police headquarters' number on his iPhone.

"M-I-P-D, go ahead."

Mazzone recognized the voice of the shift officer on duty. "Mazzone here. We have a homicide near the Wavecrest condo building on the beach. It's a Caucasian, no, uh, Asian maybe, female, early twenties, throat cut, I think. And the body is on top of a chickee hut on the beach."

"Hang on Franco. Did you say the person is on top of a chickee?"

Franco glanced down again. At least twenty people were looking up at him now, hands shielding their eyes from the sun's glare.

"Yep and there's lots of blood."

"Is she alive?"

"I can't reach her well enough to tell for sure, but there's so much blood I, I doubt it."

One of the spectators shouted to Mazzone, "What is that up there, officer?"

Franco waved as if to say "Not now."

"Lieutenant, are you sending help? The medical examiner, more cops, what? I can't get her down by myself."

"Do not, repeat, do not move the body. We're on the way. A crowd there?"

"Yeah, getting bigger, need crime scene tape and some help with these people." "Affirmative. Jesus, Franco, what a day and it's not even nine o'clock."

One of the onlookers watching the crime scene on the beach approached officer Mazzone and said, "Excuse me young man, but I noticed you using a cell phone to call your headquarters. Don't you fellas have police radios anymore?"

"Yeah, but the brass prefers we use the cell phones, so we mostly do."

"Are they cheaper or what?"

"Beats me, but they're more secure than radios, the chief says. Like, if we're on a stakeout or something you want to keep quiet you don't use the radio, because everyone could know, even other cops."

The curious man followed Mazzone as he walked to his squad car. "So, don't you guys even say stuff like 'Ten-Four?' You know, those codes like on TV."

"Naw, different cop shops sometimes have different codes and it gets confusing, so we just use plain language mostly. It's a lot better."

The civilian nodded a small thank you and strolled away, clearly disappointed.

Officer Mazzone noticed that. *Geez you'd think seeing a dead body bleeding out on top of a chickee would be enough excitement for one day at the beach.*

—

"Did you see this, Mike?"

Heather West was in the WAND-TV newsroom in Fort Myers, holding up her cell phone.

"Some guy is tweeting from Marco Island, saying cops found a body on top of a beachfront chickee. Here's a photo, no kidding, Mike, a dead body, blood all over the place. "Wait. Now it says it's a woman and her throat is cut."

Heather, twenty-four years old, was relatively new to TV news. She was the anchor of the Noon News, a redhead who wore it pulled back, trying to appear older or at least more credible.

Mike Dykstra, the assignment manager, was already on the phone to Larry Pendleton, a cameraman who lived in East Naples and mostly worked out of the station's small news bureau in that part of the county. He was closest to Marco and drove the station's live truck, equipped with microwave capability and a backpack sized LiveU unit for live reports and video feeds from the field.

Larry was on his way to Marco Island's beach within five minutes of the call from the station. *This could be it, my ticket outta this market. If I do a great shoot, this body on the chickee could make GNS or at least the Florida News Network. Yeah, I'll follow-up with résumé videos showing me at work in the field. Sure hope this is a murder and not just a jumper. Gotta be, I mean whoever heard of somebody killing herself by cutting her own throat and then jumping off a building? Man, this may be the one.*

Larry knew he'd have a tough time getting onto the beach at the private residents' entrance. The retired gatekeepers in their cranberry golf shirts and pith helmets were tough as Terminators when it came to keeping people out unless they had a membership pass.

The cameraman turned off Collier Boulevard before he reached the private beach and headed toward Tigertail, a public beach with trails, a café and a gift shop where anyone could pay twelve dollars or so to park and get onto the beach for the day.

Two elderly women walking past the concession stand at Tigertail almost were blown over when the WAND Mobile Bureau sped by, down the ramp designed for beach vehicles and onto the expanse of white sand.

Larry turned south, breaking at least three county and state laws as he headed down the beach and parked near the spectators already crowding the crime scene.

He slapped the video camera onto his shoulder and elbowed his way through the bystanders until he could get a clean shot of the chickee, the coroner on the ladder and the body on the roof. He hit the on button, zoomed in on Lia's face, then panned down to the bloody mess that was her throat.

The coroner's assistant was under the chickee, using large plastic sandwich bags to collect blood-soaked clumps of sand. Every bloodstain went into the bags along with any other bits of anything found in the surrounding sand.

Officer Mazzone was standing a few feet away, talking with Lorene and Gary. Another officer was trying to herd people back from the scene, wishing more police would come to help him put up crime scene tape.

Two other cops were walking, head down, along the grass path between the Wavecrest condo and the hotel next door. Occasionally one would kick a divot or pick up a piece of litter.

"Officer Mazzone, come here, please," the coroner said to Franco from atop the ladder. "Bring me more baggies from my van there, thanks."

Larry moved his lens to a close-up of the coroner, then widened the shot to show the body as well. *This is great! I have a body on a beach chickee hut, cops everywhere, tourists buzzing about something they never expected to see on their day at the beach. Terrific.* He panned his camera up to show the other onlookers on their hotel balconies, most of them taking smart phone pictures. *They're probably emailing and tweeting their fingers off. But I'm the only TV shooter here. Yes!*

The coroner spotted a bulky object in the pocket of Lia's robe. He leaned across the thatch and poked a ballpoint pen into the pocket. The sun glinted off metal. The coroner prodded the object with the pen until it came free of the pocket and lay on Lia's thigh.

Larry zoomed in for a close up of the lighter. He had never seen a cigarette lighter that expensive, the gold, that satellite logo set in diamonds.

The coroner scooped the lighter into the plastic bag, then put the paper money, the bills, into a separate bag.

Police Detective Chico Belliard walked from his unmarked car to the chickee hut.

"Hey, Doc, whattaya think?"

"Come see this, Chico. This is no jumper. She didn't do this to herself. And I think she's been up here for an hour or so."

Larry smiled. *I'm getting it all, the cop and the coroner, the cigarette lighter, whatever it means, and that face. Wow, was she something! Need to get some sound from the bystanders, eyewitness stuff, then I'm outta here with a story. I sure hope GNS picks it up.*

Larry's luck continued. The second person into whose face he thrust his camera and mic turned out to be Lorene. She was standing back from the crowd, her son holding onto her upper leg.

"So, ma'am, what did you see?" Larry asked, while getting a tight shot of Lorene's face.

"See, what did I see? I saw it all. I was just there, reading my vampire recipe book, when the blood started dripping all over the page," Lorene said, sucking in her breath after every third or fourth word.

Oh Geez, she's a wacko, vampire, blood, yeah, right.

"So, um, Lorene, did you see the vampire that attacked that woman up there?"

"No, I didn't even see the dead person, but the blood…"

"Ma'am, did you say you were reading a vampire recipe book? Was that…oh never mind, that'll do it for now, thanks," Larry said, turning the camera away, wondering how the one nut case on the beach that day somehow found him and his camera.

Larry was laughing softly as he began scouting his next video prey, hoping he or she would not be a vampire.

"No, wait, it's true, the blood was dripping and I hollered for Gary and it dripped on him, too. Don't you want to hear our story?"

She was into it now, panting as she talked, but Larry moved away to an elderly man who might say something sane.

A half hour later, Larry phoned the WAND-TV newsroom, ready to feed his video to the station. He had elevated the mast on his microwave truck to its full height. Heather West was on the line with him in the feed-room near the assignment desk.

"Yeah, Larry, it's a clean feed, no snow and no audio problems."

"Hey, Heather, sweetie, do me a favor will you? Call GNS and tell 'em what we have. See if they want to take it in on the next feed to Atlanta."

"Well, Larry, what's in it for me then?" Heather asked with a smile.

"Dinner out, tonight."

"Where, Lare?"

"If GNS buys my stuff, Mangrove Café. If they don't, Dairy Queen."

"Oh, they'll want it when I tell 'em about the beauty with her throat cut on the beach. Hell, Lare, Judge Judy might even buy it from us, too."

He grinned, then confirmed the video was in-house at WAND-TV and began packing up to head back toward Naples.

Collier County deputies canvassed the nearby beachfront condos and hotels, questioning residents and guests, trying to identify the dead girl. Nobody knew her.

Blood on the sand made it clear she had not fallen or jumped from one of the two buildings. She had been killed on the ground, then tossed onto the top of the chickee.

Local TV, radio and the next day's *Naples Daily News and Fort Myers News Press* all had versions of the same story:

Beauty's Throat Slashed on Beach
Murder Mystery on Marco
Chickee Hut Slaying Perplexes Cops

Tourists Flock to Scene of Scenic Slicer
Marco's Cutthroat Killer
Unkindest Cut Disrupts Beachgoers' Vacations

GNS took in the video feed of Larry's story, shortened it to a fifty-five second voice-over by the anchor with video of the body, the lighter, the blood. Then sound bites with bystanders, one five seconds, the other seven. Then, more narration over pictures of the crime scene, ending with a close-up of the cigarette lighter.

The script ended with the anchor reading:

"Authorities say the cigarette lighter found on the body of the unidentified woman may be of some help in their investigation. They did not elaborate."

ATLANTA

The news story ran four times on GNS in the next twenty-four-hours.

Cassie Page saw it in the Channel 3 newsroom and called Hagan, breathless.

"Jimmy, did you see the GNS story on the Asian girl killed in Florida?"

The muscles in his stomach tightened. He forced his voice to stay calm. "What story, Cass? Asian girl?"

"Jimmy, it's her, Lia Lee, no question. Had her throat cut, found her on some beach hut or something. And Jimmy, she had a PTV cigarette lighter on her, the Phelps lighter. Jimmy, it has to be her!"

"Where was it in Florida?"

"Not sure, Jimmy, Gulf Coast, maybe Naples or little town near there. GNS will know. It's their video."

"Thanks Cass, call you soon. I'm outa here. Thanks, babe."

Ralph McIntosh saw the third GNS report from Marco Island and was on the phone to Hagan shortly after Jimmy talked to Cassie.

"Yes, Jesus, help me, yes, it's her, it's Lia, no question," he told Hagan. McIntosh sobbed harder, uncontrollably.

"Tia, now Lia, both dead, my God, Detective, what did we do to deserve this? Why? Why our precious girls?" he screamed, then hung up.

NewsBlitz3 did a live news update as soon as it fed the GNS video to the station. Other Atlanta TV stations did the same within the half hour.

Hagan's office already was in touch with the Marco Island Police Department. That office faxed and emailed a photo of the dead girl to Atlanta PD's Homicide Task Force within the hour.

Chief Lutz called Hagan and told him to come to his office and bring the photo. "Can we go ahead and announce it's the girl we want? Are we absolutely sure, Detective?"

Covering your ass, you slimy bastard. It'll be my butt if we're wrong on this. "Well, Chief, we always want a relative to make an eyeball positive ID, as you know. That is policy, Chief, unless you authorize us to bypass it."

"That'll cost us another twenty-four hours. Don't have time, Detective, don't have it. Let's go with the father ID from TV."

"Your call, Chief, fine with me. Oh, Chief, I wanna pick up this guy Phelps for questioning. He's connected somehow to that girl and he hates Bren Forrest and he smells."

Lutz coughed nervously. "We don't have anything on him, you know that. Do not pick him up. He's a VIP and he'll be around for a while, the Olympics and all, so, no, Detective, you are not to pick up Phelps. Watch him if you want, use a tail, but leave him alone unless otherwise instructed, understood?"

Jimmy scrolled the "favorites" list on his phone and tapped on Cassie's name.

"Cassie, Jimmy here. Listen, you might want to report police are investigating Ian Phelps in this case. Yeah, no, wait…just wait a sec… listen to me. Just say 'Sources say Phelps may be questioned by police.' It's about the lighter thing. Keep it vague, but say his name a lot, as much as you can. What? Yes, it is true, I don't have the go-ahead to nail him yet. But we're tailing him, so just say he may be a suspect and let's see what he does."

45

SOUTHWEST FLORIDA

"Here it is, Sarge. Atlanta PD says the girl's name probably is Lia Lee," Officer Wally Nettles shouted to the duty sergeant across the room. He was reading an email from Atlanta PD to Marco Island Police.

Nettles was printing the message when Larry Pendleton walked in. He finished his microwave feed to WAND-TV and was hoping to get a fresh sound bite or two for the six o'clock local news.

"Hey, Wally, did ya see my stuff on GNS? Just like we sent it, every shot, cool eh?"

The policeman smiled.

"Way ahead of you, my boy," he said. "We already have an ID on the dead woman."

Larry reached for the paper in the deputy's hand. Nettles pulled it away.

"Not so fast there, Clark Kent," he teased Larry. "We'll have to clear this before we release it, ya know?"

Sergeant Dwight Grissom walked over from his desk.

"Atlanta has a detective and a forensics man on the way here now," he said. Noticing Larry, he whispered to the officer, hand curled over his mouth.

"Email says she was wanted for questioning in a murder in Atlanta. And they're asking about a cigarette lighter found on the body."

Larry fidgeted with the keys to his mobile bureau truck.

"Sarge, help me out here. Give me the girl's ID and whatever, and then you can call a news conference and get yourself some big-time TV exposure. I just need a half- hour head start."

Sergeant Grissom realized Larry's plan made sense. He could put the local TV guy in his debt, plus get a hit on GNS with a TV news conference. He would show off that fancy cigarette lighter. Perfect.

"Larry, we'll do it for cameras in forty-five minutes, here. Meantime, you can report the dead woman on Marco Island was a homicide victim, an Asian or Asian-American, name, Lia Lee, L-E-E, estimated age twenty-two to twenty-four. Her throat was cut. So far, no suspects, no motive. All right?"

Larry hollered his thanks as he dashed to his TV live truck and phoned the WAND-TV newsroom.

—

Ian Phelps was in 4D, the last first class seat available on Delta's mid-morning flight from Fort Myers to Atlanta. O'Reilly and Jax were in coach, Jax fuming in a middle seat near the rear. O'Reilly lucked out with an aisle seat over the wing.

Phelps plugged his smart phone into the in-flight Internet access at his seat and sent a message to GNS board member Jim Jenkins in Atlanta.

"Jim, Ian here, in the air, on my way. Just wanted to get a briefing before the board meeting this afternoon. Leave me a message at the Ritz Buckhead. I should be there in, say, about ninety minutes. Talk to you then."

Phelps was relaxing a little now, two scotches, no ice, and about seven hours after the situation with Lia. Bloody bitch, better off with her dead, as it turns out. By the time they find her, I'll be in Atlanta, no trace of me ever seeing her on the island.

He was lucky to get on this flight. From the Wavecrest, Phelps had driven the mile or so back to his house and called Delta. Jax threw the clothes he was wearing in a dumpster at a garden apartment complex. He had not seen any blood on them, but he took no chances.

O'Reilly made the fifty-mile drive from Marco Island to the Fort Myers airport in fifty-five minutes, cautiously staying within the speed limit. They snared three of the few seats left on the Delta flight.

I'll be in Atlanta a little earlier than I planned but what the hell, so what? I'll have time to grab a nap before the board meeting. If the other partners lean on her, Forrest will make a deal.

He dozed restlessly, wishing he could attend that meeting of the GNS board of directors. *I'd like to watch her squirm as the boys get it done. Fly on the wall I'd like to be, I would. Maybe I should change the name of GNS, maybe PGNS, yeah, love that, the Phelps Global News Service. Or maybe I'll just add it to my existing Phelps Television brand, PTV. That way I wouldn't have to change my logo!*

ATLANTA

"Yes, Art, NewsBlitz3 has learned the board of directors of GNS is meeting today to consider a sale of the all-news channel."

Cassie was on live, doing an update on the investigation into the murder of Cav Campbell, the discovery of Lia Lee's body and the dead woman's possible connection to the killing.

"We've also learned Lia Lee, the woman found murdered on a beach in Florida, is one of several persons whose names have surfaced in a drug scandal brewing at GNS."

Her beloved Detective Hagan came through for Cassie again. He had told her about Lia's name on the list of customers the GNS drug pusher had produced.

—

"Here's the rundown, Chief," Jimmy Hagan said, standing in front of Chief Lutz's desk. "We know Lia Lee was at the party and was seen talking to Campbell. We believe when Campbell went off the balcony, he had a PTV lighter in his hand and it landed in the fountain.

"We know when Lee was killed, in Florida, she had a Phelps TV lighter with her.

"There's a lotta talk around that Ian Phelps has been pressuring Bren Forrest again to sell GNS to him. One of the minority partners said as much when we talked to him.

"That's what we know. Here's what we think, Cav Campbell was using cocaine, a lot of it. Connection unknown. We think Lia Lee was a cokehead, too. We're waiting for the autopsy to see whether it's in her system.

"The rat at GNS, Bastige, thinks his drug supplier has a place in Europe and one in Florida. Phelps fits that, Chief. Marco PD thinks Phelps may have a residence on the island and they're working on that. Marco is the town where Lia Lee was murdered overnight."

Lutz frowned and brushed a fleck of dandruff off the braid of his uniform.

"So, what's your next step, Detective?"

"Sir, I think we should pick up Phelps, bring him in, lean on him a little. I think he's our guy, he's behind this whole thing and..."

"Get real, Hagan," Lutz erupted. "You have nothing concrete on Phelps. And he is a heavy hitter, not the sort we 'bring in' as you call it, without something concrete to go on. No way do we arrest him, not unless you get the smoking gun on him, you understand?"

Hagan fumed, knowing there was no point in arguing.

"Well, how about we just chat with him someplace, you know, a casual meeting, maybe at the GNS sky box tonight, at the Olympics opening ceremonies?"

Lutz frowned again and thought for a moment before he answered.

"I want full security there for Ms. Forrest, of course. If, in the course of your duties, you engage Mr. Phelps in conversation, so be it. But, Jimmy, don't screw this up. I have enough VIPs on my butt now, understand?"

Hagan smiled, nodded and walked out. He knew where he had to go next and was in a hurry to get there.

46

GNS HEADQUARTERS

"Like I told the narcs, I don't know the guy or for sure where he is."

Ned Bastige was sitting with Jimmy Hagan on the patio at GNS, a leafy, brick-floored, outdoor extension of the break room. In cooler weather, a lot of GNS employees sat out there for coffee or snacks, but in this July heat, Bastige and Hagan were alone.

"You gave the other detectives a log-on address, right? Well what about a screen name. What was your screen name?"

Bastige avoided eye contact and shook his head slightly."It doesn't mean anything bad, just a name I picked, same as the nickname of my all-time favorite ball player."

"What's the word, Ned?" Hagan's irritation and impatience was in his voice. *I don't have time to sit out here and sweat with this asshole.*

"Um, Hammer," Bastige said, almost in a whisper.

"Hammer?" Jimmy was almost shouting. "You named your drug-dealing computer name after Hank Aaron? You silly bastard! Hammer, my ass," Jimmy said as he stood up.

"You're lucky I don't tell Hank and have him and a few of his fans come down here and show you what a real hammer is."

He sat down abruptly and put his face within an inch of Ned's nose.

"Now, Ned, listen very carefully," Hagan said in a semi-whisper. "I have another question for you. I already know the answer, so if you give me the wrong answer, 'Enngghh'—the buzzer goes off and you lose, big, big time, you dig?"

Bastige nodded, sweating now from more than the heat.

"Ned, how long were you selling drugs to Cav Campbell?"

Ned looked up slowly, smiling slightly. "Detective, Cav Campbell stopped paying for his drugs a long time ago. Oh sure, he still used cocaine. He just didn't pay for it. That sonofabitch was a deadbeat. I mean, he probably didn't pay for the last six or eight orders. It was always, 'Hey, you know you can trust me for it, I mean, Bren's good for it, right?' I never knew whether she knew, but he lived off her anyway, so what the hell."

Bastige was a gusher of information now. "I kept reporting his non-payments to the boss, but he said keep on supplying Campbell, just like normal."

"When did he tell you that last?"

Bastige lit a cigarette. "I guess about three weeks ago."

"How does he communicate with you, computer only?"

"Yep. Detective, you'll protect me on this, right? I mean I'm telling you guys every damn thing, so no jail time for me, right? Right?"

"You keep talkin', Ned, you keep walkin'. For now, anyway. Tell you what, let's you and me try to contact your guy on the computer right now."

———

"Mr. Jenkins, we've been down this road before. I do not see why I should sell out to Phelps, just because you and the other partners think it's a good idea."

Bren Forrest was sitting in her usual seat at a round oak table, perhaps twenty feet across. Her executive officers and directors were the only shareholders invited to this meeting in the GNS boardroom, and therefore, Phelps was not there.

Somebody in the Human Resources Department told Bren Forrest a couple of years ago that a round conference table in a board room was more conducive to consensus and conviviality. She thought it was a crock, but she agreed to get the big, round table. So far today, it wasn't working.

"Ms. Forrest, it's simple. We want out. GNS has had a good run but the truth is, the action is moving elsewhere now. All news is not news anymore. We want to get even more heavily into social media, interactive, multi-media, blah, blah, blah, you know the bit."

"Yes, I do, and it doesn't wash. We are doing all those things now, and you know it. And we're spending a bundle on research and development, the next platform, the next Silicon Valley magic, all that…."

Jenkins interrupted. "Yes, and at enormous expense. We want to take our money and buy into smaller companies that are doing these things already. But on a smaller scale, more innovative, less derivative."

Bren stood, leaning forward, the tips of her fingers touching the table.

"Mr. Jenkins, gentlemen, you asked for this meeting, telling me you had new information of significance to proffer. I have heard nothing new so far. So, unless you have something else, I suggest we adjourn until after the Olympics."

Jenkins exchanged glances with the others at the table. Then he stood and faced Bren, who remained on her feet.

"Ms. Forrest, Bren, I am sorry to tell you this. I hoped I would not have to. I hoped we could come to an agreement. Bren, we have waited longer than we wanted, because of your personal tragedy, the untimely death of Mr. Campbell."

She started to speak, but Jenkins held up his hand gently. She nodded, crossing her arms now.

"Please, please listen carefully, Bren. Those of us, who together own forty-eight percent of GNS, have agreed to sell our interests, all of it, all forty-eight percent in one package, to Ian Phelps."

Bren's body shifted, sagged a little. She was stunned. She knew nothing of that deal, assumed at least half the minority partners would refuse to sell, keeping her control safe. She blinked and swallowed.

"I, I can't, I mean why? That puts him so close!"

"Ms. Forrest, you are correct. Phelps is so close now that if he launches a hostile takeover, he'll no doubt succeed. He can offer enough to the small shareholders, kick up the stock so many of them will sell. We figure he can get fifty-one percent, controlling interest, in six months, maybe less."

Bren sat down slowly, melting back into her chair, her face drained. She started to speak, then stopped. Her hand fluttered to her face, then to the silver brooch above her left breast. Campbell gave it to her several months before.

Jim Jenkins rose and walked over to Bren's chair.

"Bren, dear," he said, touching her shoulder, then moving a step away, "Bren, sell. Sell to Phelps now and you'll get top dollar. You'll have a fortune. You can jump on the next wave in this business and pioneer another level. Do it, Bren, for your own sake."

She lowered her head, moving it slowly side to side, her mind racing, emotions and thoughts neck and neck. *These guys really don't get what GNS means to me, and maybe there's no way they could know. All they care about is the money they've invested. How about the success we have had in building the network, slowly, steadily, from those first days in our so-called headquarters. That rundown, rented frame house on West Peachtree Street. Thirty or forty of us sharing enormous enthusiasm and too few restrooms, preparing to go on the air in less than three months.*

These money men thought I was going to run through the millions Whit left me like shit through a goose, as Dad used to say. It took me a year to convince them that a global TV news network was viable. They scoffed when I told them someday the GNS brand name would be as big as Coke.

But enough of them knew eventually Whit and I shared this dream. We were talking seriously about it just a week or two before the, the crash...

Maybe they didn't realize Whit's death spurred me on, and after I recovered from my injuries—what a long ordeal that was— I made it happen!

Now, now after fifteen years, at the top of our game, this bunch wants me to sell to a conniving bastard who thinks I'm a weak, crybaby socialite? Well. It's time to let them know GNS not only stands for Global News Service. In terms of their conspiracy, GNS also stands for Gonads Not Succeeding.

Bren looked around the table, fixing her eyes on each of the men, one at a time, her backbone now as strong as the rod in her left leg.

"Do you gentlemen also know who killed Cav?" Their reaction made it obvious the testosterone in the room had just gone out for a smoke.

She said it with a quizzical smile, a little sly, almost flirtatious.

"Is that your next little missile to fire here? I mean," she said rising to her feet again, "are you here for the reward money, too?" She was almost shouting now. No smiling.

"You want me to give up my company? Did you all have him killed to make me crazy? Is that it? Yeah, that's the ticket. Let's kill Bren Forrest and take over GNS. No, wait, that's too obvious. We'll kill her celebrity boyfriend instead, and she'll be so sad she'll just want to go hide at her snooty stables and talk to her horses. Is that what you thought?"

Mumbles of protest bubbled up from the table, but she waved them down.

"Well, gentlemen, I have made my decision. If Mr. Phelps wants to own GNS, he'll have to get it a few shares at a time. I am not afraid of him, and I'm not afraid of any of you. So, whichever among you are his toadies, his little info-gatherers, his GNS spies, go tell Mr. Phelps for me, quote, 'Go fuck yourself!'"

47

ATLANTA

Ian Phelps was torn between panic and triumph.

He stood at the window of his suite at the Ritz Carlton in Buckhead looking out at Phipps Plaza, Atlanta's most upscale close-in shopping mall, and on to the northwest.

The phrase, *one big, bleedin' suburb,* flitted through his thoughts as he stared out, barely focused on the cityscape. Phelps was digesting the news he'd received in the past fifteen minutes.

"Yes, her words exactly, Ian," Jim Jenkins had said into the phone. "She dared you to go get the stock you need to take control. And she shouted some gibberish about whether we were demanding the reward money for Cav Campbell's death. It's as though she thought we had a hand in it. She even said as much."

"What in hell is she on about, the reward money?" he asked. "Come on then, Jim, you were there, what'd she mean? I mean, is she serious or off her nut or what?"

"No, she's not crazy, crazed maybe about Campbell's death and all that, but she knows what she's doing. And she's going public tonight, telling the world she's standing alone against the evil men around her and your satanic effort to take away her precious G-N-goddam-S."

"What do you mean she's 'going public?'"

She's called a news conference in the GNS skybox, well, up there somewhere, tonight before the opening ceremonies. Shit, half the world press will be there, some going live. Ian, you are screwed, my friend, unless you have something else up your sleeve.

Shoulda done her, too, along with Campbell, I should. So, now what? Maybe I'll just go confront her in front of the press and announce...

274

"Ian? Ian, you there?"

Phelps coughed and cleared his throat.

"Jim, yes, I hear you. Jim, I think Ms. Bren Forrest has been stubborn long enough. We'll just have to take her company the hard way. Jim you might want to attend that news conference at the skybox tonight. I will be there, too, to announce our friendly effort to acquire GNS and how it now will be a definite event, whether she likes it or not."

———

Jimmy Hagan walked quickly up the four steps of Atlanta homicide headquarters and into the office, a smile on his face. He tossed his poplin suit jacket onto a wooden table and grabbed the cordless phone at his desk on the fourth ring.

"Jimmy, hey, what's new, Copperhead?"

Cassie called him Copperhead when she wanted to tease him. It always brought a smile. Copper was what the neighborhood kids back in Cabbagetown called policemen when Jimmy was growing up. Some kid saw Edward G. Robinson use the term in a gangster movie and it spread among the boys in the neighborhood who liked to sound tough and disrespectful.

Jimmy wished sometimes he had never told Cassie about that, but he actually liked it when she used the term. She reminded him the "head" part of the loving nickname was for the copperish color of his hair. She used it most when they were making love. She laughed a lot during sex, and Jimmy thought that was the coolest thing he ever saw from a woman in passion.

"What's new? More than I can tell you, Cass. What's up with you??"

"Jimmy, geez, what more do you guys need to go get Phelps? The Lee girl had his lighter, or one of 'em, on her when she was killed. Phelps has a place on that island and..."

"Hey, slow down Cass. Listen to Copper and learn, darlin'."

"Well, I just think he's a likely susp..."

"Cassie, wait a minute, wait. Now, listen to me."

Hagan turned to a window, his back to the day room and cupped the phone in his hand. "Where are you going to be about seven o'clock? I have something you'll want, but we can't talk about it right now."

"Probably on the air, Jimmy. We'll be going live with Bren Forrest's news conference from the stadium, then I'll do a package report for the late show on the opening ceremonies. So, yeah, I'll be at the stadium then."

"Outside or inside?"

"Hell, outside, you know they won't let us in. We will take the pool feed from GNS, then do our own live commentary from the designated camera zone outside the east side of the stadium."

"Okay, can you meet me at Winners, that bar between the stadium and the expressway at, say six forty-five?"

"Well, sure, for a couple of minutes, yeah, see you there, Copper!"

—

The Tower of Babble didn't have as many languages in use as did the news media gathered at the camera zone outside Olympic Stadium. At least forty-five video cameras on tripods lined the chalk marker, each focused on one or two on-air reporters, jabbering about the Games to begin officially with opening ceremonies in about an hour.

Only GNS reporters and cameras were allowed inside the stadium, along with pool reporters from Associated Press, Reuters, CBS Radio News, the Los Angeles Times, Deutsche Welle, the German broadcast service, and a Spanish-speaking radio reporter from Univision Audio.

They would have to make their coverage, audio and video, available to all the world's TV and news outlets from the media center, set up in a swarm of doublewide mobile homes directly south of the stadium.

Pool video from GNS's thirty live cameras would be fed to local stations that paid a fee for the service. With that video, NewsBlitz3 and the other stations could go on live for short bursts, featuring their reporters, lined up on the chalk.

Cassie walked into Winners, its air-conditioned semi-darkness washing over her. She saw Jimmy in a booth in the back, idly watching a bowling tournament on one of the many ESPN channels.

She slid into the booth alongside him and rubbed his leg with her hand.

"Why so tense, police boy," she grinned, stroking his leg. He reached down and took her hand.

"Well, I think we have a killer on our hands here. Any interest, or are you just down here to cover the ceremonial symbols of brotherhood and world peace?"

Cassie reached inside his leg and nudged him in the crotch.

"I got your brotherhood right here, copper," she said, smiling as he sat up with a start.

"Whoa, madam, this is a public place, and I'll have you know I am not that kind of man."

"Sure feels like it to me."

She pulled her hand away, sat in a mock prim fashion, hands locked on the table.

"Well, Detective, why did you call this meeting?"

He touched her leg under the table and frowned.

"Cassie, I think you ought to report Ian Phelps is a definite suspect in the murder of Cav Campbell. Source it 'authorities,' not even Atlanta PD, understand?"

"Great, but can I give 'em something concrete when they ask why?"

"We traced some computer messages to him, or at least to his office in London. He definitely had something to do with Cav Campbell's death. Probably set up the hit, hired that Asian girl. We have no proof yet, but I intend to smoke him out at the stadium tonight, see if I can get him to stumble."

—

The GNS skybox was the size of a four-car garage, jutting out along the east edge of the venue. Still, the box was way too small to handle the TV and other media that turned out for Bren Forrest's news conference.

The Olympics committee relented and let in all accredited media people for Bren's news conference. They would have to leave immediately afterward. Those who were there early managed to crowd into the skybox. Late arrivals were shunted to the concourse where they could watch the GNS coverage of the news conference on the big screens mounted around the stadium.

At seven o'clock, Bren Forrest stepped out of a small dressing room at the rear of the skybox and walked to the bank of microphones. It was a good TV shot, Bren up close, her bright blue suit in brilliant contrast to the slightly darkened backdrop of the entire stadium interior.

"Ladies and gentlemen," Bren began, her hand raised, a slight smile on her face. "Please, if I could have your attention. I have a statement, a brief one, and then I'll take your questions.

"First, let me dispel the rumors about the future of Global News Service. I created it. I built it with the help of many wonderful people. And I am going to continue to own GNS."

"Ms. Forrest, what about..."

"Let me finish, please," she said to the grizzled reporter from the *Dunwoody Crier* who interrupted her.

"There is talk of an effort to take over GNS by some of the minority partners. The fact is, soon there will be only one other person with a significant block of GNS stock. All my partners are selling their stock to Mr. Ian Phelps, who most of you know about, the owner of PTV in London.

"Mr. Phelps wants to control GNS. I gather he will try to do so with a hostile takeover attempt. Mr. Phelps convinced the partners to sell out to him. And the key word here is, sellout, if you get my drift."

Bren took a deep breath and a dozen or more reporters filled the space with questions, a jumble of noise. Bren waited, saying nothing. After a few seconds the questions subsided, but as Bren started to speak, a loud voice interrupted from the rear of the room.

"Ms. Forrest, perhaps you should point out that all of your partners want to sell and the only 'hostile' part of this nonsense is you!"

The voice was that of Ian Phelps, who was standing on his toes, straining to see and be seen over the crowd of press people. He was shouting to be heard. Most of the TV photographers swiveled their cameras on the tripods to focus on Phelps.

"Use the mics!" one cameraman shouted to Phelps, who by now was jostling forward, trying to get to the makeshift mic stand.

"Mr. Phelps, you are not welcome here," Bren said, her eyes blazing with anger. "Get your own forum, sir," she hissed.

Phelps pushed his way to the front, stood to the side of the microphones and leaned in.

"My friends, there is no reason for anger here. This is business. Just business. I want Ms..."

"Yes, it's my business," Bren interrupted, "and you're trying to steal it, Mr. Phelps. So, take your little armed robbery somewhere else!"

Phelps was shouting now, his face red.

"See this?" he gestured to the cameras, showing the PTV logo on his gold and diamond pinkie ring. "See this logo? PTV covers a fifth of the world already and soon we'll be merging these two giants.

"GNS will be better than it is now and the smaller stockholders will be thrilled!"

"Well, you don't own it yet! So I invite you to get the hell out of my skybox until you do. Out, Phelps, get out now!" Bren pointed toward the exit, her arm arched, her long forefinger aimed at the door, like a school teacher ordering a fourth grader to go to the principal's office.

Some of the reporters were stunned by the scene unfolding in front of them. Outside the box, many of the print reporters stared up at the big screens, on the stadium walls. Some were scribbling notes. Others were talking into their smart phones or small, digital recorders.

"Mr. Phelps, Mr. Phelps, question, sir!" a local television reporter shouted. Phelps turned.

"Mr. Phelps, there's a TV report here that you are a suspect in the murder of Cav Campbell. What's your comment on that?"

The room shifted into what seemed like slow motion. Phelps turned his head from side to side as though he expected an attack from his flank. He frowned, then snarled at the reporter.

"You bloody asshole. You little shit, ya, keep your crap to yourself, hear me?"

Bren slowly turned toward to Phelps, seeming to stare through him as he yelled at the reporter.

"Now listen, you lot. You cannot smear the name of Ian Phelps and PTV with such nonsense and anybody who does will pay the price, know what I mean?"

"But, Mr. Phelps, what about that re...."

"I am out of here now and finished with you bunch of wankers," Phelps spat, as he pushed his way through the news people toward the door.

Bren watched him go, seeming not to be touched by the clamor. She didn't move, just glared.

"Are you a killer, Mr. Phelps?" shouted a reporter for a TV tabloid show.

"Up yours, mate," Phelps hissed as he pushed out the door and into the concourse. Jax was waiting for him there.

"Keep these assholes away from me," he shouted to Jax as they bolted from the news conference. As they half jogged toward an exit, stirring music filled the stadium.

The Olympics opening ceremonies were about to start.

"People of the world, in a few moments, please join us in tribute to the athletes of the world as they enter this place of peace and good will." The voice of the stadium announcer boomed through the place, reverberating off the walls, bringing a roar from the seventy thousand spectators, all standing now.

—

As Phelps jogged around a corner on the concourse, he saw two uniformed Atlanta policemen and a third man in a rumpled suit, tie loose. They were no more than two hundred feet away. Phelps froze.

"Hey, Mr. Phelps," Jimmy Hagan shouted. "We need to speak with you."

Phelps ran to his left, sweat dripping into his eyes. To him, the cops suddenly looked like the Hobby Bobbies in the down-and-out neighborhood in Manchester, England, where Phelps grew up. As a kid, he took after his no-account father and became a petty criminal, stealing apples or sweets from neighborhood merchants. He ran a lot there, always outrunning the law and the angry shopkeepers.

Those escapes filled him with euphoria and with feelings he would be successful one day, respectable, too.

No way I'm going to give in and give that up now...so close to it....so close... need to get away from these assholes, get away to the island maybe...lay low...then get back...somehow, get those BBC pricks.

Now, as he and Jax ran toward the exit ramp, Phelps's brain was abuzz with fleeting images—himself in handcuffs, behind bars, a judge with a gavel, Lia's face. He envisioned his empire crumbling, his veneer of success smashed, his dream of besting the BBC evaporating.

They ran faster, down the ramp and out to the sedan, with O'Reilly at the wheel, engine on, doors open. They were away and out of the stadium grounds by the time Jimmy and the other police officers reached ground level.

48

MARCO ISLAND

Phelps was scared and giddy at the same time.

His escape from Olympic Stadium, O'Reilly's skillful driving and their quick takeoff from DeKalb Peachtree Airport had eluded Atlanta police.

Criminal activity was old hat to him, but he'd never actually been the subject of a high-speed police chase before. It was a scary, but thrilling experience, hence the giddiness, still with him as his private jet landed at Marco Island airport.

The field was quiet, the office closed, the landing lights on the single runway controlled from the air by the pilot. No welcoming party wanted, none present, except for the roomy sedan that awaited his arrival, courtesy of the A-Action Transportation Company. O'Reilly had phoned them from the plane and reserved the car to take the three men to Phelps's home on the island.

Phelps heard his jet taking off, even as his taxi already was on the road, almost to the bridge and over the water to Marco.

The taxi driver, Peter, was wondering about this client, whom he had driven a few times before. *I know the one guy is O'Reilly and the tough-looking one seems like a bodyguard. But the boss? Never heard his name, pays in cash. Seems aloof, his mind elsewhere. Oh well, not my business. And the tips are great.*

Phelps relaxed as they neared his home on Landmark Bay. Nobody on Marco knew where he lived except this taxi driver and he didn't know Phelps's name. The house, his car and his boat all were registered to an offshore dummy company.

This should be the safest place to be. The cops in Atlanta will think I scooted back to Europe or someplace as far away as I can get. We can regroup here, low profile, and figure out the next step. Seems we have everything we need.

In the house, Jax turned on the TV, hoping to find an ultimate fighting match, a sport he liked a lot more than boxing.

"Bloody hell, Jax, find GNS will ya," Phelps snapped, wanting a news update that well could include him. What he saw was recap coverage of the opening ceremonies of the Olympics. Even though he just "left" that building a few hours before, the pomp and ceremony, the athletes on parade, the dancers and all the rest seemed a world away.

ATLANTA POLICE HEADQUARTERS

Jimmy Hagan was in what passed for Police Chief Lutz's woodshed.

"Detective, how am I going to explain to the mayor that a man wanted for three murders eluded you and your men and apparently flew out of town, flew on a private jet to who knows where?"

"Chief, listen, please, can I just say we don't have time for that right now? You can beat me up later, but we have to find out where he might have gone and ..."

"No, you listen. You, you..." The chief sighed, his shoulders slumped, and he said in almost a whisper, "Jimmy, do what you have to do, but realize my career and yours are on the line. You know the rules, but get creative and get him, one way or the other."

Jimmy was on the phone with Cassie as soon as the chief was out of earshot.

"That's amazing," Cassie said, when Jimmy told her what the chief said.

"The suits here at the TV station just told me to forget any Olympics stories and focus on the manhunt for Phelps. They're even authorizing travel if it's absolutely necessary. By the way how'd he get away, do you know?"

"We'll talk about that later. Right now I have a load of calls to make and I may have to go to Florida tomorrow to try to find Phelps, if he's there. And I think he is."

"Great, I'm sure I can get a photog and we can go together," Cassie said, excitement in her voice. "Marco Island, right?"

"Yeah, the odds are he's around there somewhere, and I think he'll hide out there before he uses a private plane to get farther away. It's worth a shot."

"That works, Jimmy, see you at home in an hour or so. I'll call Delta and book a flight to Fort Myers and see about a rental car and a place to stay on the island. If we can, let's try to leave here before noon."

49

MARCO ISLAND

"Welcome, it's a great day at the Marco Beach Hilton," said the perky young woman at the reception desk. "Are you checking in?"

"Yes, thank you," Cassie replied, "We have two rooms reserved, under the names Cassandra Page and Daryl Evans."

Because Daryl, the NewsBlitz3 cameraman, was assigned to the story with Cassie, she and Jimmy had debated on the flight from Atlanta what to do about the sleeping and room arrangements.

"We'll just tell Daryl not to mention you and I shared a room," Jimmy had said. "You know, what happens on the road stays on the road, right?"

"Sure, no problem," Cassie responded sarcastically. "He can keep a secret, no question. Get real, Jimmy. You do know Daryl is a news photographer, don't you? News, Jimmy. You know, finding out stuff and then telling everybody. We'd be the talk of Atlanta."

"Maybe, but…"

"Jimmy, in our business the news photogs know everything. And they tell everything. It's their currency."

"Well, then let's just tell Daryl at the hotel and see whether he'd be comfortable with it. He might even think maybe it's the least he could do for landing this cushy Florida sun and fun assignment."

As Cassie, Jimmy and Daryl waited in the lobby for an elevator, Jimmy said, as casually as he could, "Everybody on board with the room situation?"

"I hope we have a good view of the beach and the gulf," Daryl said.

"The lady at the desk said we both do," Cassie said, "I mean both rooms do. I mean not the exact same view, but both are beach view. Same beach, different rooms, I mean…"

"Guys, I'm cool with, as you put it, 'the room situation.' Not to worry."

Jimmy started to talk, stopped, then said, "Well, are you surprised or…?

"Detective, Cassie, don't worry about it. "

"So then when we get back to Atlanta you'll keep it to yourself?" Jimmy asked.

"Yeah, sure. Anyway, it's not my day to watch you."

—

"Welcome, I'm Jeff Packer, glad to meet you," the Marco Island chief of police said to Jimmy, as he walked into the police department headquarters, next to the fire department complex.

"Let me brief you on what we're doing and then we'll show you how to get to the airport. You'll be working with Collier County Sheriff's personnel there, because the airport is off the island, not in the Marco city limits. But on a case like this, we work together.

"The airport is out there, not far from a lot of wild things. And that's just in the bar at the nearby golf course," the chief said with a grin."

Jimmy knew about the jurisdiction situation, having set up his meetings with local authorities in a phone call from Atlanta. Already sheriff's deputies had a man at the Marco airport in case Phelps showed up there.

"Since mid-morning, we've had two officers canvassing the island," Chief Packer told Jimmy, "convenience stores, drugstores, gas stations, dry cleaners and so forth. They're showing everybody the cell phone photo of Phelps, the one your guys in Atlanta e-mailed to us late last night.

"So far, no hits, Detective," Packer said, "but we'll be checking restaurants and bars, too. And, you said on the phone you'd have a TV news team with you. Are they here now?"

Jimmy nodded. "Yes, the reporter is Cassandra Page and her cameraman's name is Daryl Evans. They dropped me off here at your office, and they're out getting some general cover video around the island. Cassie probably will want to interview you soon for her report to Atlanta for the six o'clock local news there. So, she should be back here shortly."

A heavy rain was pelting Cassie's rental Ford Escape as she turned off San Marco Drive into police headquarters.

The downpour was one of those almost daily thundershowers that subtropical places endure, the kind of rain that can go from gentle showers to frog stranglers to puffy clouds in no time. Jimmy was waiting at the door, watching for Cassie's car and when it pulled up, he ran through the rain and piled into the back seat, laughing at the fast-changing weather.

"The cops here say this won't last long," he said, brushing water from both shoulders.

"Well, we didn't get much video and don't have a lot of time," Cassie said.

"So let's go in and get the interview, then we'll head out to the airport."

"Cassie, this is Chief Packer, Marco PD. Chief, one of Atlanta's best reporters, Cassandra Page."

Cassie did a quick on-camera interview with Chief Packer. In a nutshell, he told her they think Phelps might be on Marco and the search continues.

"Okay, Cassie, we're going to the Marco airport."

Chief Packer told Jimmy the Sheriff's Department said there were no private planes parked at the airstrip that morning, but someone could fly in or out of there at night and only the reptiles would notice.

At the airport, Daryl recorded video of the long runway and the airport terminal building. Boring, and maybe not even relevant, Daryl thought. But his news photographer's spirits rose when he saw the nest of crocodiles near the low berm that ran alongside the runway. He counted eight crocs for sure, but also saw some movement in the dark water that could have been more.

He was right, but didn't know it. The eight crocs he saw were females, but at least a couple of males lurked nearby.

Not sure how we'll use that video, but you don't see crocodiles at an airport every day. So, I know we'll figure a way to work it in. I can hear the promo already, "Manhunt in the Everglades— Reptiles restless—is Media Mogul hiding in the swamp?"

"Let's go, Daryl," Cassie said, throwing her oversized tote over her shoulder. "They said the TV station's East Naples bureau is at least twenty-five minutes from here."

They made it in twenty. As they walked into the bureau, a producer was on the phone, nodding, then, seeing Daryl and Cassie, said, "If you're Cassandra, this is for you. Atlanta."

"Cassie, you're all set at the WAND-TV bureau to do a report for Atlanta to use for the top of the six o'clock show."

It was Chuck at the NewsBlitz3 assignment desk. "Keep it to two minutes and include your on-camera closer."

"I need three minutes," she said firmly, knowing the moon landing wouldn't even get three minutes if it happened in these "modern" times of short attention spans by newsies and viewers alike.

"Unless you have video of Ian Phelps being drawn and quartered alive, you cannot go more than two and a half. Period. We have a little thing called the Olympics, remember?"

"Chuck," she said, softly now, almost coyly or as coyly as Cassie ever was, with anyone but Jimmy Hagan, "Chuckie, how about crocodiles, live, ugly crocodiles and they're not at Disney World either. Crocs, Chuck. So, two-forty-five, right?"

When she hung up, Daryl was already editing the video, starting with the restless reptiles.

50

ATLANTA

Bren Forrest's feelings of hatred and revenge toward Ian Phelps washed over her in waves of adrenalin, anxiety and alarm. Gone, temporarily at least, was the euphoria she felt about GNS's fifteenth anniversary, the GNS wall-to-wall coverage of the Olympics, still in its early stages, and her resolve to keep the company Phelps tried to take away.

With him at large, she felt she had to do something, anything to make sure he didn't get away without paying for his crimes.

She thought about calling Chief Lutz but quickly discarded idea. Max Ippolito. Yes, Max will know the latest and give me some guidance.

He answered on the second ring.

"Yes, ma'am, yes. For sure. We know Phelps has not been found. Did you see Cassandra Page's report at six from Florida? No, not to my knowledge, but I do know Detective Hagan is down there, working with the local law enforcement.

"Yes, ma'am, Jimmy, uh, Detective Hagan, is pretty sure Phelps is on Marco Island or nearby…of course, yes, the lighter, it was found near Lia Lee's body on the chickee hut thing at the beach.

"Ms. Forrest, would you like me to get Jimmy to call you? Tell him what you just told me about the reward money? It could help a lot. Yes. Should he call you upstairs, at home?"

"No, I'll find out how to reach the detective from Chief Lutz and call him myself. Thanks, Max."

Jimmy was in the hotel room when his cell phone rang. He assumed it was Cassie.

"Hey, Cass, I'll bet you're ready for a glass of wine or three, right? Did the piece for your six o'clock show go well?"

"Actually, I would love 'a glass of wine or three,' maybe four, Detective, but that's not why I called."

"Uh oh. Is this, I mean, uh, Ms. Forrest, is that you?"

She apologized for bothering him and asked if there were any new developments in the hunt for Phelps.

"Not really, but we're working all the obvious possible sources and the local cops are very helpful. We can tell you confidentially we really do think he's here. Because he's an international fugitive, all the airports and seaports and so forth are on alert in case he tries to leave the country.

"Oh, and his chartered plane is too short range to fly from here to Europe. But even if he made it there, Interpol is on alert. So are Scotland Yard and the emmies."

"The what?" Bren asked. "The Emmys?"

Jimmy chuckled and said, "No, not the TV awards Emmys, the emmies. It's slang, maybe mostly cop slang, for MI5 and MI6, the Brits' intelligence services. Sorry."

"Detective, you made me laugh and I thank you for that. Now, I want to know whether you could spread the word down there that my offer of a half-million-dollar reward for Phelps's capture is still available. Maybe someone there knows something, somehow. And I wasn't kidding when I said it's for his capture, dead or alive."

"Will do, ma'am, will do."

"And there's one more thing, just between us, Detective. When you return from this assignment I have a serious proposal for your consideration, a great opportunity."

"Well, of course, but, uh, could you give me a little more information now?"

"No, just focus on finding Phelps. And please give Ms. Page my regards if you run into her down there. I saw her report on Channel 3. I'd like to meet with her, too, when all this is over. Goodbye for now, Detective, and thank you very much."

MARCO ISLAND

As Jimmy clicked off his cell, the "missed call" light began to blink. Seeing it was Cassie, he called it immediately. She left a message.

"Hi, Copper, Daryl and I are leaving the TV news bureau in Naples now. We'll be back on Marco Island in twenty minutes or so. Can't wait."

Jimmy picked up the room phone and called the concierge desk. He made notes as the concierge answered his questions.

"Well, if you want casual food and drink, maybe some live music, is that what you mean by local color? I'd try Marek's Bistro up on Bald Eagle Drive. It has a friendly bar and a big local clientele. It's casual, but everything is around here. Remember that old TV show, *Cheers*? It's sort of like that, where everybody knows everybody else.

"Check out Porky's, too. Some say the food is better than the name suggests. And some nights they have an all-girl band that rocks the place.

"Another spot would be the Snook Inn. It's on the water and the grouper sandwiches are terrific. Not far from there is Arturo's. The bar is popular and the Italian food's nice.

"Then if you still want to play, the piano bar at the Marco Polo restaurant is usually lively. You may be among the younger people there, but so what? Stop by my desk in the lobby when you go out and I'll have a map for you for your pub crawl this evening."

Jimmy had more than beer and good cheer on his mind. He wanted to show Phelps's photo around town, especially to the locals, thinking if Phelps ever did leave his hiding place on Marco, he'd stick to local hangouts, not the hotels where a lot of out-of-towners tend to stay and play.

—

"Well, that's two strikes," Jimmy said with a grimace as they drove up Collier Boulevard and then left on Bald Eagle toward the Snook Inn.

The Bistro and Porky's bar both seemed like fun, friendly places, but none of the hostesses and bartenders remembered seeing the man in the photo Jimmy showed them. None of the customers recognized him either.

"Anybody else hungry?" Daryl asked as they parked at the Snook Inn.

"Yea, Jimmy, can we grab a bite here?" Cassie asked, waving toward the outdoor waterside tables.

"Sure, but let's see if any of the employees here have seen Phelps," Jimmy said, walking over to the counter where a hostess was checking names on a list of people waiting for a table.

"Excuse me, miss, could you tell me whether you've seen this man here or anywhere else in town lately?"

She hadn't. Cassie heard similar answers from the bartender, the bar back and a server waiting for a drinks order she brought to the bar from diners sitting at one of the picnic tables that lined the water's edge.

"But I haven't been at work for the past three days," the server said, "so you might want to check with the girls who were on duty then. I know Liz and Shea were here. They're off tonight, but Liz'll be here tomorrow. We open for lunch at eleven. Do you want to leave a message for her?"

"Maybe I'll stop by then. But thanks anyway, appreciate it."

As advertised, the grouper sandwiches at the Snook were very good, especially to the three visiting Atlantans, who hadn't eaten since early that morning.

Before they went back to their beachfront hotel, they wanted to check in with the deputy on stakeout at the Marco Airport, across the Marco bridge, about fifteen minutes from the restaurant. In the darkness, they saw a squad car parked on the side of the airport office. An incoming plane would not be able to see it until it taxied off the runway onto the ramp area.

Jimmy turned off the headlights, pulled next to the police car and spoke to the deputy behind the wheel.

"Detective Jimmy Hagan, Atlanta PD, officer. Everything quiet out here tonight?"

"You bet, Detective. I'm Deputy Johnny Hunter and I'll be here until O-six hundred, when my relief is scheduled."

"That's great, thanks. Your dispatcher has my cell number and the hotel number, so we'll be up and out early."

Cassie tugged on Jimmy's sleeve and whispered in his ear. Jimmy smiled and turned back to the deputy.

"By the way, Deputy, is the beach open at this hour and is it safe to take a walk out there at night?"

"Not a problem, Detective, you can get to the beach from any of the hotels over there, and it's safe. Just be sure not to trip over a turtles' nest in the darkness."

As they drove back to the hotel, Jimmy asked Cassie and Daryl, "What do you suppose he meant by 'don't trip over a turtle's nest?'"

"Maybe it's some kinda code, some local knowledge stuff," Cassie said.

"Yeah, maybe its code for people who take walks on Marco's beach after dark," Daryl added.

"So, what's it mean, 'turtles' nests'?" Jimmy asked again.

"Probably it means keep your pants on."

51

MARCO ISLAND

"Look, Jimmy, that keep-your-pants-on stuff isn't code at all," Cassie said, leaning over the railing of their balcony at the beachfront Hilton hotel.

"There's one of those cordoned-off turtle places on the beach. See the yellow tape around it? Is that crime scene tape or what?"

"I guess that's what the deputy was talking about out at the airport," Jimmy said, smiling as he recalled their long, lingering walk on the beach the night before.

They hadn't seen any turtle nests and they did keep their pants on, mostly. Their time together was intensified by the situation. Neither of them could have imagined a week ago that within a few days they'd be alone on a beautiful beach in Southwest Florida, working together to catch a killer of Bren Forrest's movie star fiancé and probably two young women.

The intimacy and their shared "mission" flared into their senses, blocking out other thoughts until early in the morning, soon after the sun came up.

Jimmy phoned for room service, then suggested they await breakfast on their balcony. It was time to talk with Cassie about his phone conversation with Bren Forrest, the personal part. He went through that phone call in detail, as Cassie's interest increased by the minute.

"So what do you make of that, Cass, her wanting to talk to both of us about a serious proposal, some 'great opportunity,' as she put it?"

"I don't know, really, but she seems so focused on Ian Phelps, you know that 'dead or alive' thing. I'm not sure we can count on anything for sure about her until her horrible nightmare is over."

"Well, the part about you obviously could be about hiring you at GNS," Jimmy said. "But how could you live without a daily dose of NewsBlitz3?"

They both laughed, as Cassie added, "You mean like when the promotions people make us dress up with antlers on our heads and dance with the weatherman for Christmas season feel-good, 'Happy Holidays' videos? You're right, Copper, how could I live without all that?"

———

"We meet again," Jimmy said, as they joined Daryl in the hotel lobby, "the three of us, The Mod Squad, right, Cassie?"

"True dat," Cassie said, making a sort of fake aggressive stand, legs akimbo. "One black, one white, one blond!"

Daryl looked blank. "The Mod Squad?"

"Nothing, it's a joke," Cassie said, "just the name of a TV show from a million years ago about a trio of crime fighters. And when we all get our big movie contract after this case, the blond will have to be you, Daryl."

"It'll cost you extra," Daryl said over his shoulder as he walked toward their rental SUV out front.

Their first stop was at Hoots, a casual breakfast and lunch place known for omelets, huge home fries, black beans and rice and friendly service. The "Mod Squad" showed Phelps's photo around the tables and to the servers and kitchen staff. No hits.

"If he's local, he's new, I'm thinkin'," said one waitress," because I've been here going on ten years, and I sure don't recollect seeing him. This guy win the lottery or somethin'?"

"Not so far as we know," Jimmy said with a smile. "Not yet."

Next stop was Kretch's, one of the island's dining landmarks. Apparently not, however, for Ian Phelps.

"Let's go back to the Snook Inn and find that server, Liz, the one the girl last night said would be at work today," Jimmy said.

A warm breeze was blowing across the outdoor tables and the chickee bar at the Snook, as the locals called it. Three or four staffers were setting up for the brunch and lunch crowd, expected soon after the place opened at eleven o'clock.

Cassie was with Daryl as he recorded video of the Snook, overlooking the wide waters of the Big Marco Pass separating Marco Island from its neighboring community, the Isles of Capri.

The dock slips at the Snook were still empty, but would not be for long. Some islanders would go to the Snook by boat rather than by car, even though it took five times longer to make the trip.

As one local explained it, "If you drive around here, when you could be on a boat, you'll never have a pod of dolphins swimming alongside your car."

"Hi, I'm Detective Hagan, Atlanta Police Department," Jimmy said to the twenty-something hostess at the front desk. "I'm working with the Marco police on a case and I wanted to..."

"Is it about that woman who was killed over on the beach the other day?"

"We just have a few questions," Jimmy dodged, showing her Phelps's picture on the cell. Have you seen this man here recently?"

"No, I don't think I've seen him here. But you should ask Liz and Bonnie, if they're here."

The bartender, Miguel, overheard the Liz and Bonnie part and said loudly, "No, Liz just called and said she'll be at least an hour late. Something about a speeding ticket on Alligator Alley."

The hostess shrugged, "Sorry, Detective, but Bonnie may be here, in the kitchen.

She was, but said she had never seen the guy in the photo.

"You might check with Liz, though. She seems to know everybody. Should be here any minute."

Jimmy knew that wasn't going to happen.

The bartender motioned to Jimmy, who walked over to the bar.

"What's going on?" Jimmy asked casually.

"You might try a few places in Goodland that draw good crowds on weekends. One is called Chuckles. It's pure Goodland, but don't be fooled if they're dressed like derelicts and don't have all their teeth. Some of those peckerwoods have more millions than Bill Gates, having made a ton of money from the square grouper, ya know, and all that.

"Then there's Stan's Idle Hour, packed on Sundays with bikers, bankers and everything in between. Lots of women there too, so if your guy's a player, well…"

"Great," Jimmy said. "Anything else?"

"Yeah, I'd check out the Little Bar too. I think the Raiford Starke Band is playing there. Great stuff. Starke's a guitar genius and his bass player, Stevie, is very cool and…"

"Sounds good, I appreciate it. Goodland, is it? Where's that from here?" Jimmy asked, pulling out the map the hotel concierge gave him.

—

"If you're going to make a quick trip to those three places and then come back here," Cassie said, as Jimmy headed toward the car. "Daryl and I'll stay and get whatever else we can for the report I'll feed to Atlanta this afternoon."

Jimmy nodded and started the motor, saying over his shoulder, "If I get a good lead in Goodland, I'll call you. Otherwise, I'll be back."

Chuckles was located in a crack in time, as well as at a marina. It was part run down chickee, part old-time country store and part the bar scene from Star Wars, only with characters dressed as swamp things or squeegee bums.

In one corner, a woman with lipstick redder than Mao and scarecrow hair was showing off her pet parrot by feeding it out of her mouth. Every time she put a handful of unshelled peanuts in her mouth, she'd open wide and the parrot would reach in with its beak and share, after shelling the nuts itself, of course.

Jimmy could not imagine Ian Phelps, or anybody else he'd know on the planet, being a parrot's snack food delivery system. So, after a quick, "ever see this guy in here?" to a zombie he assumed was the bartender, Jimmy clawed his way out of there and back into the twenty-first century.

Five minutes later, he pulled up to Stan's Idle Hour, parked his rental among the Harleys and a few rice rockets and went inside. Stan's was rustic and rockin' as well, but it seemed like the Oak Room at the Plaza Hotel in New York compared to Chuckles.

After fifteen minutes of showing Phelps's photo around, Jimmy cooled off with a Coke and then walked next door to the Little Bar. The friendly woman there studied the photo and shook her head.

"Sorry, detective, I haven't seen that one around here. But we'll have a good crowd in here tonight if you want to come back and show this picture around. Be sure to show it to the musicians if you come. Raiford and Stevie are playin' and they know everybody. Also Raiford has a great memory. People say he can play and sing more than three hundred songs, knows them by heart. So, he might recall this guy's face, ya never know."

Jimmy laughed, gave the woman his card and asked her to call him on his cell or at the Hilton if the man in the photo showed up.

"I haven't seen much of your little fishing village, but I like what I see," Jimmy said.

"Well, we're pretty laid back, here," she said with a small shoulder shrug. "We try to keep it real."

"This could be the official outpost of real," Jimmy said with a laugh. "Is there more of the town than I can see from here?"

"Not much more. See those T-shirts on that shelf next to the bar? The message on the front pretty much sums it up."

Jimmy picked up a black shirt off the stack and read the words in white letters, "Where the Hell is Downtown Goodland Anyway?"

"Keep the shirt and come back and see us."

—

The WAND-TV truck was straddling two parking spaces at the Snook Inn when Jimmy pulled in. The local station's reporter-photographer, Larry Pendleton, was pulling equipment from the rear double door.

"Hey, Detective, Cassie's on the balcony patio up those stairs," Pendleton said. "It's a great place for a standup, with a view of the island, the bridge, even out toward the Marco airport."

"You doing a report for your station, Larry?"

"Yeah, and I'll take Cassie's report and take care of feeding it to her station there."

Jimmy asked Larry to alert Cassie he was going to find the waitress who may have seen Phelps.

Larry was getting excited. He knew he was on a hot story and GNS would continue to use his video in its worldwide coverage. And the more help he gave Cassie and Jimmy, well, things might turn out just great.

"Liz, is it? Liz, I'm an Atlanta police detective working with Marco police and the Collier County Sheriff's Department."

Jimmy started by asking Liz about her delay getting back to the Snook Inn and her encounter with a Florida Highway Patrolman.

She was still mad about it, having been pulled over on Alligator Alley, the stretch of Interstate 75 connecting Florida's east and west coasts.

"I had to sit there on the side of the road forever," she told Jimmy with a grimace. Her mood was darkened as she realized her tips for that day would no way cover the cost of her speeding ticket.

"So, have you seen this man, the past few days or so?"

Seeing the photo of Ian Phelps in Jimmy's phone produced an immediate reaction.

"Yeah, yes, I'm pretty sure. Yep, he was here, came by boat. He and a couple of other guys. They're not from around here. That would have been Thursday 'cause I was off Friday and yesterday."

"What can you tell us about him, the conversation maybe, what they ate or drank?"

"What I remember most was his boat. Well, I don't know whose boat it is for sure, but he seemed to be in charge. They docked right there," she said, pointing at a slip attached to the sea wall."

"What else, anything?"

"Yeah, the name of the boat, the *BeebKiller,* like all run together. I asked him what it meant. Funny, he corrected the way I said it. Imagine, with that accent of his, correcting me. Seemed really important to him."

"Anything else? Did you by any chance see the number on the side of the boat?"

"No, but I probably could one fine day," she said, smiling now. "What I mean is, he went on about the name 'Beeb,' saying it stands for the BBC, then 'Killer.' *BeebKiller*.

"Then he asked me out, said he'd take me on his boat that night and tell me all about its strange name. I told him I already had plans but would take a rain check. Said he was leaving town soon but would be back 'cause he has a house here. He called me 'Liz, me lovely.' That's so cute. So, I asked him his name and ya know what he sez? He sez, 'Liz, me lovely, you can just call me 'Killer.'"

Jimmy glanced over to where Cassie was recording video with Daryl and waved at her to join him, then turned back to Liz.

"Would you like to be on TV, Liz? That woman heading this way is my friend, Cassie, and she would like you to tell her what you told me about this 'Killer' guy."

Cassie made small talk with Liz while Daryl put up a tripod on which the video camera would be mounted for the on-camera interview. Jimmy went over to the water's edge and made calls to Police Chief Packer and to Atlanta PD Homicide.

Chief Packer notified his officer in charge of the marine patrol unit to see whether they had a vessel named *BeebKiller* on file. He also sent two officers to check public boat dock locations and marinas.

Some boat service companies were closed Sundays, but Packer's office gave Jimmy their emergency phone numbers. He had a hit on his fourth phone call, to a service specialist at Intercoastal Marine, Tom Scott.

"Yeah, I know that boat, *BeebKille*r. It's a Grady White. I've serviced it myself several times. I know it's over on Liberty Drive, but I don't recall the house number. Tell you what. If you'll meet me in our office on Windward Drive in about fifteen minutes, I'll get on the computer with you."

"There, that's it," Jimmy said, looking over Scott's shoulder at the computer list of Intercoastal's clients. *BeebKiller.*

The boat's name was on the list of service calls to boats docked at residences on Marco Island. Jimmy noticed the name on the service records was some corporate name, not Phelps, not anything even close. But there it was, the address, 392 Liberty Drive.

52

MARCO ISLAND

For Ian Phelps and his guys, O'Reilly and Jax, it began as a lay-about Sunday. The three TVs in the house all were in use after the men finished a late afternoon lunch, a slab of smoked salmon Jax ordered for takeout at the Paradise Seafood Shop.

O'Reilly was watching GNS coverage from Atlanta of the Olympics, but he was mostly dozing on a living room couch, awakened now and then by the frenzied whistle-blowing of the referees.

Jax was watching reruns of *Law and Order* in the home office, rooting for the bad guys. But he laughed out loud while watching the detective characters in some of the earliest episodes of that series using pay phones before cell phones were widely available.

Phelps had a TV on in his bedroom but his mind was on his plans to get out of the country. He stared toward the TV, but with eyes glazed. His mind was searching for solutions, choices for the next safe place.

He knew he could do that with the private jet parked in Sarasota, ready to pick him up at the Marco Island airport. He needed to get to a place where he could access his assets, the cash in offshore accounts and the people who ran the drug smuggling operations in Latin America and the Caribbean.

The plane could get him to much of Mexico and any number of islands without refueling. His contacts knew how to get people and goods in and out of places without being noticed.

Yes, that's the way to go, get to some dusty or deserted place way south of here and regroup. We could go right now, but maybe late night is better? Or tomorrow? No, dark would be best. I'll tell the pilot to pick us up at ten tonight.

Suddenly the TV audio pierced his consciousness.

"Coming up on WAND-TV NewsFlash10: Have you seen this man?" A photo of Phelps, filled the screen, the one Jimmy had been showing around Marco Island.

"This suspected triple murderer has been seen here in Collier County and a manhunt is underway at this hour. He could be in your neighborhood, up your street or down the block. Be on the alert! We'll have the latest breaking, shocking new details. It's a NewsFlash10 exclusive!"

"Bloody hell!" Phelps yelled to Jax and O'Reilly. "Pack up, get the car out of the garage. We're leaving now!"

"What about the car?" O'Reilly asked, walking into Phelps's bedroom.

"We'll leave it at the Marco airport, so don't worry about it. Won't do us any bloody good anyway. Looks like I'll never be back here again."

—

At Marco Police headquarters, Chief Jeff Packer was on the radio, sending a squad car to the foot of the Jolley Bridge that connected the island to the mainland.

"Close one outbound lane and put moveable barriers on the other. Check carefully anybody who's headed off the island. You have the suspect's photo on your cell. And he might have two men with him. These guys may have killed three people. They might be armed, and we know they're dangerous."

Two more police cars were sent to the Liberty Drive address. Jimmy was in one with a policeman. Cassie and Daryl followed in their rented SUV.

Chief Packer phoned the Sheriff's Department and asked the duty officer to notify their deputy on stakeout at the airport.

"When your relief arrives, you stay on duty with him," the desk officer told the deputy at the airport. We need everybody on this, and we're sending more backup, including two plainclothes officers for surveillance.

"They should be there any minute. Pull your cars out of sight, inside a hangar if you can. Let us know if anything moves out there, in the air or on the ground. Our suspect may be going there from Marco by car and a plane may be flying in to pick him up."

At the house on Liberty Drive, one Marco cop and Jimmy went to the front door, guns drawn. Two other officers went around back quietly, noticing a boat was on the dock's electric lift, just out of the water. On the side in blue letters, its name, *BeebKiller.*

Through the pool screen enclosure over the lanai, the deputies could see much of the home's interior through the expanse of sliding glass doors. Nothing moved, but they could hear voices and crowd noise, something about Argentina upsetting France. Could be volleyball, girls' beach volleyball, maybe.

"Check this out, it's the Olympics. Can we stop and watch a while?" whispered one uniform, grinning.

"No, it's just Argentina and France."

"Yeah, but it's Argentine and France girls' beach volleyball," said the other cop.

At the front double glass doors, the policeman knocked. "Ian Phelps, police, open the door, Mr. Phelps." Nothing. The officer repeated the order, waited a few seconds, then motioned they were going in.

With his service revolver, he broke the glass pane, reached through and turned the lock button, opened the door and they rushed in.

Within moments, the police and Jimmy knew Phelps was gone. The TVs were on, closets and drawers in the bedrooms open. One deputy slowly opened a door from the kitchen to the garage. No car, but a small puddle of water under where a car was parked not long ago.

—

O'Reilly was going exactly the speed limit along Collier Boulevard, through Marco's main business district. As he reached and drove onto the bridge, he saw in his rear view mirror, a policeman taking orange cones out of the trunk of his squad car, preparing to close the outbound lane of the bridge, part of the manhunt.

"Okay, boss, we just made it before the coppers set up their check point at the bridge." He had to twist around to see Phelps, huddled on the floor in the back seat area of the white SUV. Phelps sat up a bit.

"The plane should be at the airport within a few minutes after we get there, if the pilot had the right flying time from Sarasota. So, stay cool, you two, and drive right up next to the runway when we get there."

Chief Packer told the cops at the Liberty Drive house to knock on neighbors' doors and ask what they may have seen or heard at the house.

Jimmy, Cassie and Daryl headed to the airport. At the bridge, Jimmy showed his shield to the police at the roadblock.

"Having a lot of traffic today, officer?"

"No, Detective, but we have this guy's photo, so if he comes this way we'll get 'em."

At the airport, a casual observer would see a quiet evening and not much else. Two men, civilians by the look of their khaki pants and golf shirts, sat on a bench outside the airport manager's office, part of the small terminal building.

One of the men was thumbing casually through the Sunday edition of the *Naples Daily News*, having already discarded two inserted advertising sections, one selling auto parts and tires, the other touting vitamin supplements and skin products.

The other guy, also in his late twenties, was practicing that feat of seemingly pulling a quarter out of someone's ear. Over and over, he would cuff his hand, reach for the other man's ear, then pull his hand away with a quarter between his thumb and forefinger, smiling a lot, apparently trying to make up for his bench mate's towering lack of interest in such magic.

"Dipshit," his partner mumbled, half-heartedly swatting the other man with the paper. He then pulled out the sports section.

"How'd the Marlins do last night?" the quarter trickster asked.

"Won, beat the Phillies seven-four. That's six in a row for the fish, but they're streaky, been that way all year. Hell, they could lose the next nine or ten in a row. Weird."

"So? Are the Rays doing any better?"

"Yep. They're just a game, maybe game and a half, behind the Yankees in their division. But I like the National League better, without that designated hitter system."

"Why is that? Talk about boring, having pitchers bat. What a waste of time."

"Tell you what, how about you put your quarters away and read the paper like a normal person?"

"What, you don't like a little magic on a beautiful evening?"

"No, no, I love it, Jack, love it. In fact I may pick up a limb on one of those trees over there and put it in one of your orifices. How about that for a magic trick?"

They both looked at the thick stand of cypress trees, knowing four deputies, SWAT team members, were in there, hidden by the trees and even more so by the Ghilli suits they wore, basically camouflage outfits, with tactical vests.

Several sheriffs' department squad cars were hidden inside a large hangar so a pilot landing from the north would not see them until the plane touched down on the lone runway and taxied up to the hangar door. Jimmy's rental SUV was behind the hangar, out of sight.

Cassie and Daryl waited in the car while Jimmy walked over to the office, entered and spoke to a supervisor whom police already vetted. He had no criminal record.

"If a plane comes in unannounced and lands, what normally happens next?"

"The pilot would taxi over to the ramp area, let the passengers off and then either refuel or park the plane," the supervisor said.

"Well, if it's who we think it is, he won't be refueling or parking," Jimmy said. "We need to surround the plane as soon as it comes to a stop."

Phelps's chartered jet was flying along the Gulf Coast, turning to glide over the coastline and over north Naples for a landing at the Marco airport to the south. The pilot had not filed a flight plan, and airport personnel would have no idea he was going to land until they saw the plane on approach.

As the Citation CJ4 went lower and slower, the airport manager alerted the sheriff's deputies.

"We don't know whether this is the plane we want or not, but we'll want to talk to the pilot and any passengers right away," a deputy said.

As the plane touched down, Phelps's white SUV, with O'Reilly at the wheel, drove past the parking lot and toward the tarmac where arriving passengers routinely would wait for luggage to be unloaded.

"There's your plane, boss, just now landing," O'Reilly said excitedly. "Like clockwork it is, boss, bleedin' clockwork."

The plane didn't taxi to the ramp area, as is customary. It slowed, then stopped on the runway, engines idling, but not off.

"Go, go, go, O'Reilly, to the plane door!" Phelps's heart was pounding, his face flushed.

As O'Reilly floored the gas pedal, the car lurched forward, onto the runway toward the plane. All the squad cars tore out from behind the hangar in pursuit, sirens on. One car careened to a stop in front of the plane, preventing a possible effort at a quick takeoff.

Phelps's car stopped about twenty yards from the aircraft. He scooted out the back door and began running.

Jimmy slammed on his brakes almost under a wing of the aircraft, and Daryl jumped out of the backseat, his video camera on his shoulder, shaky as he ran forward, recording the scene. Cassie trailed, wanting to see everything but not get in Daryl's way.

The two plainclothes deputies darted off their bench in pursuit, guns in hand.

"Stop, Phelps, stop or we'll shoot," the quarter-in-the-ear guy shouted. They had no plans to shoot the fugitive unless he showed a weapon, but Phelps didn't know that.

All the cops were now running, but one slowed to shout into his cell phone.

"Keep the chopper ready," he shouted, "but we probably won't need it. The subject is running toward the swamp and the mangroves, so just stand by."

Phelps ran past the Citation and across the runway, looking over his shoulder, panicked, zigzagging, trying to find cover. Ahead he saw grass, then some watery areas and behind that, thick mangroves.

Dry ground, has to be, maybe I can lose them in there, escape maybe.

Two of the officers pulled Tasers off their belts, ready to use if they could get close enough to Phelps. Almost there. Almost.

Sweat dripping into his eyes, Phelps plunged across and over the narrow, grassy berm into the swamp alongside, lurching and reaching, the water up to his ankles, then his shins, tripping, stumbling, trying to stay upright, falling to his knees, slogging forward.

Daryl stopped and steadied his camera, zooming in as far as he could. Cassie crept up and put her hand on Daryl's shoulder as they watched and recorded Phelps's last stand.

A stab of pain shot through Phelps's left leg, and he felt himself being tugged down and to the left. For a second he was running in place, his flailing arms propelling him nowhere.

A jolt hit him hard in his right shoulder, the pain blinding him, but it wasn't coming from his arm and hand, which he saw for a second as they left his torso forever.

He looked down at his leg in the water and recoiled in horror as he saw the crocodile tugging, pulling, twisting him down, its strong jaw pressure and sharp teeth doing evolution's work.

He then saw the eyes of one crocodile, seeming to smile as she bit into his groin, then pulled what was left of him down, down into the water, twisting as she hung on with a bite force of more than twenty thousand pounds per square inch.

Phelps, already numb, didn't know the numbers, never knew each of these critters dining on his flesh and blood had in their jaws the power of a T. Rex dinosaur. Another croc struck, latching onto and twisting his prey's midsection into and under the water.

It was the last thing on earth Ian Phelps knew.

Daryl slowly zoomed out to a wide angle when he saw the lawmen trying to maneuver to get a clear shot at the attacking crocs, but realized it would be futile; too many crocs. The lawmen's instinct and training told them to take Phelps alive, if possible, but there was no way. He was in a half dozen pieces, the crocs now competing with each other for their entrée for the day, or maybe for several months. Crocs can survive on a couple of big meals a year like this one.

"He's dead meat," said one deputy, a comment worthy of the redundancy-of-the- month award.

One officer turned toward the Citation and saw the pilot still in the cockpit, staring at the scene. The lawman pointed his gun at the plane and shouted to the pilot to shut off the engines and to leave the plane with his hands in the air.

He did, slowly, his eyes glazed as though he was in a trance. His previous version of Chuck Yeager had, so to speak, left the building.

"Daryl, are you confident about the video you have on camera?" Cassie asked, knowing even NewsBlitz3 might not air the gory, gruesome demise of Ian Phelps.

"You bet, Cassie," Daryl said, his eyes wide and bright. "Now, that's not something ya see every day."

One of the deputies explained to Jimmy and Cassie that Phelps was a goner when the first croc had the first bite.

"And even if he missed the croc's nest here and run farther up the runway, the gators would have nailed him there. There are lots of alligators all over the place. Oh, and the pythons would have been pleased to make his acquaintance as well."

The End

Epilogue

ATLANTA & MARCO ISLAND

The sensational events at the Marco Island airport prompted Atlanta Police Chief Lutz to call a news conference. He wanted to make sure he became the face and voice of the successful effort. As he put it to the media who crowded into his office lobby, "The search for the killer is over. He has been brought to justice."

The chief also had plans for Jimmy Hagan.

"While I preside over the comprehensive after-action investigation, I am instructing homicide Detective James Hagan to remain in Florida to coordinate with the authorities there. And I'll include his information in my daily briefings."

This guy is somehow a media favorite and I need to have him out of the picture for a while.

—

Staying on the case in Marco was fine with Jimmy, especially when the NewsBlitz3 suits insisted Cassie stay on the story there, too. They even offered to send a producer down there to help her, Rita Runner.

"Gee, thanks," Cassie said in a phone call to the news director, "but Daryl and I can handle it for now. You don't need to spend the money to send Rita. All we need is a Fed EX account and some cash, an advance, maybe a thousand each, please. Thank you, so much."

"Cassie," the news director said in a hesitant voice, "would it be all right if you guys moved to a less expensive hotel, maybe one not on the beach? We are getting some cost control heat from down the hall and…"

"There's no way we can do that," Cassie interrupted. All the hotels are full on the island and more media is showing up. If we check out now we'd have to camp out on the beach and the mosquitos might carry us away."

"Come on, Cass, gimme a break."

"Well, if you think we'll be here for a month or so, we might find a condo for rent on Marco. It is the slow season after all. That might be cheaper in the long run." Cassie held the phone away from her ear, anticipating her boss's reaction to that.

"A month?" the news director asked, his voice going from baritone to soprano. "A month?"

"I have to run, seriously, we can talk later," Cassie said. "Thanks for everything."

—

On the Marco bridge, it looked as though some sort of techno-vehicular parade was about to hit town, as TV vans from GNS and TV stations from Tampa, Miami, Orlando and points north crowded both southbound lanes of the twin span. The major TV networks also sent reporters and cameramen and the BBC had a camera-reporter team on the way.

The story of TV tower impalement was red meat to the British media from the start, and when word spread the man who died trying to escape police was a British media baron, the UK tabloids went into full, stop-the-presses spasms of delight.

Law enforcement authorities on Marco began daily media briefings. It was clear early on the reporters preferred to hear from Detective Jimmy Hagan with relevant input from The Sheriff's Department and Marco Island PD. Not the other way around.

Even the Atlanta TV stations preferred to focus most of their efforts and attention to Marco rather than on Chief Lutz's daily droning in Atlanta.

As one reporter from Atlanta's News9NOW quipped, "What would you rather watch, Chief Lutz up there bloviating in his gaudy

Hessian operetta costume or swamps full of crocs, gators, pythons and other deadly newsmakers? Not to mention a nightly eyeful of Cassandra Page."

—

The publicity swirling around the Ian Phelps case led to media inquiries about the Phelps drug smuggling operation and that led to the FBI and the DEA starting to pay attention. Their tentacles spread to Europe, Aruba, Curacao and beyond, but the trail always seemed to lead to Southwest Florida.

Agents began poking around Marco, but it took weeks to make any progress, partly because there was no way a federal agent could pass himself off as just one of the guys at, say, Chuckles or Stan's Idle Hour.

The media, eager to prolong the story, eventually focused on a handful of self-described "nature preservationists," who were outraged at the treatment accorded the crocodiles that consumed Ian Phelps.

At a news conference staged outside the Sheriff's Department substation on Marco Island, the group announced a "Rally for Reptiles" and called for a fund-raising effort to raise awareness of the human intrusion the airport reptiles endured.

Thus, the "Coins for Crocs" campaign was born. The salivating media took the bait and made "Coins for Crocs" known far and wide.

—

Bren Forrest began to assume more daily, hands-on control of GNS, partly out of excitement over the prospects of her new passion, the crime and corruption unit. And partly because she sniffed competition in the air.

Getting consumers' attention was getting tougher, in a world with a thousand TV channels, not to mention the tens of thousands of video offerings via the Internet. As she often said in pep talks to her staff and at inside–the-industry gatherings, "The Koreans already are working to perfect video receivers that fit inside the human eye, not unlike contact lenses. So our job is to create media content so compelling nobody will ever blink again."

—

Bren wanted to hire Cassie Page and Jimmy Hagan at GNS, and she didn't want to wait any longer. With Phelps dead, her blistering desire to avenge Cav Campbell's death shifted toward another goal. She wanted to create a special investigative unit at the news network to uncover major crime and corruption around the country.

Having Cassie and Hagan run it made perfect sense, she told herself, as she called Cassie's cell phone.

"I am flattered, Ms. Forrest."

"I'm calling you first, Cassie, but I'm also going to ask Detective Hagan to join us on this project."

"It sounds like a great idea, the crime unit, and I like having a national palette to paint on. Oh, forgive me, that sounds so lame I guess, but…"

"No, not at all, but you're right, you'd be able to go anywhere the story would take you. Now, what's your contract situation with Channel 3?"

"I have about eighteen months left, but I do have an out, meaning I could quit at any time, if I were offered a job from a network, including GNS. There's some fine print, so…"

"All right, please check that out and let me know. Your bosses will have a fit, you know that."

"Maybe, we'll see."

"So, Cassie, do we have a deal?"

"Ma'am, I'd love to work for you on this at GNS, but I need a little time before I commit."

"Fair enough. I'm phoning Detective Hagan right now. If you see him later today you'll have something to talk about."

"Yes, we will, Ms. Forrest. Yes, we surely will."

—

After a lot of lawyer input and invoices, Bren Forrest decided to divvy up the half-million dollar reward in this manner:

Rally for Reptiles and Coins for Crocs, the two newly-minted conservation organizations in Southwest Florida, each received fifty-thousand dollars.

The remaining four hundred thousand was awarded to "Liz, me lovely," the sharp-eyed server at the Snook Inn who identified Phelps's photo for Detective Hagan.

In a flash, Liz's favorite TV channel became Global News Service. She also grew to like the BBC America channel. She enjoyed calling it, "The Beeb."

Liz stayed on at The Snook for a while, basking in the attention she was getting from customers who showed up primarily to see her in person.

About a year later, she and a partner opened their own beachfront restaurant on Marco Island, "Liz, Me Lovely's Killer Grille."

Acknowledgments

If we took this opportunity to thank everyone who has had some influence on DEADLY NEWS, from creation to fruition, the book would be at least a two volume boxed set.

Because that is not realistic, we want to express our gratitude to the following people (mostly in alphabetical order) and to others whose names may not appear. But you know who you are and you know you have our thanks and appreciation.

First, our thanks to Cathy Teets of Headline Books, Inc. Her patience and perseverance in leading us through our first novel is a steadying influence on what by any measure has been an exciting experience.

Neal J. Aslin—A friend since our years at the U. of Mo. School of Journalism. He is in and knows the corporate world. He offered valuable critiques of character development and even had a fine suggestion should we do a sequel. Did we say he is a cockeyed optimist?

Karna Small Bodman—An accomplished novelist, a former heavy hitter in President Reagan's White House and former TV news anchor. Her advice on the deft handling of plot progression and scene setting was enormously helpful, as was her savvy about the world of publishing today.

Neal Boortz, national radio talk show host—A student of media after forty plus years in talk radio. Neal's penchant for on-air hijinks and controversy over the years is a treasure trove of stories. Stay tuned.

Thom Carr—Marco Island Chief of Police, retired. Chief Carr is very good at noting how authors sometimes don't stick to reality when writing about police work. If we don't have it right, it's not his fault.

Claudia Curle—Our mother and mother-in-law, our first pair of eyes on the book in its early, mistake-ridden form. From the start, she made this neophyte novelist feel like a best-selling author.

Biologist Gregory M. Erickson—PhD, Florida State University, who shared his vast knowledge about the modern day prehistoric creature that is the American Crocodile. About two thousand American crocodiles live in South Florida. If we say any more at this point it might be a spoiler.

Gail Evans—A former colleague and top executive at CNN, whose knowledge of the big league news business added texture to our story.

Detective Geoff Fahringer, Collier County Sheriff's Department —His detailed knowledge of stakeouts, chases and other law enforcement situations comes from having done all these things. He's still doing them, so bad guys in southwest Florida, beware.

Laurie Farmer Thannisch—Our daughter, who loves us enough to tell the truth about some weaknesses in early drafts, and whose many skills include laser-like proofreading.

Justin Farmer—Our son, whose knowledge and insider experience in TV news gave us a window on the advanced technology which makes worldwide, up to the minute news possible.

Judy Farmer—My sister, whose lifetime as an educator helped make her a prodigious proofreader and editorial whiz-bang.

Robin and Sharon Horsman—English friends who helped us keep the British characters and their actions authentic and realistic.

Patrick Junkroski and Paul Kovak of Mytechnologypros.com, who led us through the digital world of web sites, social media and other wonders of cyberspace.

Barbara Klaus—A "Comma-kazi" about punctuation and of great counsel about nuance in the characters. Her sense of, "He wouldn't say that" was invaluable.

Richard Klaus—The late orthopedic surgeon and friend who knew how little we know about things he knew so much about and was willing to share with us.

Andrew Miller—Photographer, WINK-TV, Ft. Myers, FL. He gave us valuable technical advice about how local news gets from the scene to the TV viewer.

Mary Zachrich and Carolyn Brown - good friends, patient and helpful as test readers of early versions of **DEADLY NEWS**. Their questions and suggestions brought clarity to our sometimes-clouded minds.

Robert Tweedie - Manager of Marco Island Executive Airport, who taught us about the airport's operations relevant to our story.

About the Authors

Don Farmer and Chris Curle have been in the news business—television, radio and print—for a combined total of ninety-nine years, from the headline events and back rooms of world politics to the front lines of wars and social revolutions.

They met in a TV newsroom in Houston, Texas. She was a reporter/anchor at KTRK-TV, the ABC station there. Don was there on assignment in his role as southern bureau chief for ABC News, based in Atlanta.

They married two years later, and immediately moved to London, where Don was a key correspondent in the network's primary European bureau. They also lived for several years in Germany, where Don was ABC's bureau chief and correspondent.

During this period, Chris covered international news for radio and print in Europe, Asia and the Middle East.

Don's coverage abroad sent him to war and civil strife in Europe, the Middle East, Latin America and Asia, including Vietnam and Cambodia. He also covered the civil rights movement in the US, including Dr. Martin Luther King, Jr.'s historic movement, Dr. King's assassination and the violent aftermath in several American cities.

He covered the unsuccessful presidential campaigns of several men named George—Wallace, McGovern and Romney—and one very successful George, the forty-first president.

For five years, Don covered the US House of Representatives and the US Senate as a congressional correspondent for ABC News.

When Ted Turner created CNN, he hired Chris and Don to be among that all-news network's "pioneer" on-air news anchors. During their two-hour, live "Take Two" daily program on CNN, they interviewed thousands of interesting people, many of whom are world famous.

Some of their more memorable conversations were with presidents, prime ministers, first ladies, generals, ambassadors, potentates and celebrities in the worlds of sports, Hollywood and Broadway.

One of Don's favorite assignments was his conversation with The Beatles, all four of them, after John Lennon had created a firestorm by remarking in 1966 that the Beatles were more popular than Jesus.

Chris's career before CNN included anchoring newscasts and a live "magazine" show on the ABC TV station in Washington DC, interviewing and reporting on the capital's movers and shakers. Among her career favorites were Nancy Reagan, Barbara Bush, Bob Hope, Benjamin Netanyahu, the Rev. Billy Graham, actor James Earl Jones and wildlife expert Jim Fowler, who brought some exotic critters with him to a live, on-air interview.

Don and Chris also anchored the news for the ABC TV station in Atlanta, WSB-TV, where their coverage included visits to such interesting places as Iceland, Honduras, Saudi Arabia, the Galapagos Islands, Africa and the fall of the Berlin Wall.

Chris and Don write columns for several newspapers in Atlanta and in Southwest Florida.

Don is the co-author of *Roomies: Tales From the Worlds of TV News and Sports*, a book he wrote with his lifelong friend, the late, legendary sportscaster, Skip Caray.